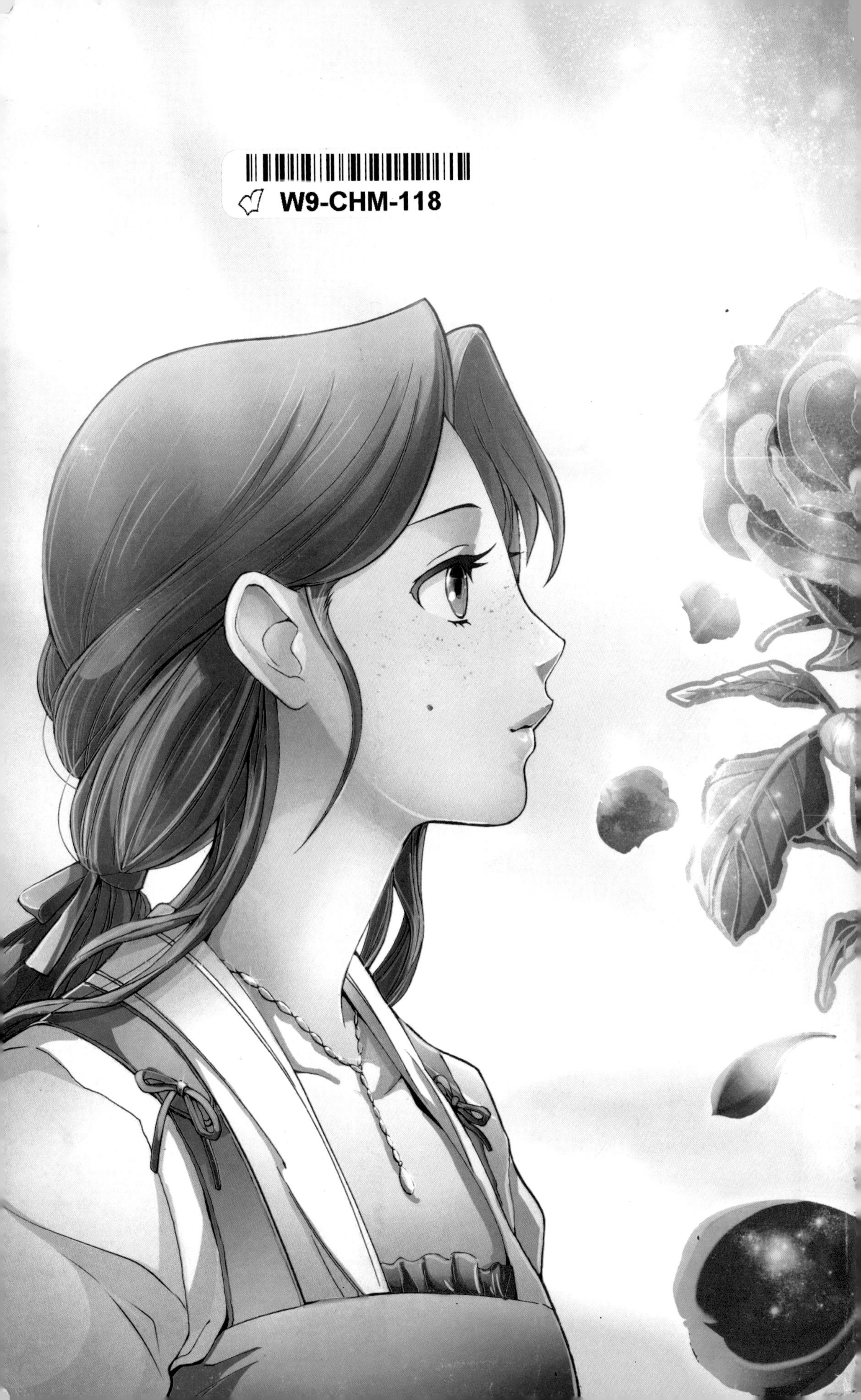

Contents

Greetings to our fellow Disney **Beauty and the Beast** fans!

It brings us great pleasure that you've decided to read *Belle's Tale*. This two-volume manga series was first released in 2017, shortly after the live-action movie release. Five years later, we are thrilled to present you with this new full-color edition of this manga! Since this series is very near and dear to our hearts, we wanted to develop two distinctly unique color concepts to represent two vastly different perspectives.

This book follows Belle, our curious, optimistic, and independent heroine, as she befriends the castle's enchanted staff and learns to look beyond the Beast's hideous exterior to find the heart and soul of the true Prince inside. So different from the Beast, her vision represents the more vibrant and exciting world outside her small town. You'll be able to see a depiction of Belle's perspective through a *shoujo anime*-inspired color style.

Also available now is *The Beast's Tale*, featuring a drastically different color style to reflect his own view on the world. We hope you enjoy this tale as old as time!

--- The TOKYOPOP Team!

Disney
BEAUTY AND THE BEAST

BELLE'S TALE

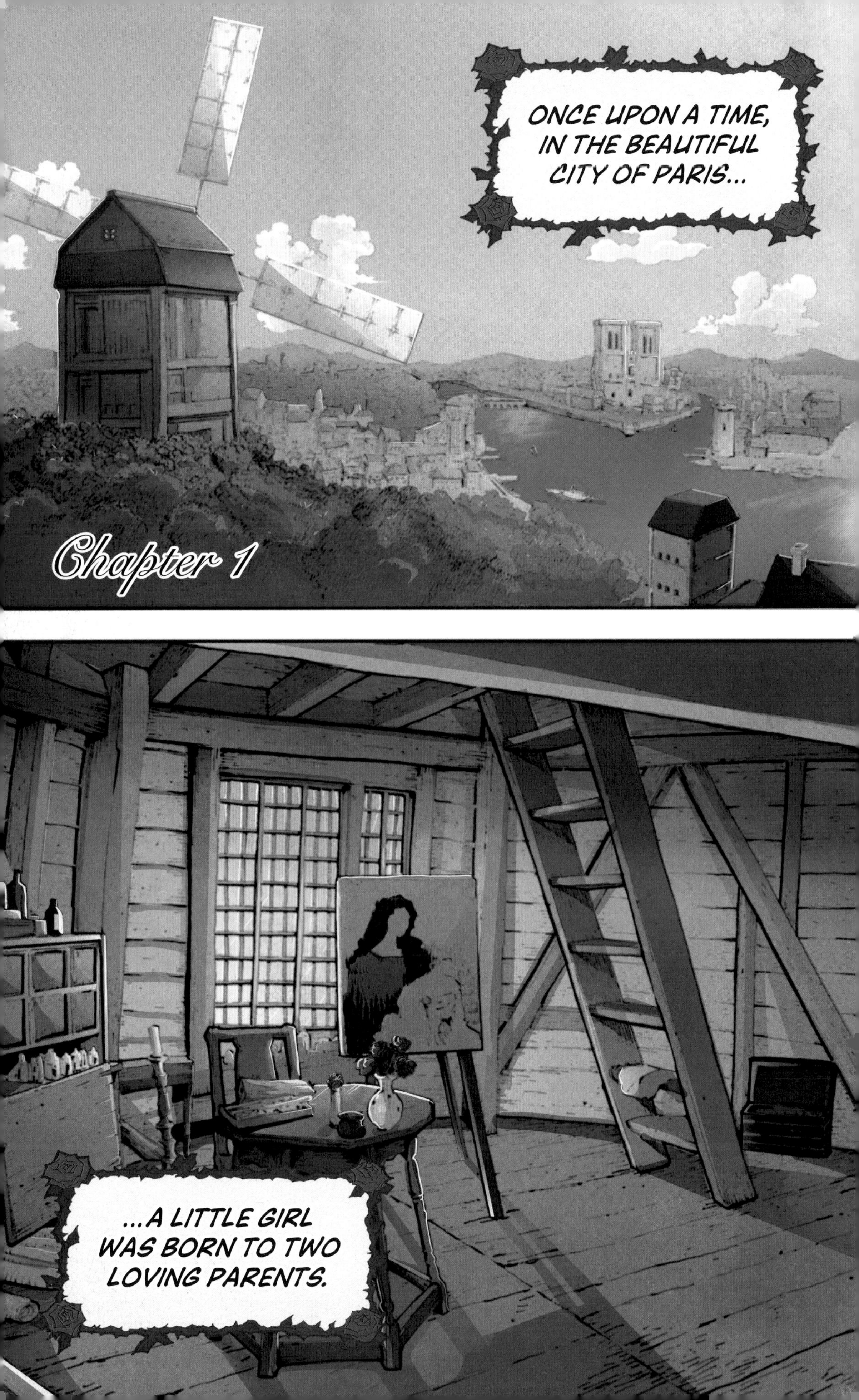
ONCE UPON A TIME, IN THE BEAUTIFUL CITY OF PARIS...
Chapter 1
...A LITTLE GIRL WAS BORN TO TWO LOVING PARENTS.

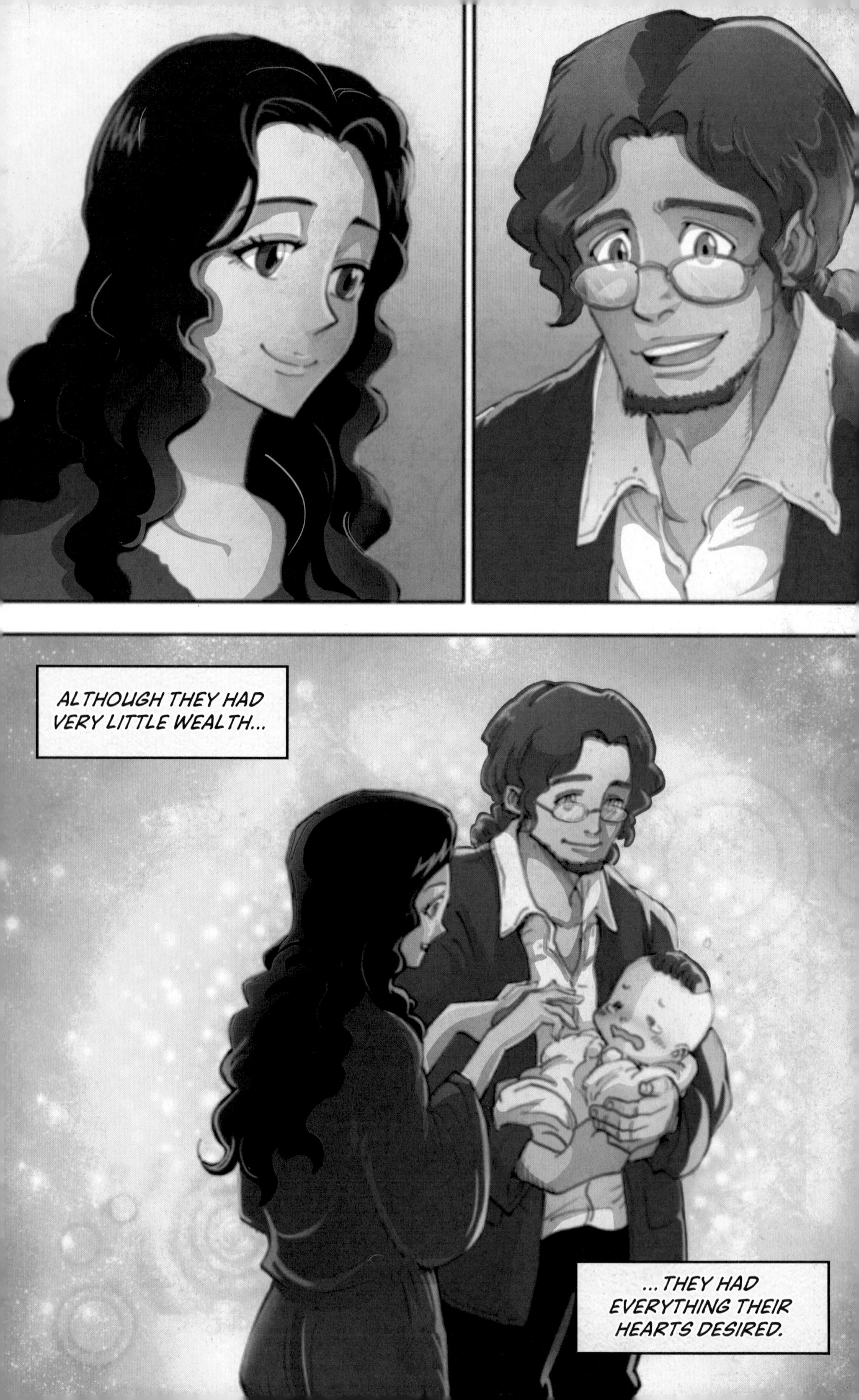
ALTHOUGH THEY HAD VERY LITTLE WEALTH...
...THEY HAD EVERYTHING THEIR HEARTS DESIRED.

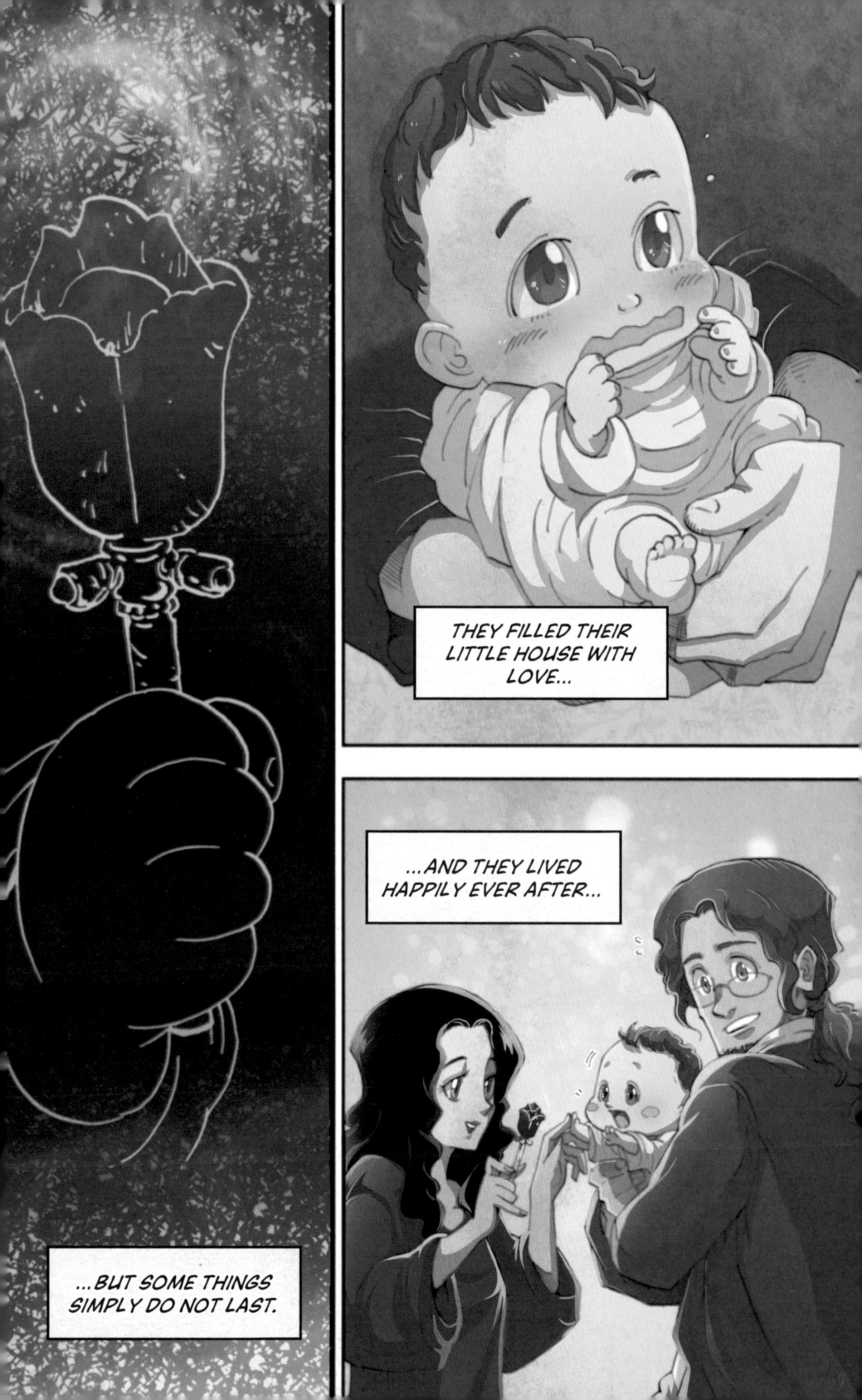
THEY FILLED THEIR LITTLE HOUSE WITH LOVE...
...AND THEY LIVED HAPPILY EVER AFTER...
...BUT SOME THINGS SIMPLY DO NOT LAST.

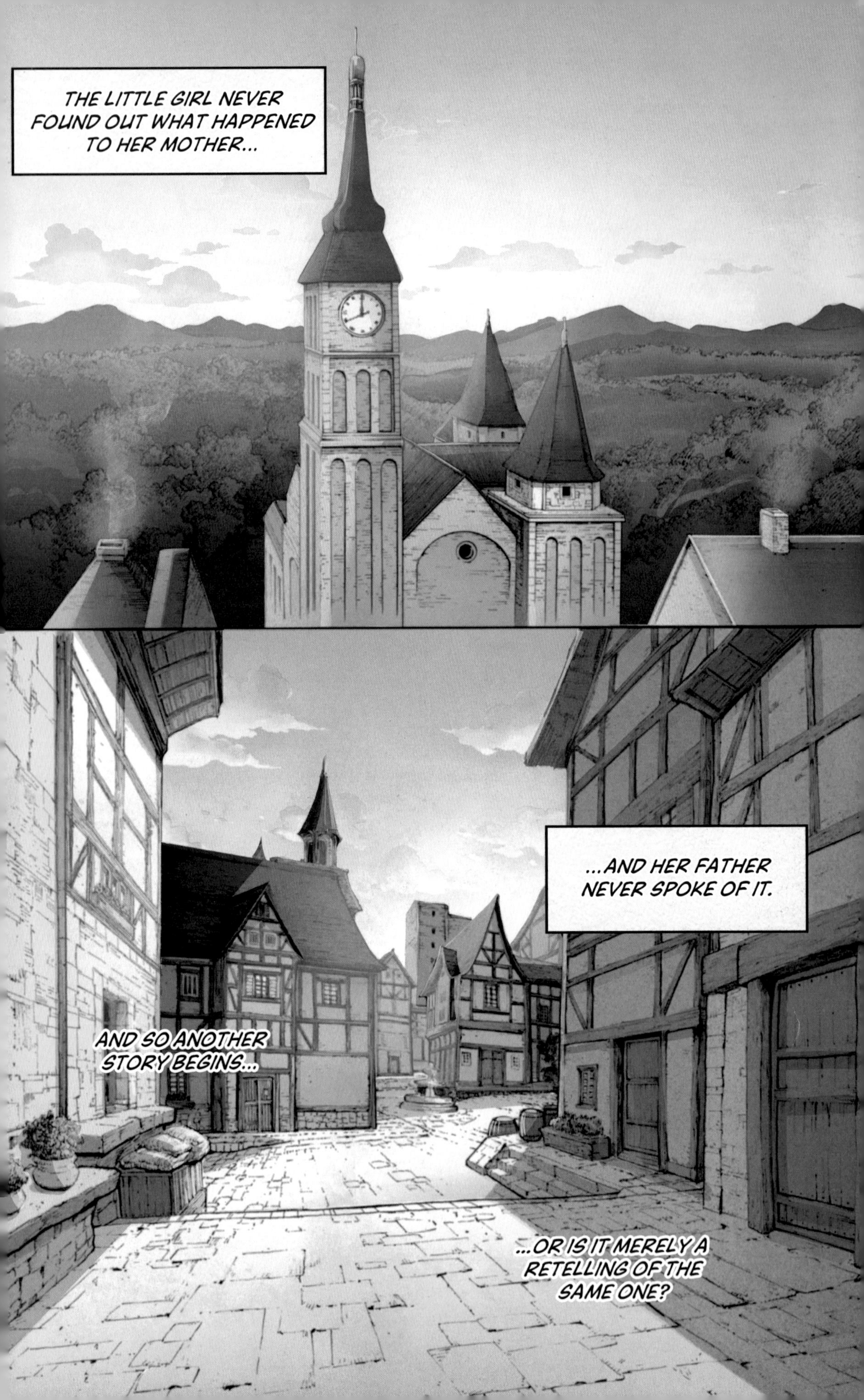
THE LITTLE GIRL NEVER FOUND OUT WHAT HAPPENED TO HER MOTHER...
...AND HER FATHER NEVER SPOKE OF IT.
AND SO ANOTHER STORY BEGINS...
...OR IS IT MERELY A RETELLING OF THE SAME ONE?

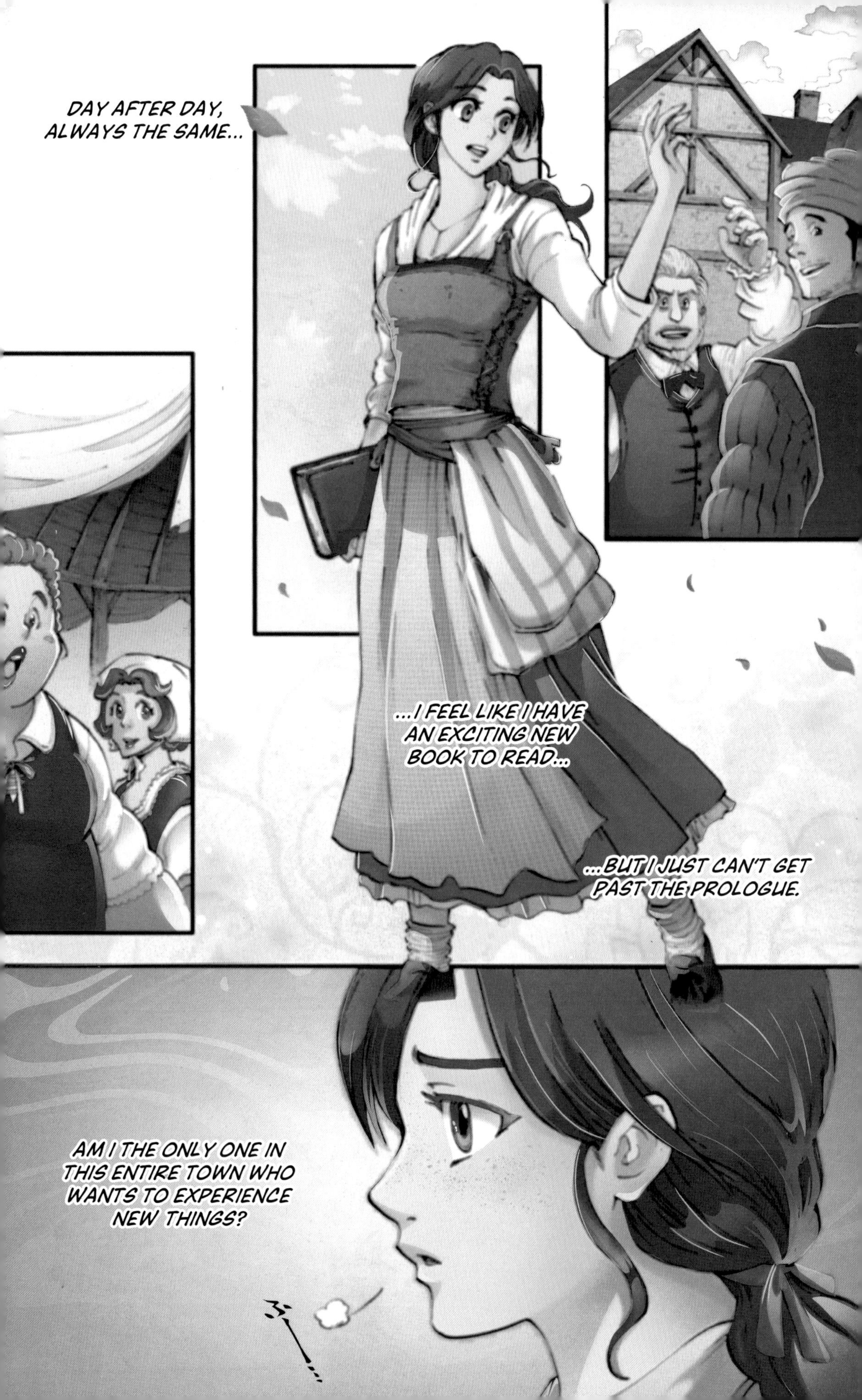
DAY AFTER DAY, ALWAYS THE SAME...
...I FEEL LIKE I HAVE AN EXCITING NEW BOOK TO READ...
...BUT I JUST CAN'T GET PAST THE PROLOGUE.
AM I THE ONLY ONE IN THIS ENTIRE TOWN WHO WANTS TO EXPERIENCE NEW THINGS?

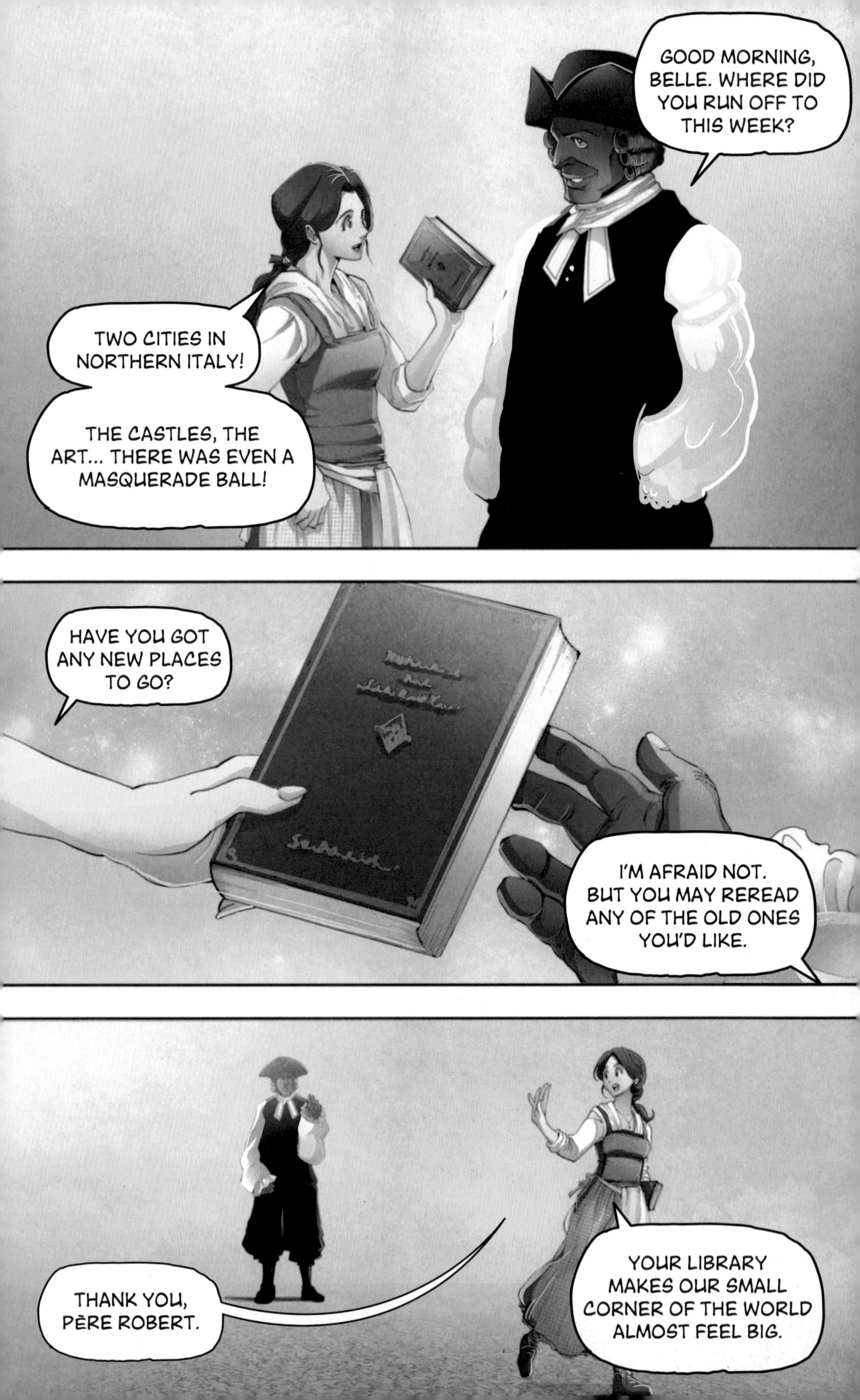
GOOD MORNING, BELLE. WHERE DID YOU RUN OFF TO THIS WEEK?
TWO CITIES IN NORTHERN ITALY!
THE CASTLES, THE ART... THERE WAS EVEN A MASQUERADE BALL!
HAVE YOU GOT ANY NEW PLACES TO GO?
I'M AFRAID NOT. BUT YOU MAY REREAD ANY OF THE OLD ONES YOU'D LIKE.
YOUR LIBRARY MAKES OUR SMALL CORNER OF THE WORLD ALMOST FEEL BIG.
THANK YOU, PÈRE ROBERT.

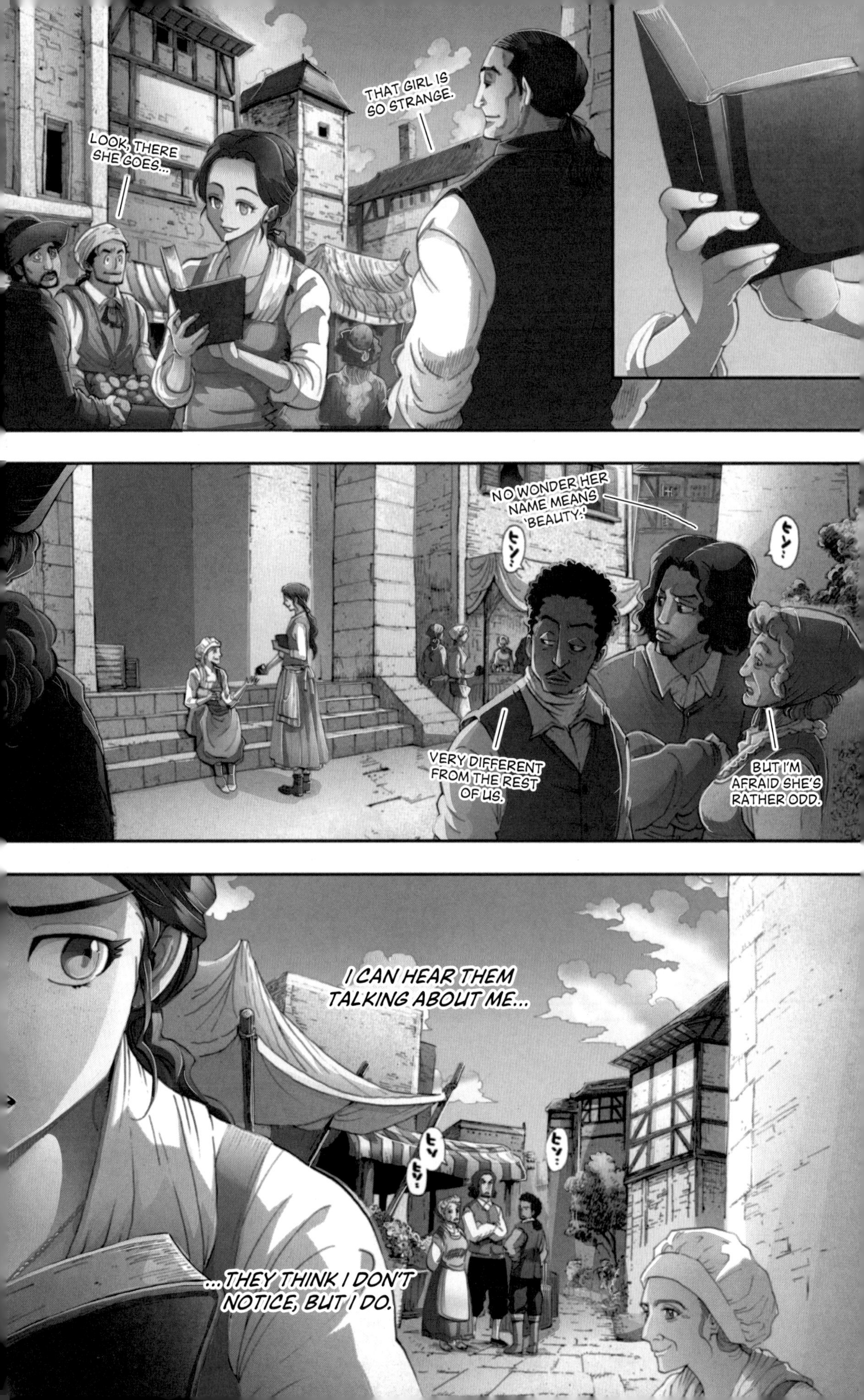
THAT GIRL IS SO STRANGE.
LOOK, THERE SHE GOES...
NO WONDER HER NAME MEANS 'BEAUTY.'
ヒソ…
ヒソ…
BUT I'M AFRAID SHE'S RATHER ODD.
VERY DIFFERENT FROM THE REST OF US.
I CAN HEAR THEM TALKING ABOUT ME...
ヒソ…
ヒソ ヒソ
...THEY THINK I DON'T NOTICE, BUT I DO.

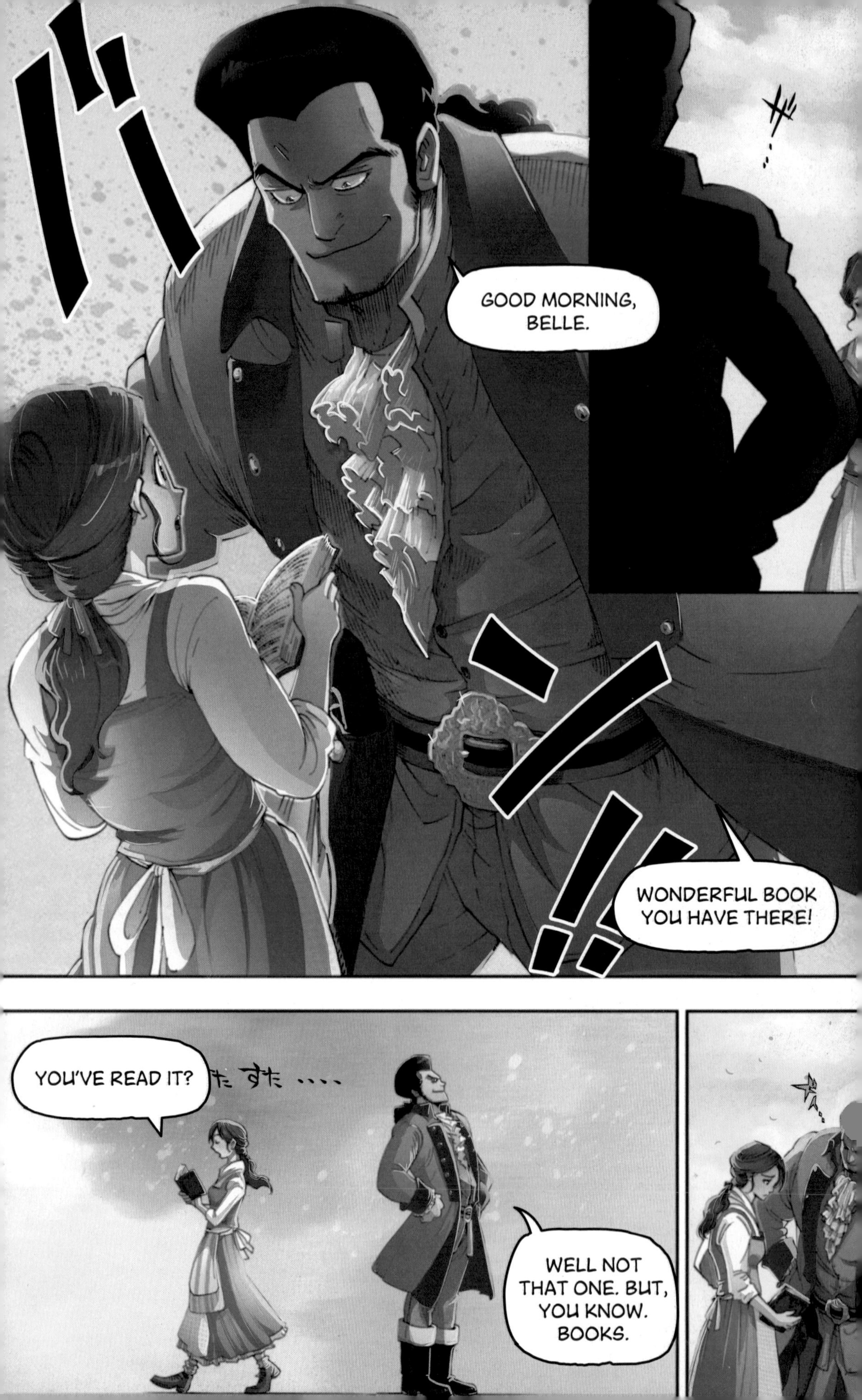
GOOD MORNING, BELLE.
WONDERFUL BOOK YOU HAVE THERE!
YOU'VE READ IT?
たすた ····
WELL NOT THAT ONE. BUT, YOU KNOW. BOOKS.

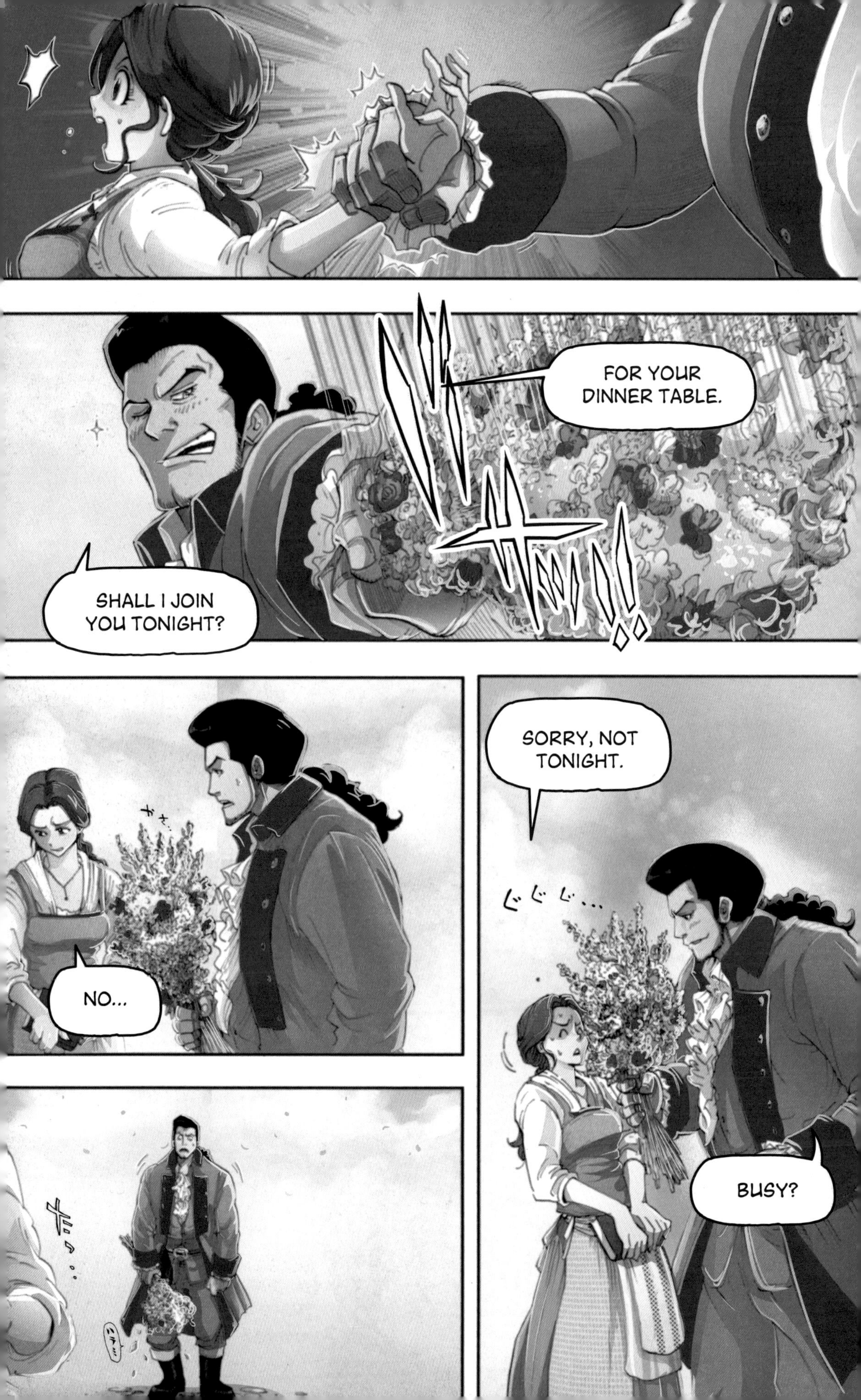
FOR YOUR DINNER TABLE.
SHALL I JOIN YOU TONIGHT?
SORRY, NOT TONIGHT.
じじじ...
BUSY?
NO...

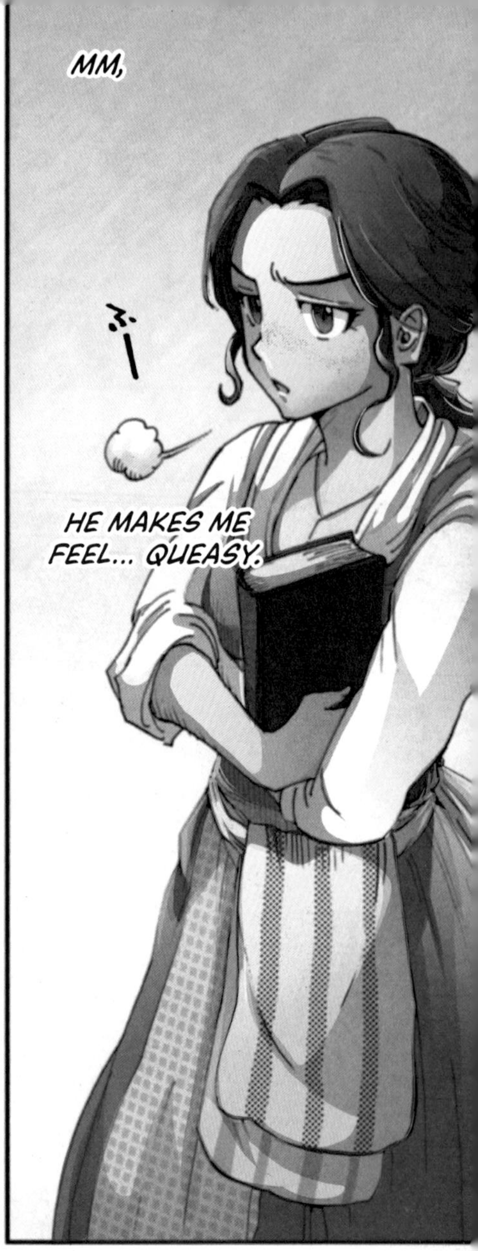
MM,
ふー
HE MAKES ME FEEL... QUEASY.
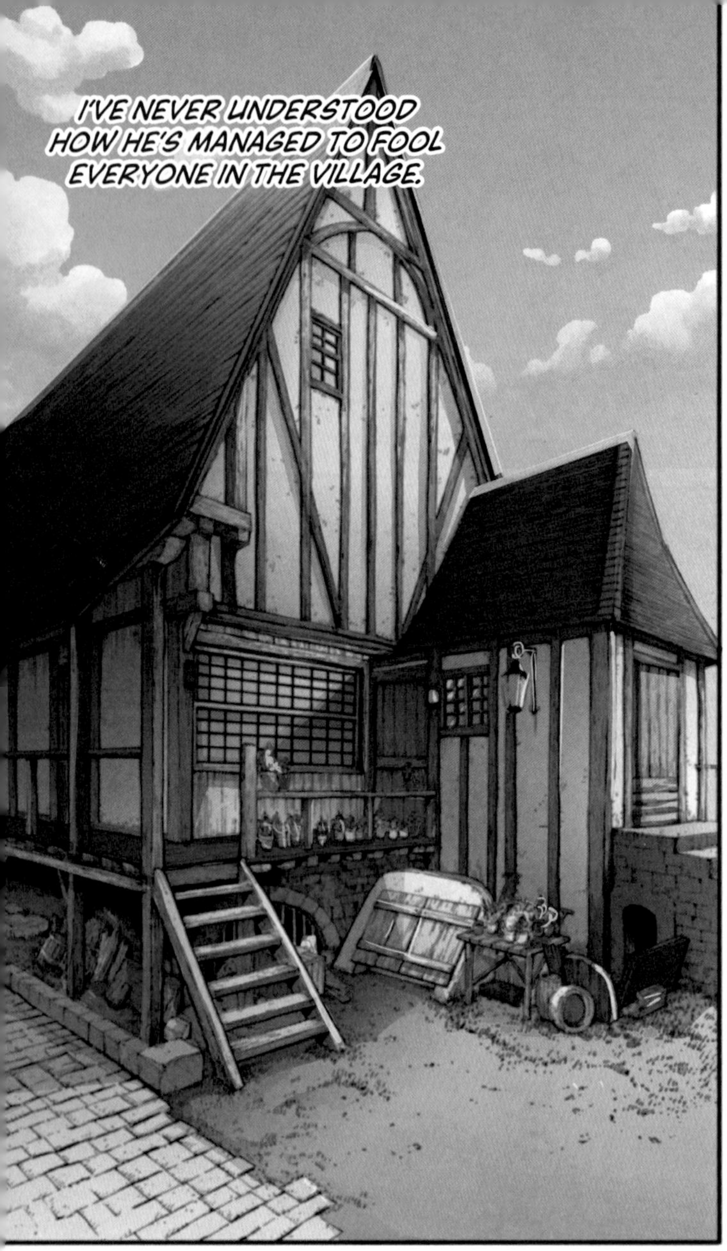
I'VE NEVER UNDERSTOOD HOW HE'S MANAGED TO FOOL EVERYONE IN THE VILLAGE.
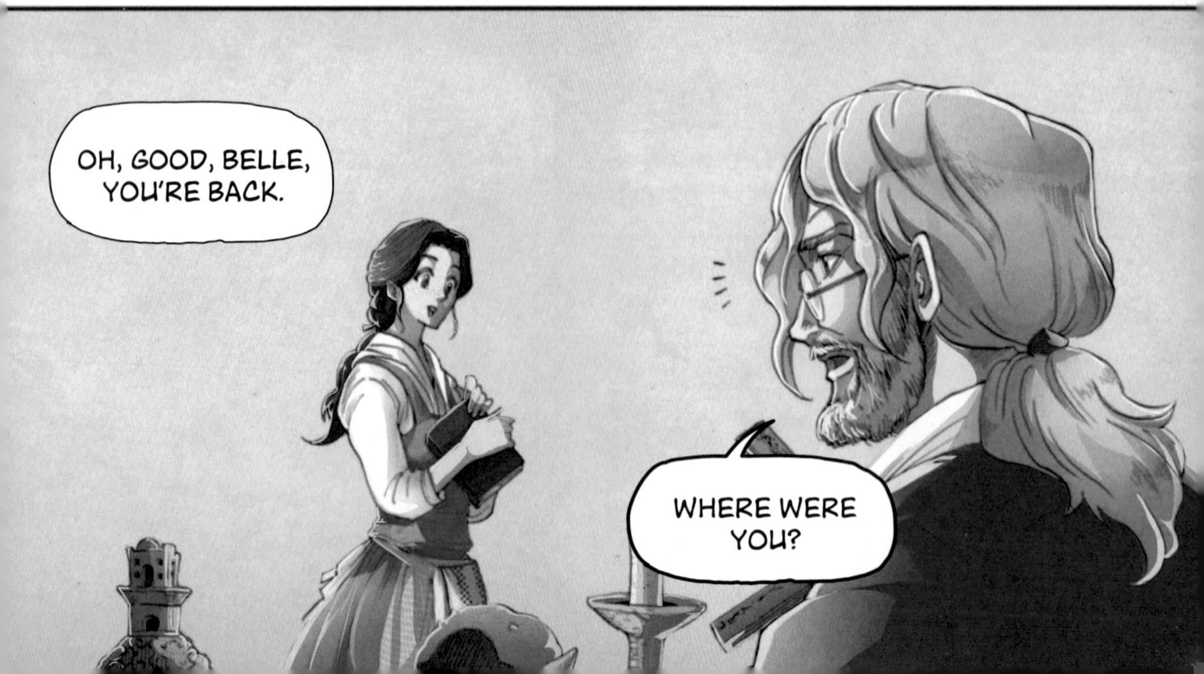
OH, GOOD, BELLE, YOU'RE BACK.
WHERE WERE YOU?

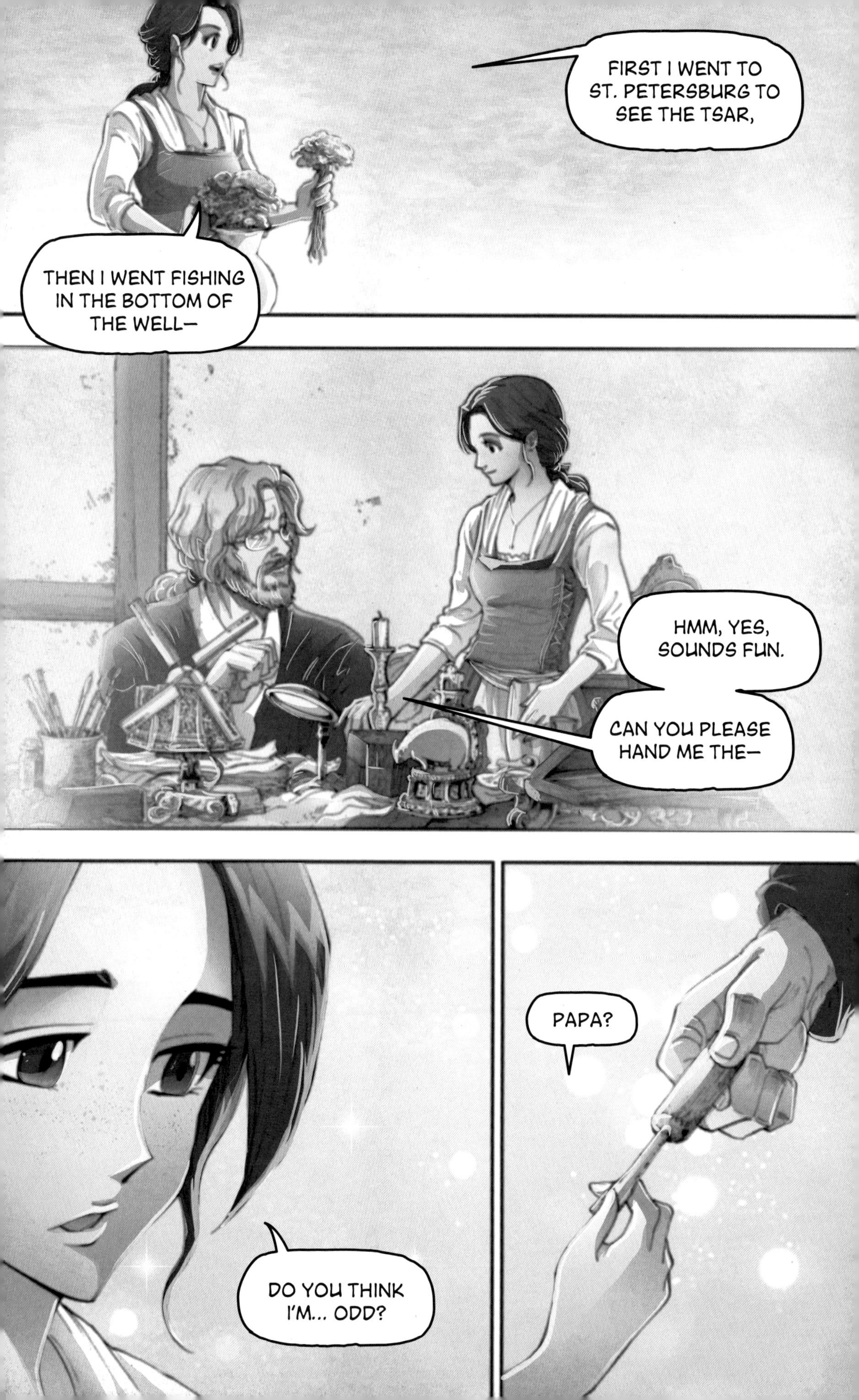
FIRST I WENT TO ST. PETERSBURG TO SEE THE TSAR,
THEN I WENT FISHING IN THE BOTTOM OF THE WELL—
HMM, YES, SOUNDS FUN.
CAN YOU PLEASE HAND ME THE—
PAPA?
DO YOU THINK I'M... ODD?

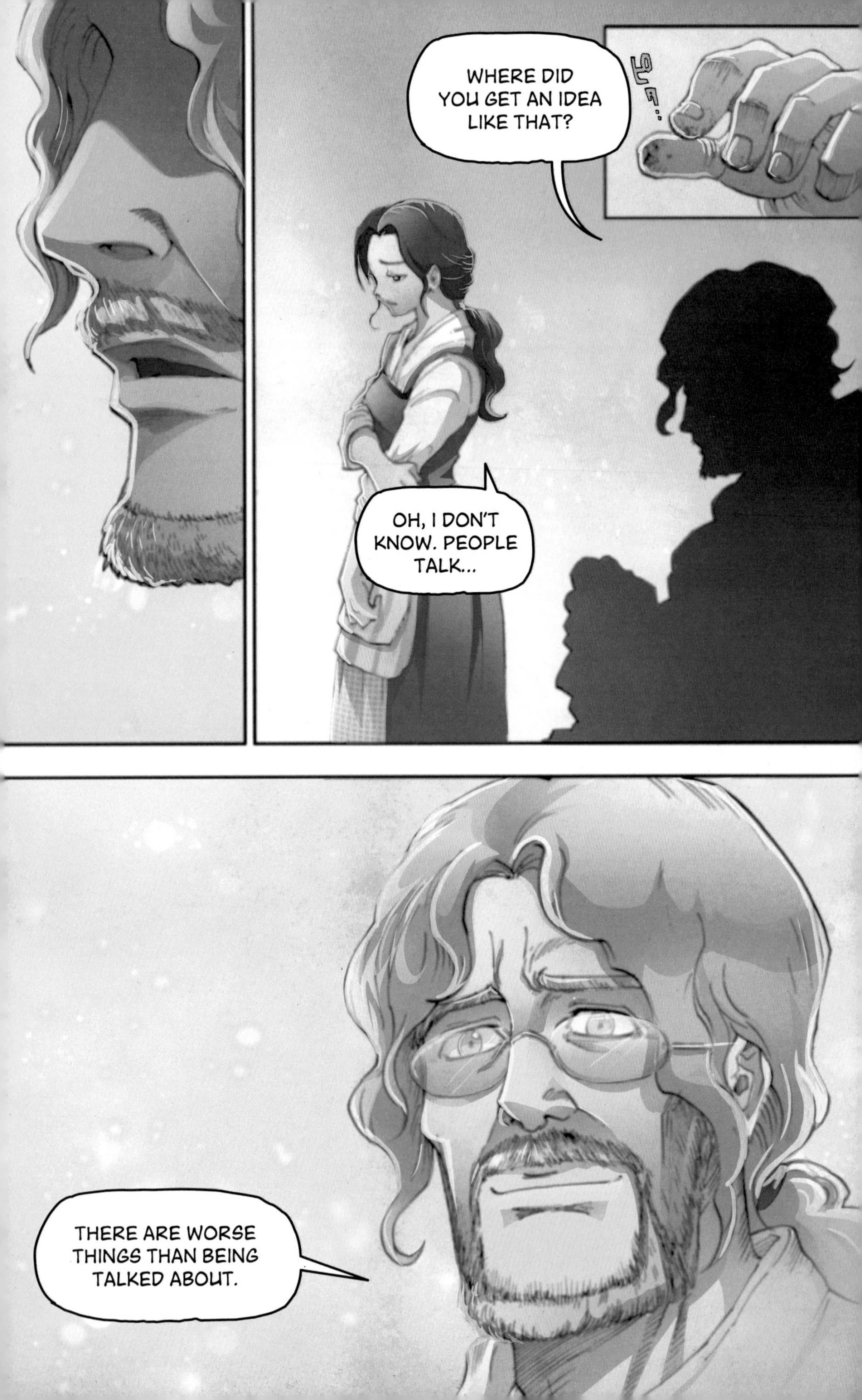
WHERE DID YOU GET AN IDEA LIKE THAT?
OH, I DON'T KNOW. PEOPLE TALK...
THERE ARE WORSE THINGS THAN BEING TALKED ABOUT.

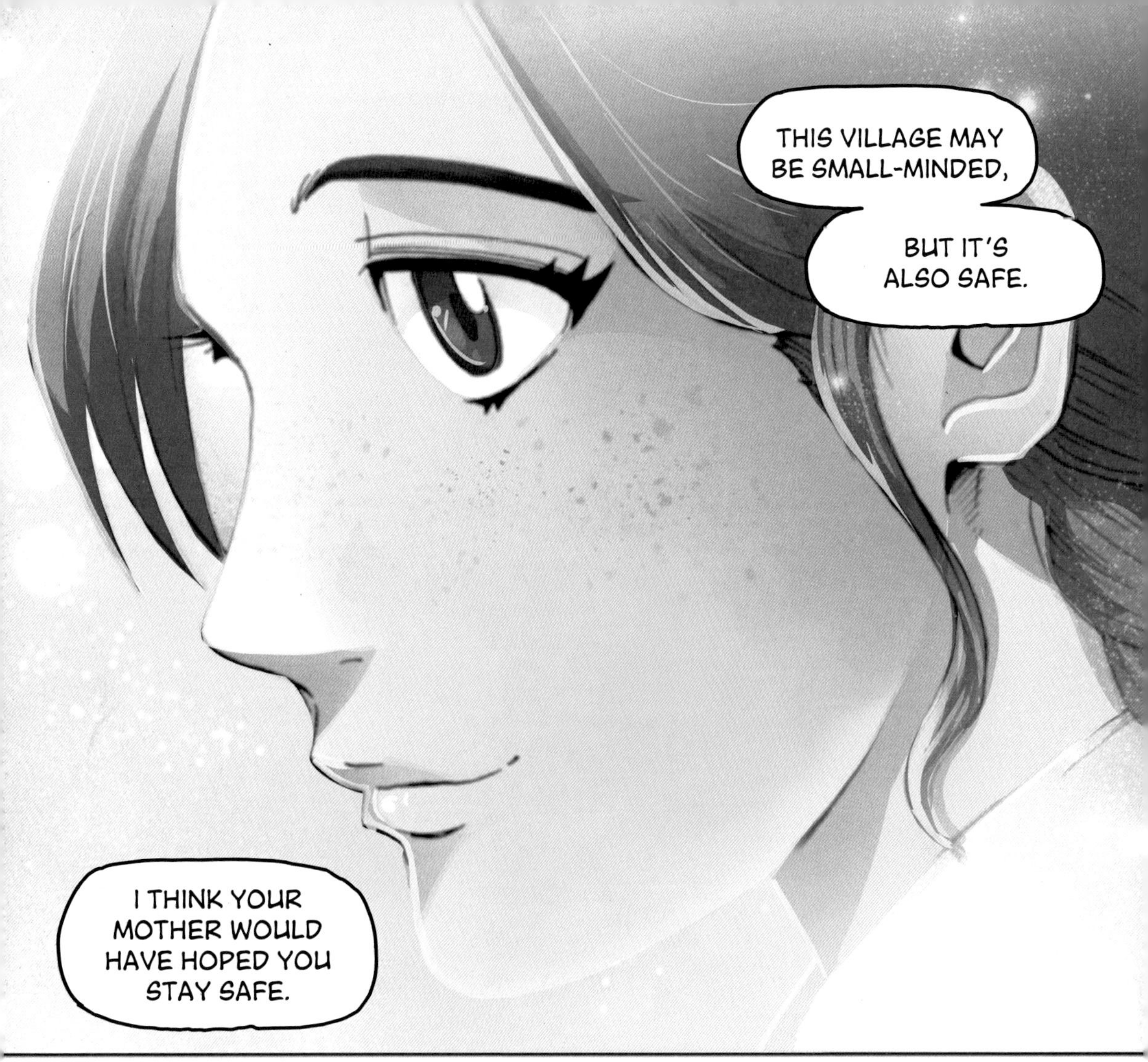
THIS VILLAGE MAY BE SMALL-MINDED,
BUT IT'S ALSO SAFE.
I THINK YOUR MOTHER WOULD HAVE HOPED YOU STAY SAFE.

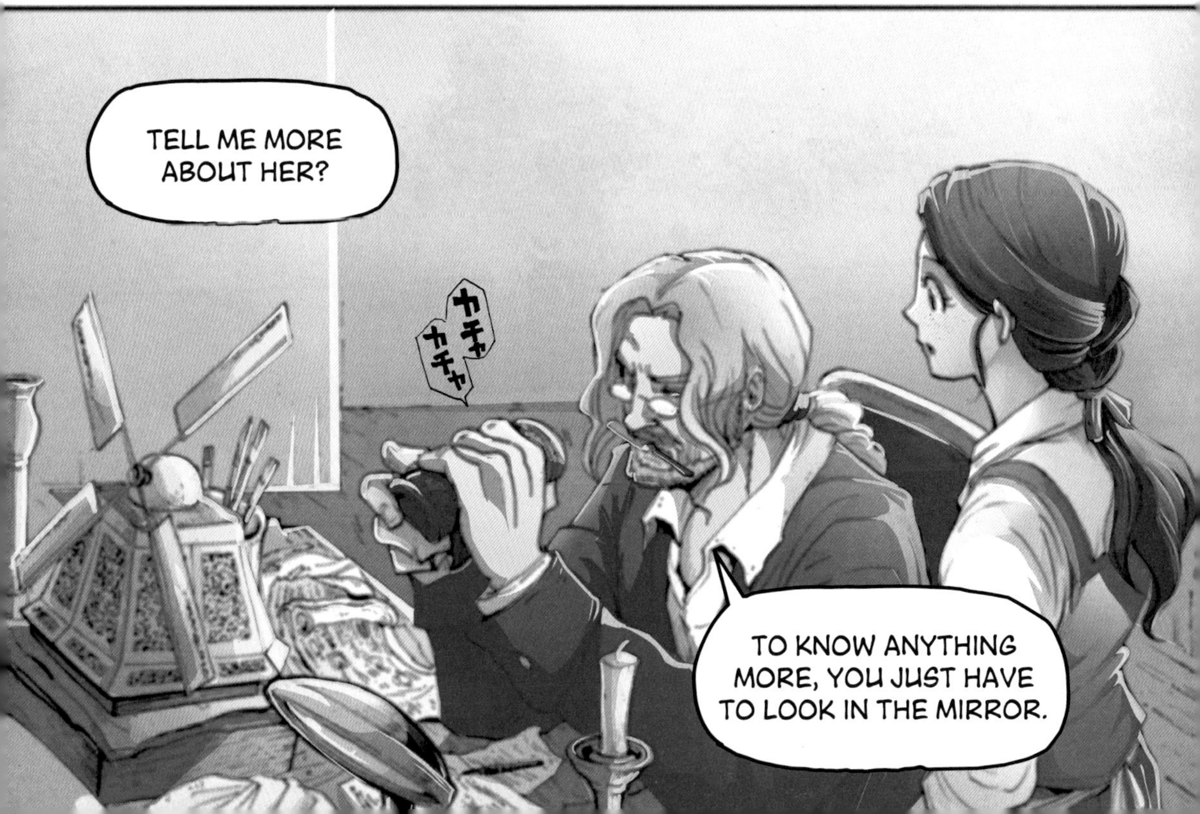
TELL ME MORE ABOUT HER?
カチャ
カチャ
TO KNOW ANYTHING MORE, YOU JUST HAVE TO LOOK IN THE MIRROR.

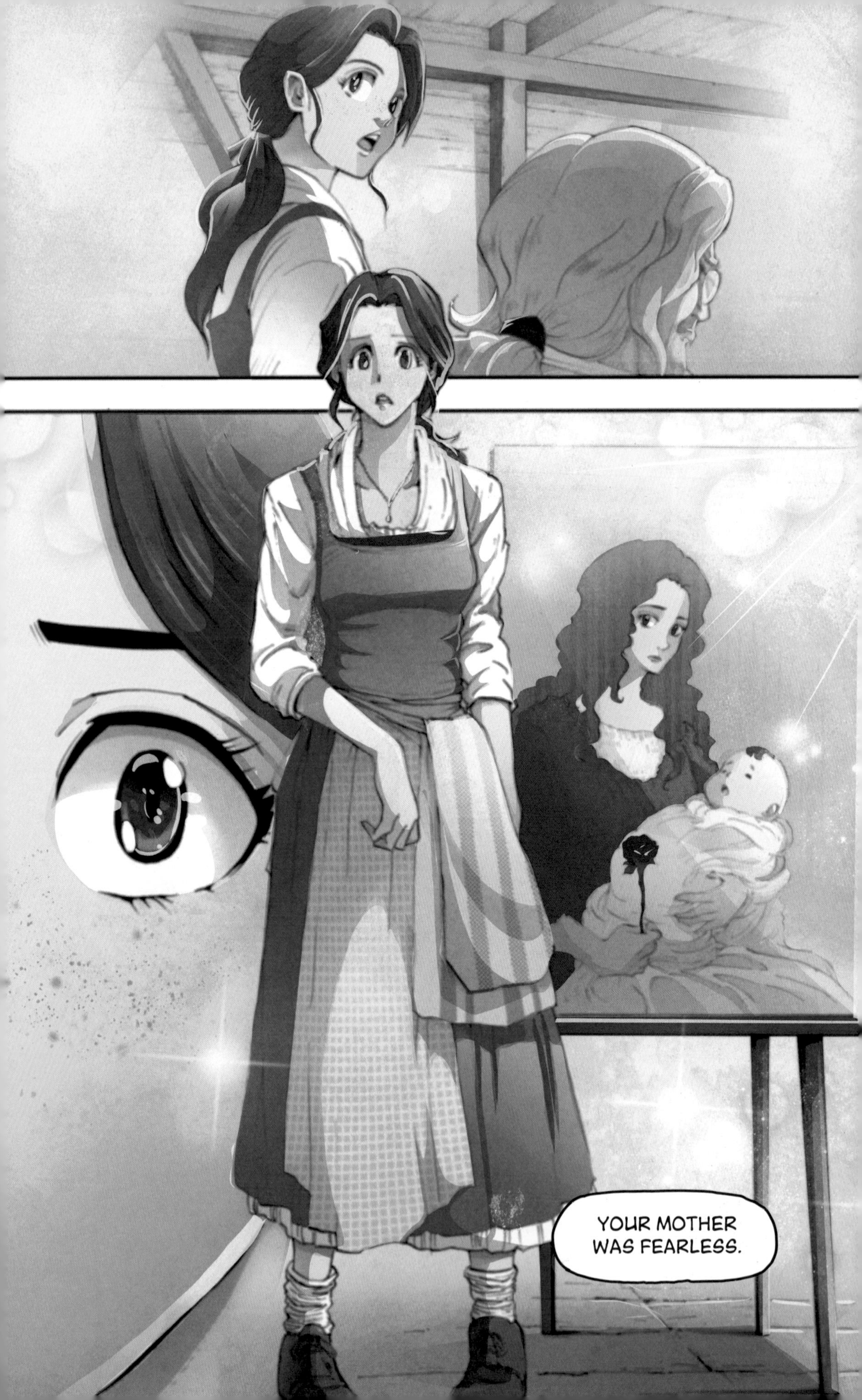
YOUR MOTHER WAS FEARLESS.

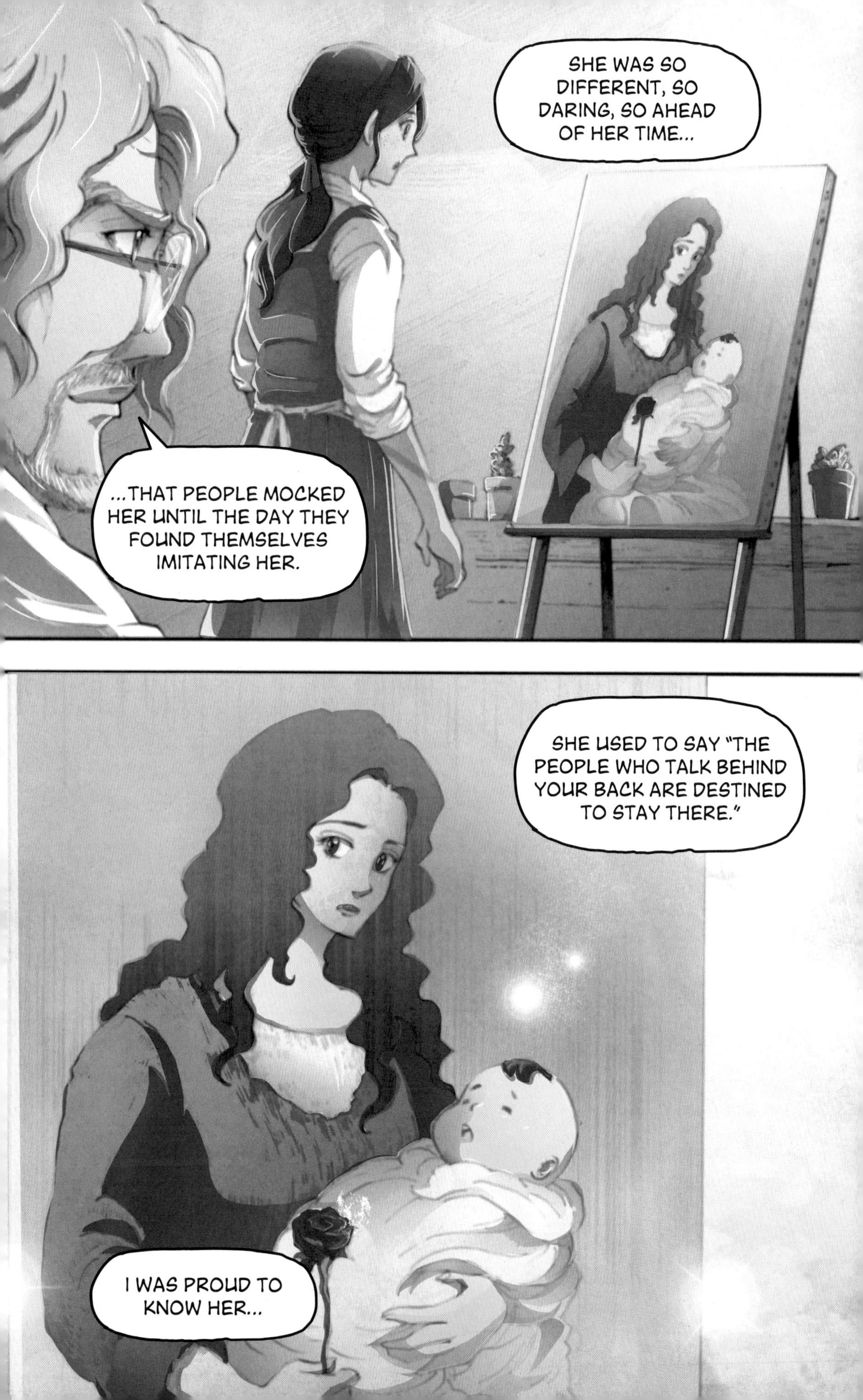
SHE WAS SO DIFFERENT, SO DARING, SO AHEAD OF HER TIME...
...THAT PEOPLE MOCKED HER UNTIL THE DAY THEY FOUND THEMSELVES IMITATING HER.
SHE USED TO SAY "THE PEOPLE WHO TALK BEHIND YOUR BACK ARE DESTINED TO STAY THERE."
I WAS PROUD TO KNOW HER...

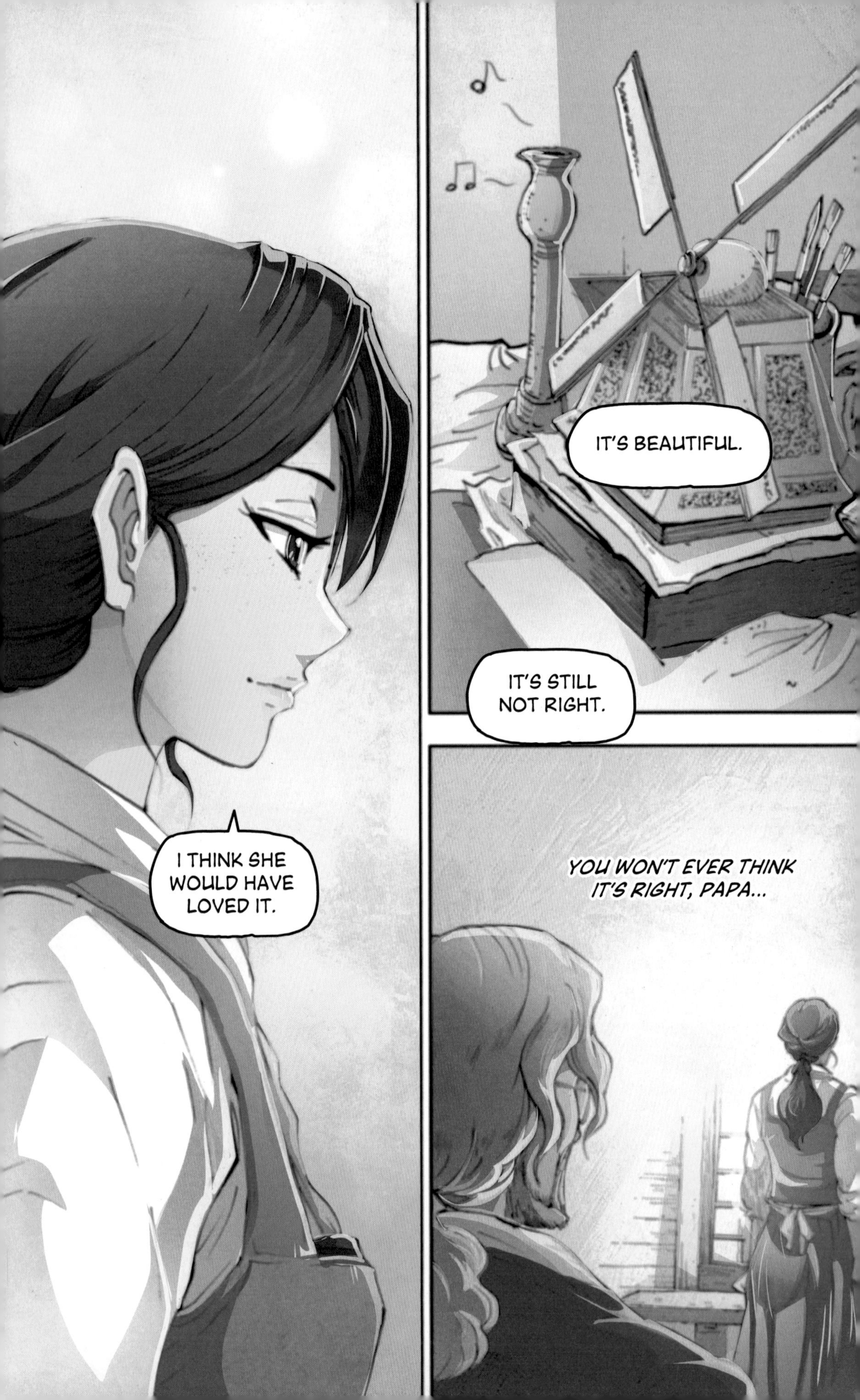
IT'S BEAUTIFUL.
IT'S STILL NOT RIGHT.
YOU WON'T EVER THINK IT'S RIGHT, PAPA...
I THINK SHE WOULD HAVE LOVED IT.

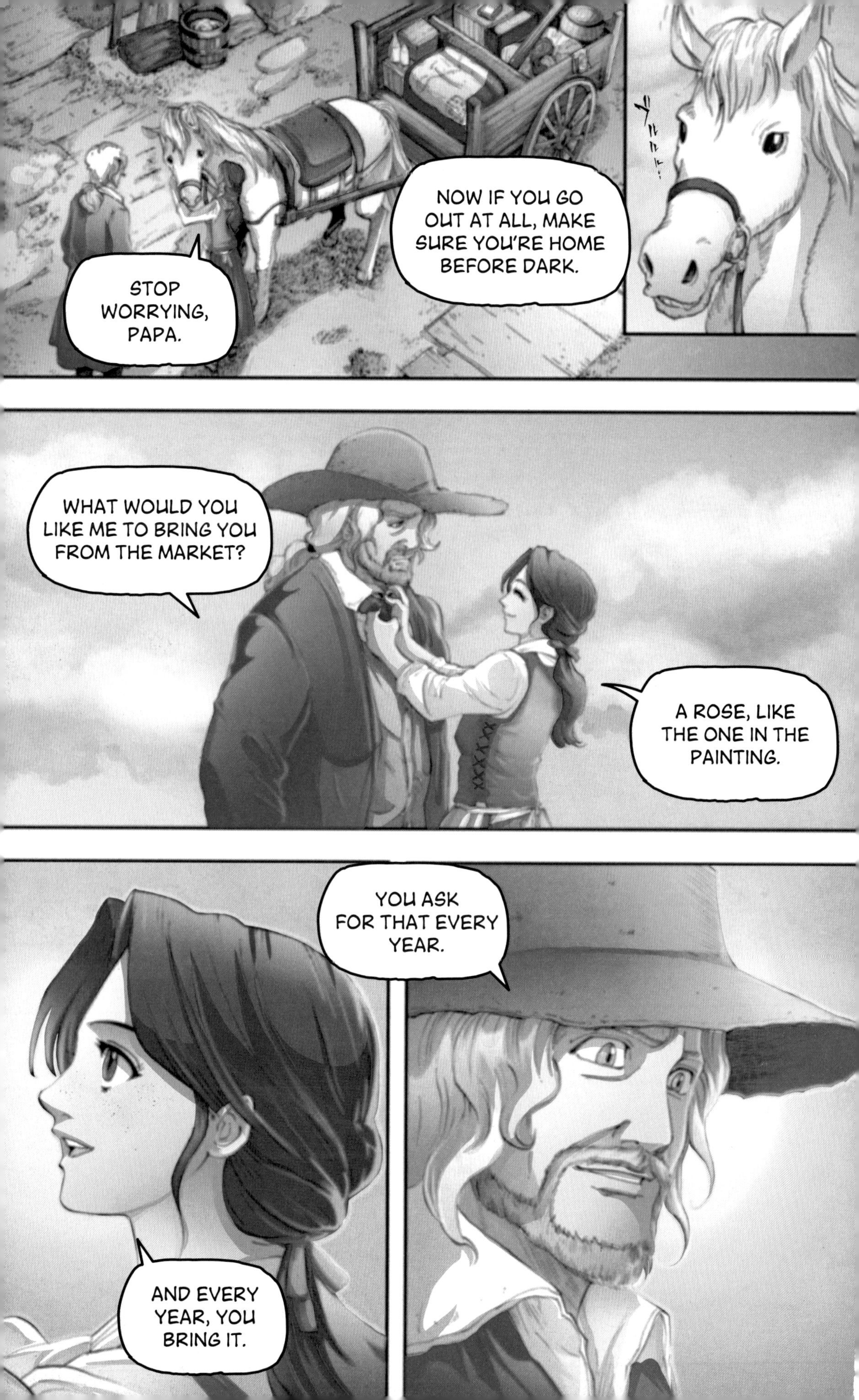
NOW IF YOU GO OUT AT ALL, MAKE SURE YOU'RE HOME BEFORE DARK.
STOP WORRYING, PAPA.
WHAT WOULD YOU LIKE ME TO BRING YOU FROM THE MARKET?
A ROSE, LIKE THE ONE IN THE PAINTING.
YOU ASK FOR THAT EVERY YEAR.
AND EVERY YEAR, YOU BRING IT.

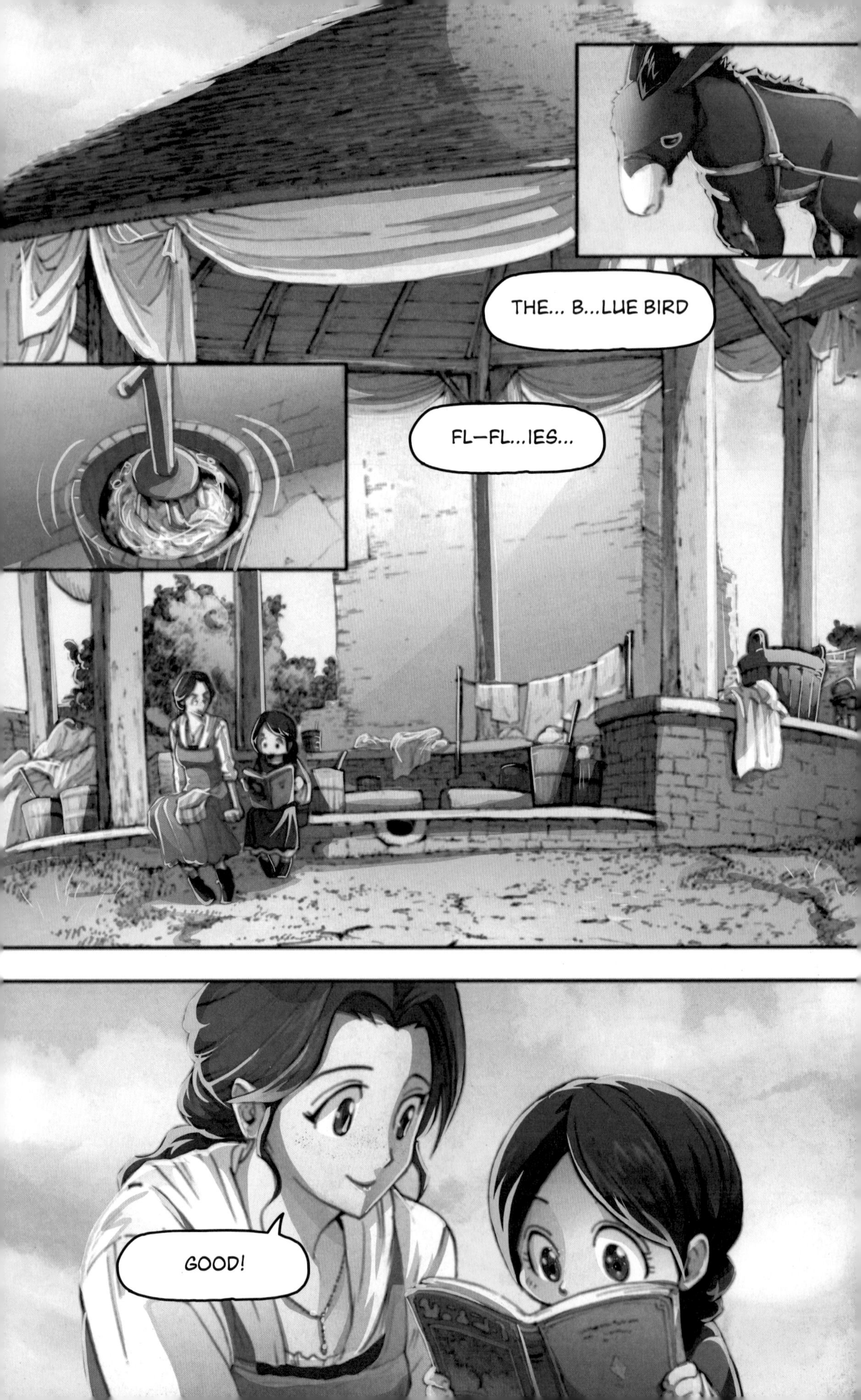
THE... B...LUE BIRD
FL—FL...IES...
GOOD!

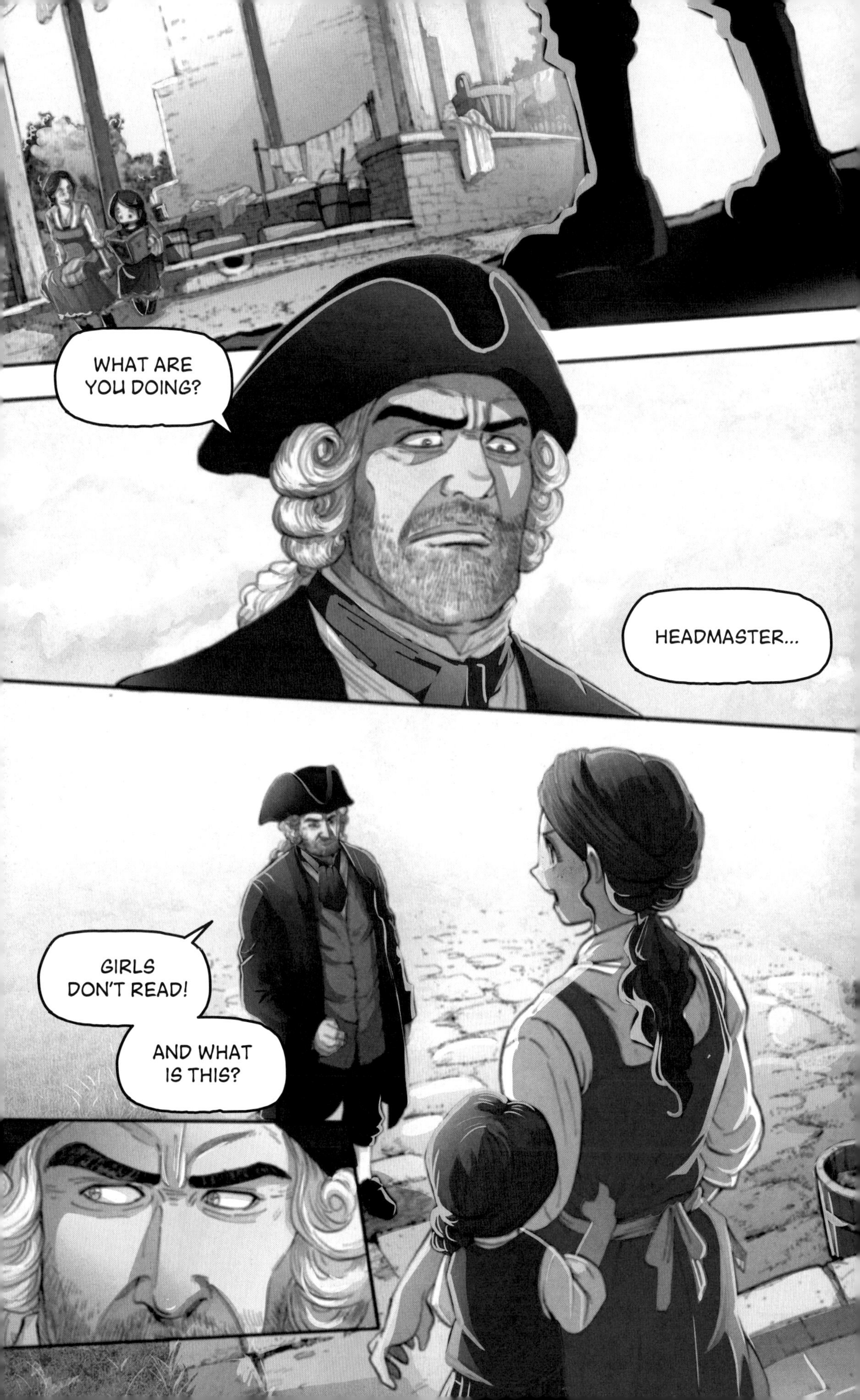
WHAT ARE YOU DOING?
HEADMASTER...
GIRLS DON'T READ!
AND WHAT IS THIS?

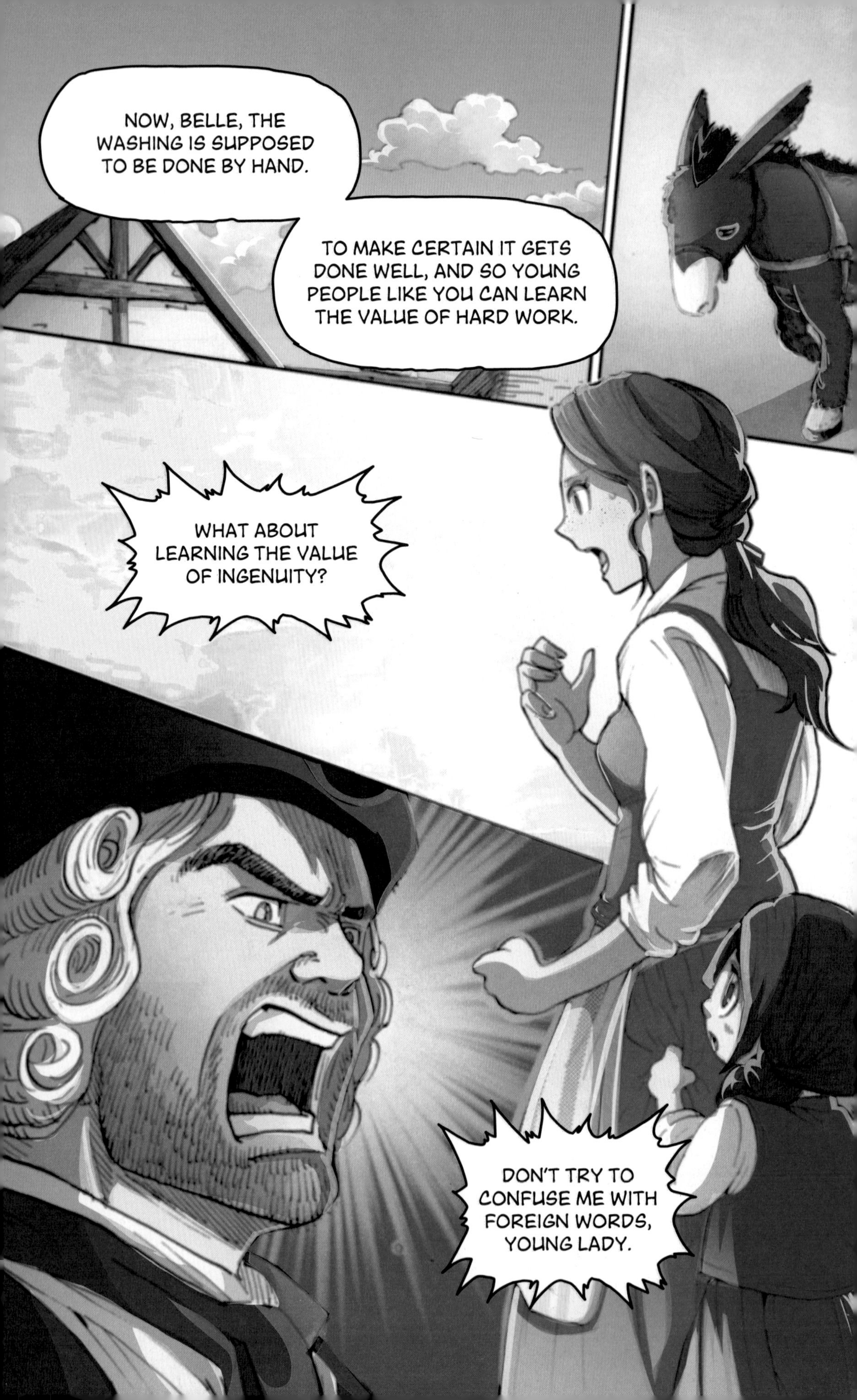
NOW, BELLE, THE WASHING IS SUPPOSED TO BE DONE BY HAND.
TO MAKE CERTAIN IT GETS DONE WELL, AND SO YOUNG PEOPLE LIKE YOU CAN LEARN THE VALUE OF HARD WORK.
WHAT ABOUT LEARNING THE VALUE OF INGENUITY?
DON'T TRY TO CONFUSE ME WITH FOREIGN WORDS, YOUNG LADY.

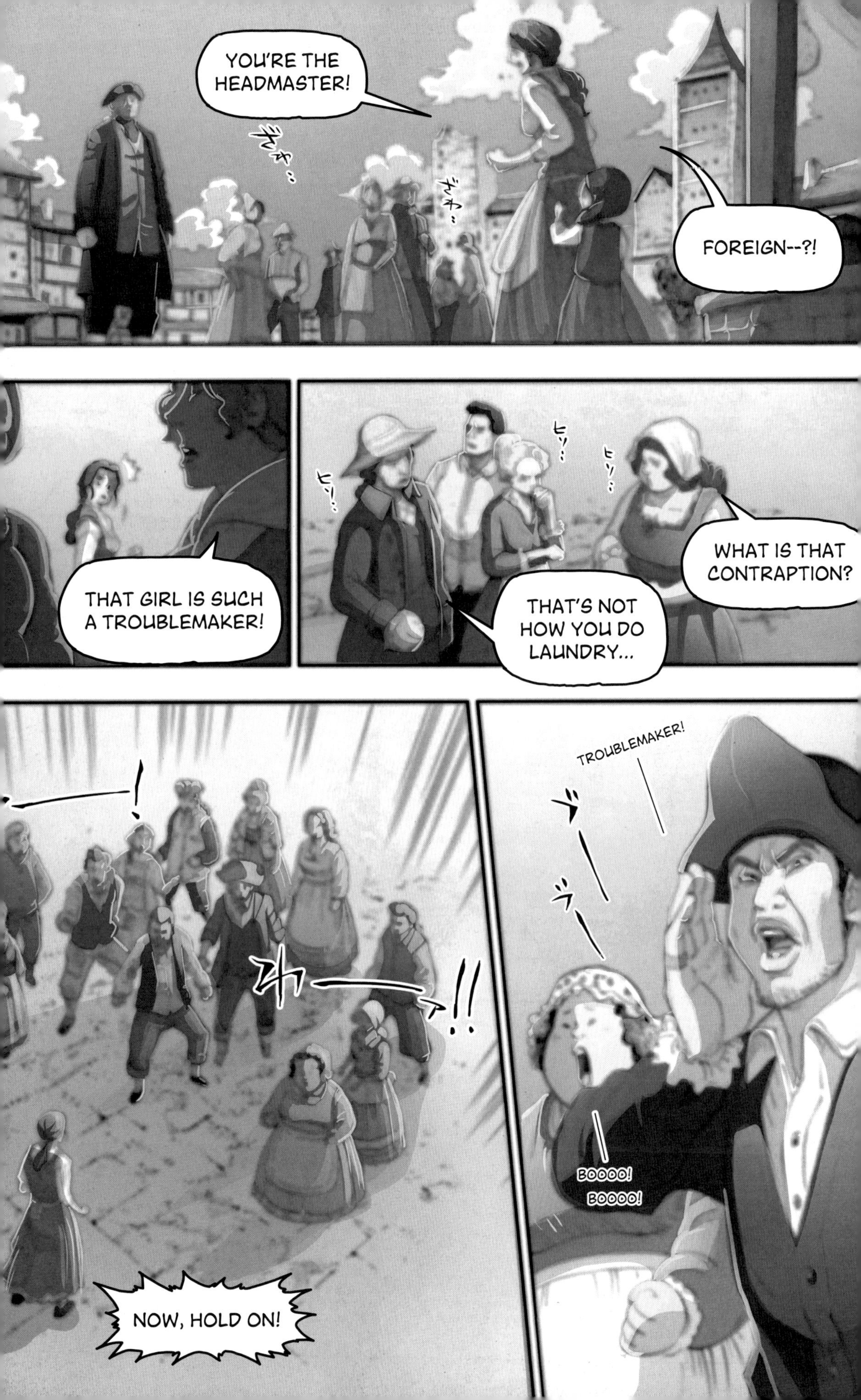
YOU'RE THE HEADMASTER!
FOREIGN--?!
WHAT IS THAT CONTRAPTION?
THAT'S NOT HOW YOU DO LAUNDRY...
THAT GIRL IS SUCH A TROUBLEMAKER!
TROUBLEMAKER!
BOOOO!
BOOOO!
NOW, HOLD ON!

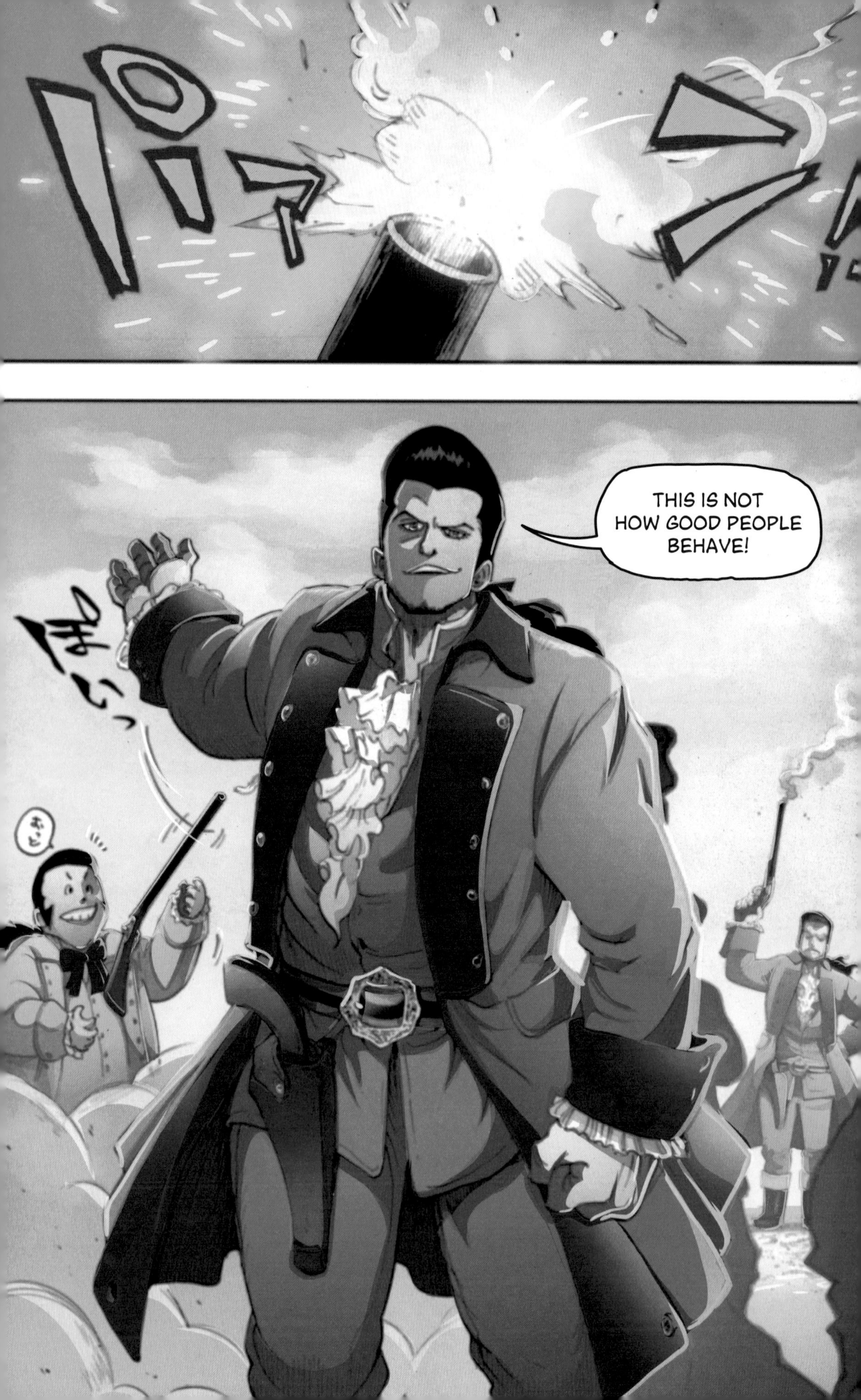
パァン!
THIS IS NOT HOW GOOD PEOPLE BEHAVE!
ぽいっ

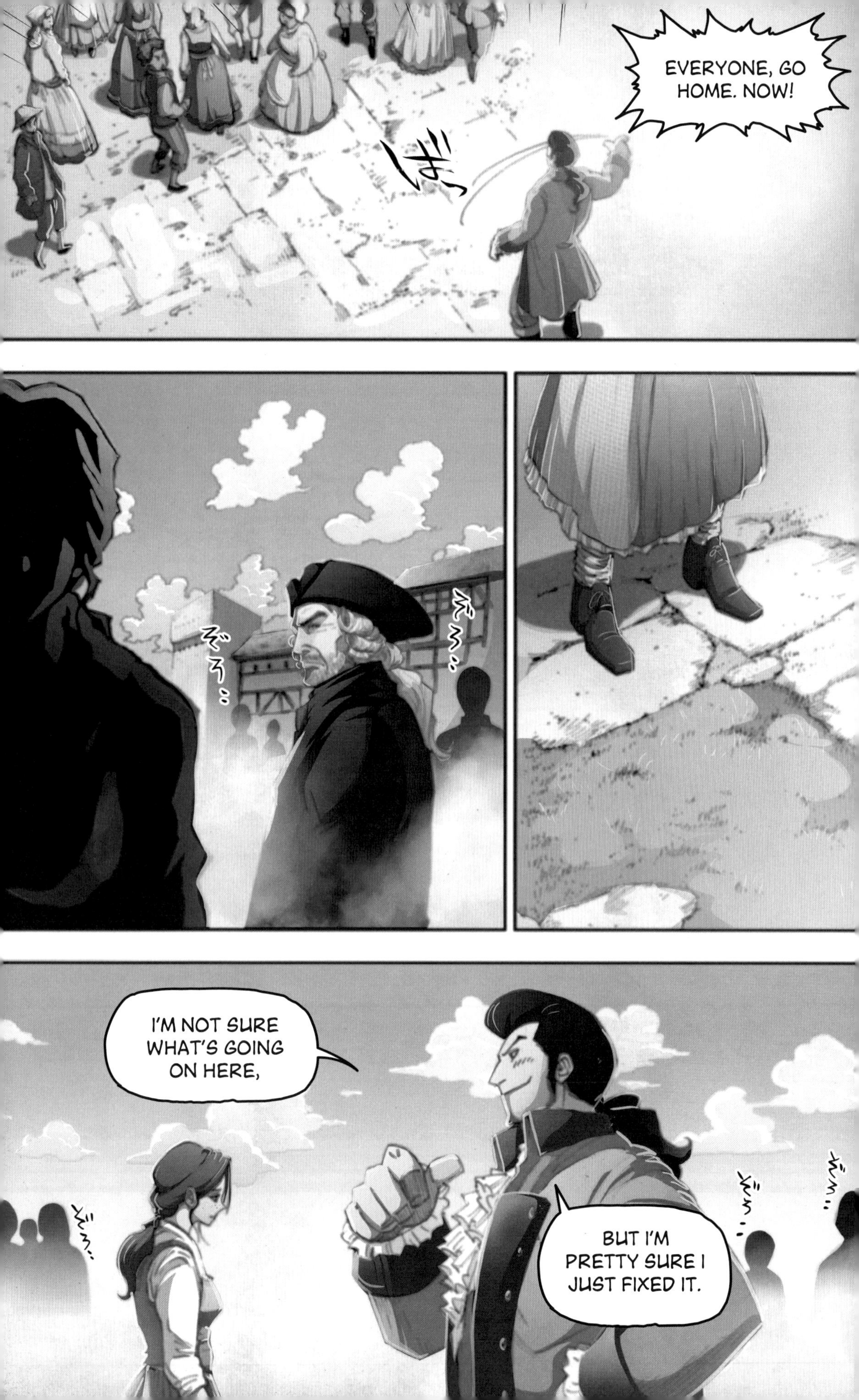
EVERYONE, GO HOME. NOW!
I'M NOT SURE WHAT'S GOING ON HERE,
BUT I'M PRETTY SURE I JUST FIXED IT.

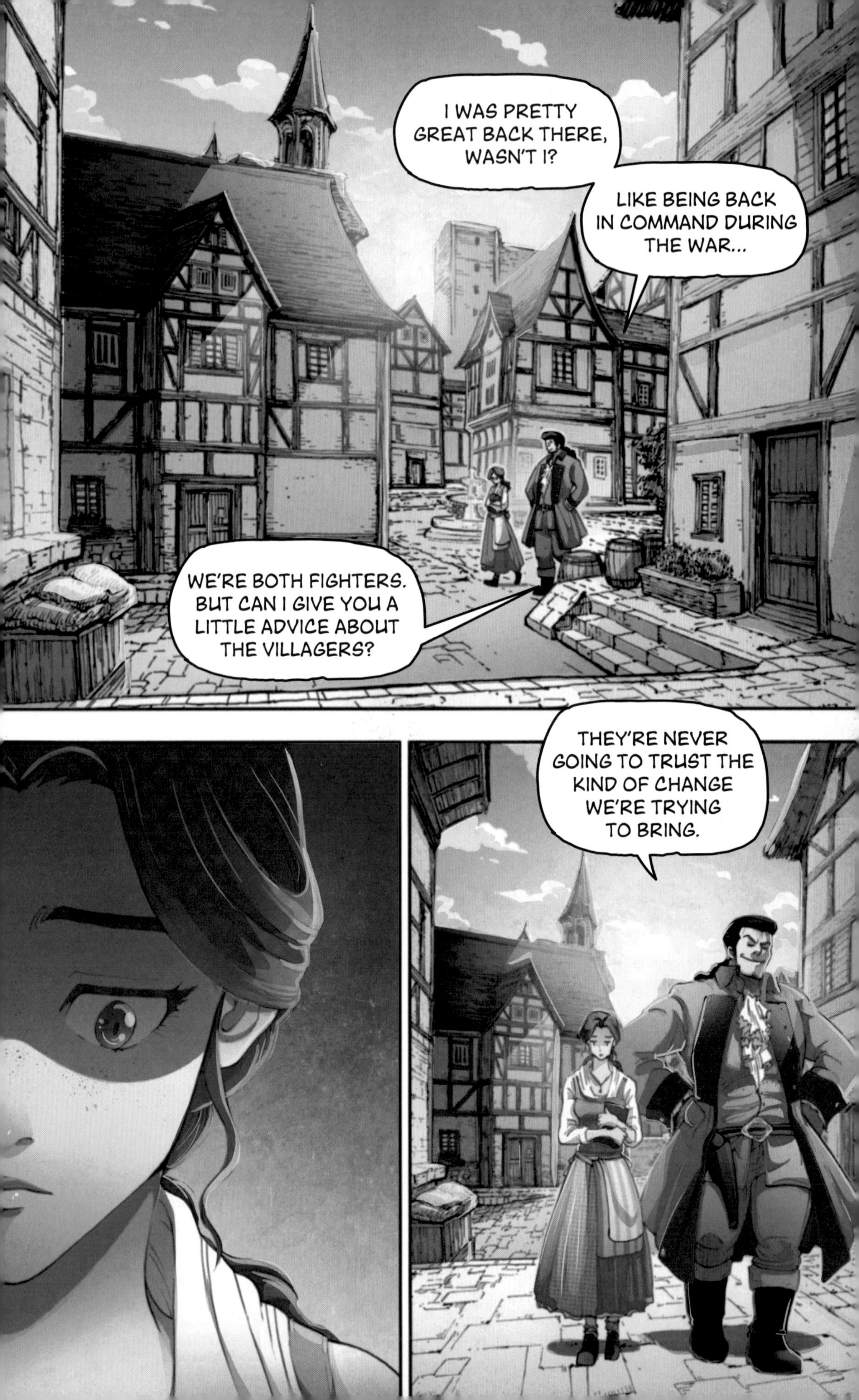
I WAS PRETTY GREAT BACK THERE, WASN'T I?
LIKE BEING BACK IN COMMAND DURING THE WAR...
WE'RE BOTH FIGHTERS. BUT CAN I GIVE YOU A LITTLE ADVICE ABOUT THE VILLAGERS?
THEY'RE NEVER GOING TO TRUST THE KIND OF CHANGE WE'RE TRYING TO BRING.

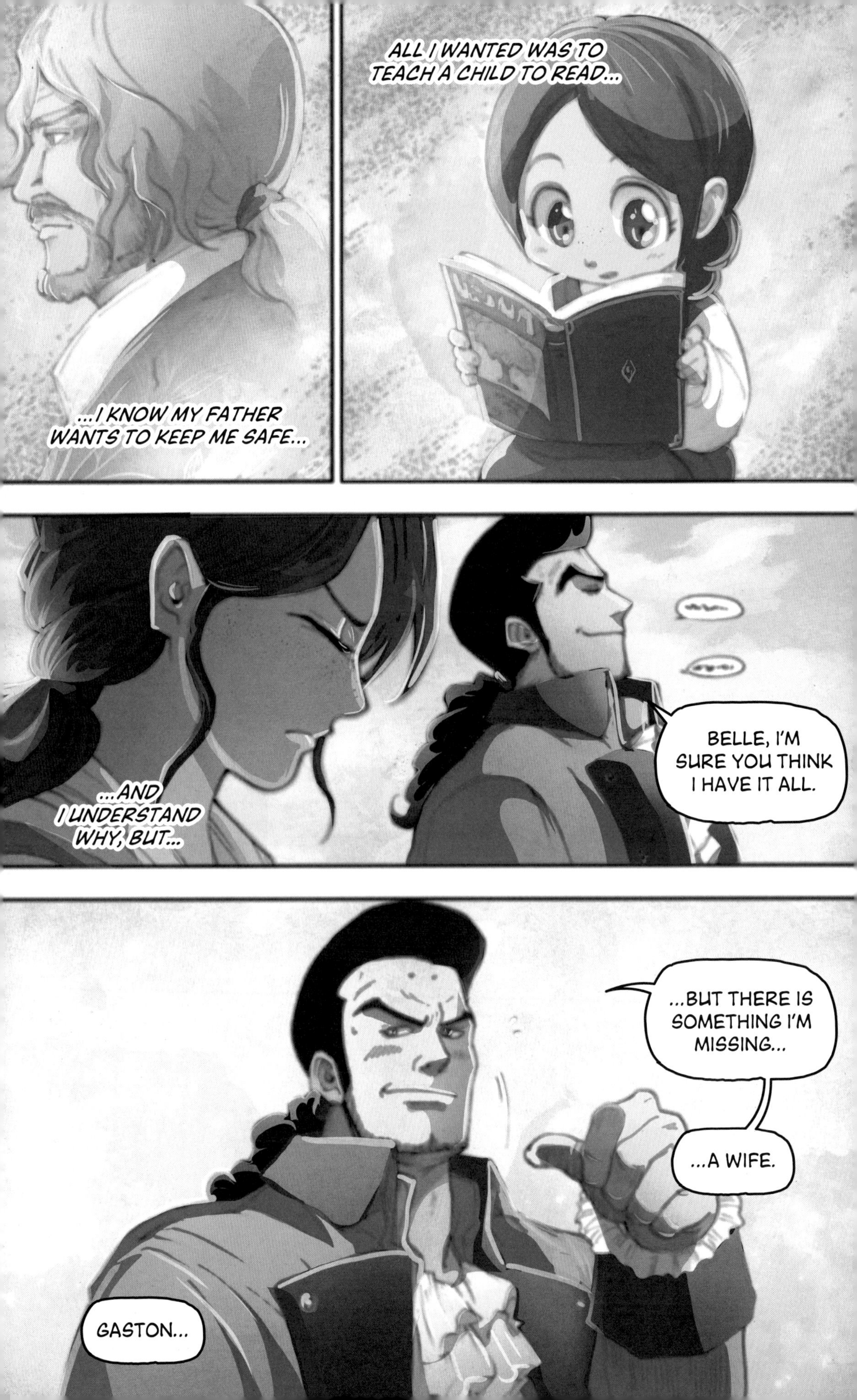
ALL I WANTED WAS TO TEACH A CHILD TO READ...
...I KNOW MY FATHER WANTS TO KEEP ME SAFE...
BELLE, I'M SURE YOU THINK I HAVE IT ALL.
...AND I UNDERSTAND WHY, BUT...
...BUT THERE IS SOMETHING I'M MISSING...
...A WIFE.
GASTON...

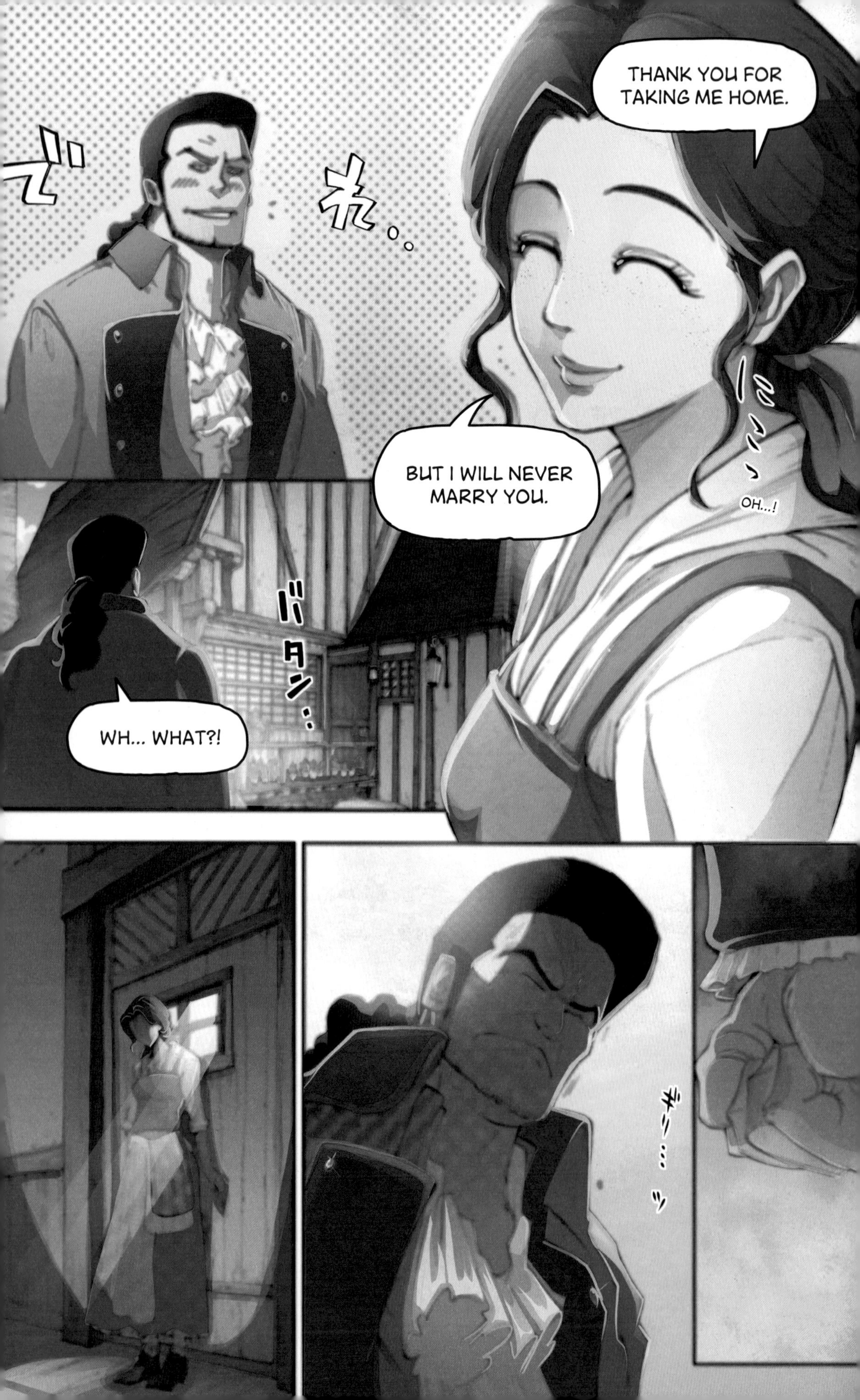
THANK YOU FOR TAKING ME HOME.
BUT I WILL NEVER MARRY YOU.
OH...!
バタン
WH... WHAT?!

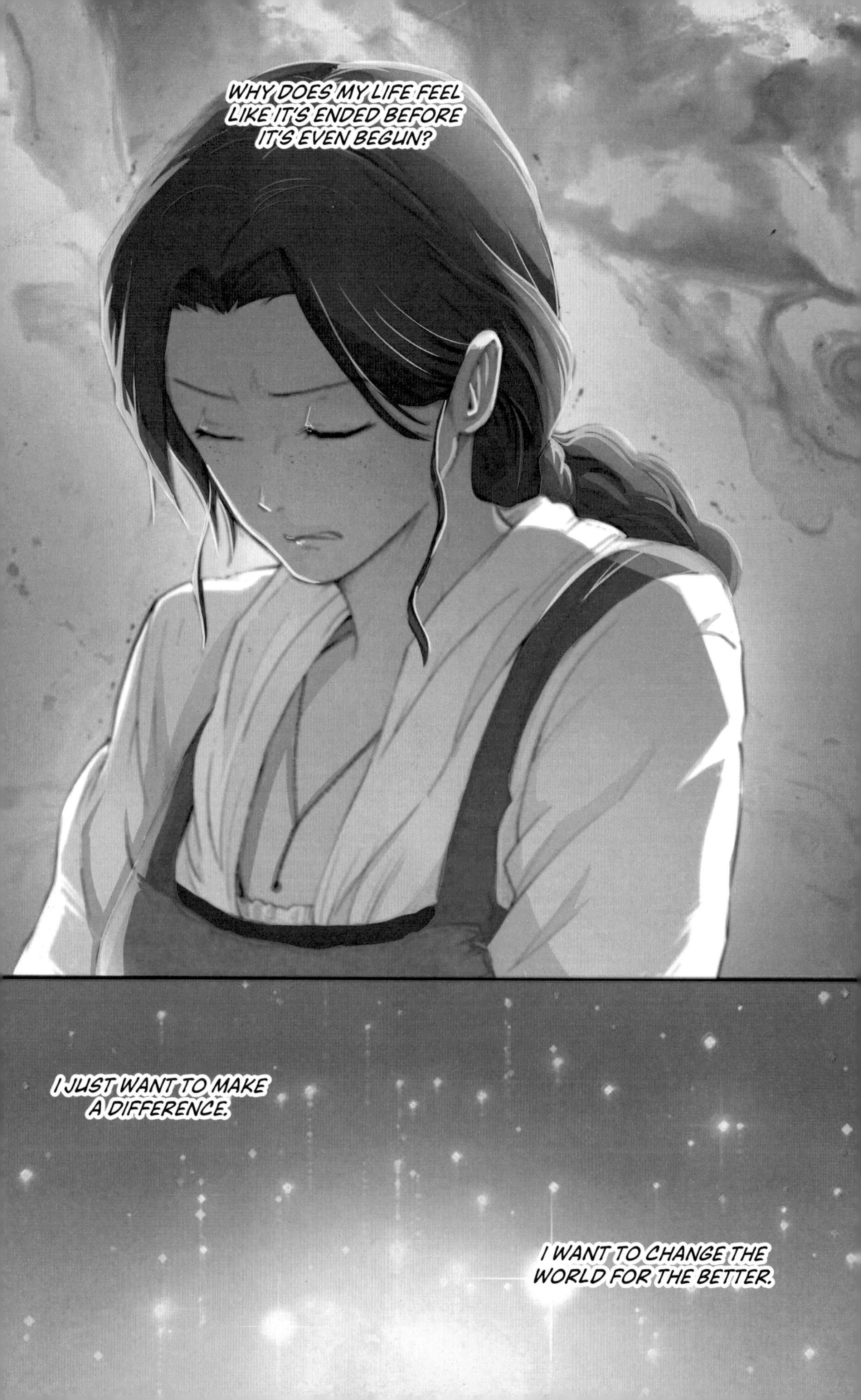
WHY DOES MY LIFE FEEL LIKE IT'S ENDED BEFORE IT'S EVEN BEGUN?
I JUST WANT TO MAKE A DIFFERENCE.
I WANT TO CHANGE THE WORLD FOR THE BETTER.

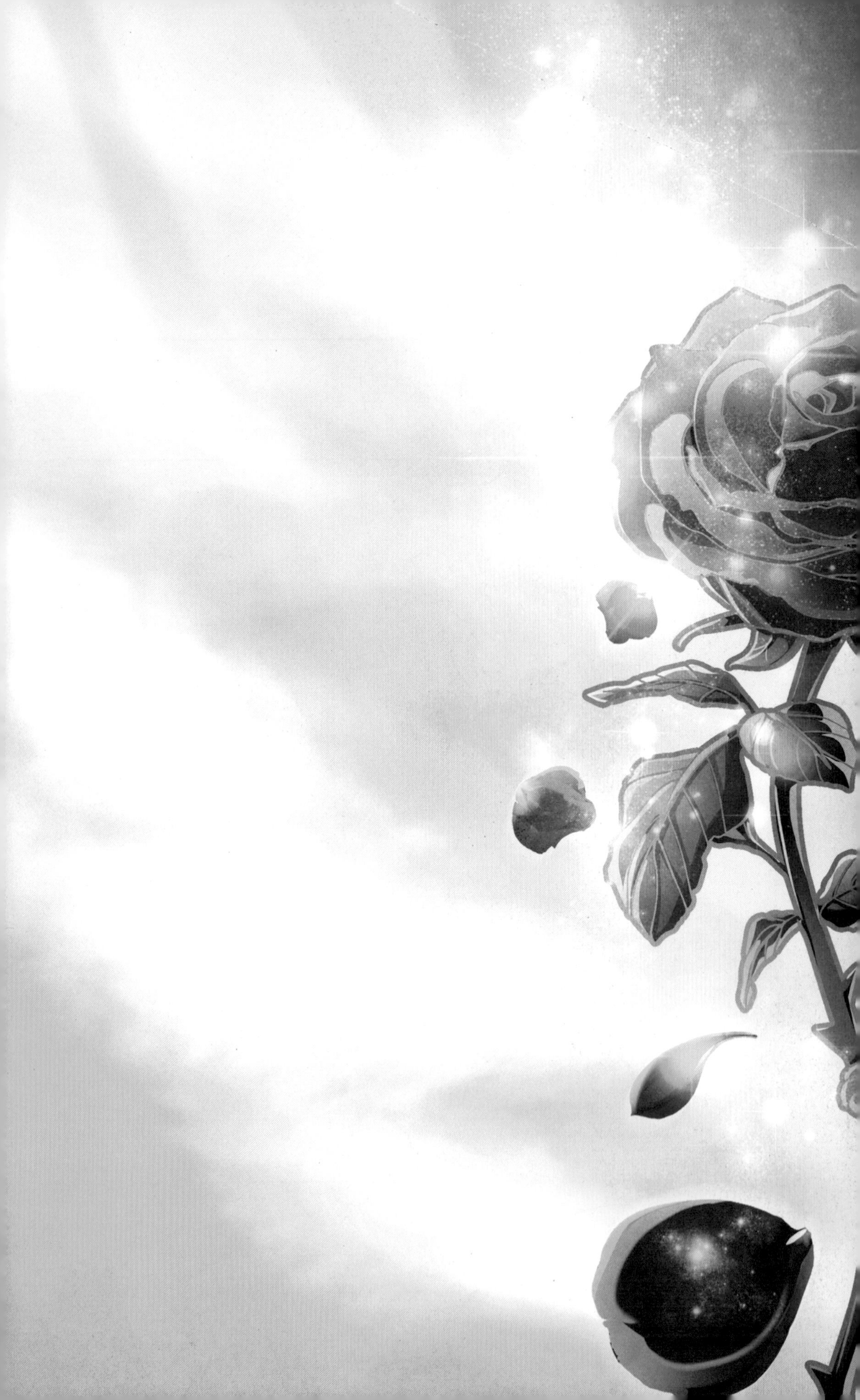

Chapter 2

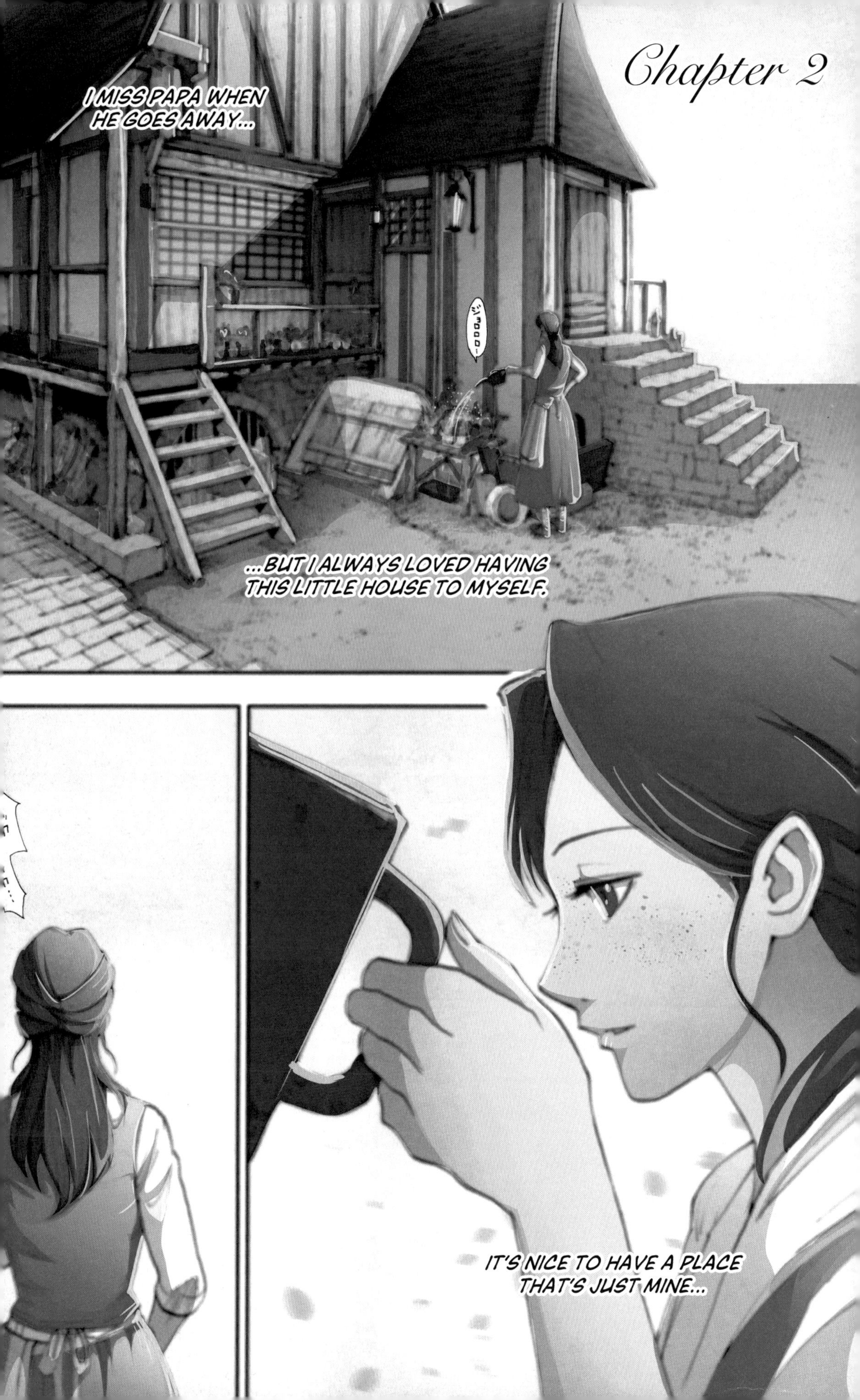
I MISS PAPA WHEN HE GOES AWAY...
...BUT I ALWAYS LOVED HAVING THIS LITTLE HOUSE TO MYSELF.
IT'S NICE TO HAVE A PLACE THAT'S JUST MINE...

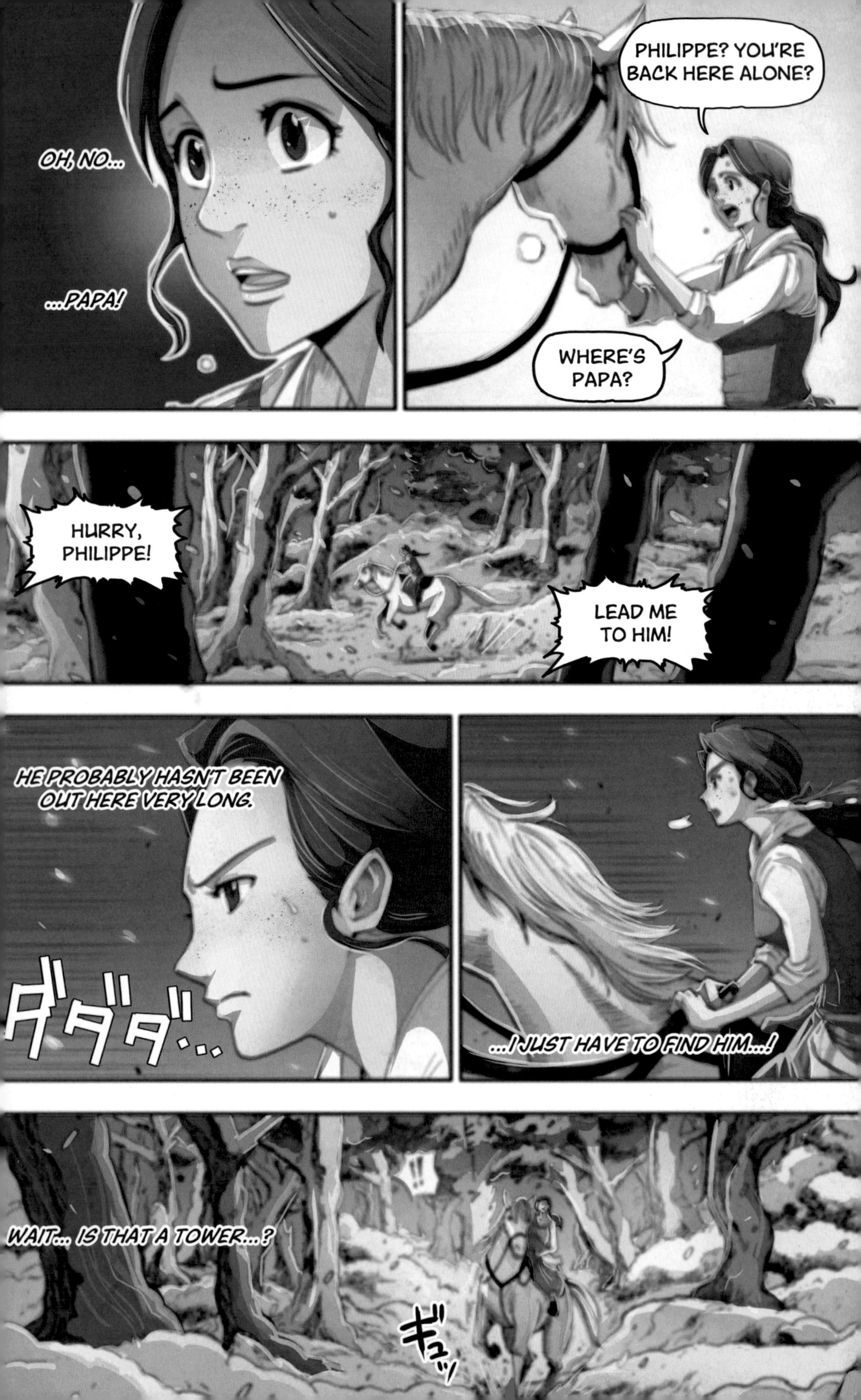
PHILIPPE? YOU'RE BACK HERE ALONE?
WHERE'S PAPA?
OH, NO...
...PAPA!
HURRY, PHILIPPE!
LEAD ME TO HIM!
...I JUST HAVE TO FIND HIM...!
HE PROBABLY HASN'T BEEN OUT HERE VERY LONG.
ダダダ...
!!
WAIT... IS THAT A TOWER...?
ギュッ

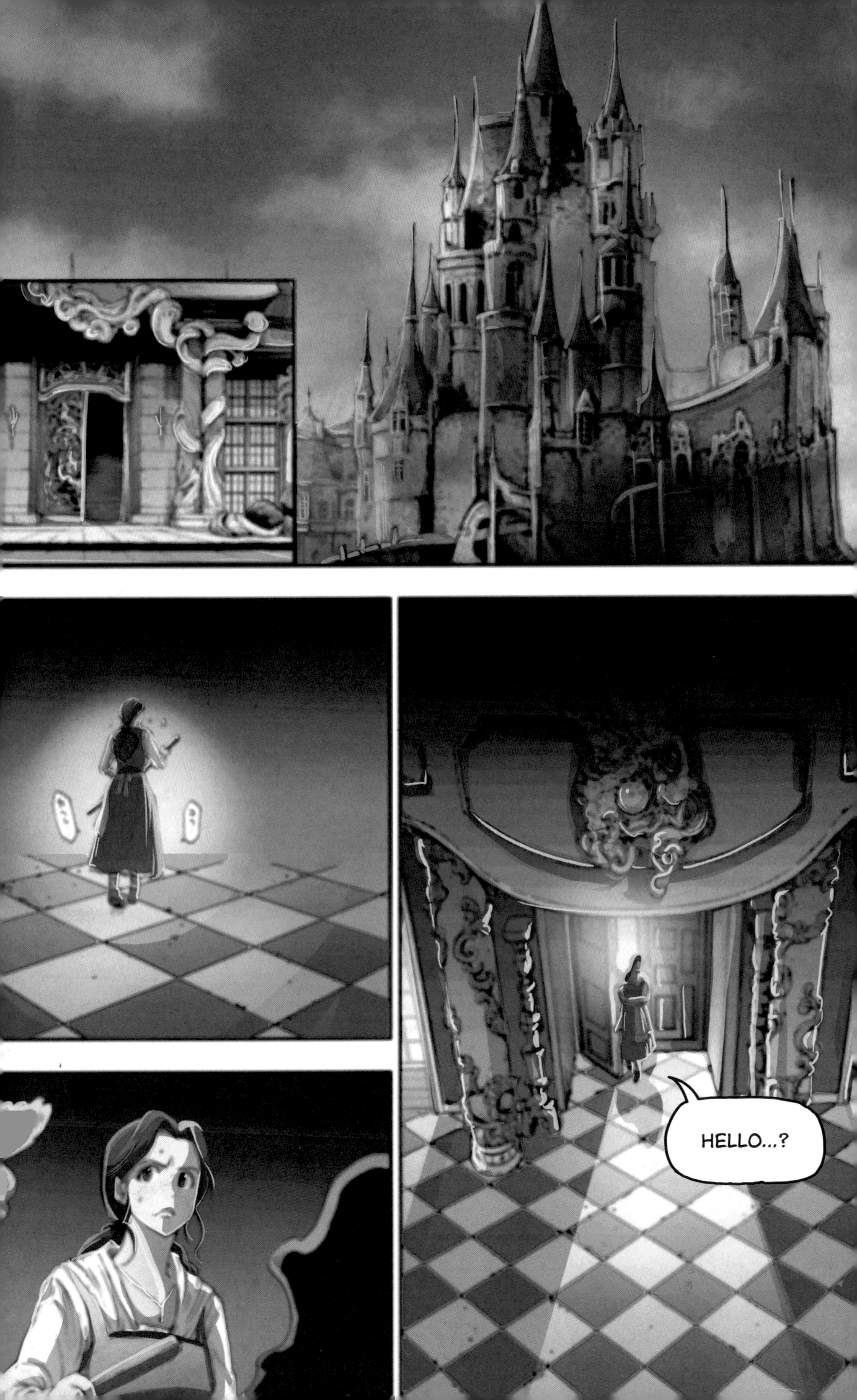
HELLO...?

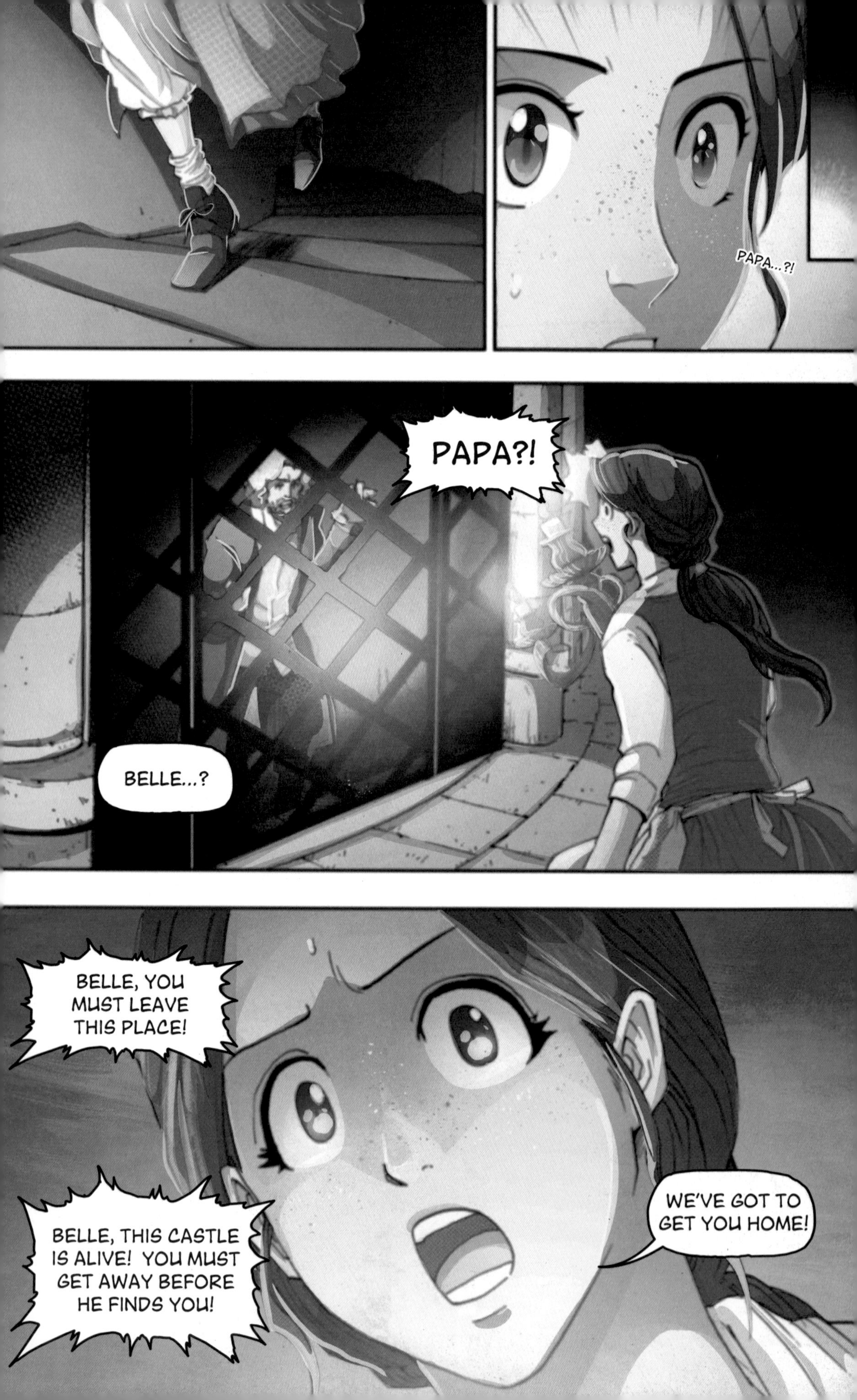
PAPA...?!
PAPA?!
BELLE...?
WE'VE GOT TO GET YOU HOME!
BELLE, YOU MUST LEAVE THIS PLACE!
BELLE, THIS CASTLE IS ALIVE! YOU MUST GET AWAY BEFORE HE FINDS YOU!

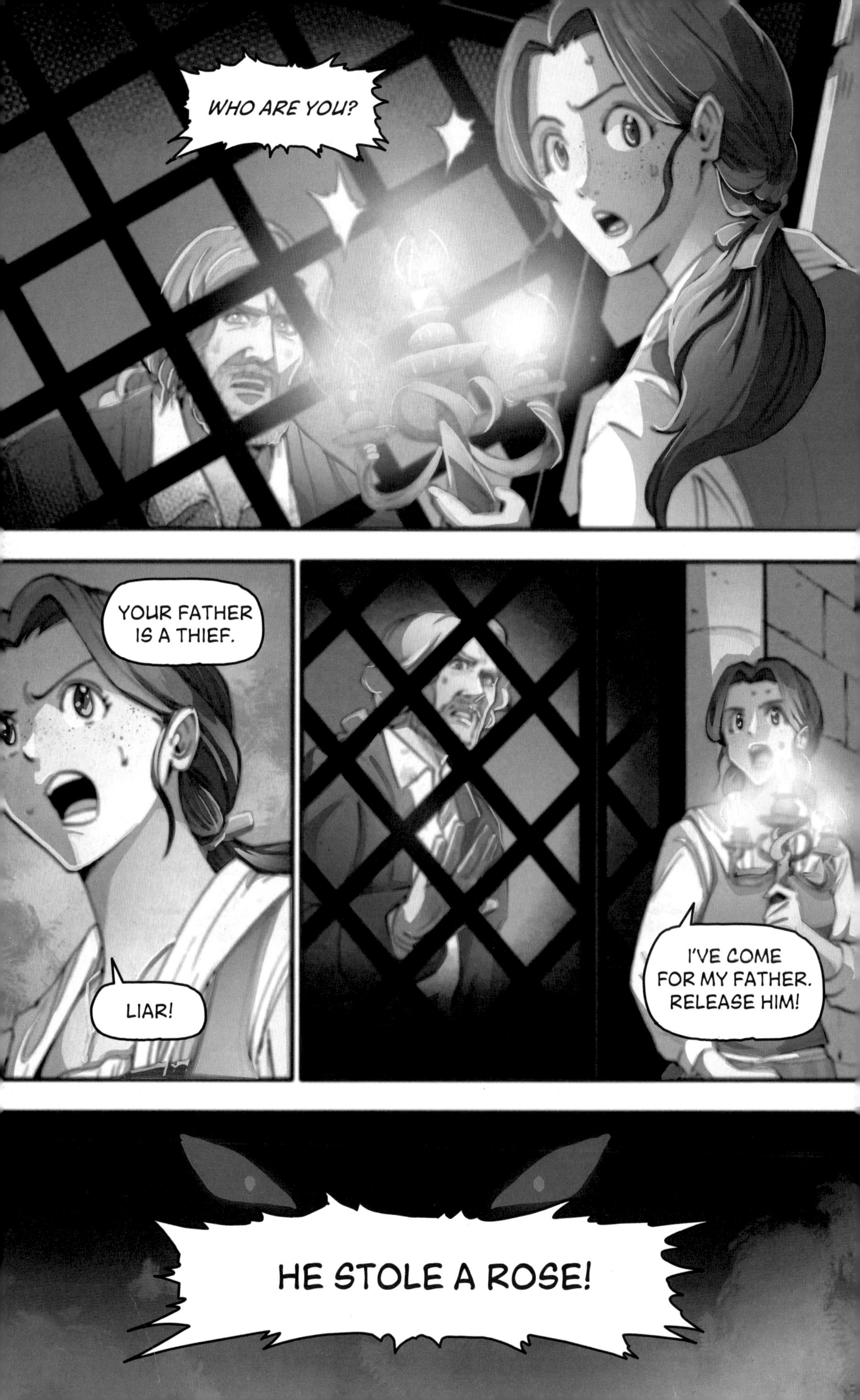
WHO ARE YOU?
I'VE COME FOR MY FATHER. RELEASE HIM!
YOUR FATHER IS A THIEF.
LIAR!
HE STOLE A ROSE!

THE ROSE WAS FOR ME...!

PUNISH ME, NOT HIM.

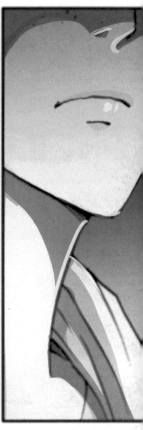

NO! HE SAID I WAS HIS PRISONER FOREVER.

A LIFE'S SENTENCE FOR A ROSE?

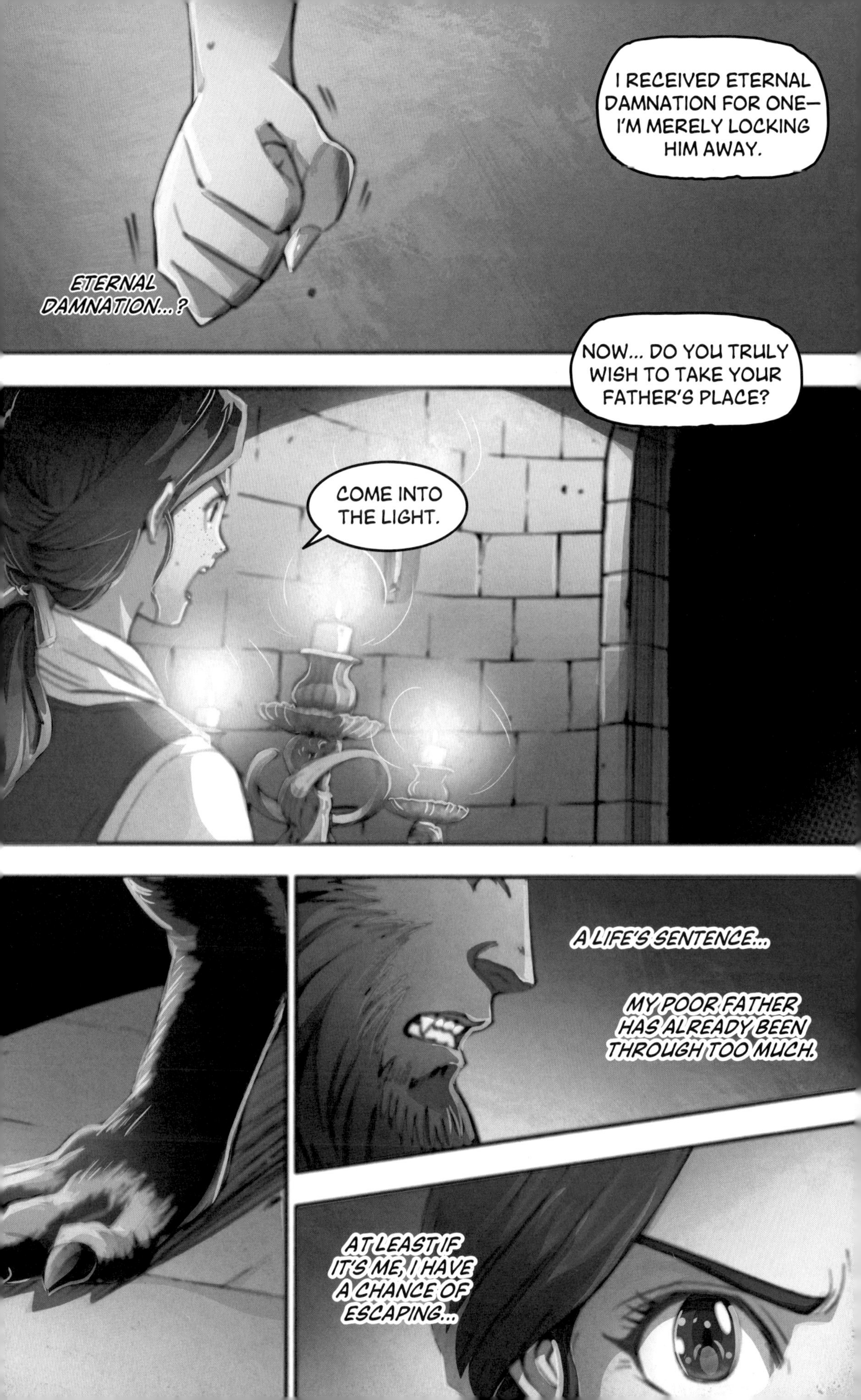
I RECEIVED ETERNAL DAMNATION FOR ONE—I'M MERELY LOCKING HIM AWAY.
ETERNAL DAMNATION...?
NOW... DO YOU TRULY WISH TO TAKE YOUR FATHER'S PLACE?
COME INTO THE LIGHT.
A LIFE'S SENTENCE...
MY POOR FATHER HAS ALREADY BEEN THROUGH TOO MUCH.
AT LEAST IF IT'S ME, I HAVE A CHANCE OF ESCAPING...

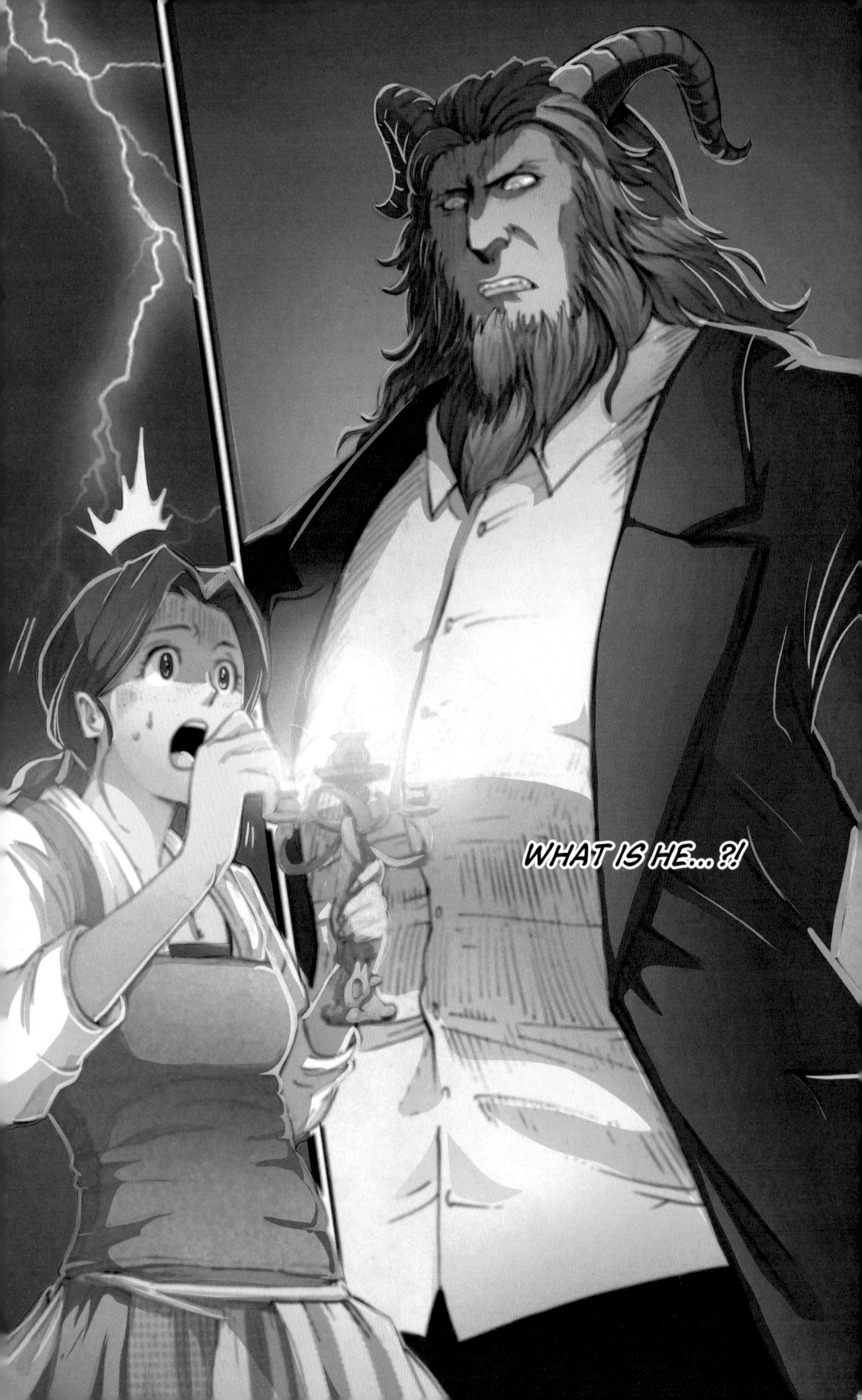
WHAT IS HE...?!

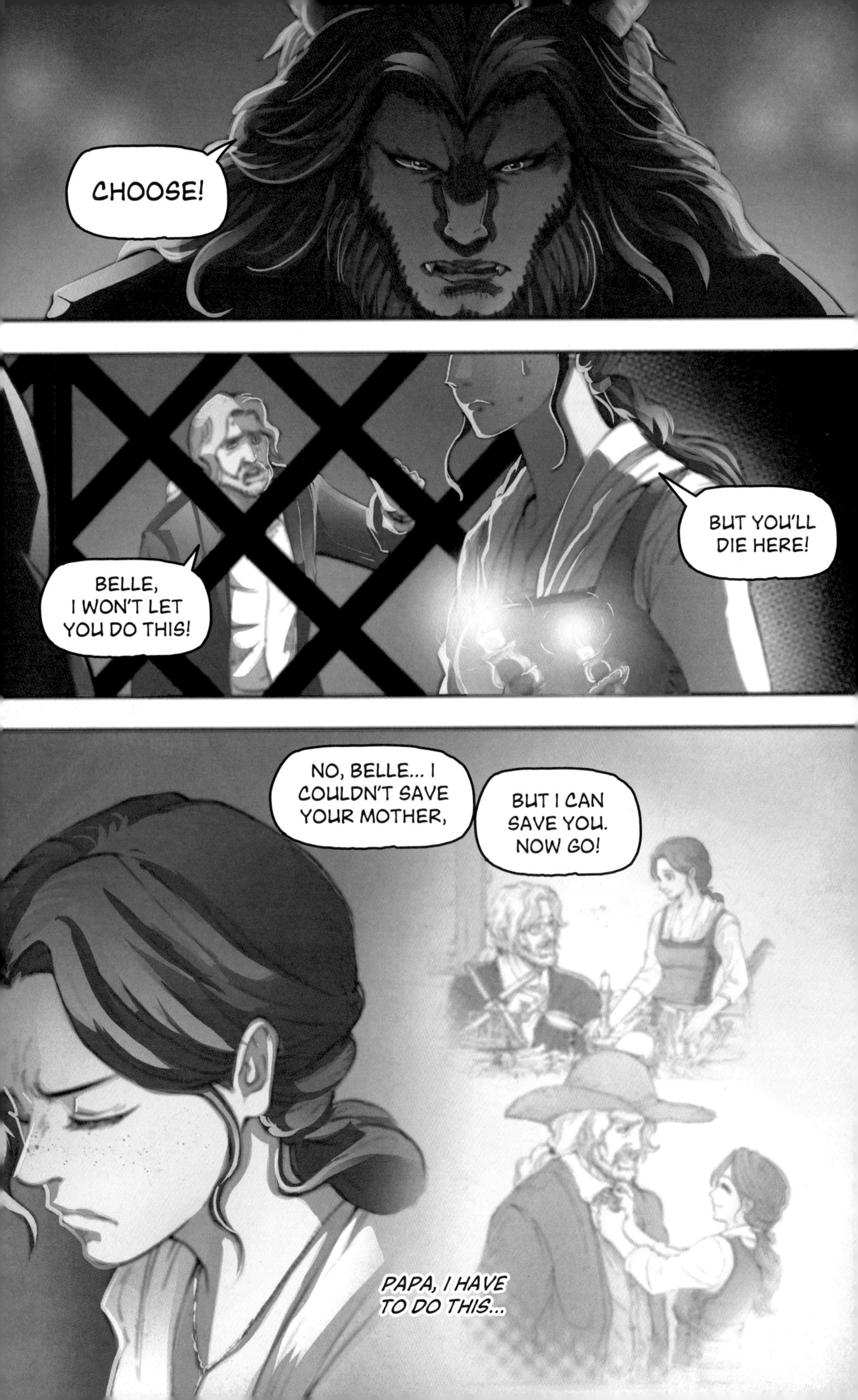
CHOOSE!
BUT YOU'LL DIE HERE!
BELLE, I WON'T LET YOU DO THIS!
NO, BELLE... I COULDN'T SAVE YOUR MOTHER,
BUT I CAN SAVE YOU. NOW GO!
PAPA, I HAVE TO DO THIS...

I WILL LEAVE.

OPEN THE DOOR. I NEED A MINUTE ALONE WITH HIM.

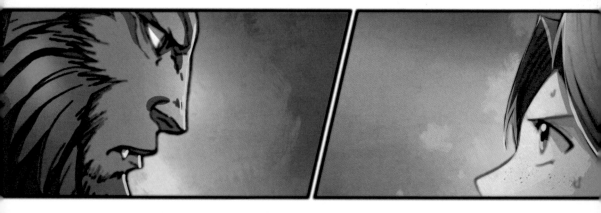

WHEN THIS DOOR CLOSES, IT WILL NOT OPEN AGAIN!

PHEW...

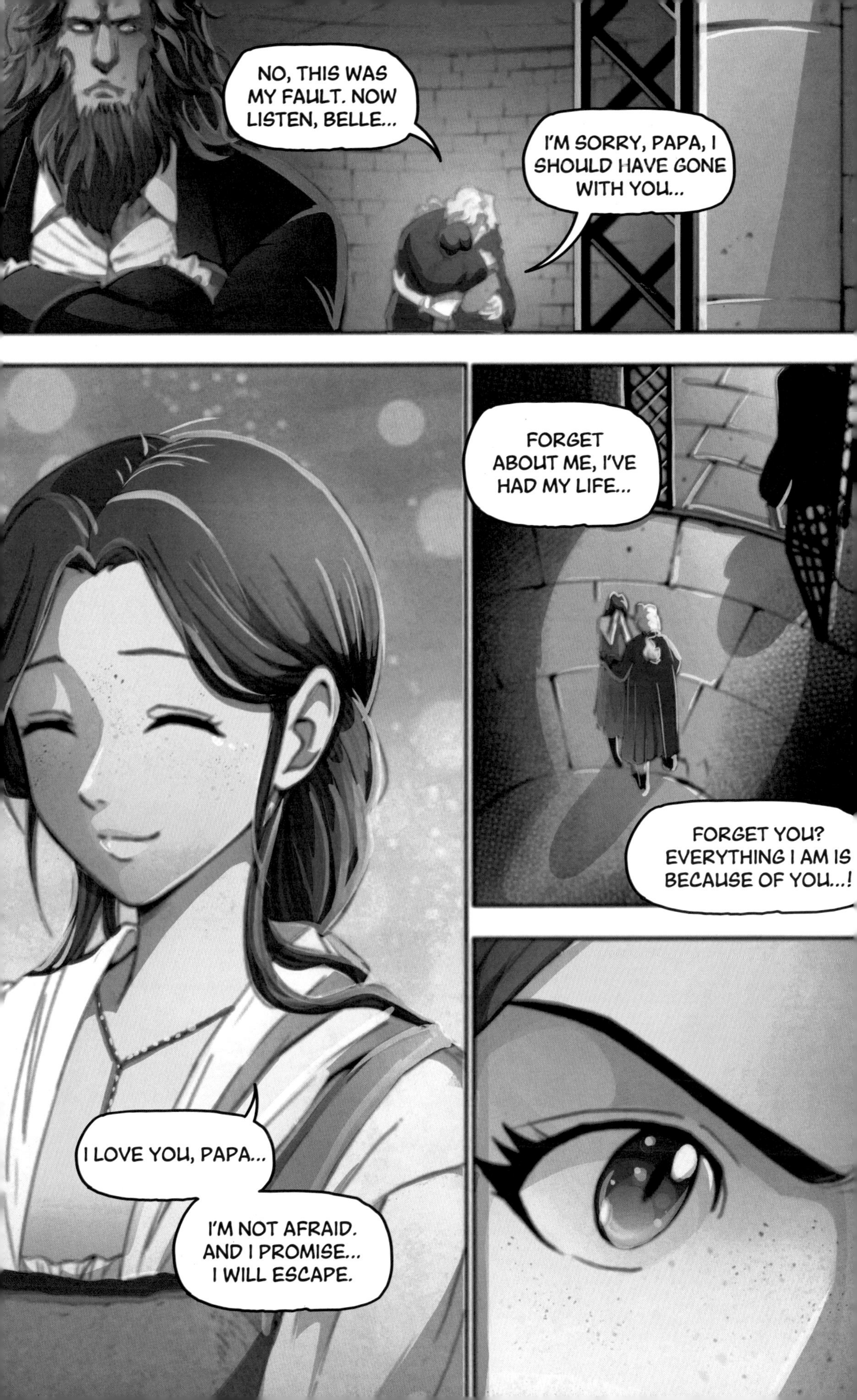
I'M SORRY, PAPA, I SHOULD HAVE GONE WITH YOU...
NO, THIS WAS MY FAULT. NOW LISTEN, BELLE...
FORGET ABOUT ME, I'VE HAD MY LIFE...
FORGET YOU? EVERYTHING I AM IS BECAUSE OF YOU...!
I LOVE YOU, PAPA...
I'M NOT AFRAID. AND I PROMISE... I WILL ESCAPE.

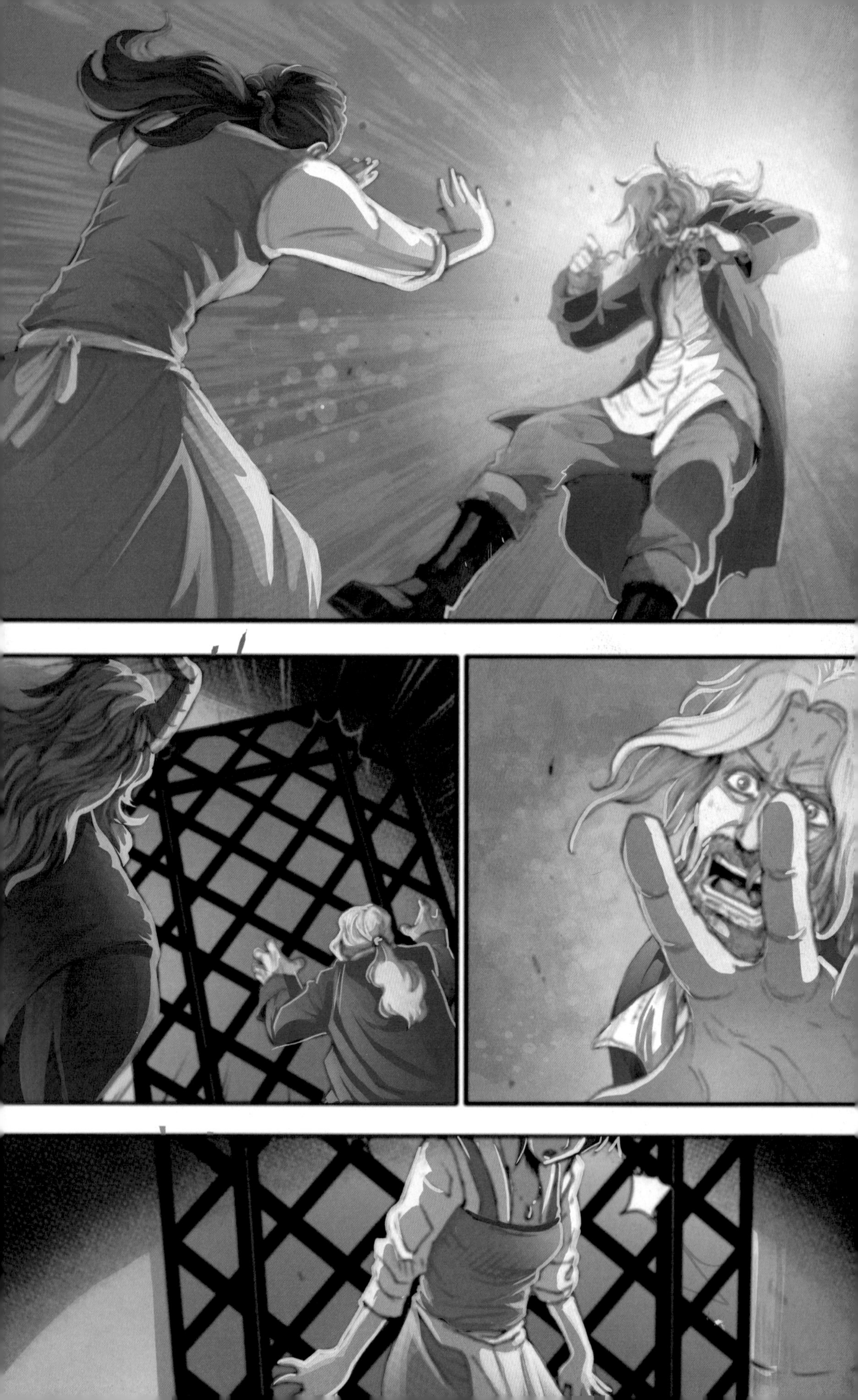

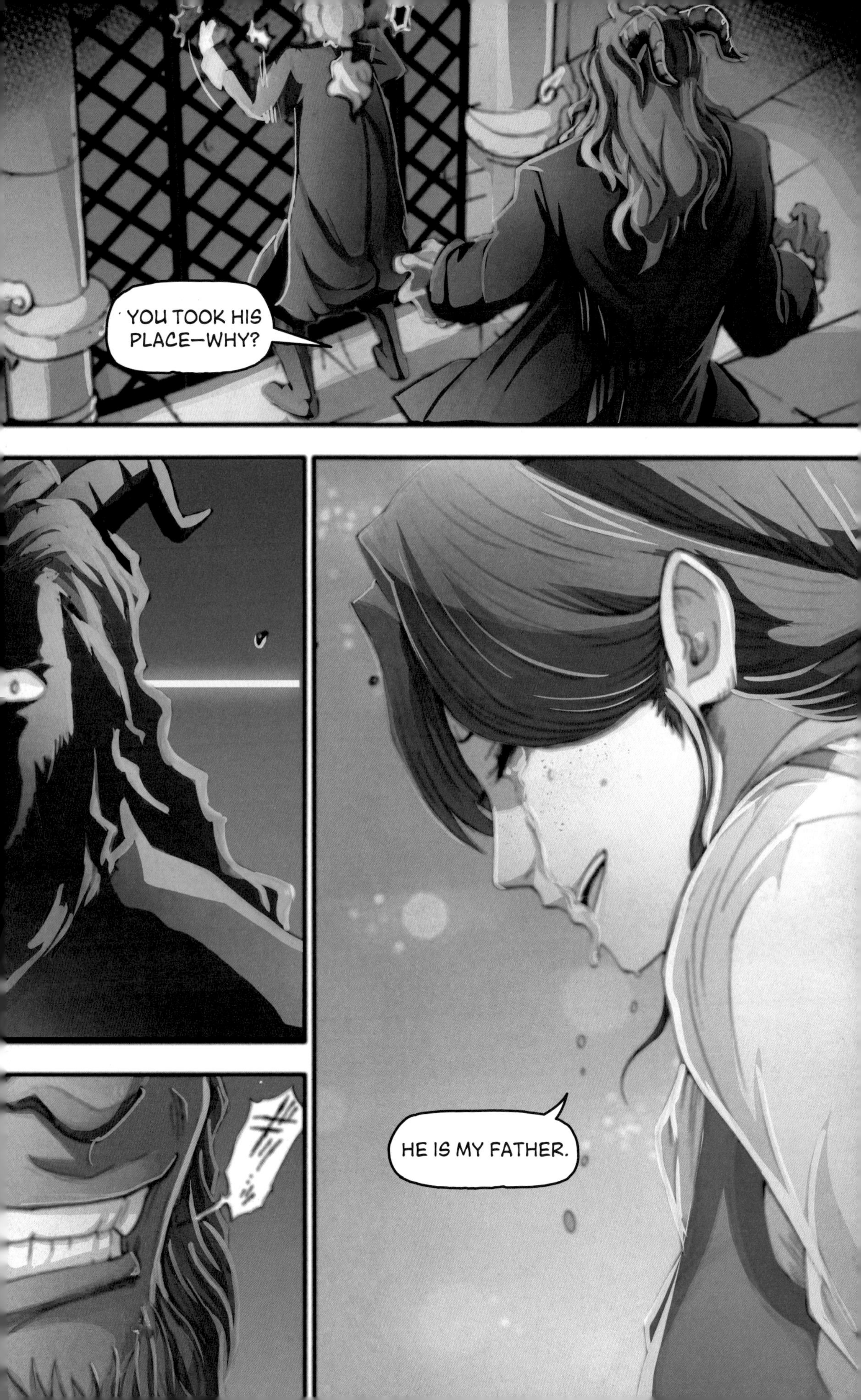
YOU TOOK HIS PLACE—WHY?
HE IS MY FATHER.

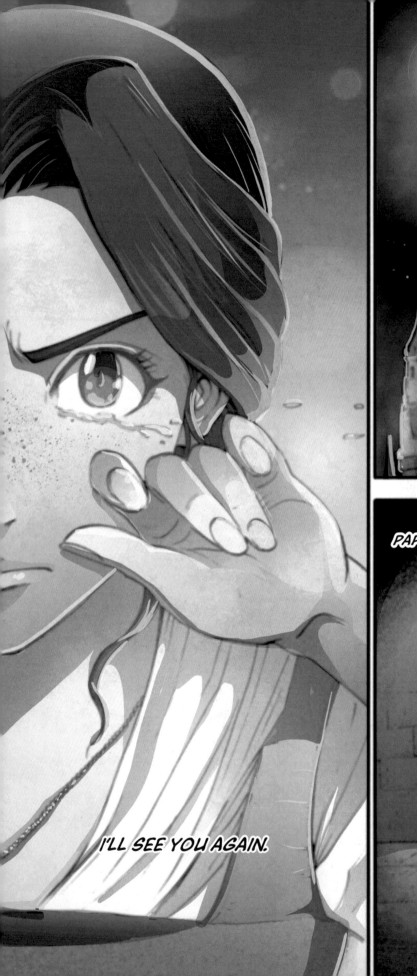

I'LL SEE YOU AGAIN.

PAPA...

I PROMISE...

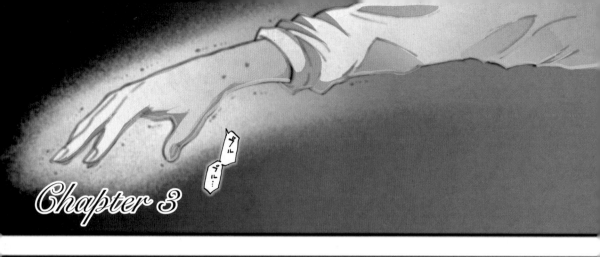

Chapter 3

FORGIVE MY INTRUSION, MADEMOISELLE...

...BUT THE MASTER HAS SENT ME TO ESCORT YOU TO YOUR ROOM.

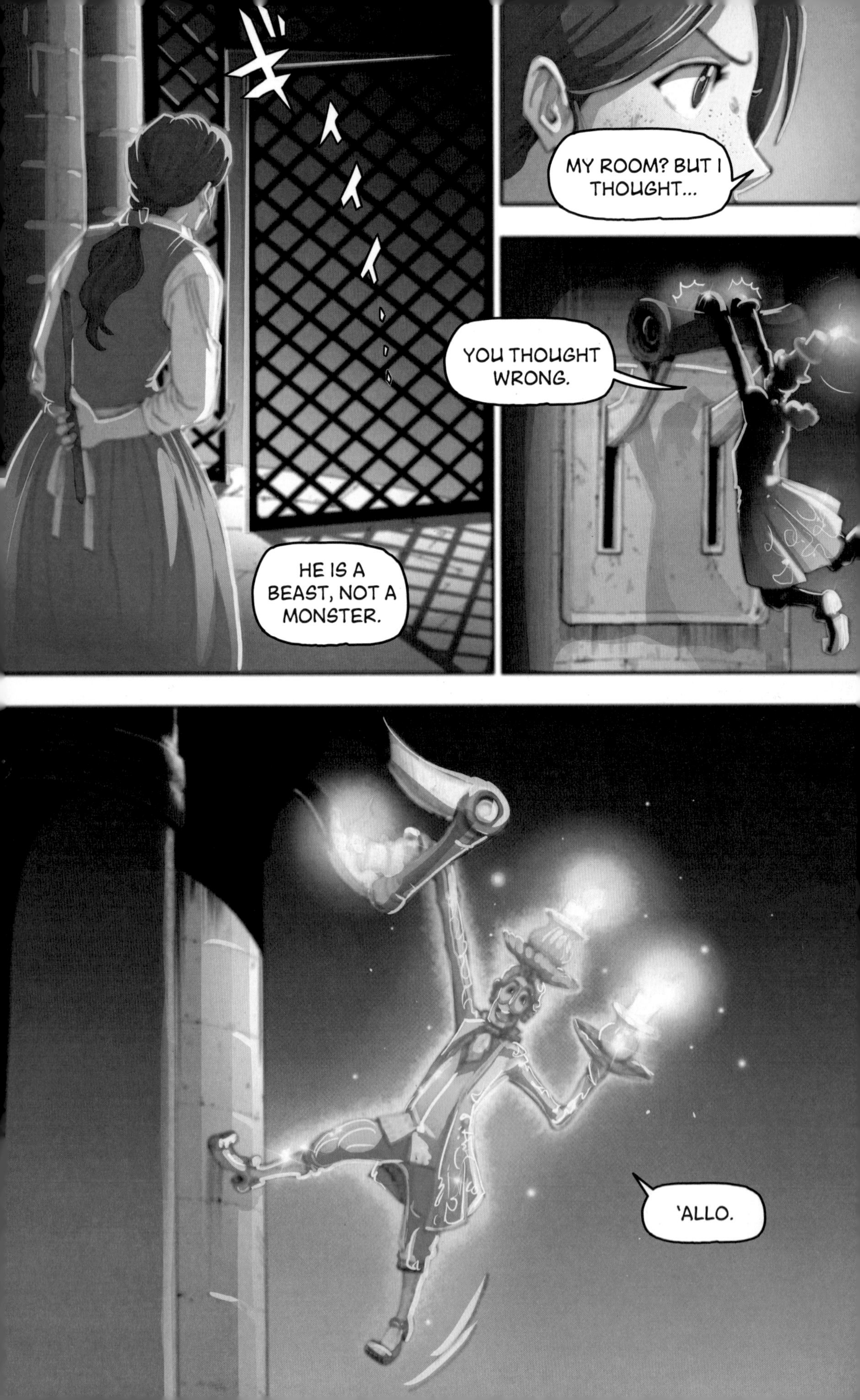
MY ROOM? BUT I THOUGHT...
YOU THOUGHT WRONG.
ギイイイ...
HE IS A BEAST, NOT A MONSTER.
'ALLO.

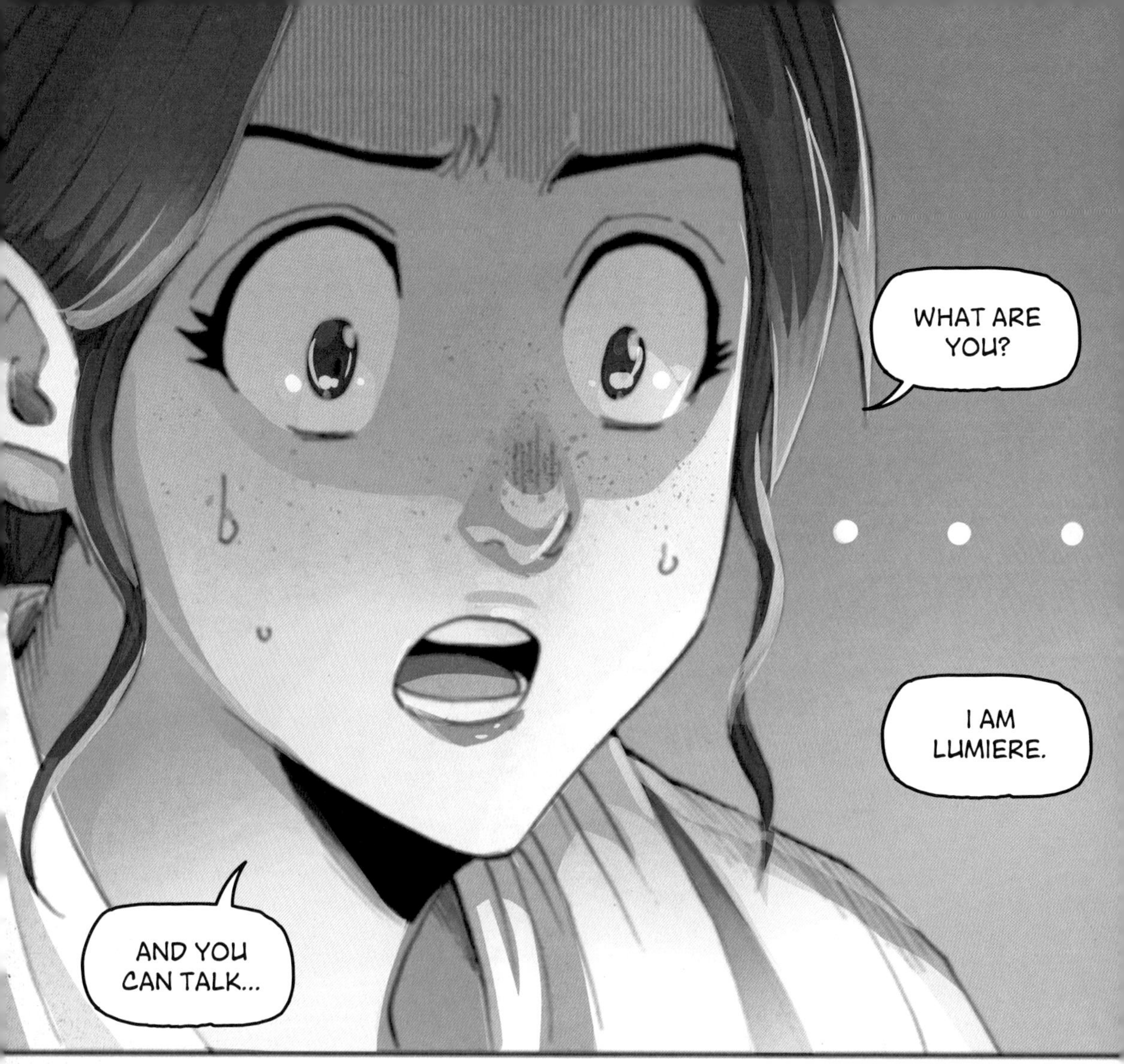
WHAT ARE YOU?
...
I AM LUMIERE.
AND YOU CAN TALK...

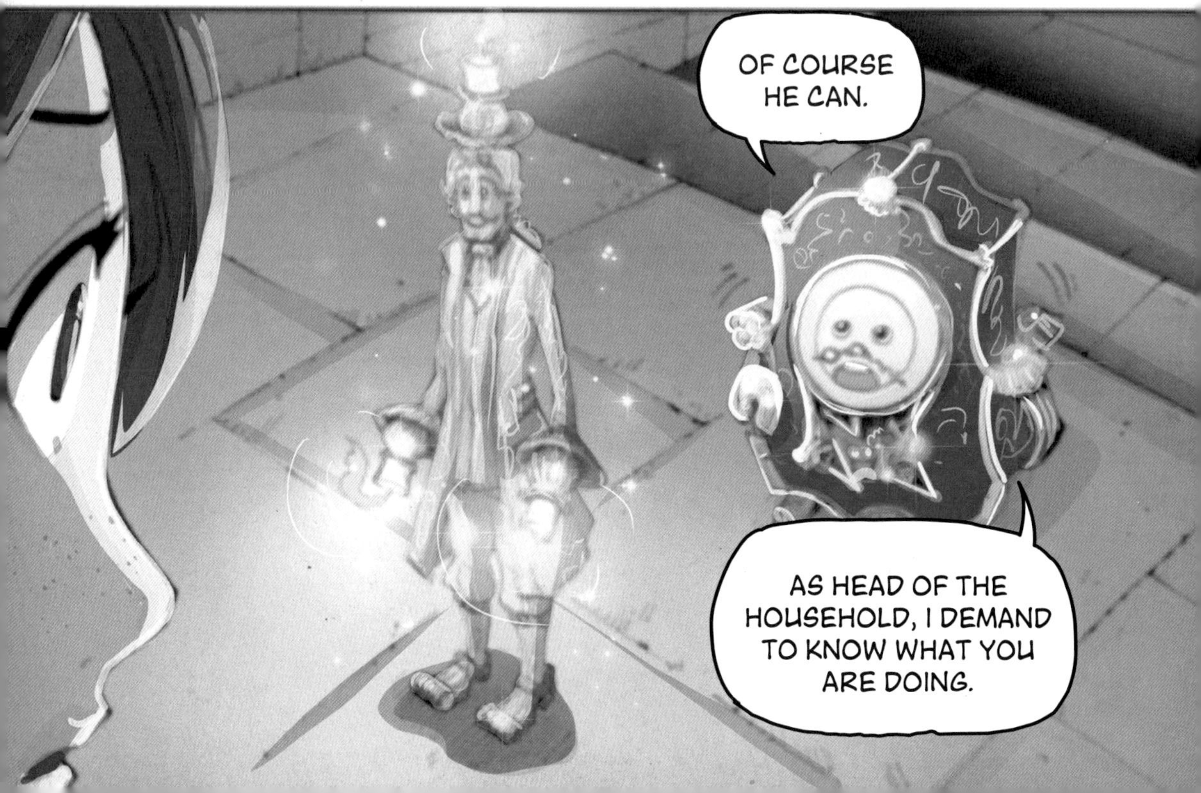
OF COURSE HE CAN.
AS HEAD OF THE HOUSEHOLD, I DEMAND TO KNOW WHAT YOU ARE DOING.

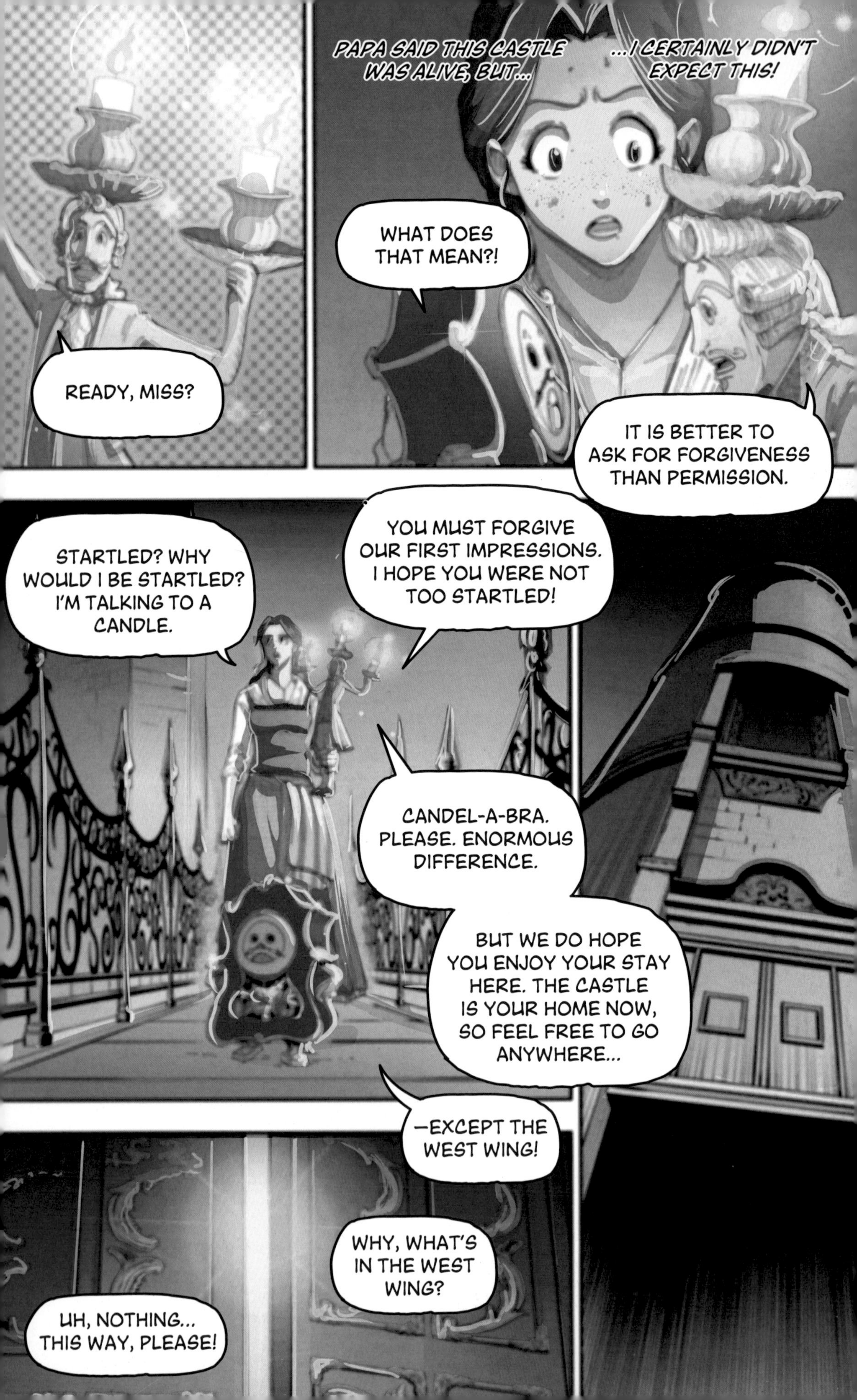
PAPA SAID THIS CASTLE WAS ALIVE, BUT...
...I CERTAINLY DIDN'T EXPECT THIS!
WHAT DOES THAT MEAN?!
IT IS BETTER TO ASK FOR FORGIVENESS THAN PERMISSION.
READY, MISS?
BUT WE DO HOPE YOU ENJOY YOUR STAY HERE. THE CASTLE IS YOUR HOME NOW, SO FEEL FREE TO GO ANYWHERE...
—EXCEPT THE WEST WING!
YOU MUST FORGIVE OUR FIRST IMPRESSIONS. I HOPE YOU WERE NOT TOO STARTLED!
STARTLED? WHY WOULD I BE STARTLED? I'M TALKING TO A CANDLE.
CANDEL-A-BRA. PLEASE. ENORMOUS DIFFERENCE.
WHY, WHAT'S IN THE WEST WING?
UH, NOTHING... THIS WAY, PLEASE!

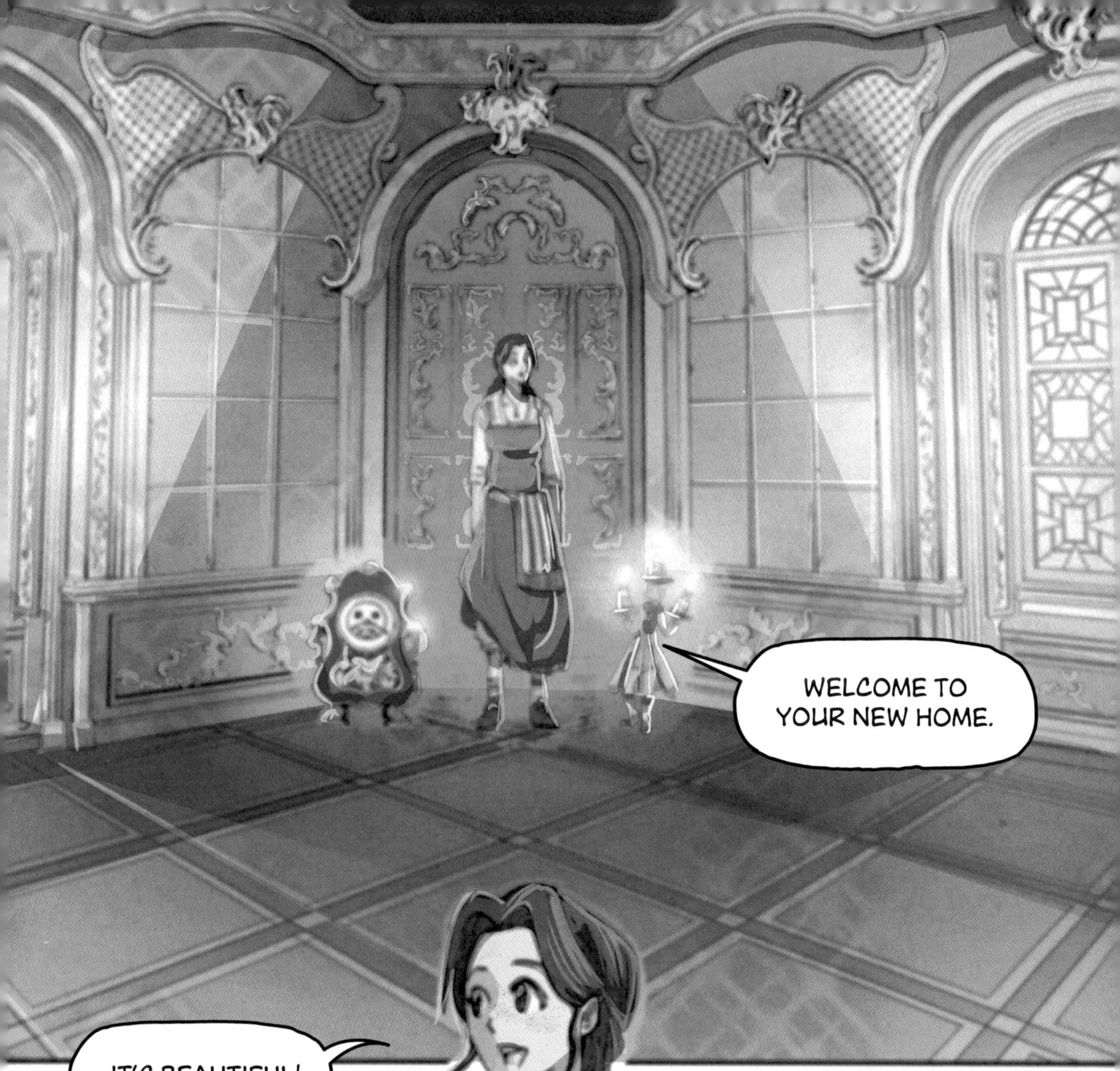
WELCOME TO YOUR NEW HOME.

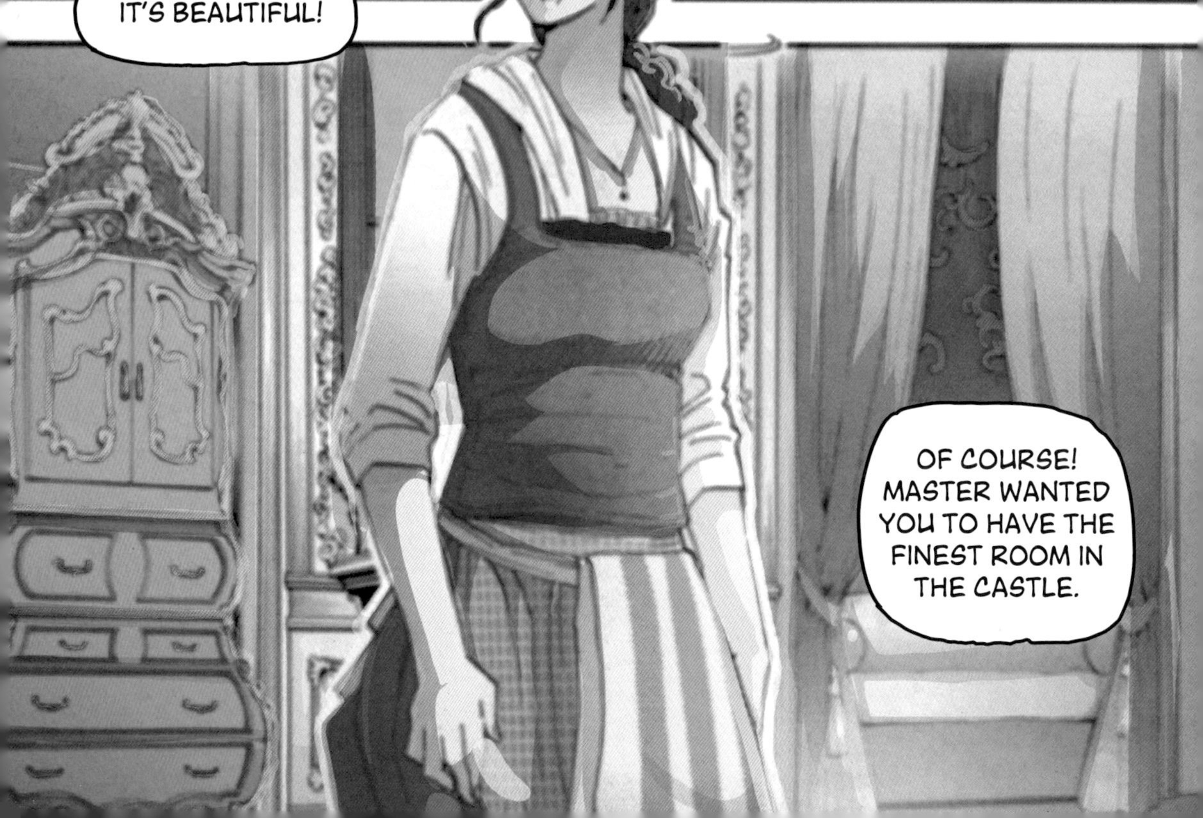
IT'S BEAUTIFUL!
OF COURSE! MASTER WANTED YOU TO HAVE THE FINEST ROOM IN THE CASTLE.

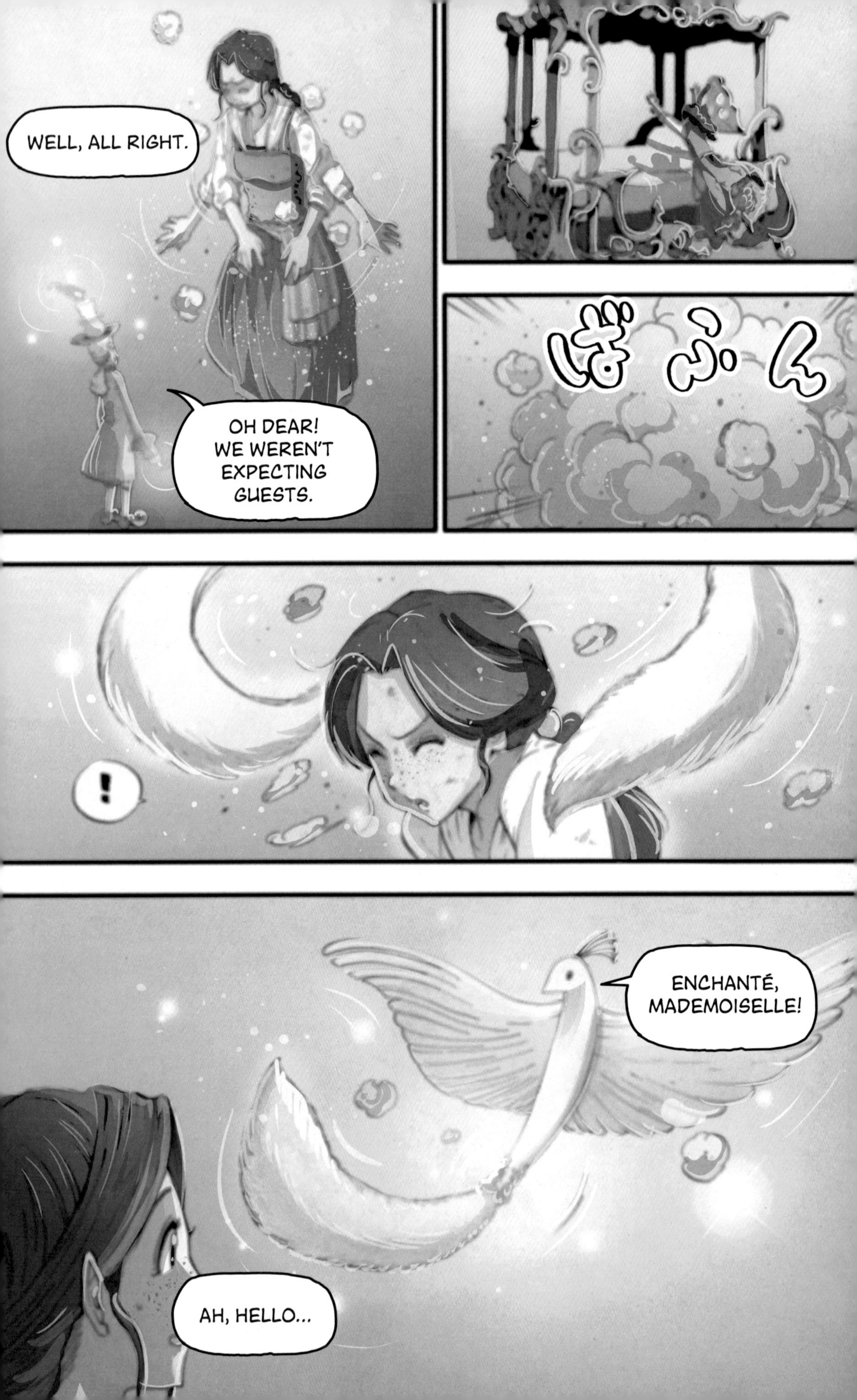
ばふん
WELL, ALL RIGHT.
OH DEAR! WE WEREN'T EXPECTING GUESTS.
!
ENCHANTÉ, MADEMOISELLE!
AH, HELLO...

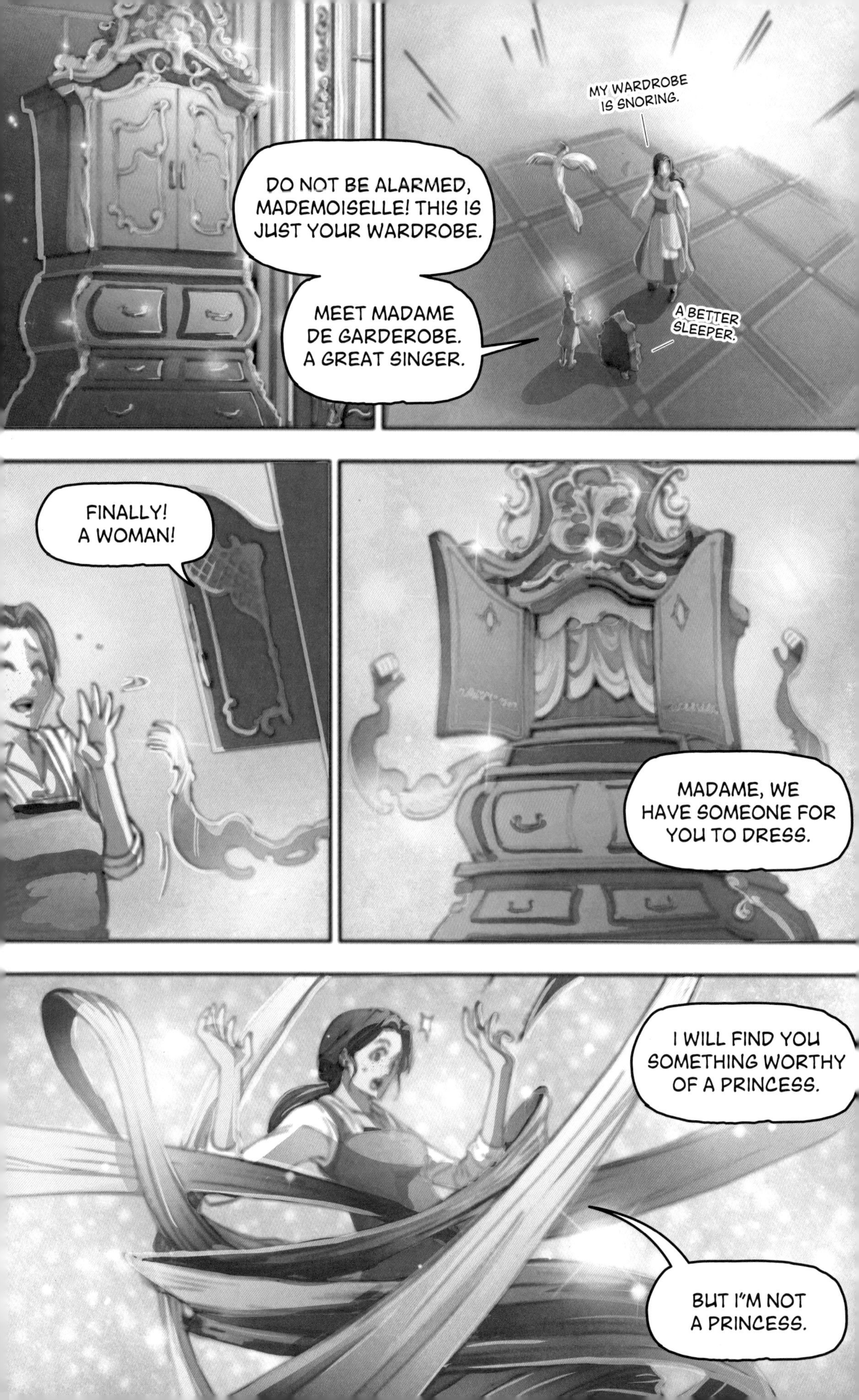
MY WARDROBE IS SNORING.
DO NOT BE ALARMED, MADEMOISELLE! THIS IS JUST YOUR WARDROBE.
MEET MADAME DE GARDEROBE. A GREAT SINGER.
A BETTER SLEEPER.
FINALLY! A WOMAN!
MADAME, WE HAVE SOMEONE FOR YOU TO DRESS.
I WILL FIND YOU SOMETHING WORTHY OF A PRINCESS.
BUT I"M NOT A PRINCESS.

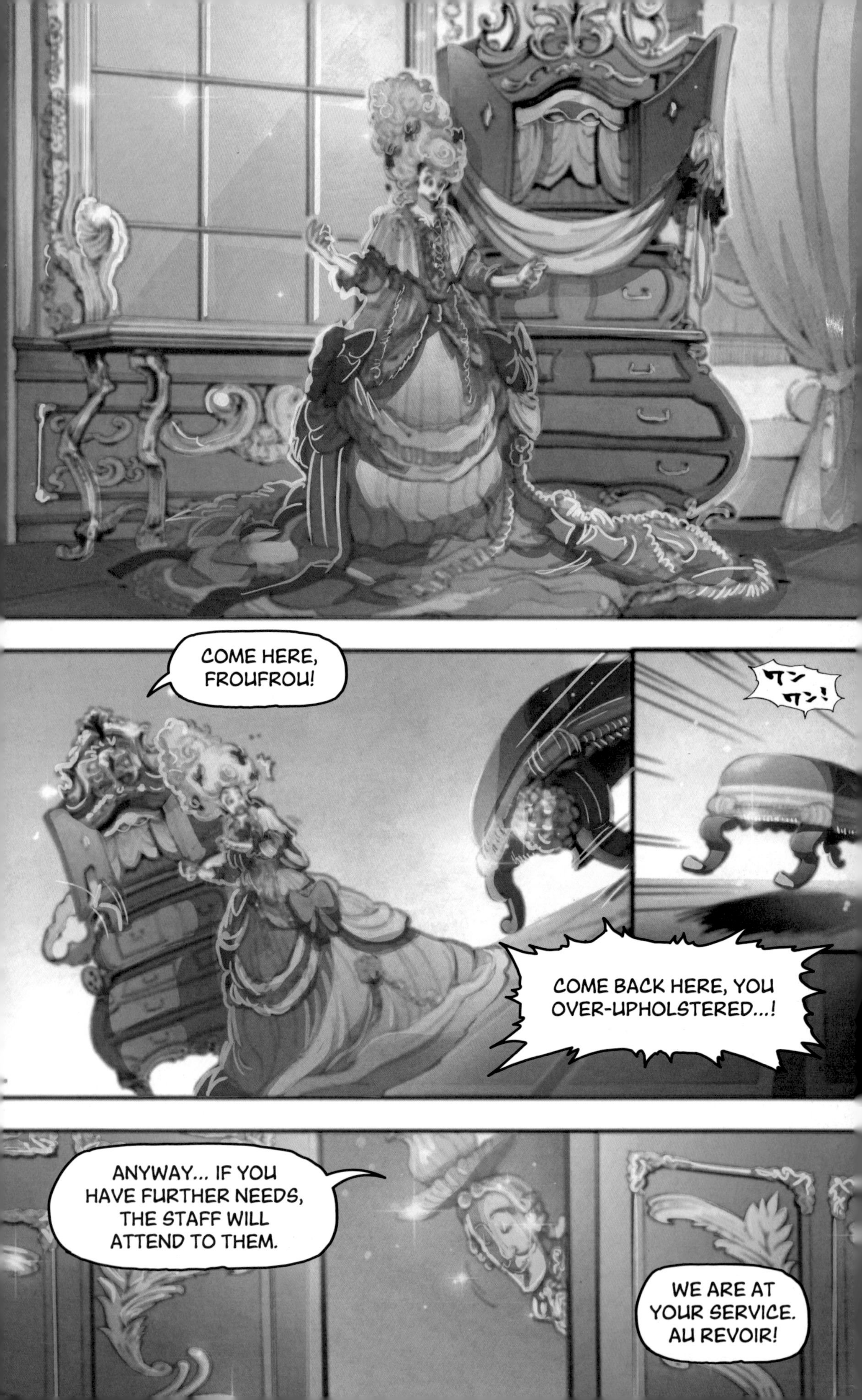
ワン ワン!
COME HERE, FROUFROU!
COME BACK HERE, YOU OVER-UPHOLSTERED...!
ANYWAY... IF YOU HAVE FURTHER NEEDS, THE STAFF WILL ATTEND TO THEM.
WE ARE AT YOUR SERVICE. AU REVOIR!

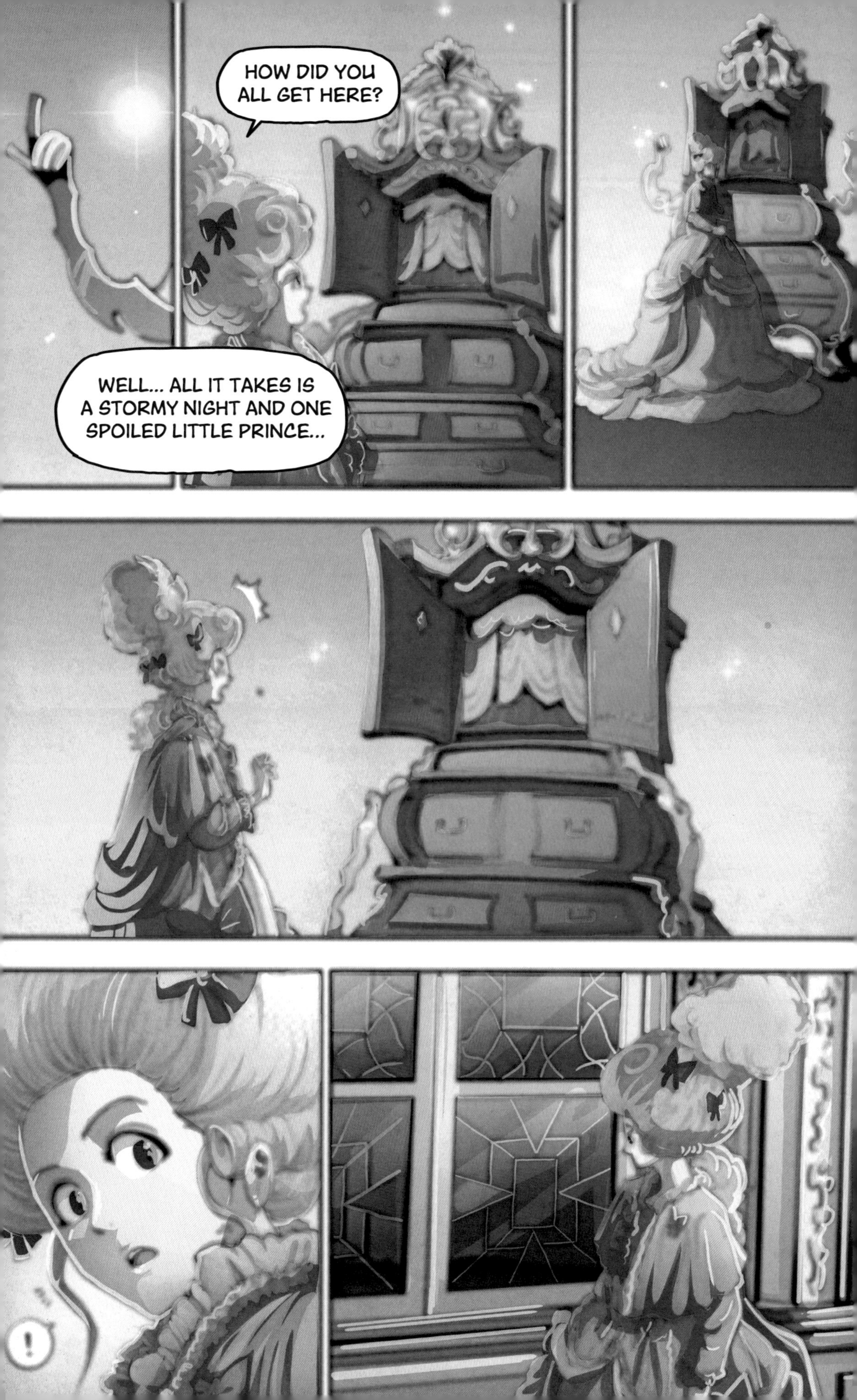
HOW DID YOU ALL GET HERE?
WELL... ALL IT TAKES IS A STORMY NIGHT AND ONE SPOILED LITTLE PRINCE...
!

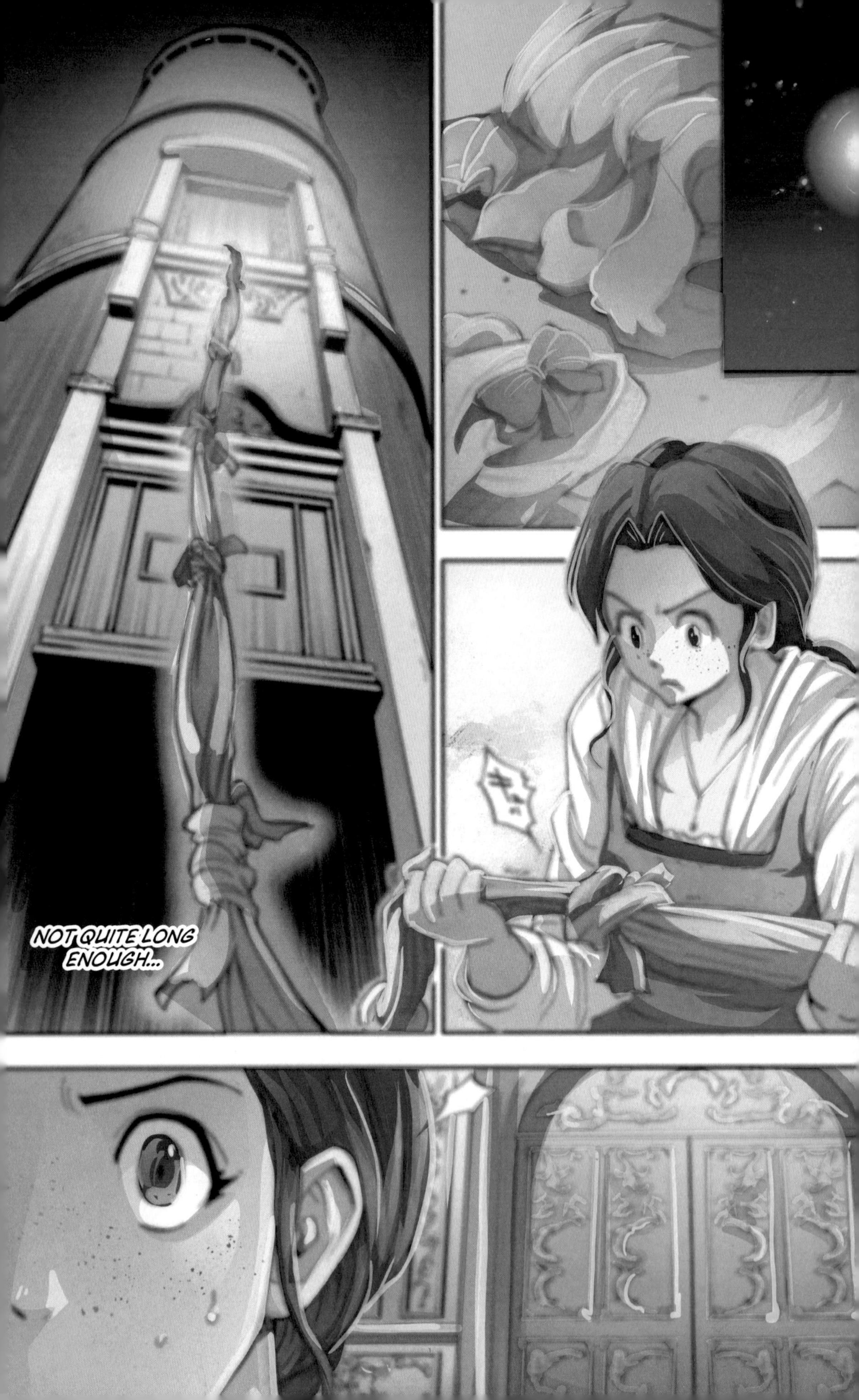
NOT QUITE LONG ENOUGH...

JUST A MINUTE!

I DON'T KNOW WHAT TO DO, BUT I KNOW I DON'T WANT TO HAVE DINNER WITH HIM!

YOU WILL JOIN ME FOR DINNER!

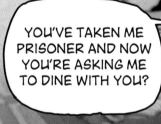

YOU'VE TAKEN ME PRISONER AND NOW YOU'RE ASKING ME TO DINE WITH YOU?

ARE YOU MAD?

IT WOULD GIVE ME GREAT PLEASURE IF YOU WOULD JOIN ME FOR DINNER...

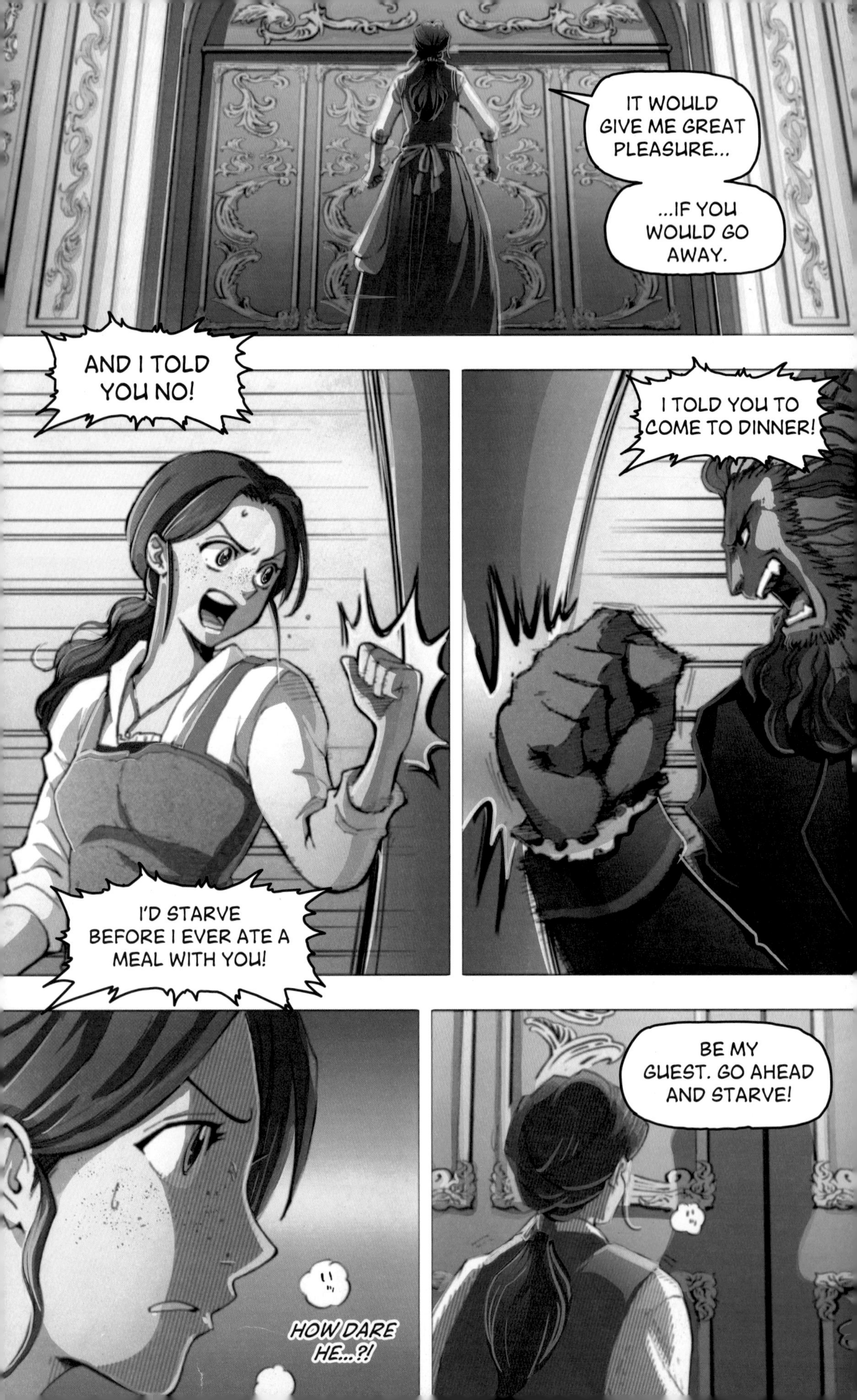
IT WOULD GIVE ME GREAT PLEASURE...
...IF YOU WOULD GO AWAY.
I TOLD YOU TO COME TO DINNER!
AND I TOLD YOU NO!
I'D STARVE BEFORE I EVER ATE A MEAL WITH YOU!
BE MY GUEST. GO AHEAD AND STARVE!
HOW DARE HE...?!

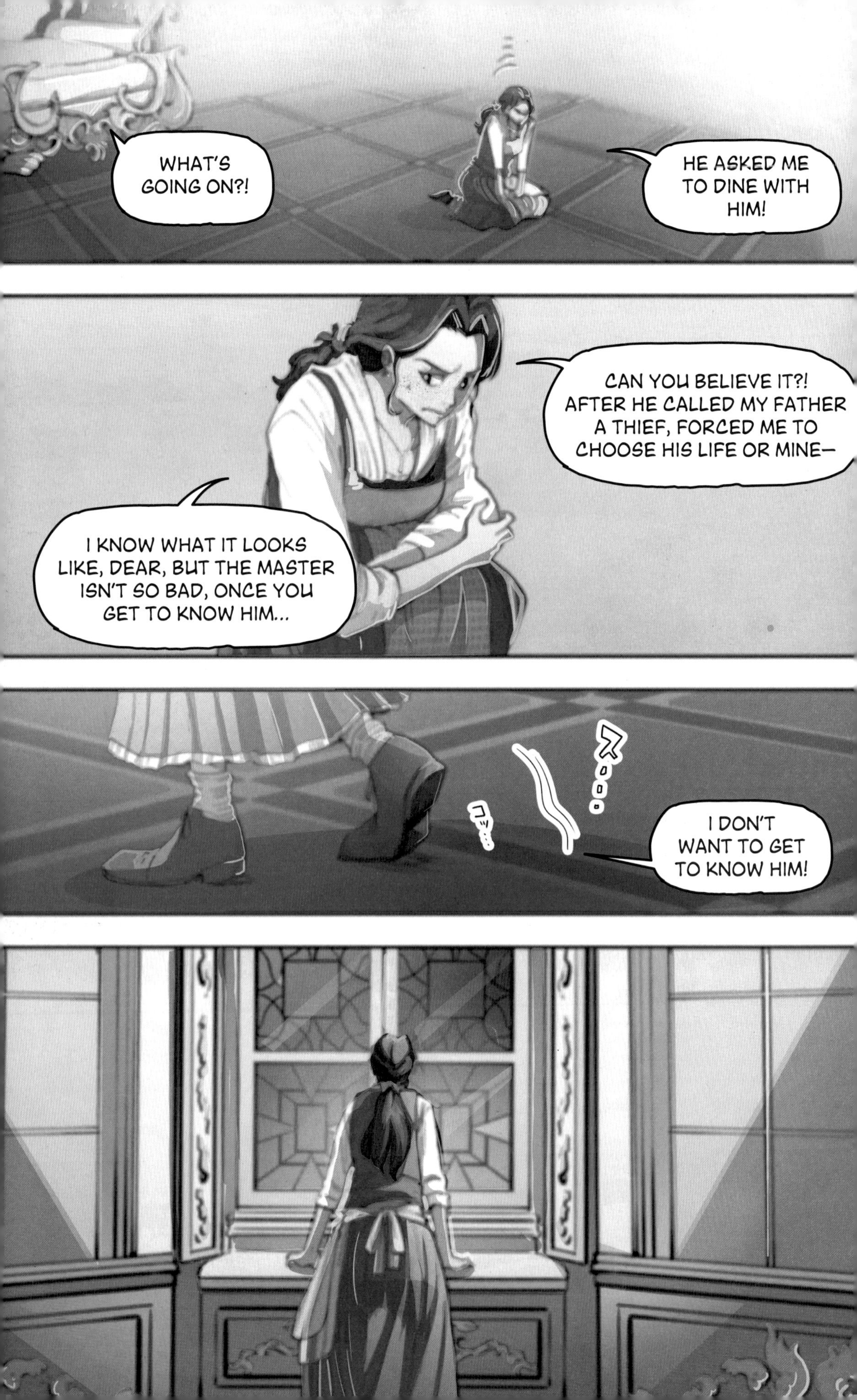
HE ASKED ME TO DINE WITH HIM!
WHAT'S GOING ON?!
CAN YOU BELIEVE IT?! AFTER HE CALLED MY FATHER A THIEF, FORCED ME TO CHOOSE HIS LIFE OR MINE—
I KNOW WHAT IT LOOKS LIKE, DEAR, BUT THE MASTER ISN'T SO BAD, ONCE YOU GET TO KNOW HIM...
I DON'T WANT TO GET TO KNOW HIM!
ズ…
コッ…

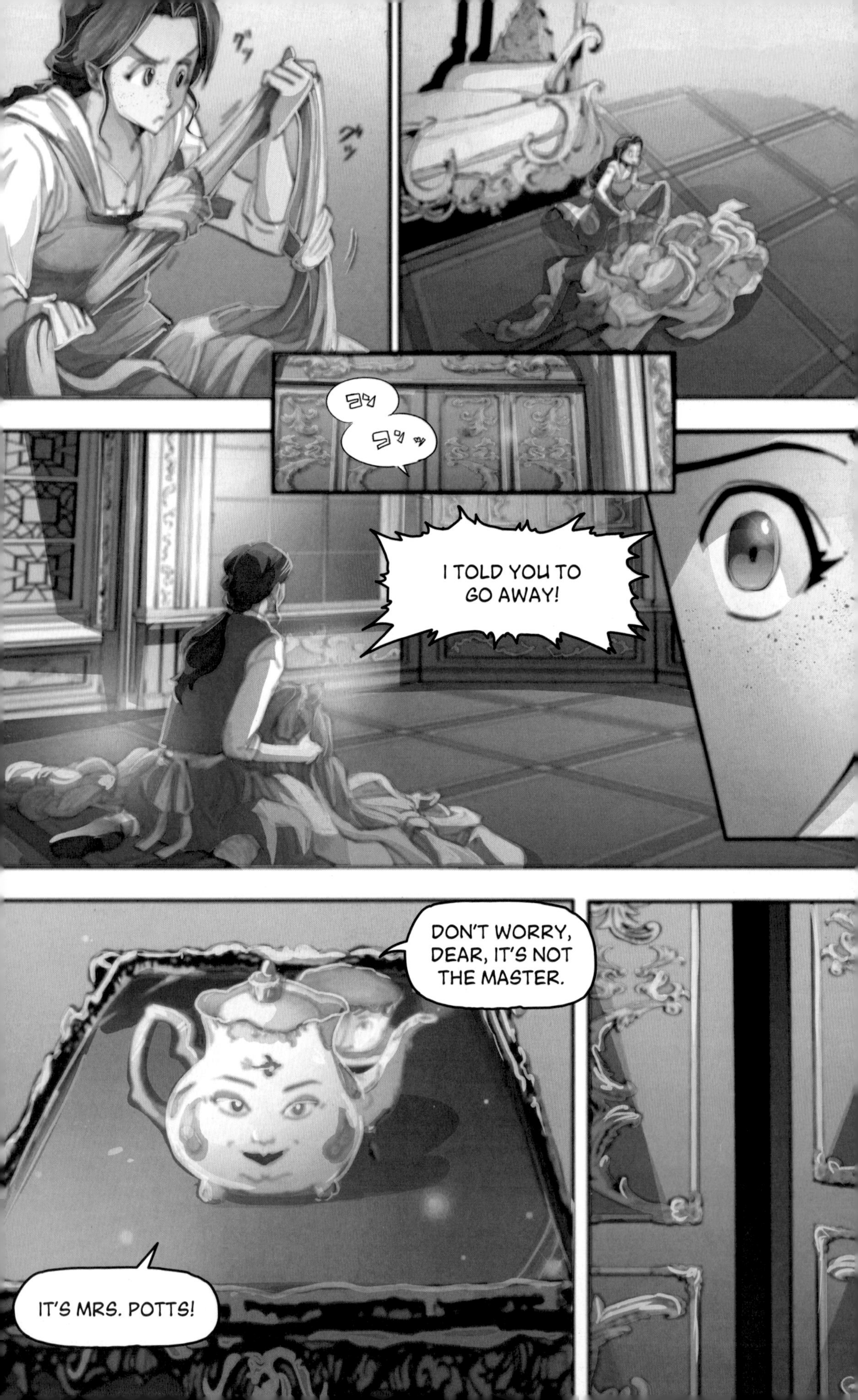

コツ
コツッ
I TOLD YOU TO GO AWAY!
DON'T WORRY, DEAR, IT'S NOT THE MASTER.
IT'S MRS. POTTS!

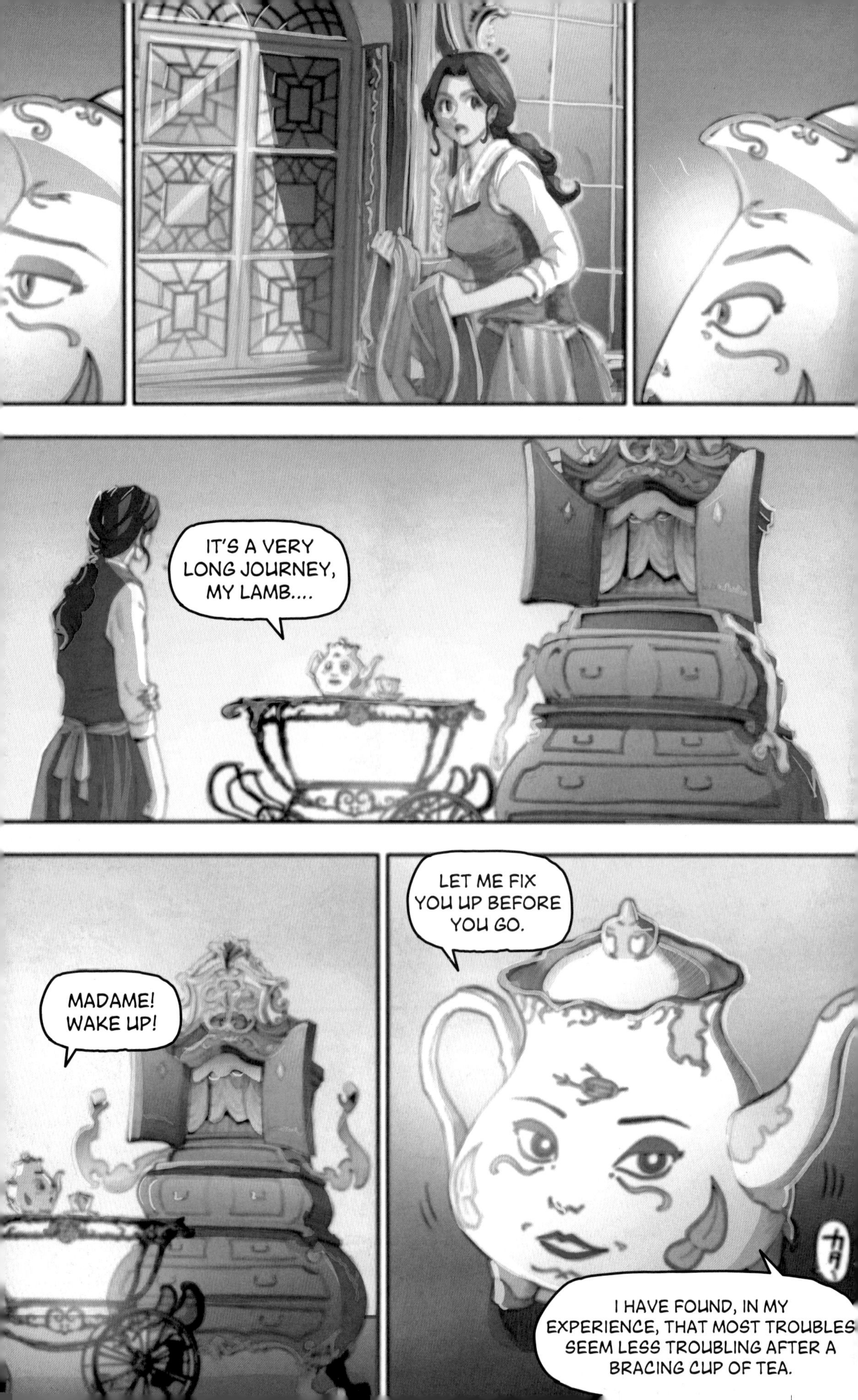
IT'S A VERY LONG JOURNEY, MY LAMB....
LET ME FIX YOU UP BEFORE YOU GO.
I HAVE FOUND, IN MY EXPERIENCE, THAT MOST TROUBLES SEEM LESS TROUBLING AFTER A BRACING CUP OF TEA.
MADAME! WAKE UP!

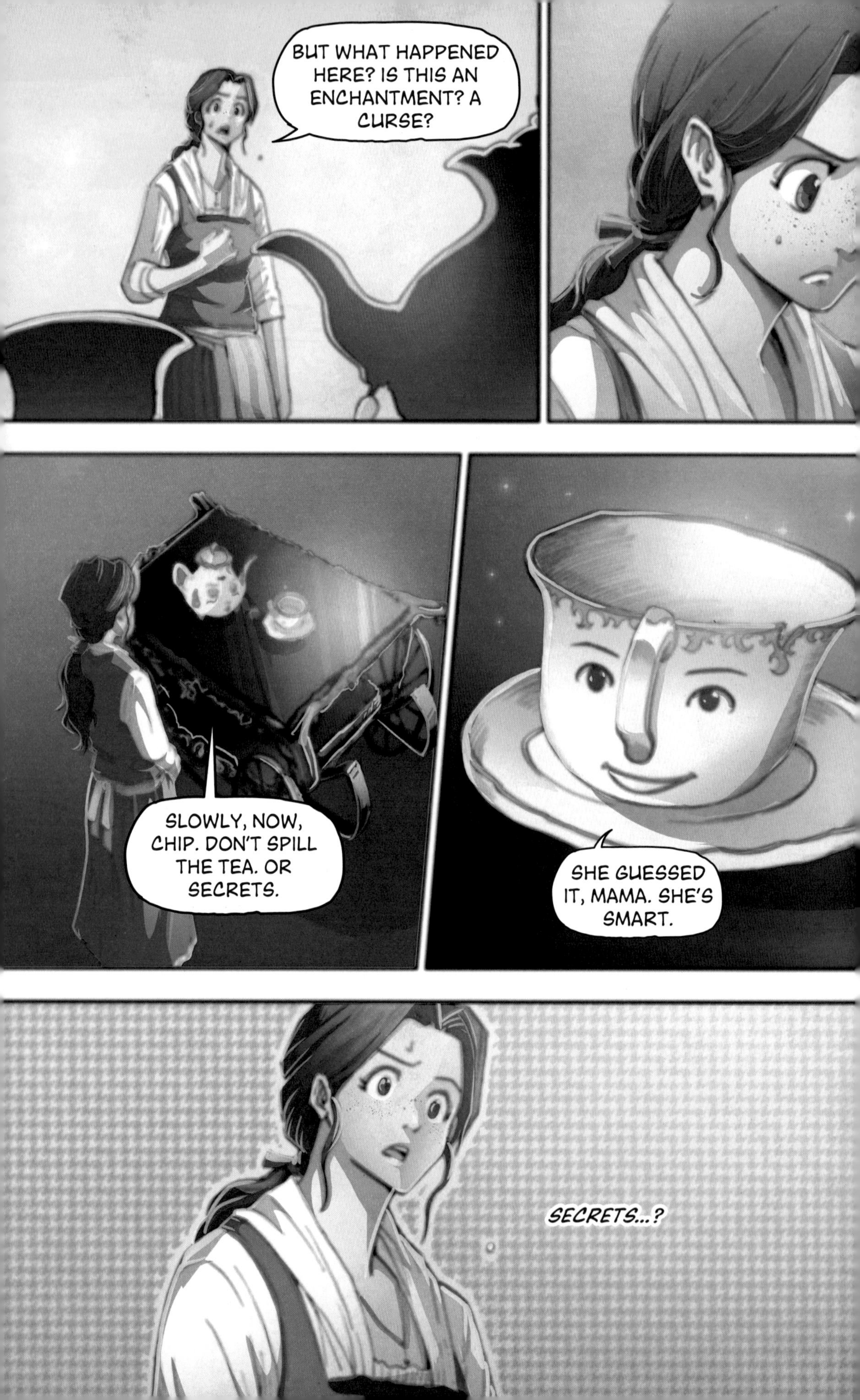
BUT WHAT HAPPENED HERE? IS THIS AN ENCHANTMENT? A CURSE?
SHE GUESSED IT, MAMA. SHE'S SMART.
SLOWLY, NOW, CHIP. DON'T SPILL THE TEA. OR SECRETS.
SECRETS...?

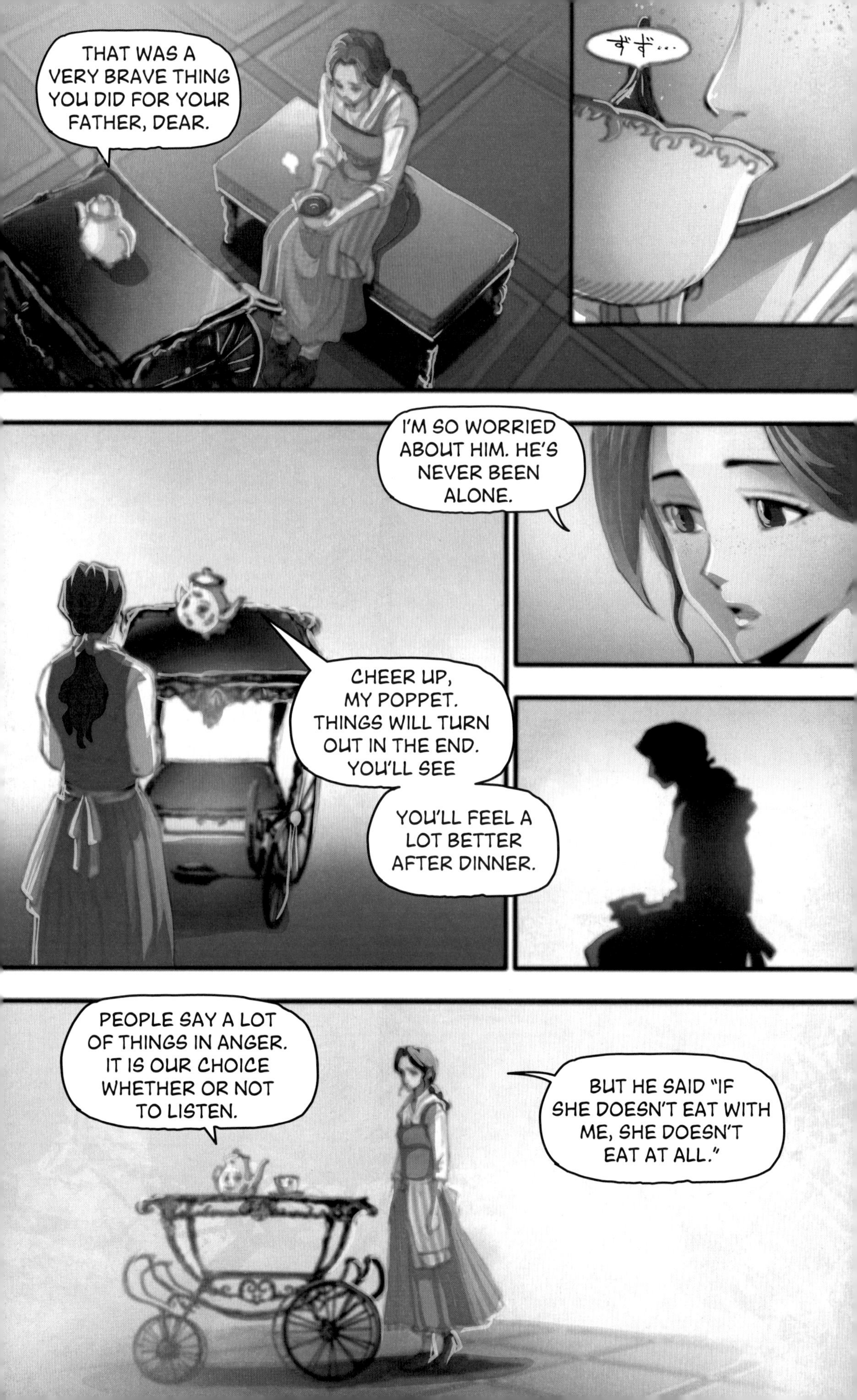
ずず…
THAT WAS A VERY BRAVE THING YOU DID FOR YOUR FATHER, DEAR.
I'M SO WORRIED ABOUT HIM. HE'S NEVER BEEN ALONE.
CHEER UP, MY POPPET. THINGS WILL TURN OUT IN THE END. YOU'LL SEE
YOU'LL FEEL A LOT BETTER AFTER DINNER.
BUT HE SAID "IF SHE DOESN'T EAT WITH ME, SHE DOESN'T EAT AT ALL."
PEOPLE SAY A LOT OF THINGS IN ANGER. IT IS OUR CHOICE WHETHER OR NOT TO LISTEN.

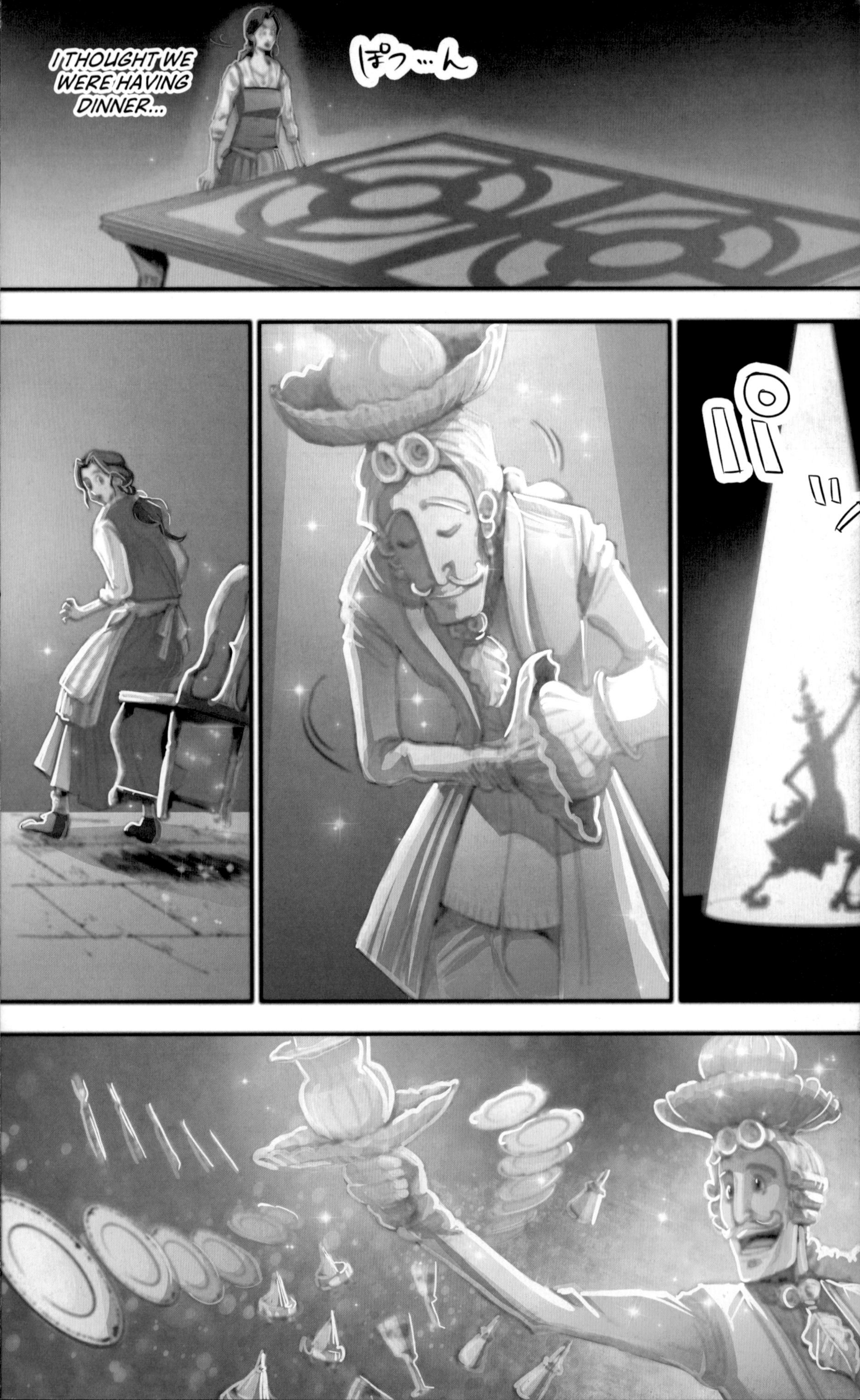
ぽつ…ん
I THOUGHT WE WERE HAVING DINNER...
パ

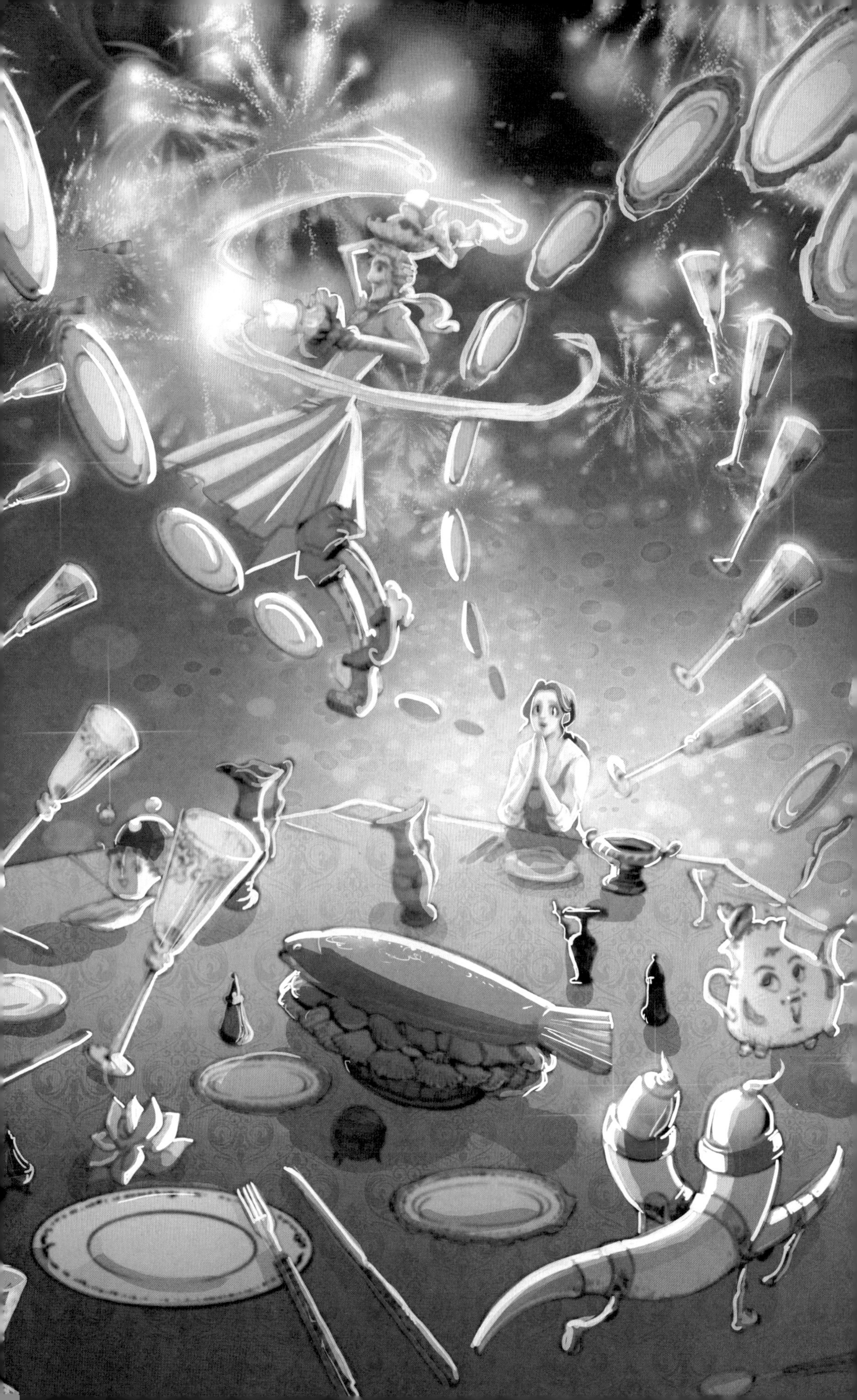

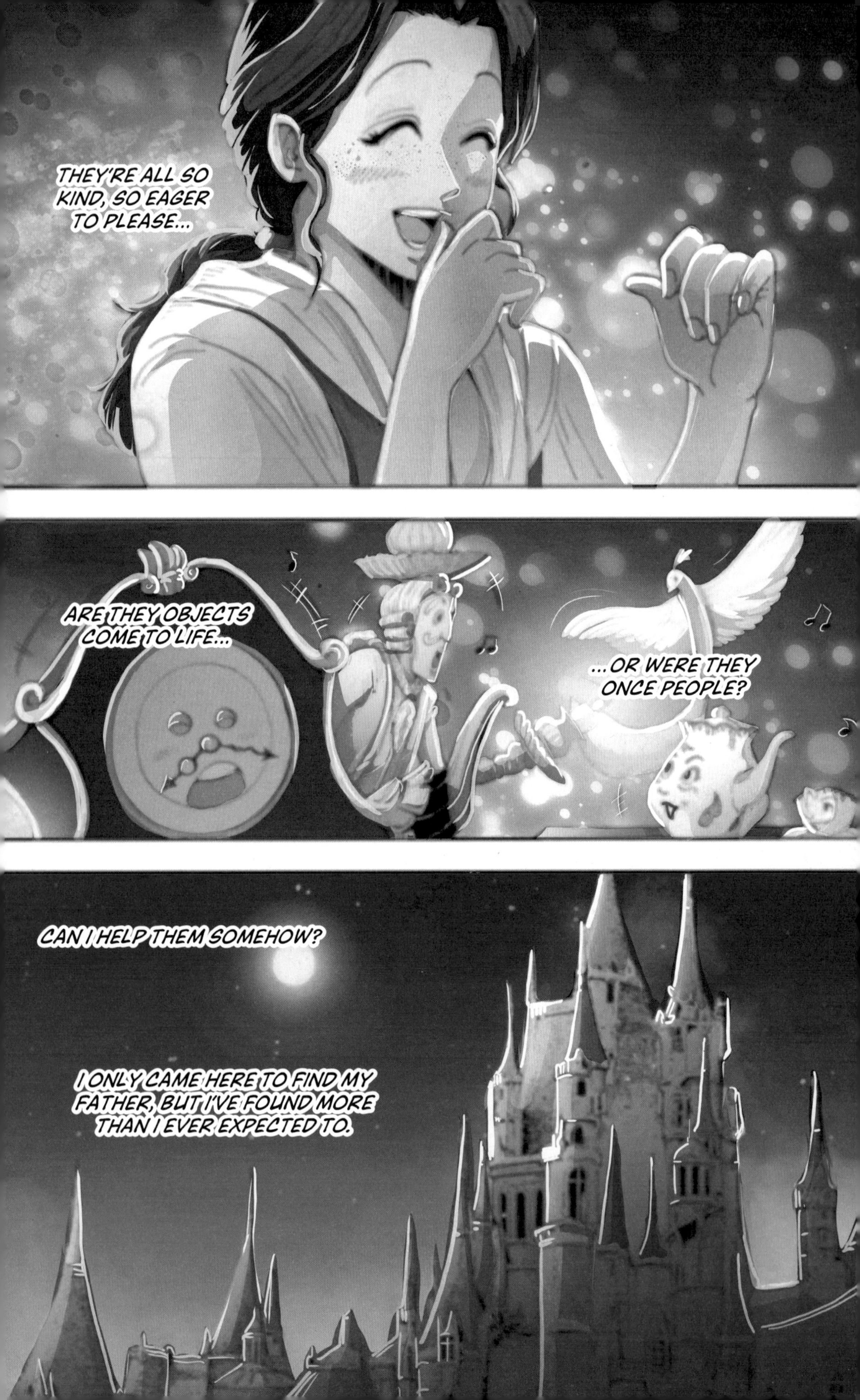
THEY'RE ALL SO KIND, SO EAGER TO PLEASE...
ARE THEY OBJECTS COME TO LIFE...
...OR WERE THEY ONCE PEOPLE?
CAN I HELP THEM SOMEHOW?
I ONLY CAME HERE TO FIND MY FATHER, BUT I'VE FOUND MORE THAN I EVER EXPECTED TO.

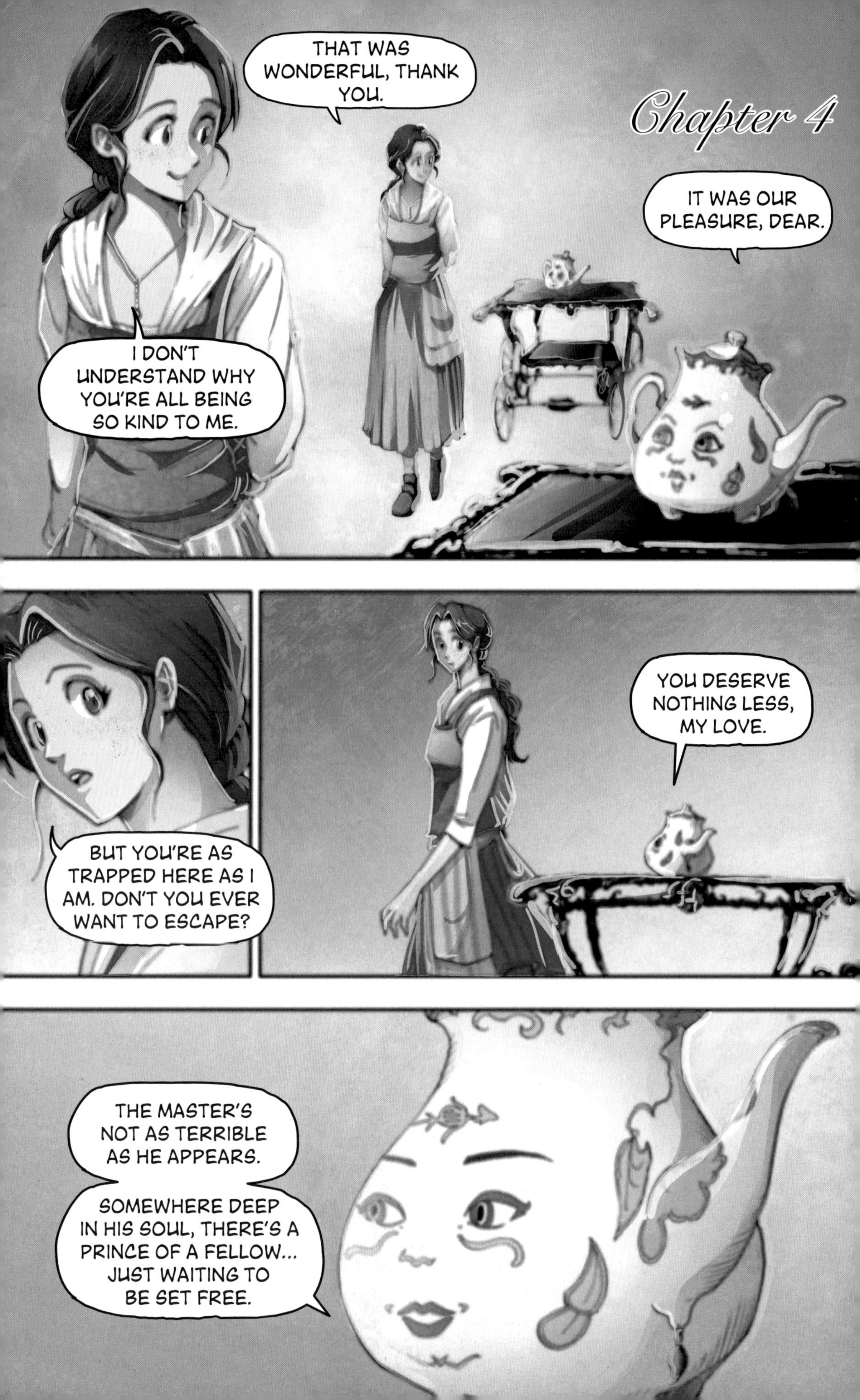
THAT WAS WONDERFUL, THANK YOU.
Chapter 4
IT WAS OUR PLEASURE, DEAR.
I DON'T UNDERSTAND WHY YOU'RE ALL BEING SO KIND TO ME.
YOU DESERVE NOTHING LESS, MY LOVE.
BUT YOU'RE AS TRAPPED HERE AS I AM. DON'T YOU EVER WANT TO ESCAPE?
THE MASTER'S NOT AS TERRIBLE AS HE APPEARS.
SOMEWHERE DEEP IN HIS SOUL, THERE'S A PRINCE OF A FELLOW... JUST WAITING TO BE SET FREE.

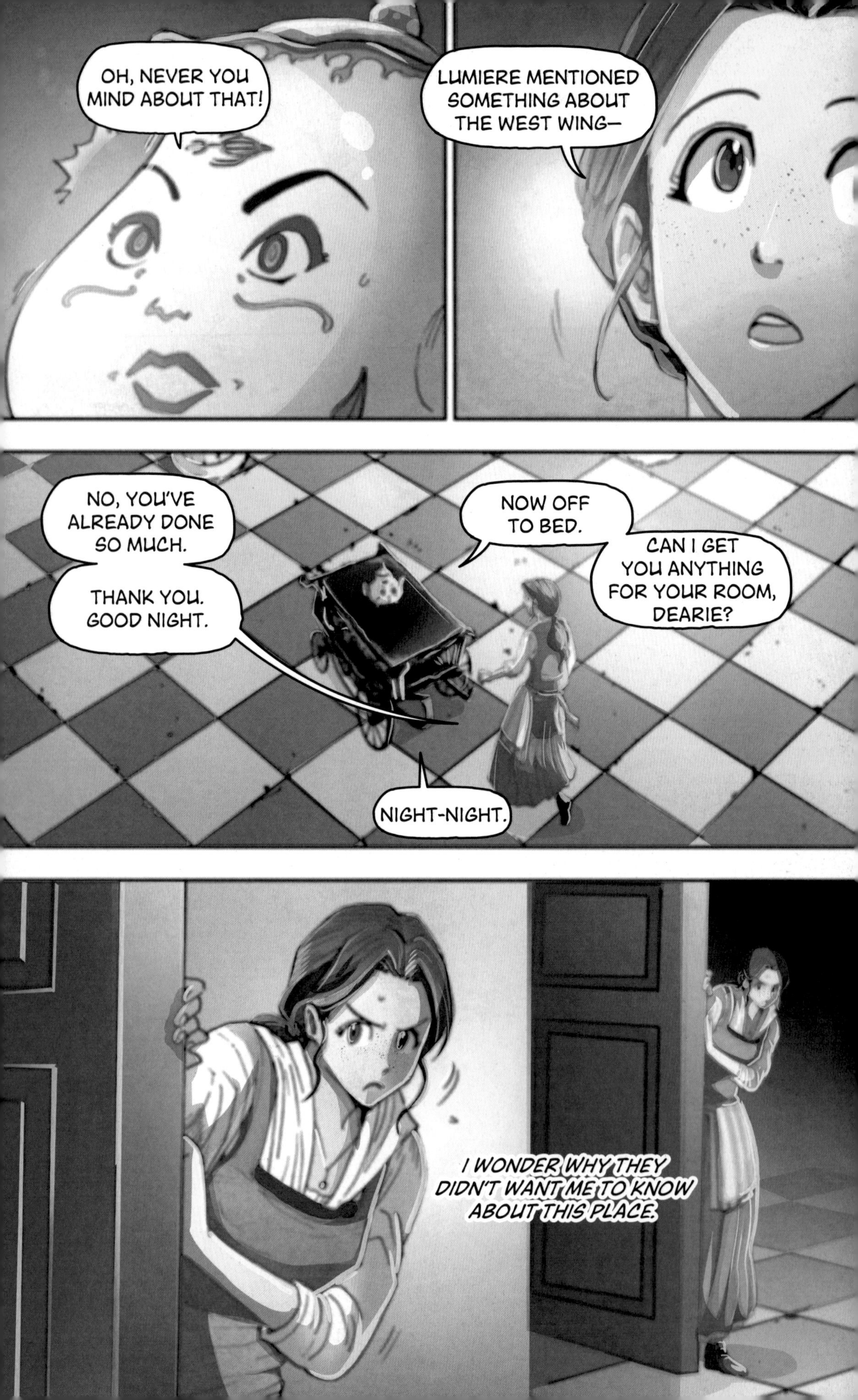
LUMIERE MENTIONED SOMETHING ABOUT THE WEST WING—
OH, NEVER YOU MIND ABOUT THAT!
NOW OFF TO BED.
CAN I GET YOU ANYTHING FOR YOUR ROOM, DEARIE?
NO, YOU'VE ALREADY DONE SO MUCH.
THANK YOU. GOOD NIGHT.
NIGHT-NIGHT.
I WONDER WHY THEY DIDN'T WANT ME TO KNOW ABOUT THIS PLACE.

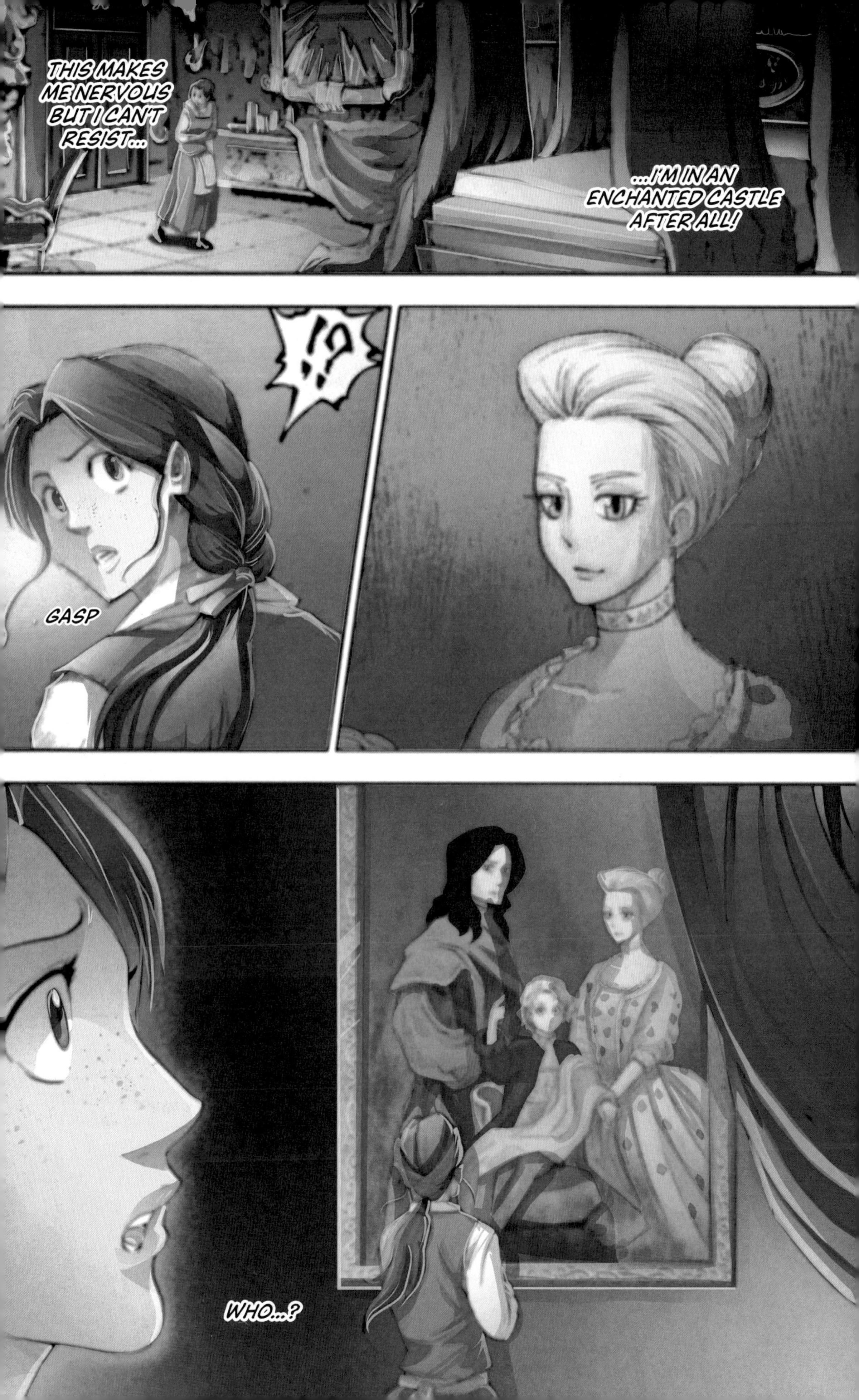
THIS MAKES ME NERVOUS BUT I CAN'T RESIST...
...I'M IN AN ENCHANTED CASTLE AFTER ALL!
!?
GASP
WHO...?

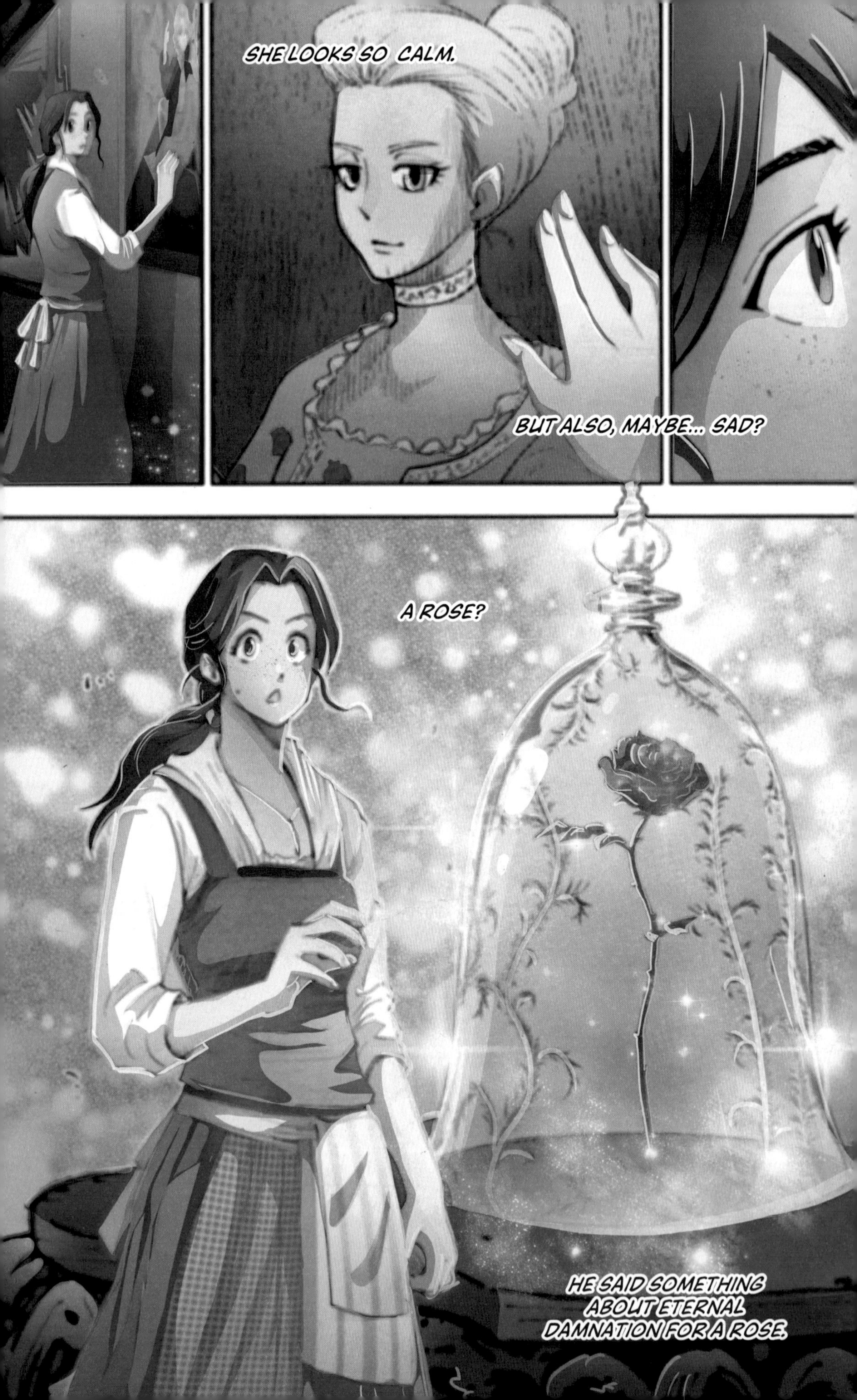
SHE LOOKS SO CALM.
BUT ALSO, MAYBE... SAD?
A ROSE?
HE SAID SOMETHING ABOUT ETERNAL DAMNATION FOR A ROSE.

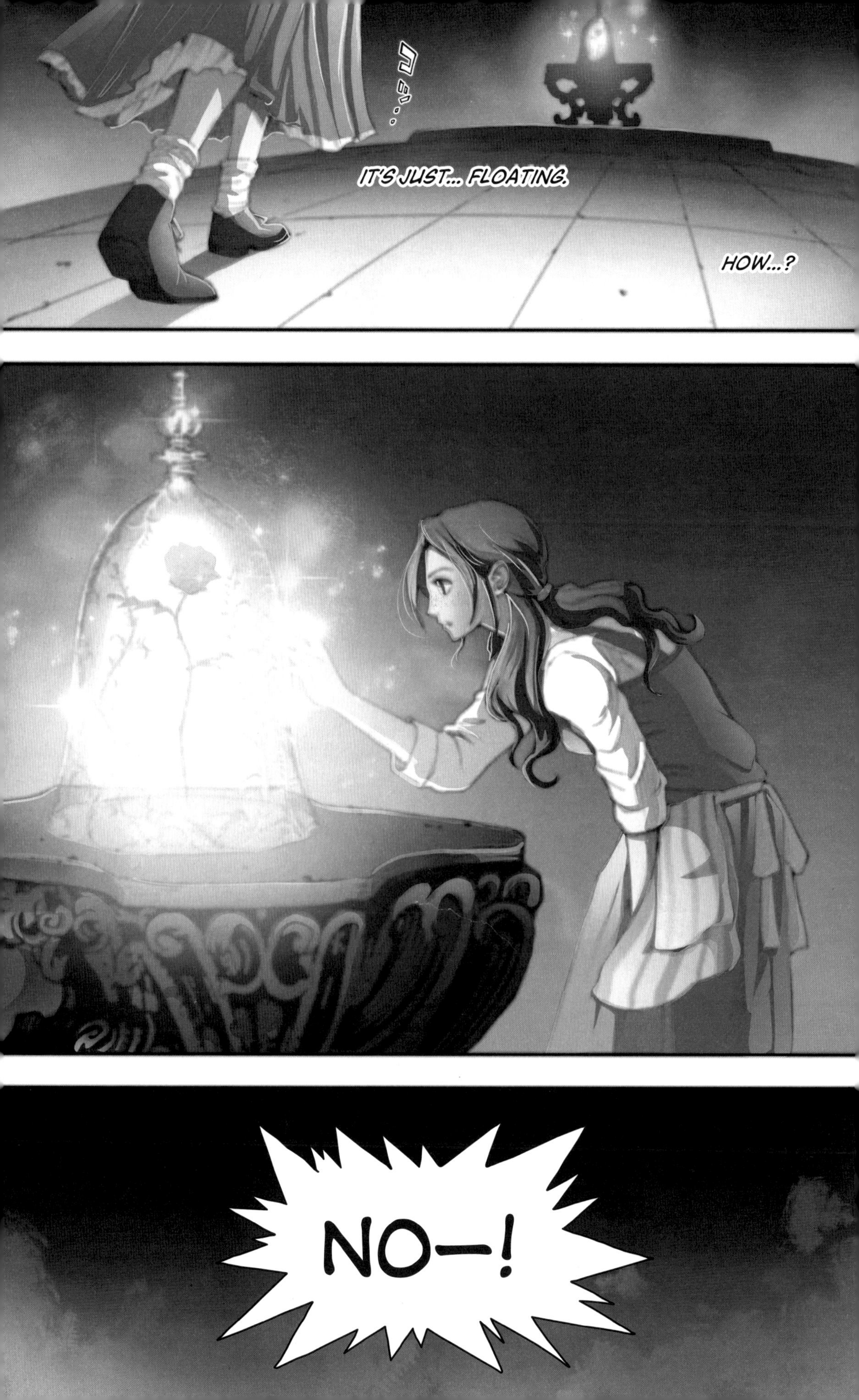
IT'S JUST... FLOATING.
HOW...?
NO—!

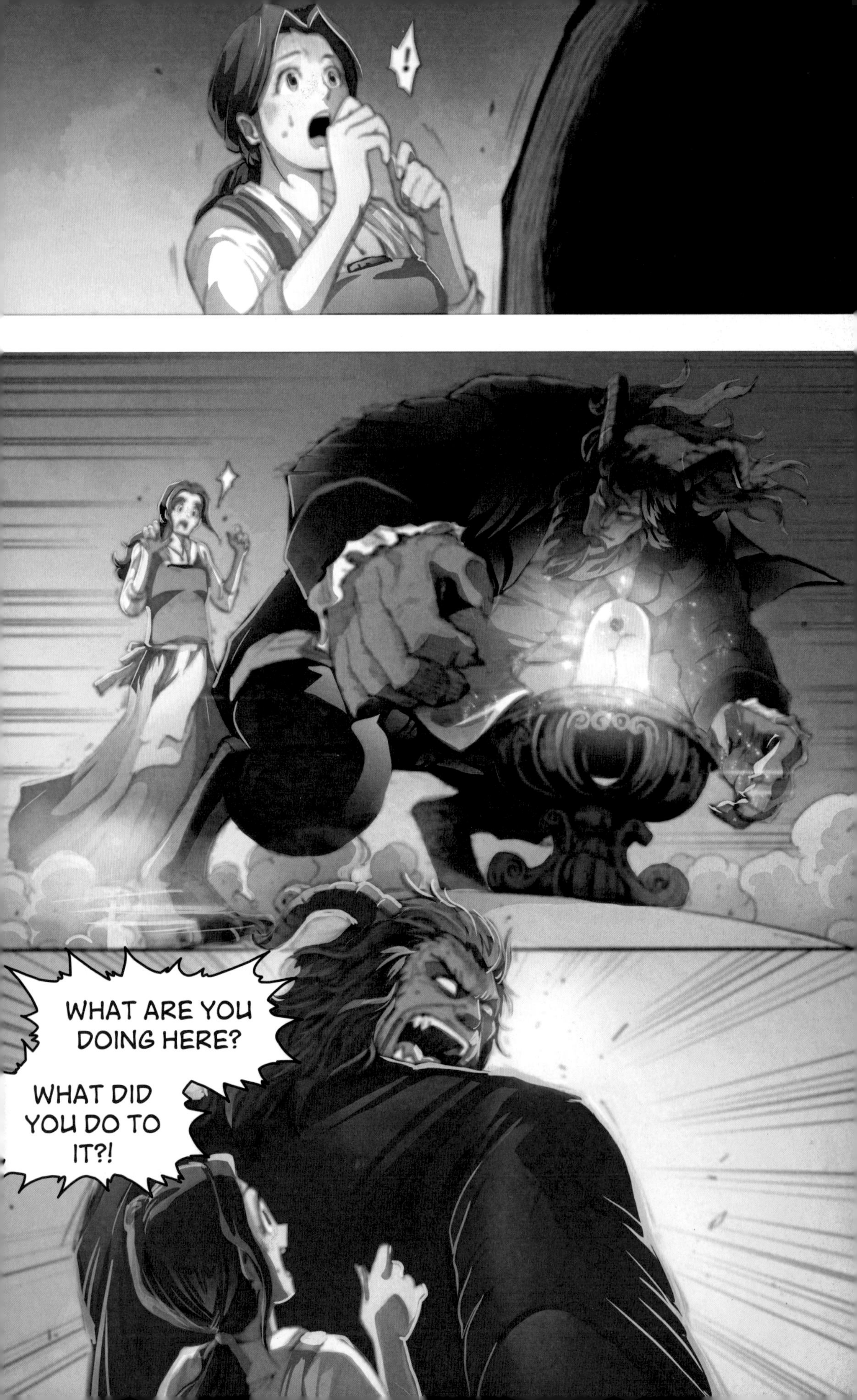
!
WHAT ARE YOU DOING HERE?
WHAT DID YOU DO TO IT?!

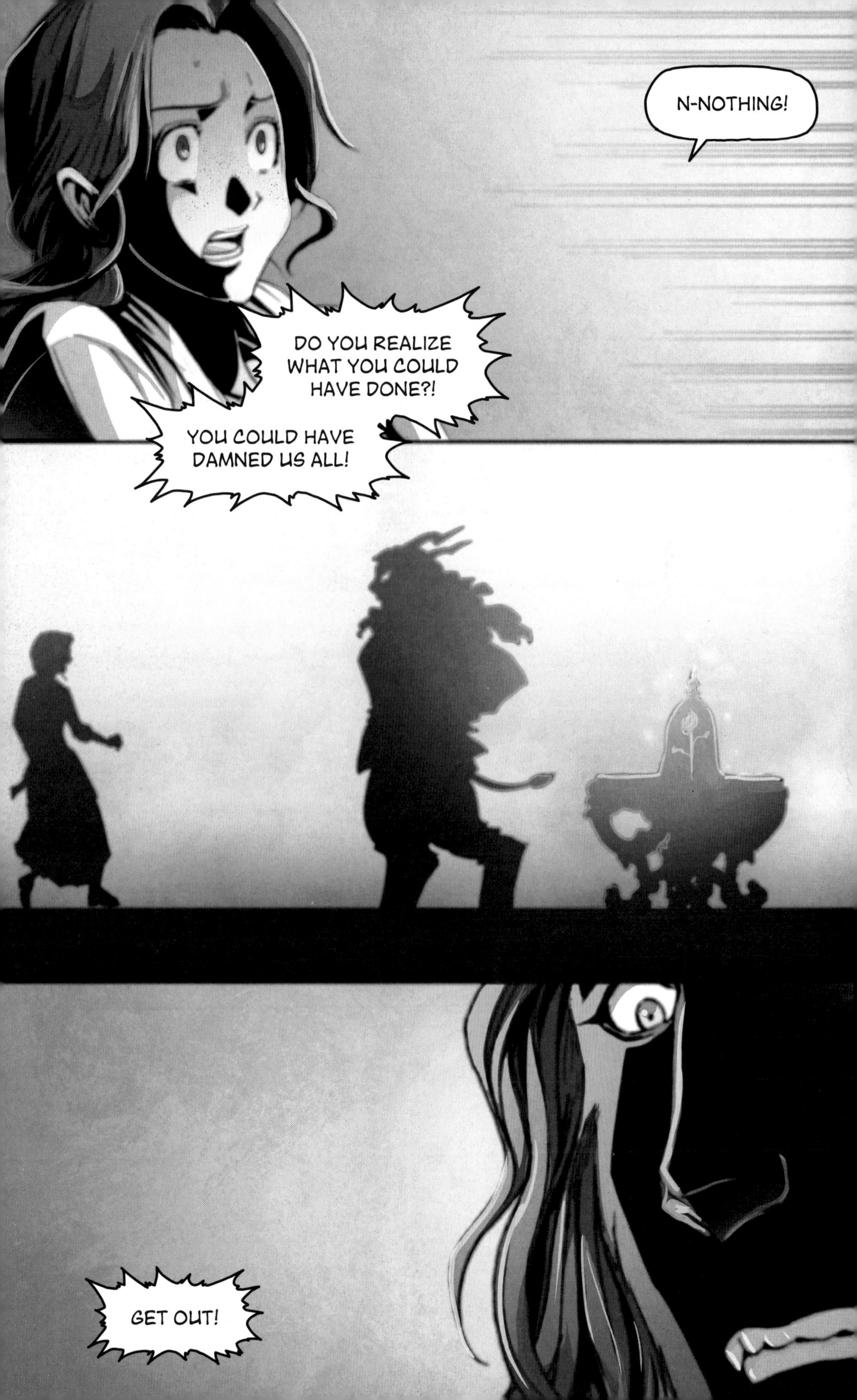
N-NOTHING!
DO YOU REALIZE WHAT YOU COULD HAVE DONE?!
YOU COULD HAVE DAMNED US ALL!
GET OUT!

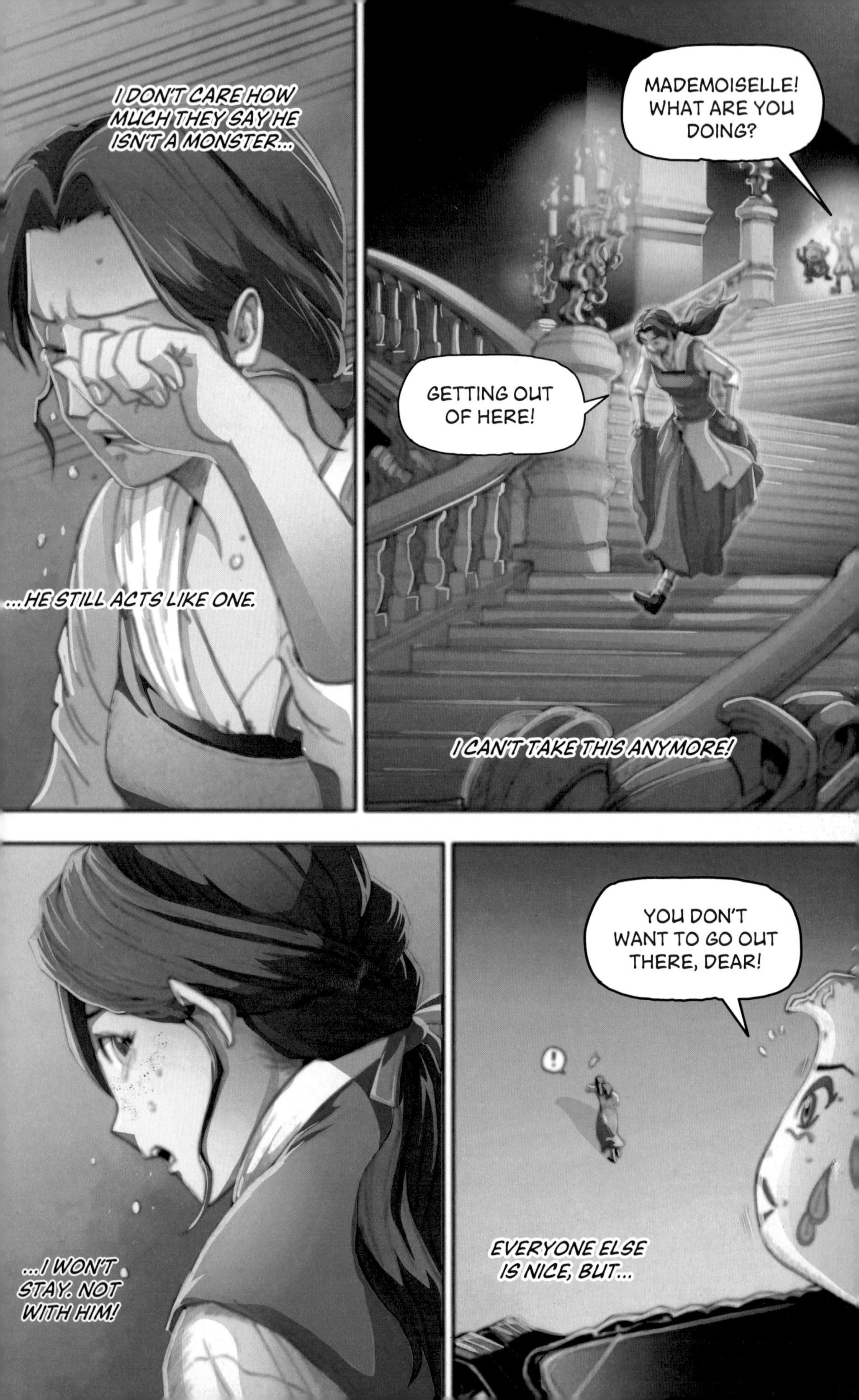
MADEMOISELLE! WHAT ARE YOU DOING?
GETTING OUT OF HERE!
I CAN'T TAKE THIS ANYMORE!
I DON'T CARE HOW MUCH THEY SAY HE ISN'T A MONSTER...
...HE STILL ACTS LIKE ONE.
YOU DON'T WANT TO GO OUT THERE, DEAR!
EVERYONE ELSE IS NICE, BUT...
...I WON'T STAY. NOT WITH HIM!

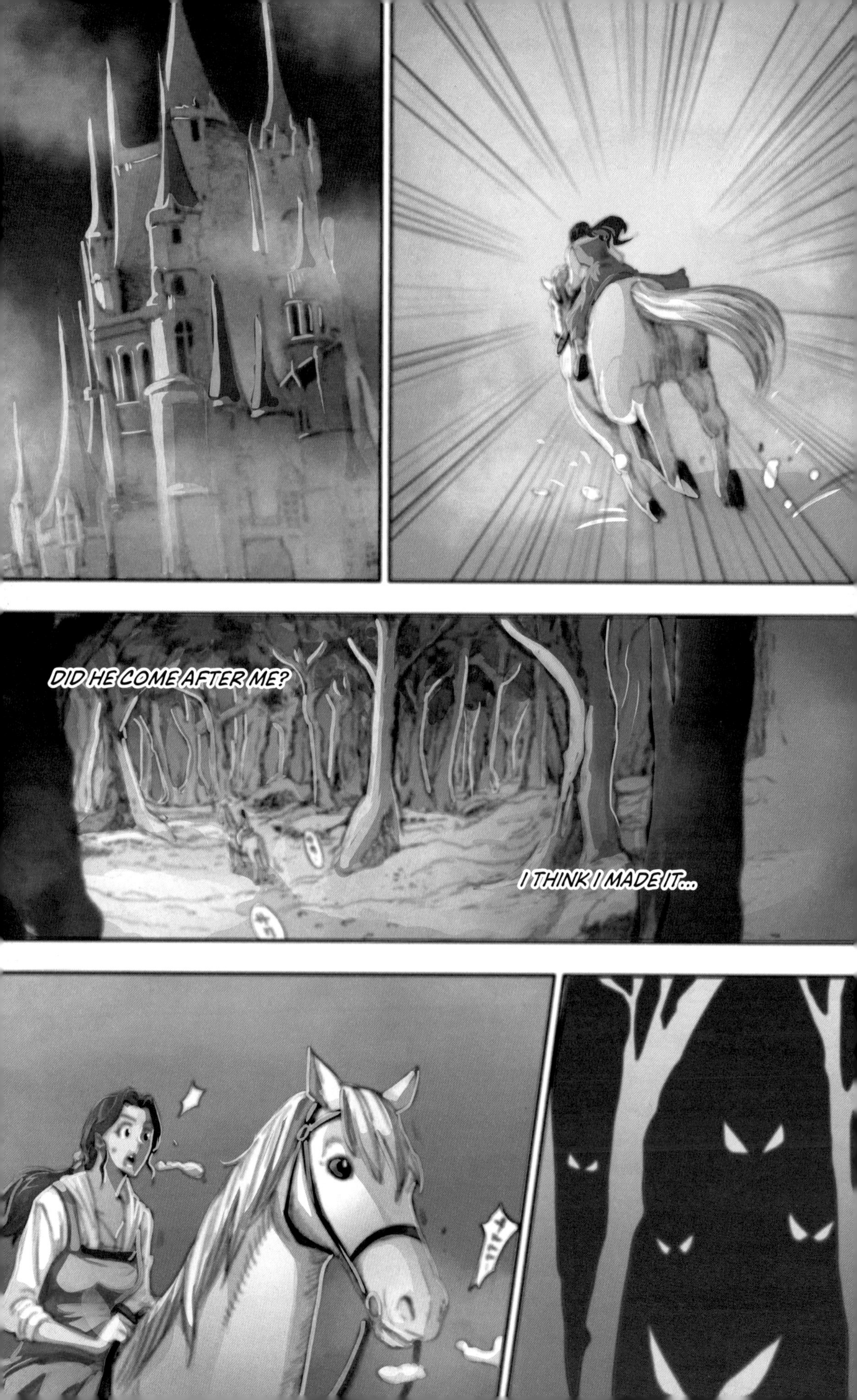
DID HE COME AFTER ME?
I THINK I MADE IT...

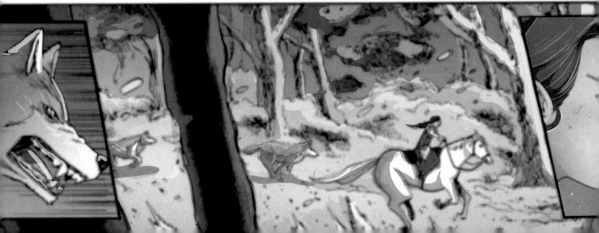

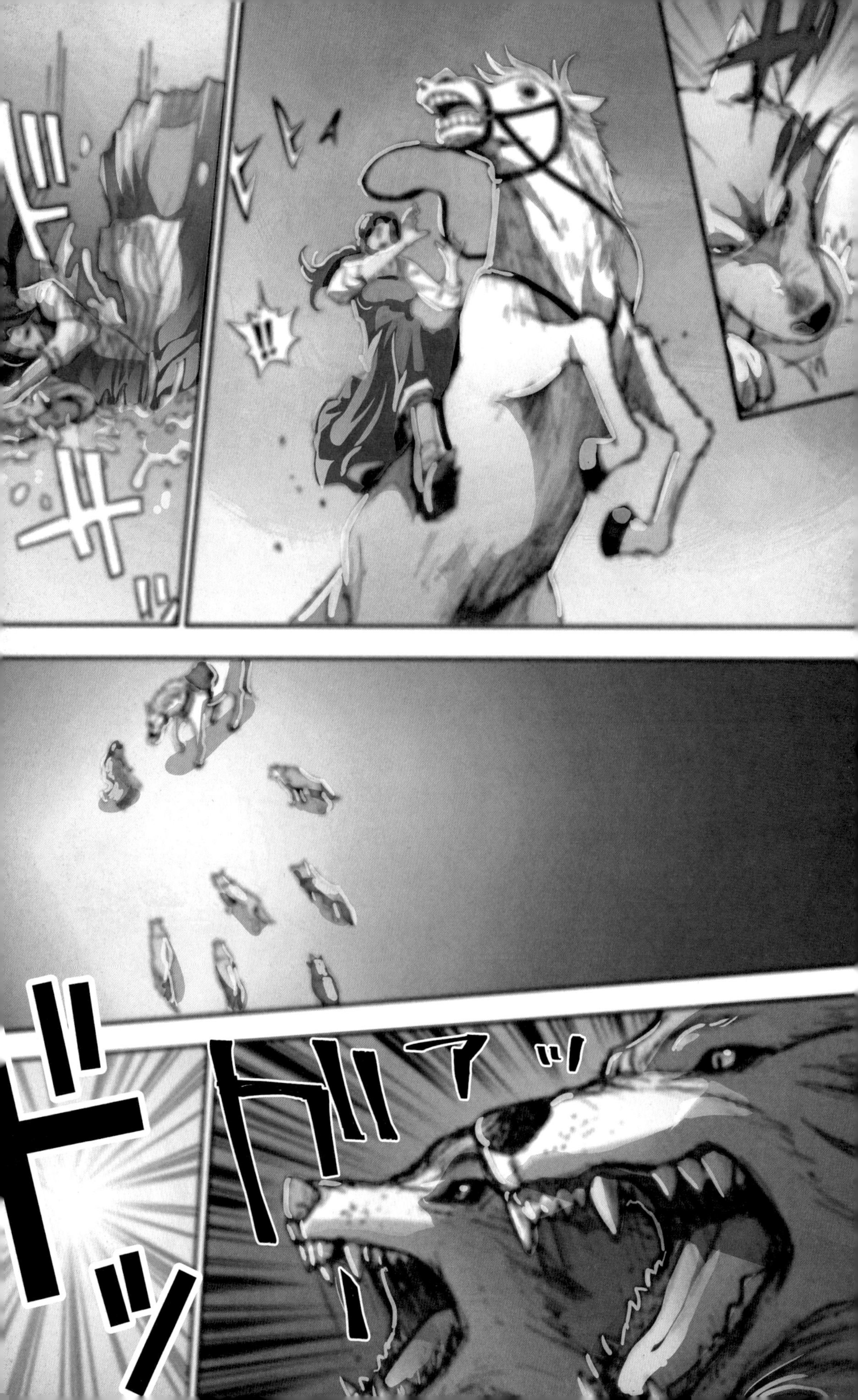
!!
ドッ
ガアッ

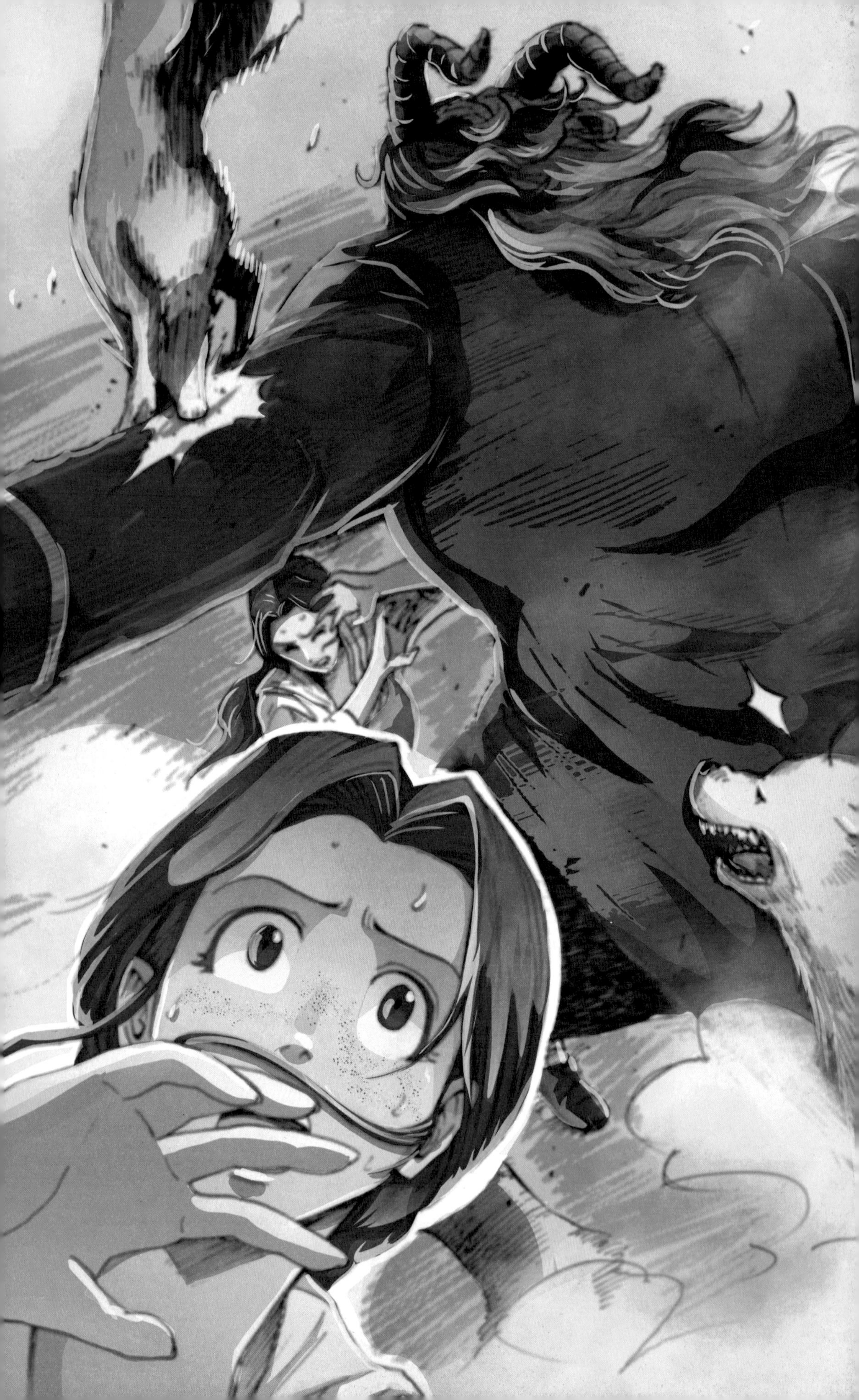

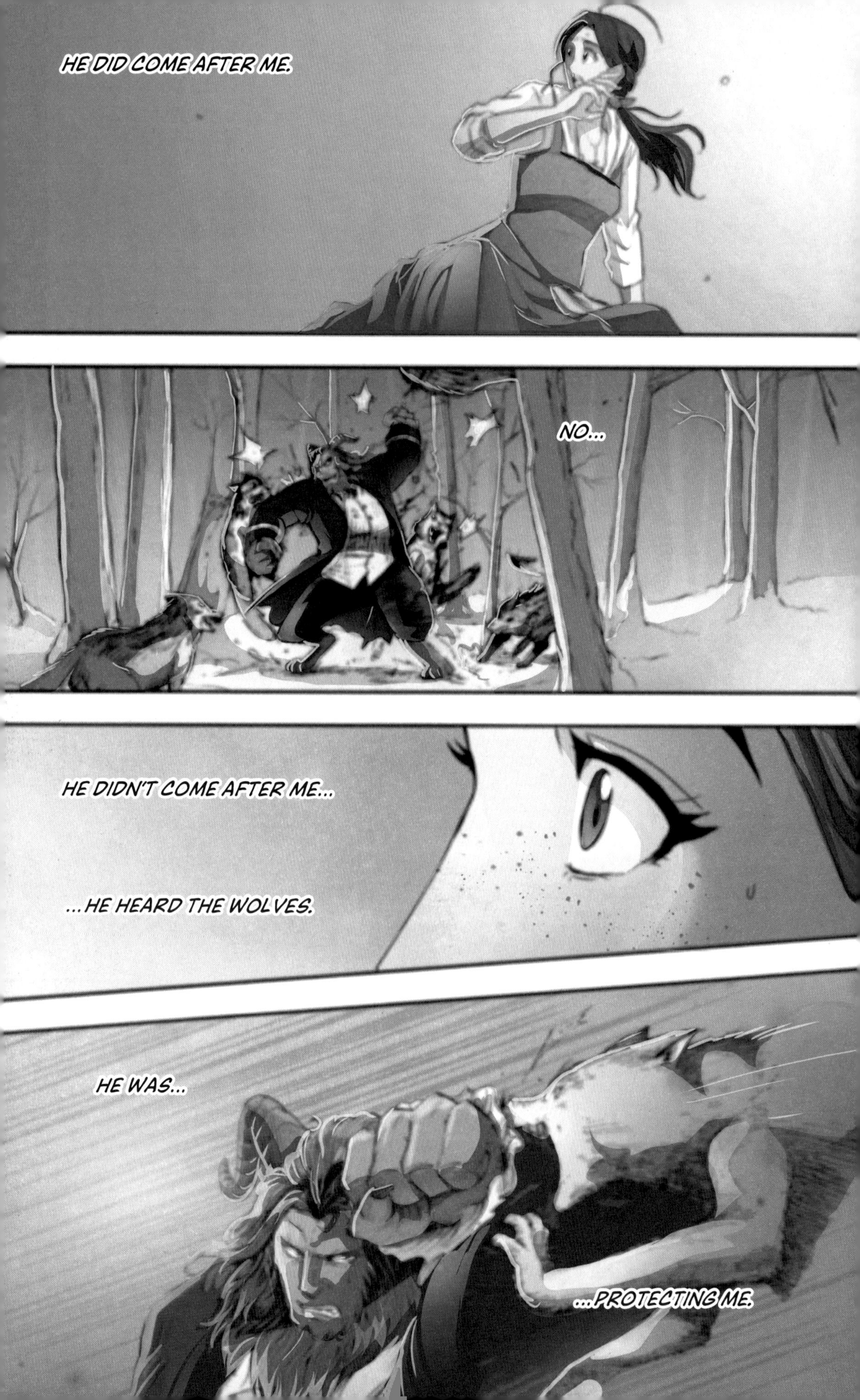
HE DID COME AFTER ME.
NO...
HE DIDN'T COME AFTER ME...
...HE HEARD THE WOLVES.
HE WAS...
...PROTECTING ME.

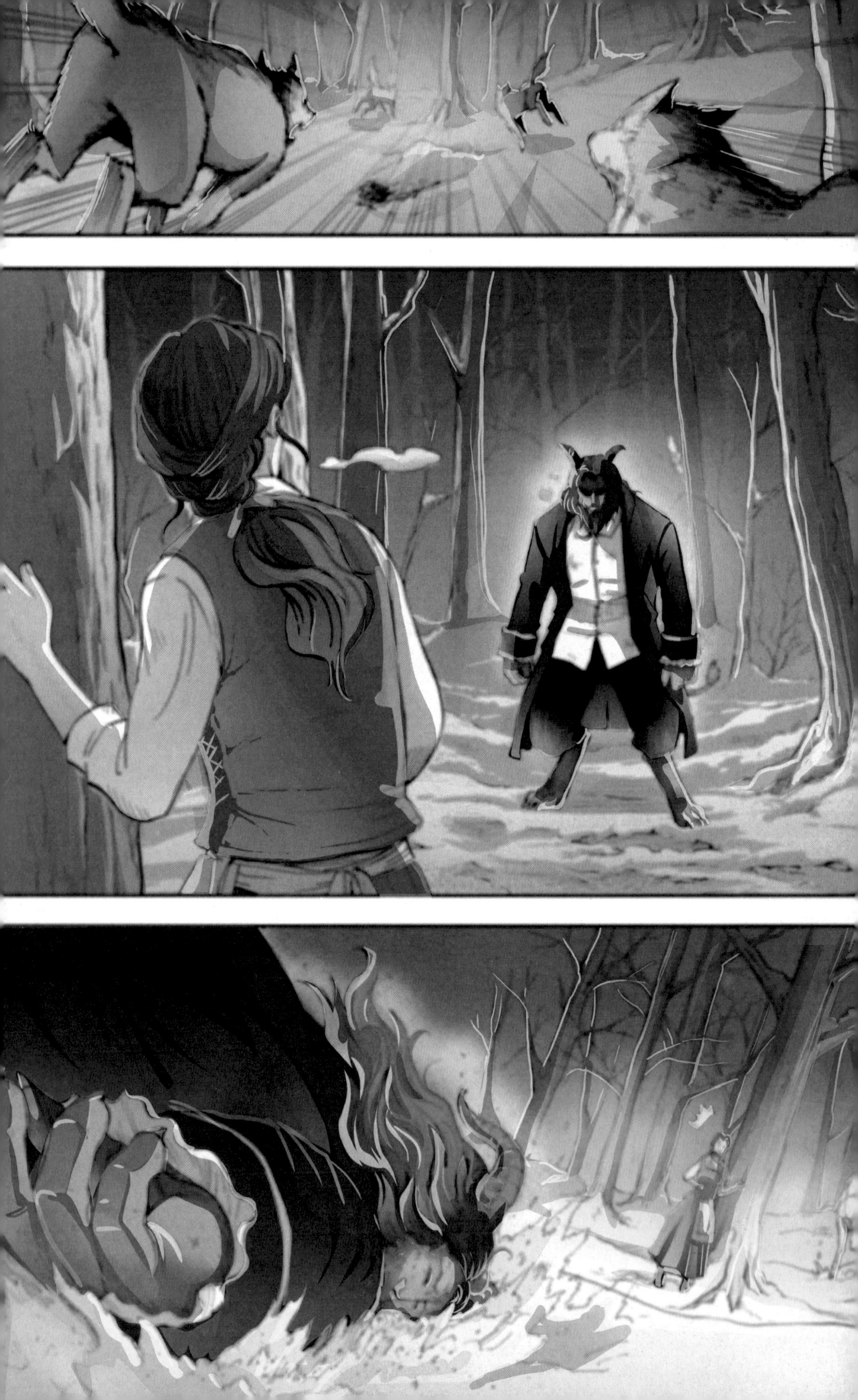

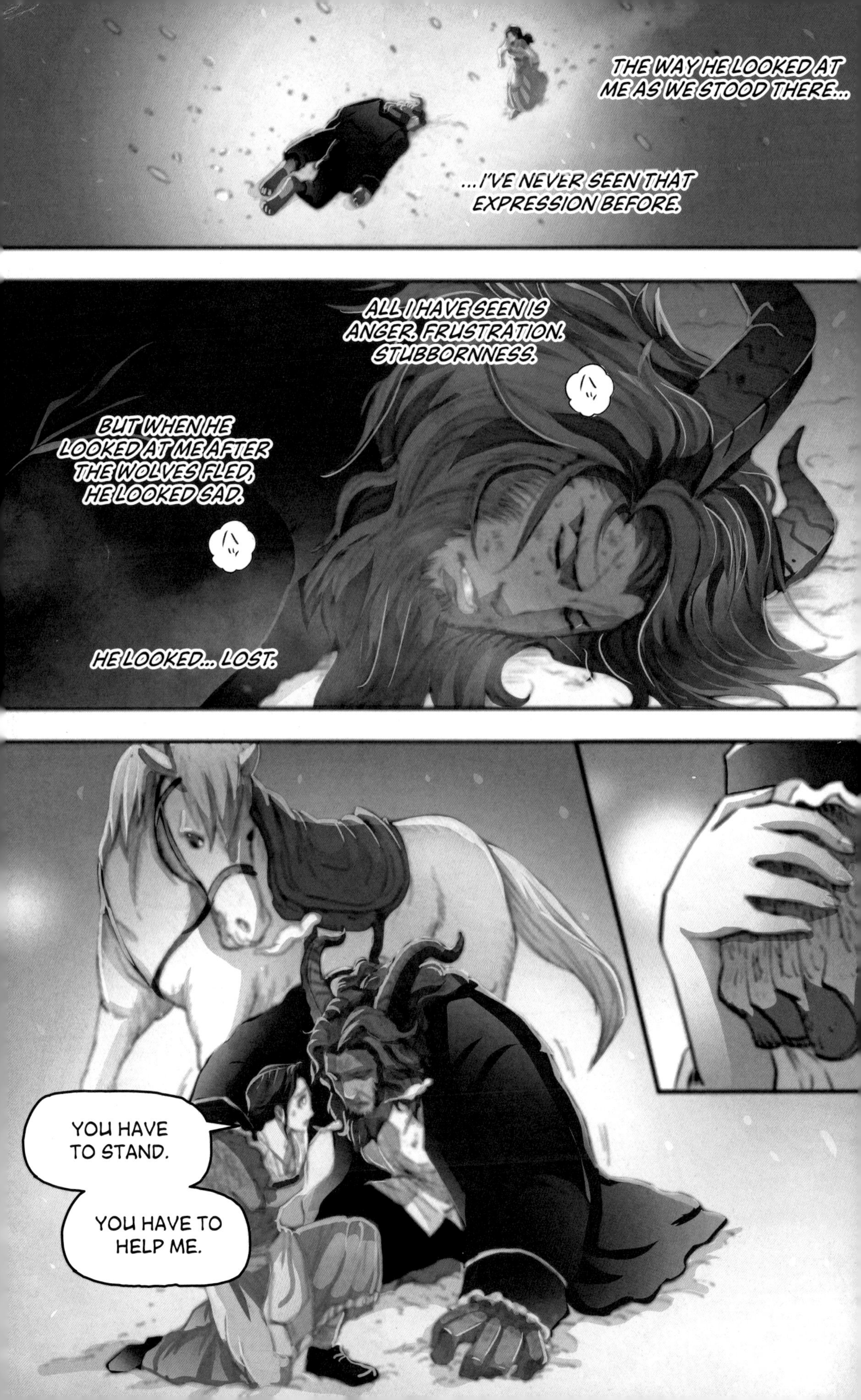
THE WAY HE LOOKED AT ME AS WE STOOD THERE...
...I'VE NEVER SEEN THAT EXPRESSION BEFORE.
ALL I HAVE SEEN IS ANGER. FRUSTRATION. STUBBORNNESS.
BUT WHEN HE LOOKED AT ME AFTER THE WOLVES FLED, HE LOOKED SAD.
HE LOOKED... LOST.
YOU HAVE TO STAND.
YOU HAVE TO HELP ME.

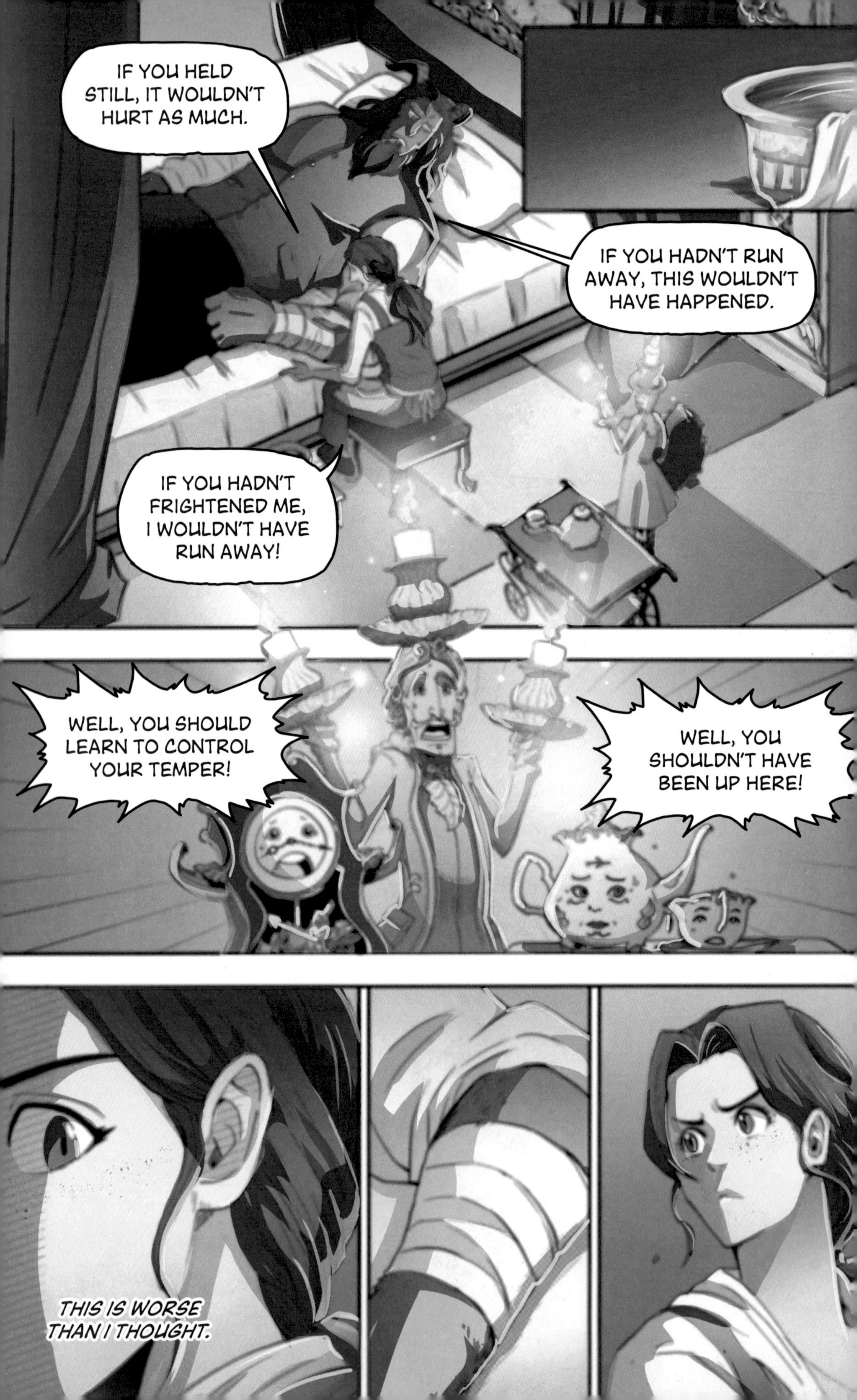
IF YOU HELD STILL, IT WOULDN'T HURT AS MUCH.
IF YOU HADN'T RUN AWAY, THIS WOULDN'T HAVE HAPPENED.
IF YOU HADN'T FRIGHTENED ME, I WOULDN'T HAVE RUN AWAY!
WELL, YOU SHOULDN'T HAVE BEEN UP HERE!
WELL, YOU SHOULD LEARN TO CONTROL YOUR TEMPER!
THIS IS WORSE THAN I THOUGHT.

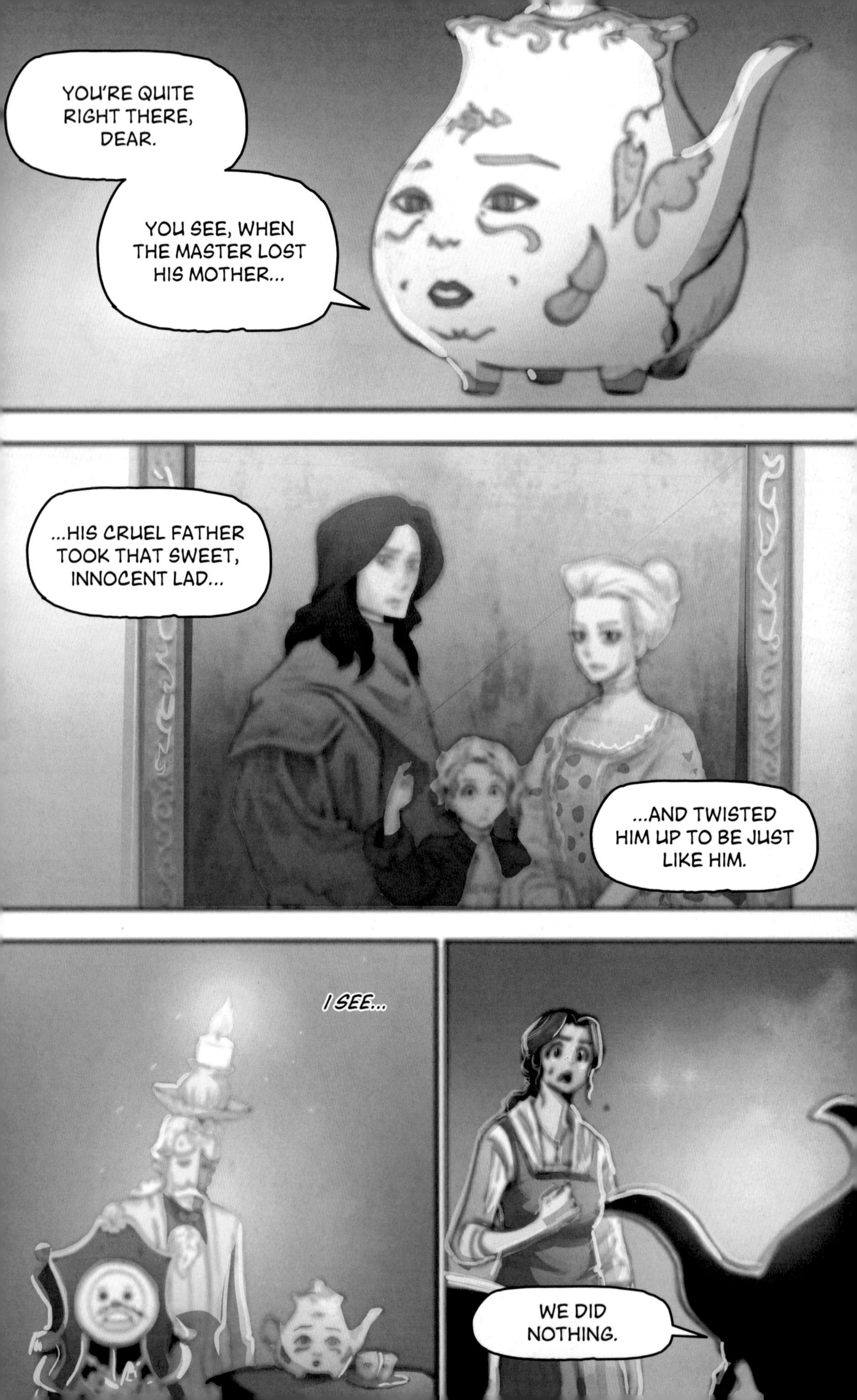
YOU'RE QUITE RIGHT THERE, DEAR.
YOU SEE, WHEN THE MASTER LOST HIS MOTHER...
...HIS CRUEL FATHER TOOK THAT SWEET, INNOCENT LAD...
...AND TWISTED HIM UP TO BE JUST LIKE HIM.
WE DID NOTHING.
I SEE...

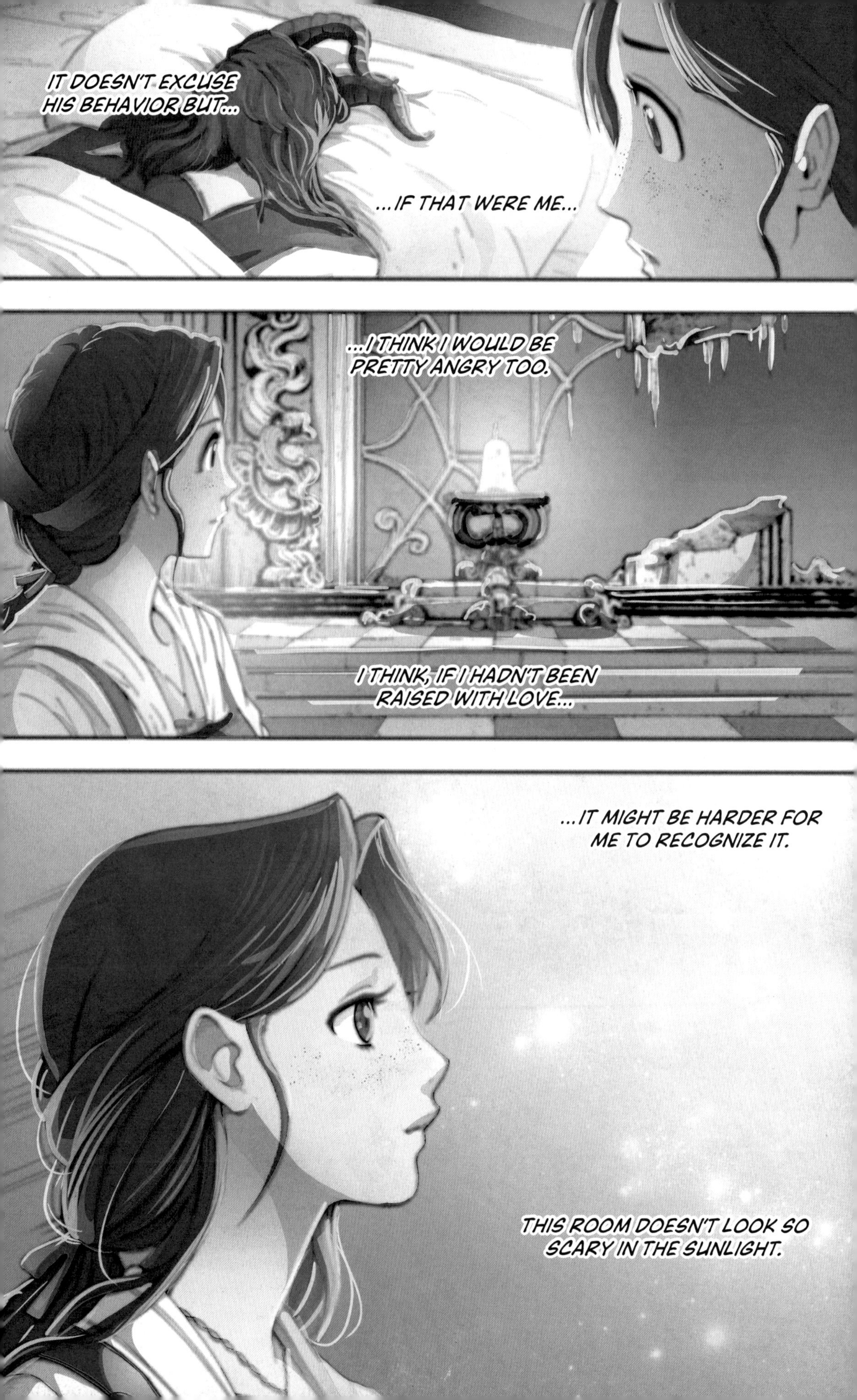
IT DOESN'T EXCUSE HIS BEHAVIOR BUT...
...IF THAT WERE ME...
...I THINK I WOULD BE PRETTY ANGRY TOO.
I THINK, IF I HADN'T BEEN RAISED WITH LOVE...
...IT MIGHT BE HARDER FOR ME TO RECOGNIZE IT.
THIS ROOM DOESN'T LOOK SO SCARY IN THE SUNLIGHT.

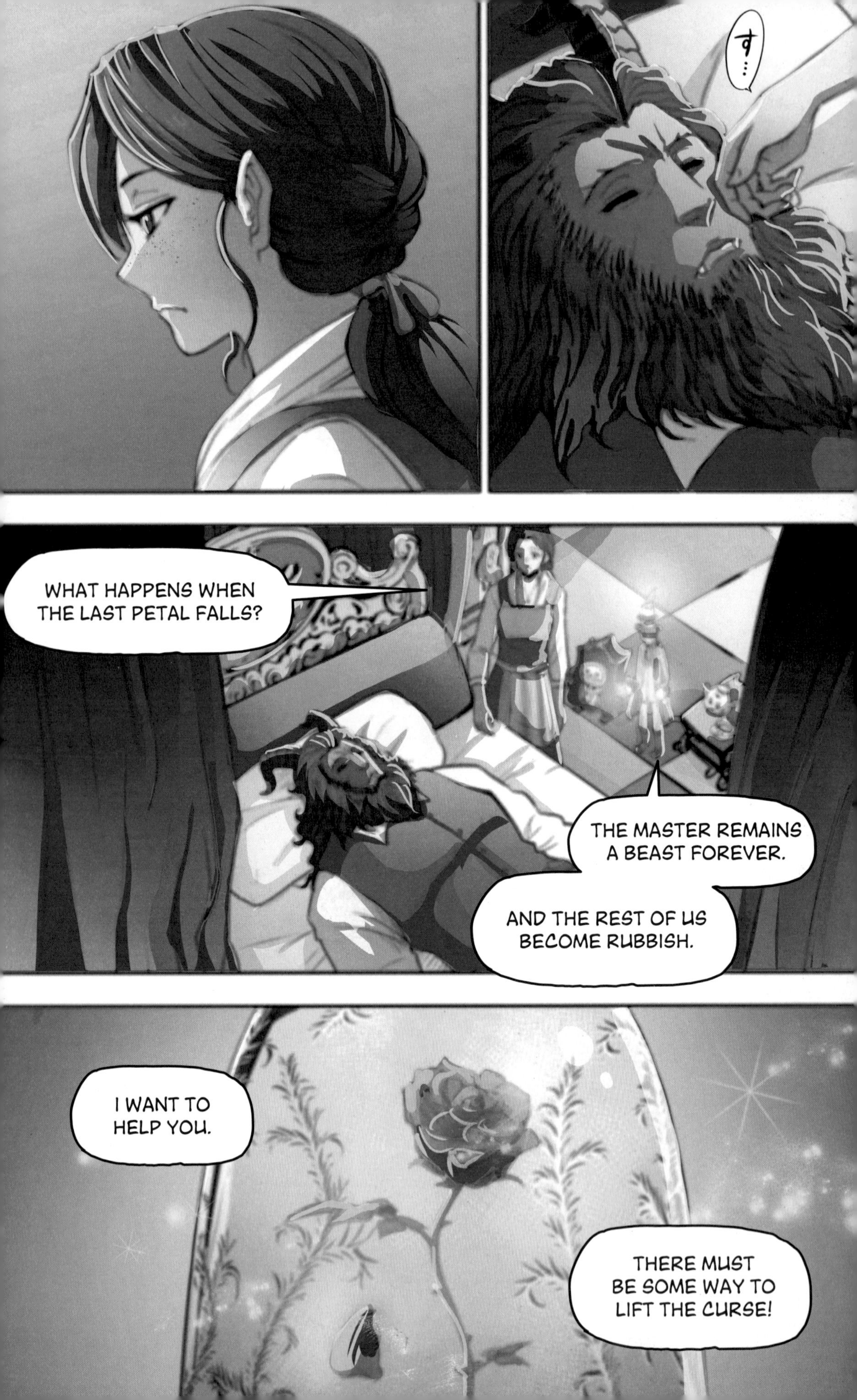
す…
WHAT HAPPENS WHEN THE LAST PETAL FALLS?
THE MASTER REMAINS A BEAST FOREVER.
AND THE REST OF US BECOME RUBBISH.
I WANT TO HELP YOU.
THERE MUST BE SOME WAY TO LIFT THE CURSE!

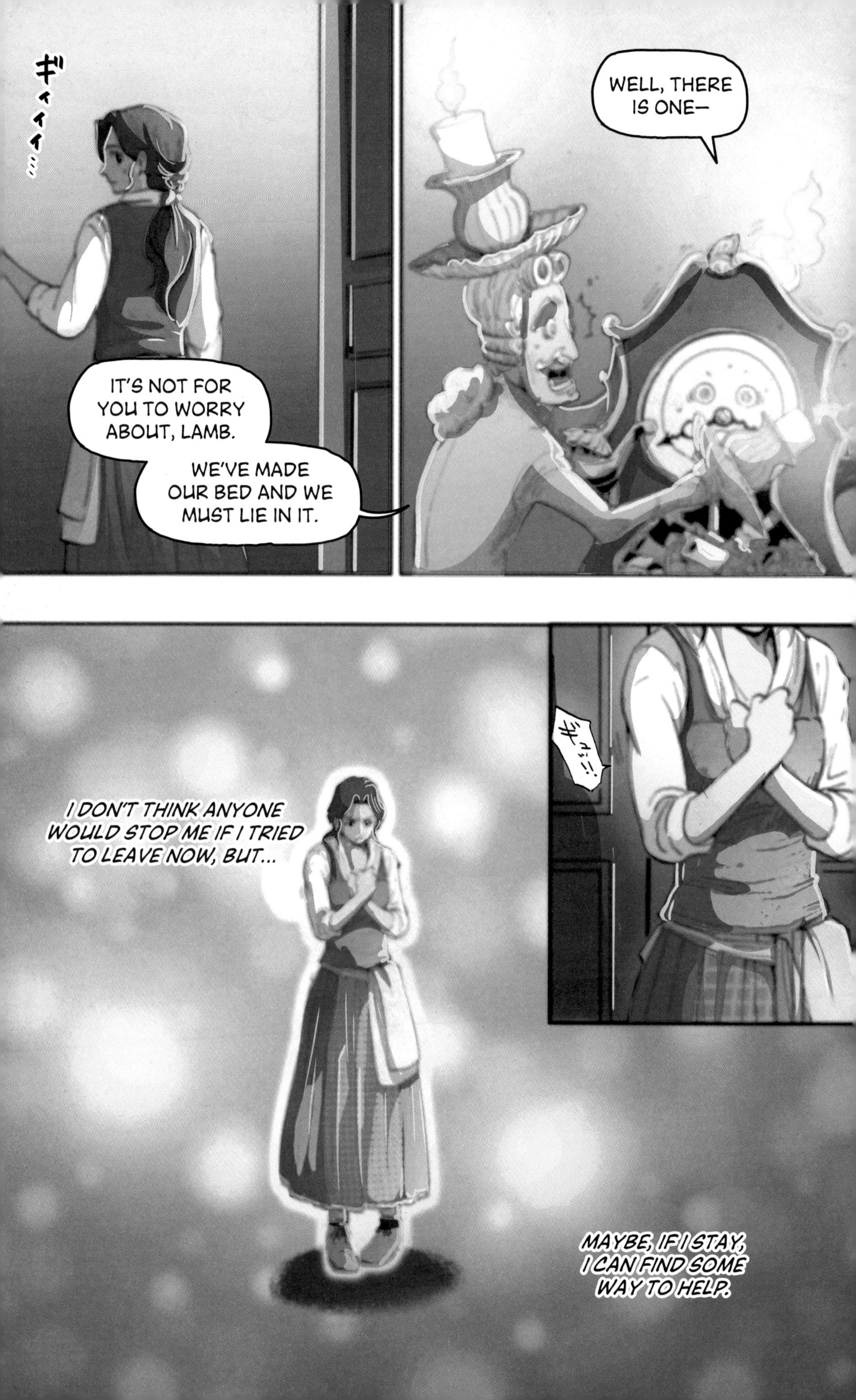
WELL, THERE IS ONE—
ギィイイ…
IT'S NOT FOR YOU TO WORRY ABOUT, LAMB.
WE'VE MADE OUR BED AND WE MUST LIE IN IT.
ギュッ!!
I DON'T THINK ANYONE WOULD STOP ME IF I TRIED TO LEAVE NOW, BUT...
MAYBE, IF I STAY, I CAN FIND SOME WAY TO HELP.

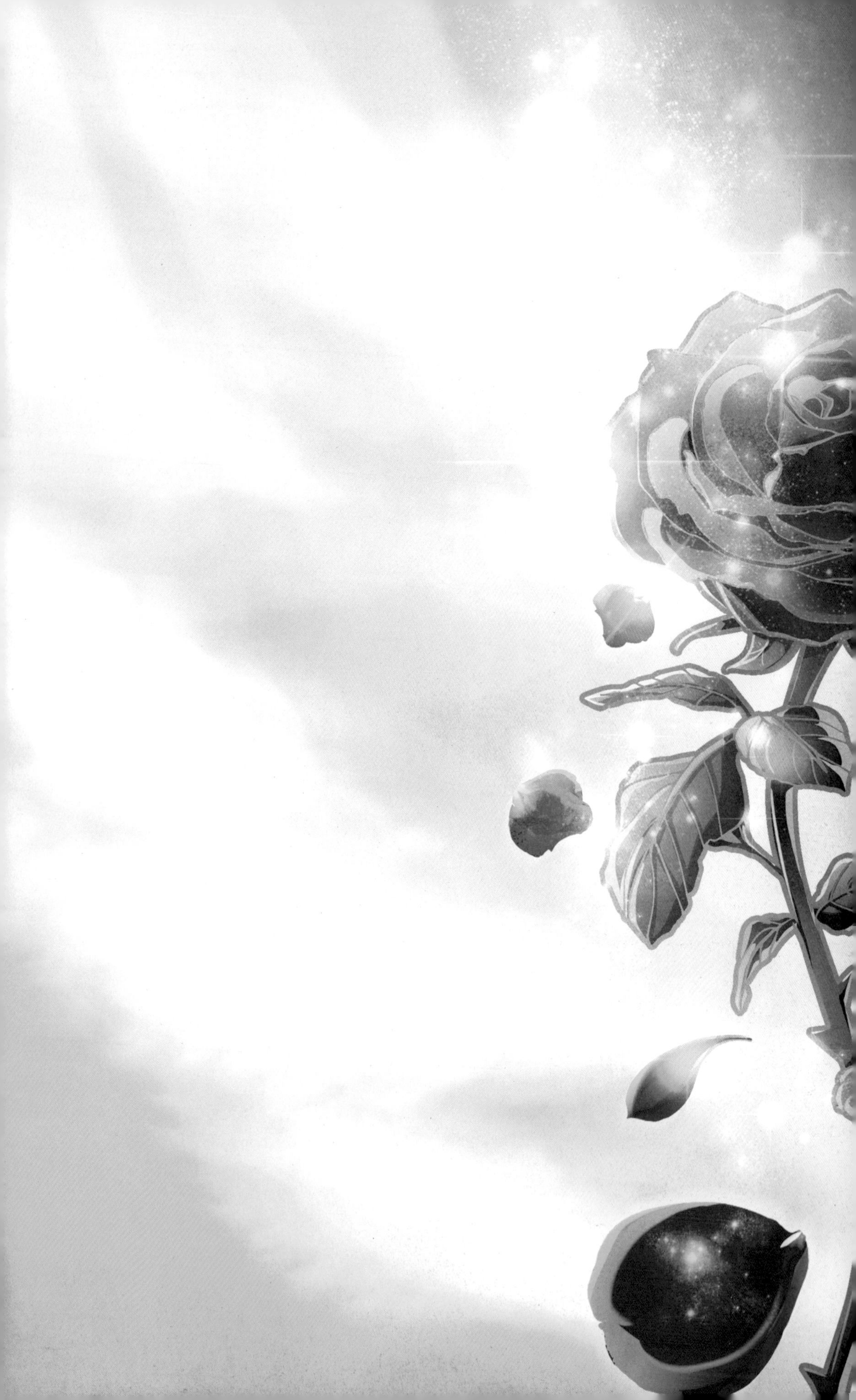

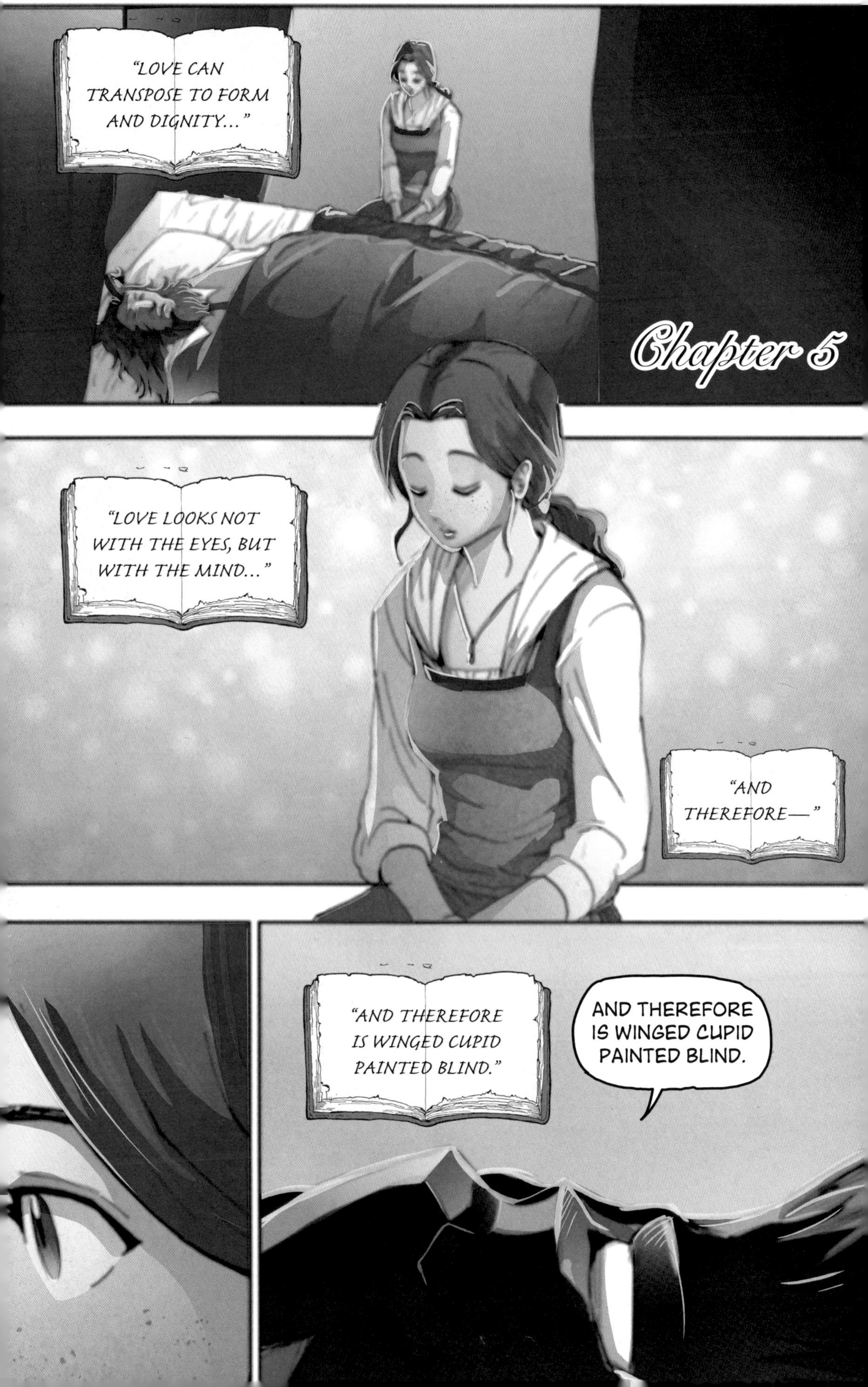
"LOVE CAN TRANSPOSE TO FORM AND DIGNITY..."
Chapter 5
"LOVE LOOKS NOT WITH THE EYES, BUT WITH THE MIND..."
"AND THEREFORE—"
"AND THEREFORE IS WINGED CUPID PAINTED BLIND."
AND THEREFORE IS WINGED CUPID PAINTED BLIND.

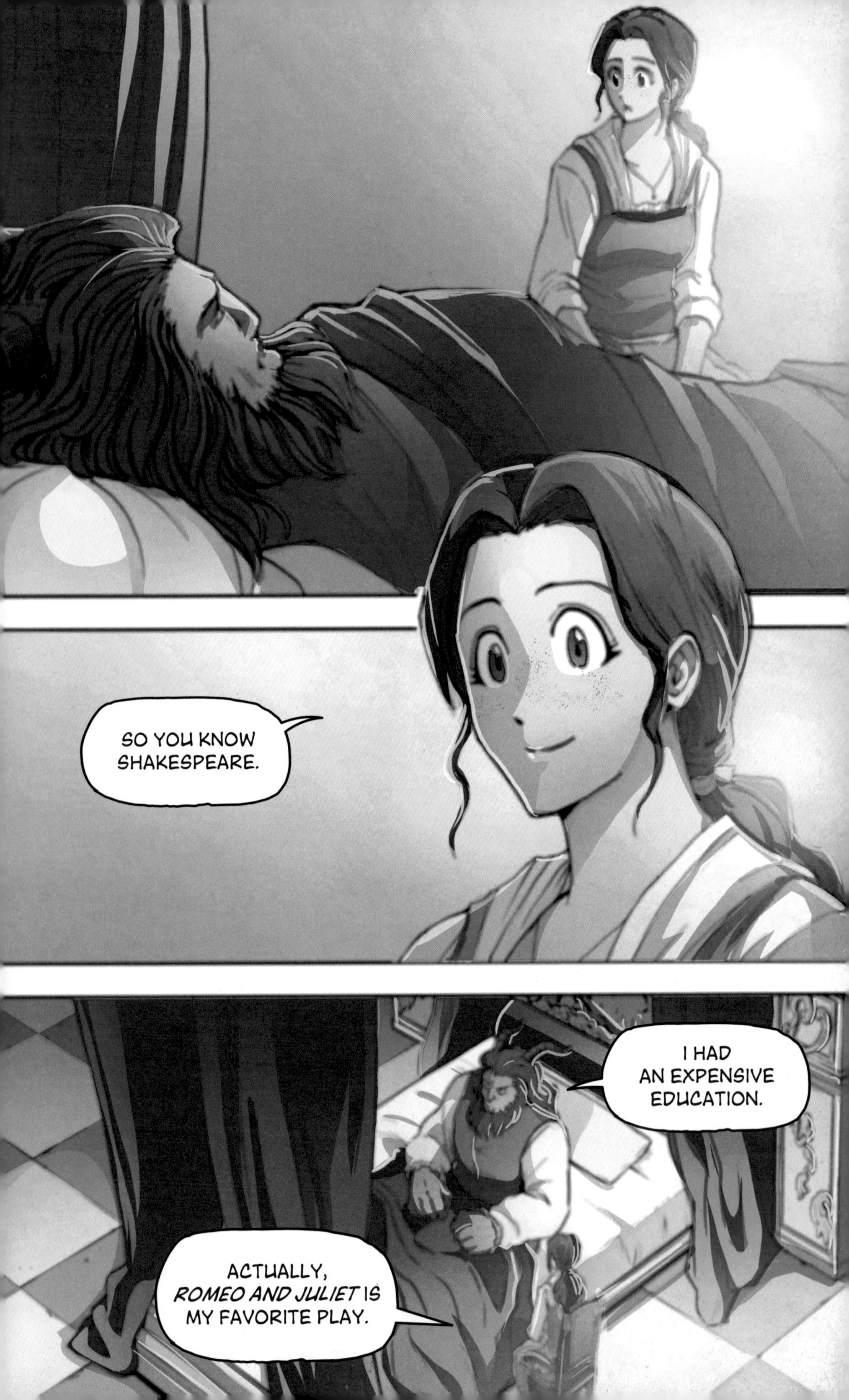
SO YOU KNOW SHAKESPEARE.
I HAD AN EXPENSIVE EDUCATION.
ACTUALLY, *ROMEO AND JULIET* IS MY FAVORITE PLAY.

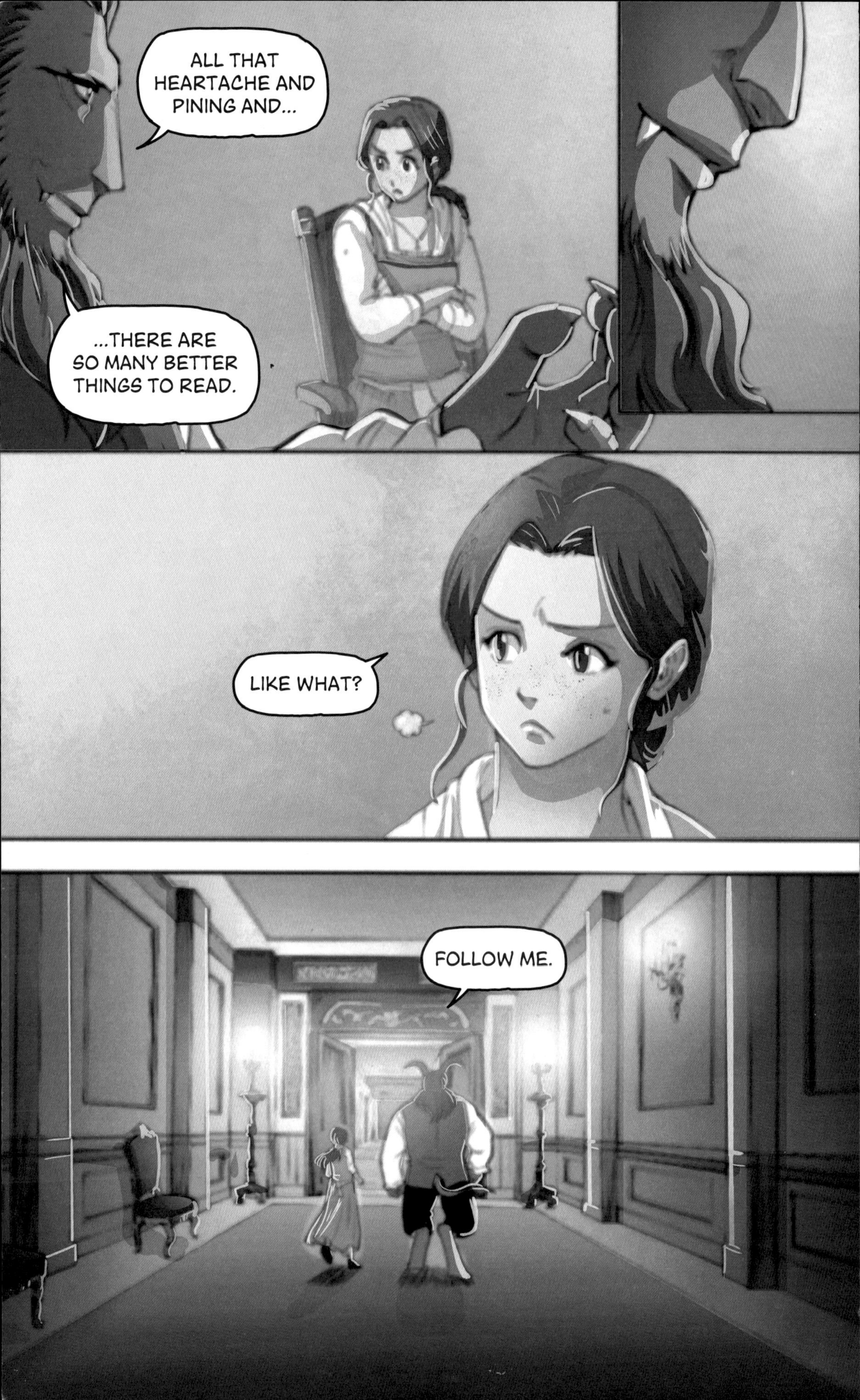
ALL THAT HEARTACHE AND PINING AND...
...THERE ARE SO MANY BETTER THINGS TO READ.
LIKE WHAT?
FOLLOW ME.

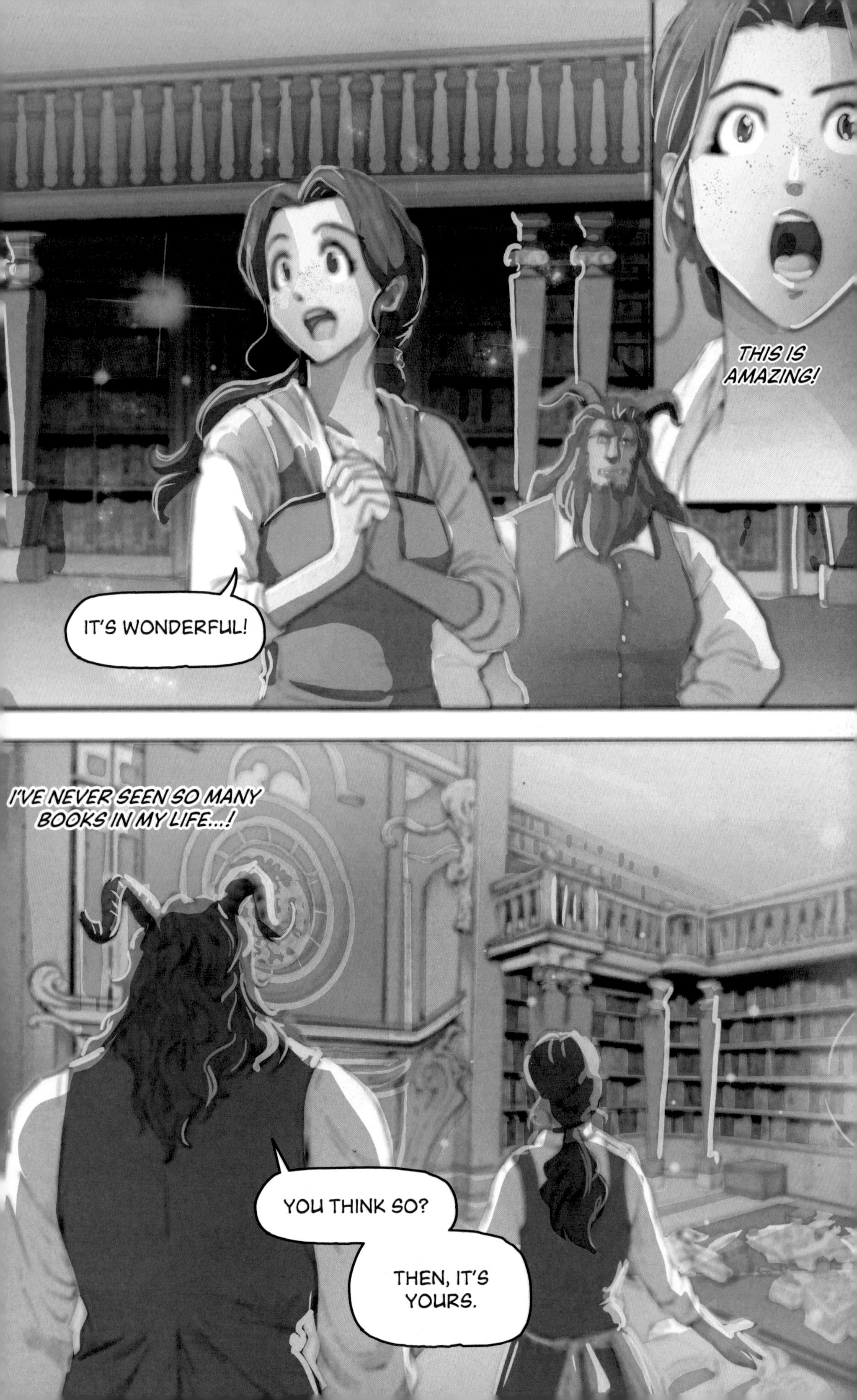
THIS IS AMAZING!
IT'S WONDERFUL!
I'VE NEVER SEEN SO MANY BOOKS IN MY LIFE...!
YOU THINK SO?
THEN, IT'S YOURS.

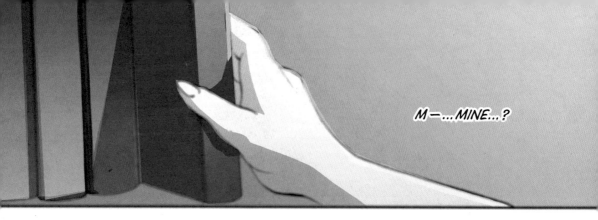

M —...MINE...?

YOU CAN BE MASTER HERE.

THAT WAS...

...SO KIND OF HIM!

I FEEL A LITTLE DIZZY.

MY HEART IS POUNDING.

I WONDER IF SOMETHING CHANGED...

...OR IF THIS SIDE OF HIM WAS ALWAYS THERE.

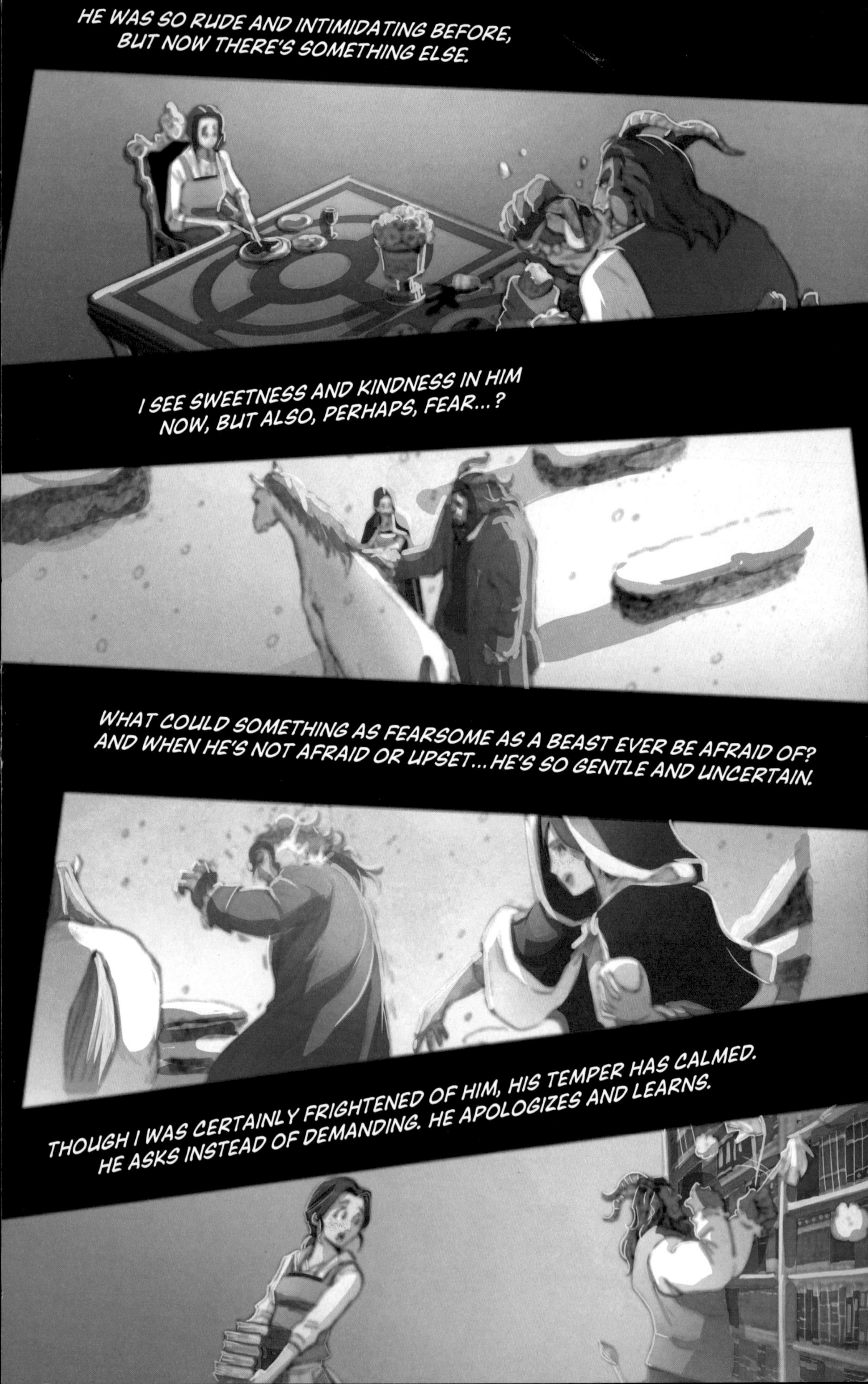
HE WAS SO RUDE AND INTIMIDATING BEFORE, BUT NOW THERE'S SOMETHING ELSE.
I SEE SWEETNESS AND KINDNESS IN HIM NOW, BUT ALSO, PERHAPS, FEAR...?
WHAT COULD SOMETHING AS FEARSOME AS A BEAST EVER BE AFRAID OF?
AND WHEN HE'S NOT AFRAID OR UPSET... HE'S SO GENTLE AND UNCERTAIN.
THOUGH I WAS CERTAINLY FRIGHTENED OF HIM, HIS TEMPER HAS CALMED. HE ASKS INSTEAD OF DEMANDING. HE APOLOGIZES AND LEARNS.

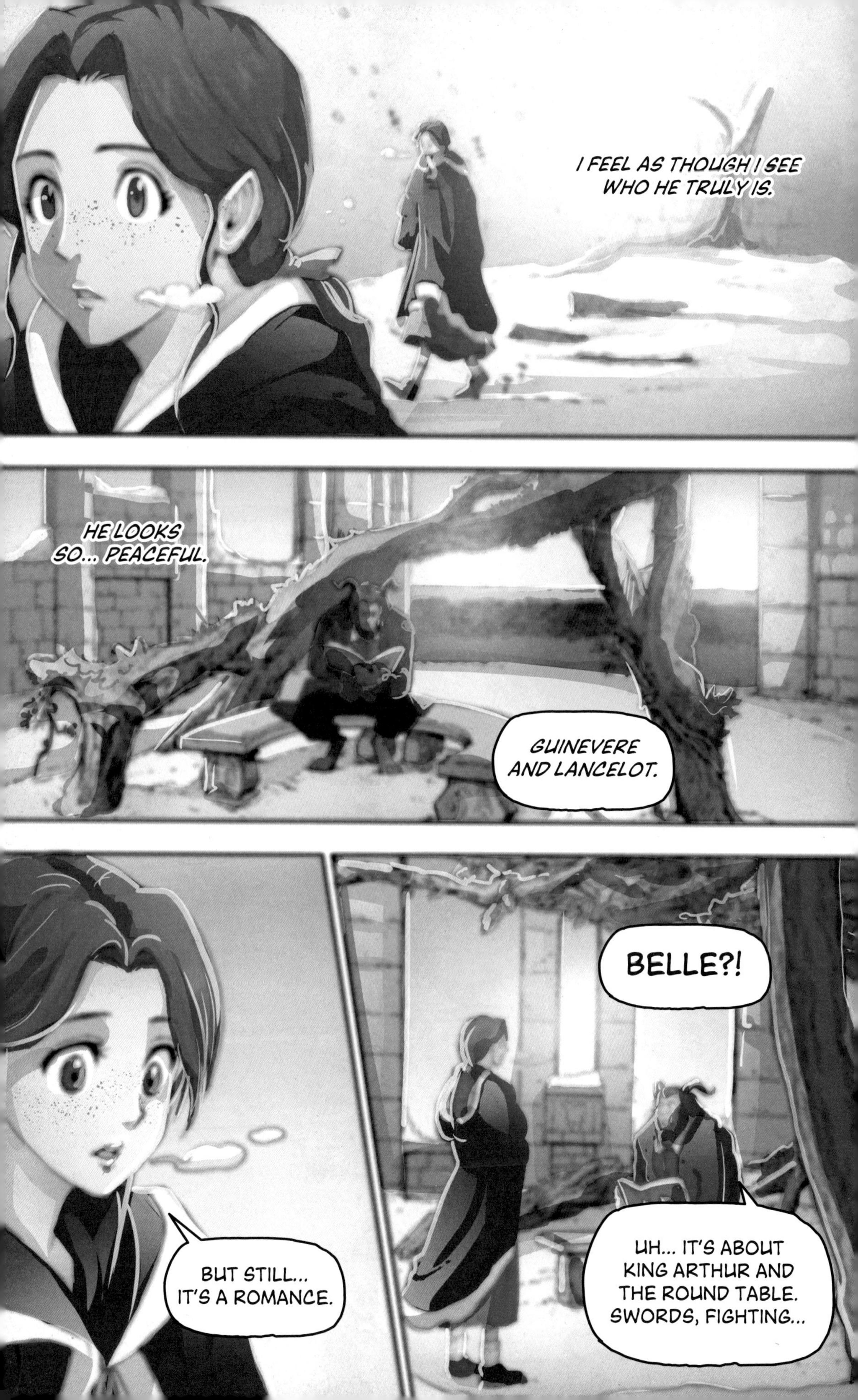
I FEEL AS THOUGH I SEE WHO HE TRULY IS.
HE LOOKS SO... PEACEFUL.
GUINEVERE AND LANCELOT.
BELLE?!
UH... IT'S ABOUT KING ARTHUR AND THE ROUND TABLE. SWORDS, FIGHTING...
BUT STILL... IT'S A ROMANCE.

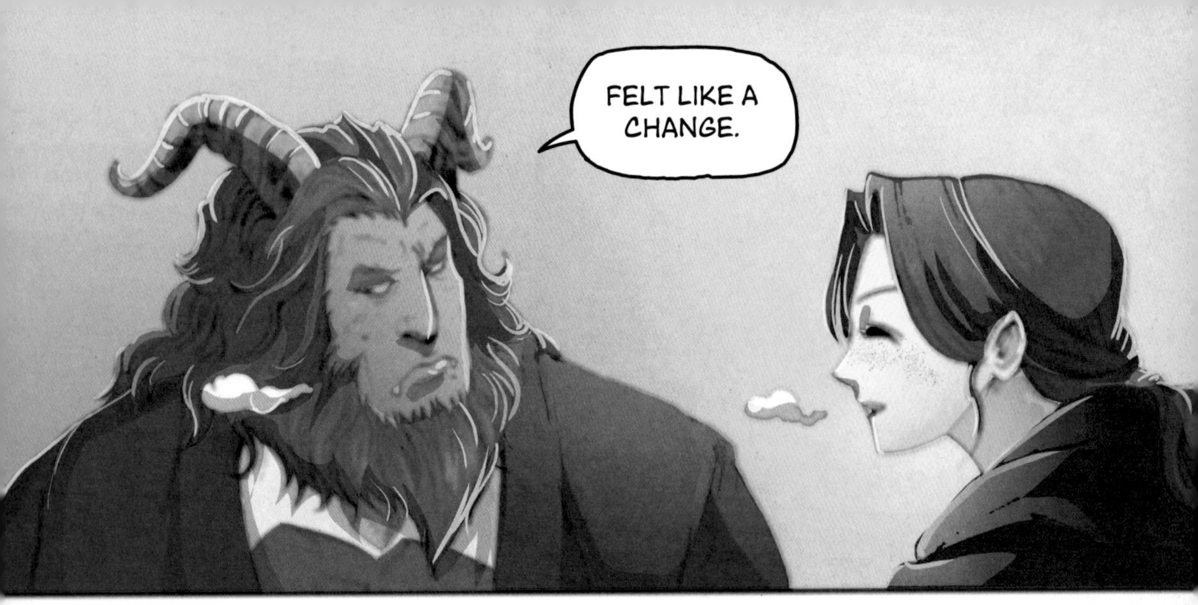
FELT LIKE A CHANGE.

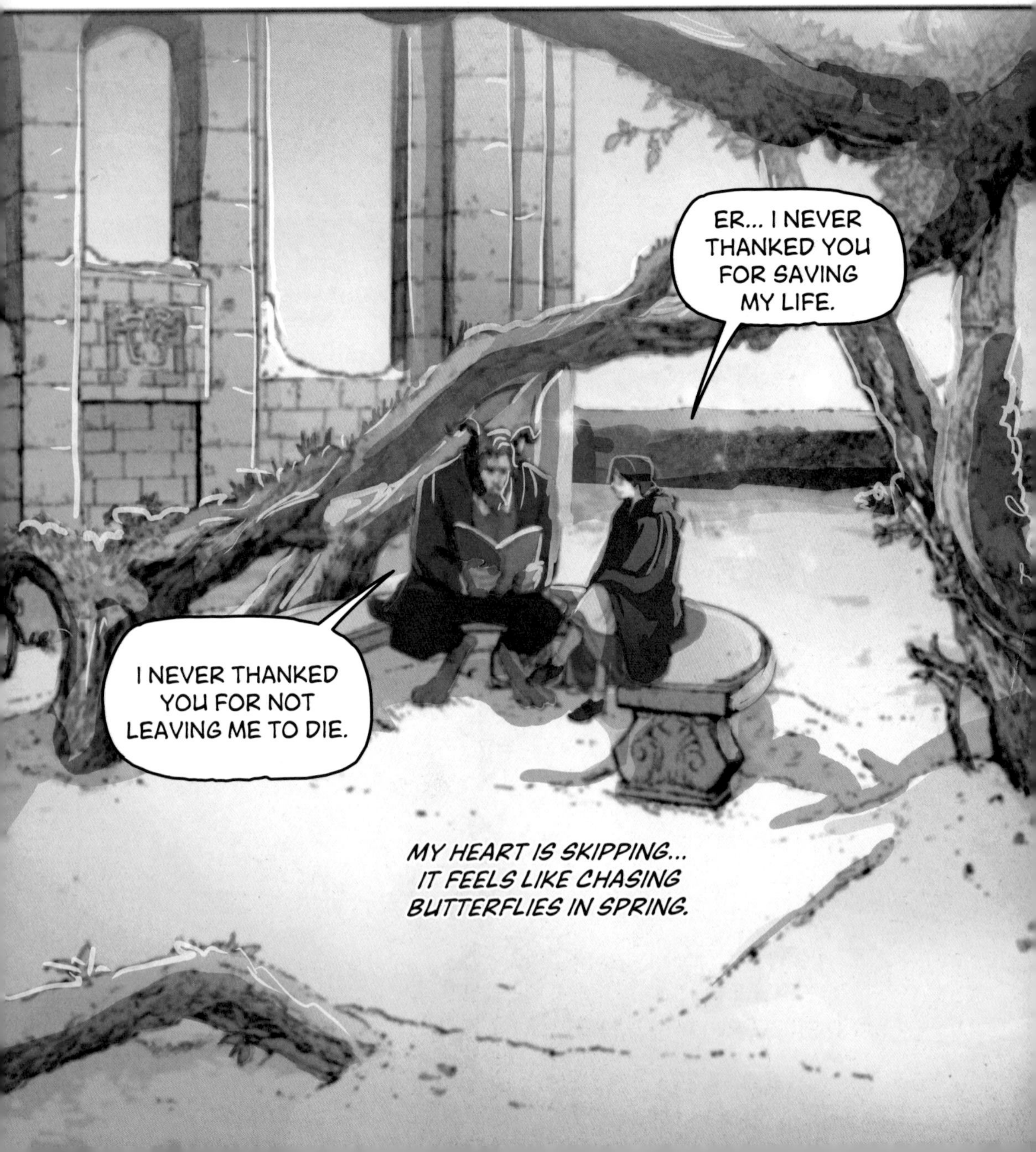
ER... I NEVER THANKED YOU FOR SAVING MY LIFE.
I NEVER THANKED YOU FOR NOT LEAVING ME TO DIE.
MY HEART IS SKIPPING... IT FEELS LIKE CHASING BUTTERFLIES IN SPRING.

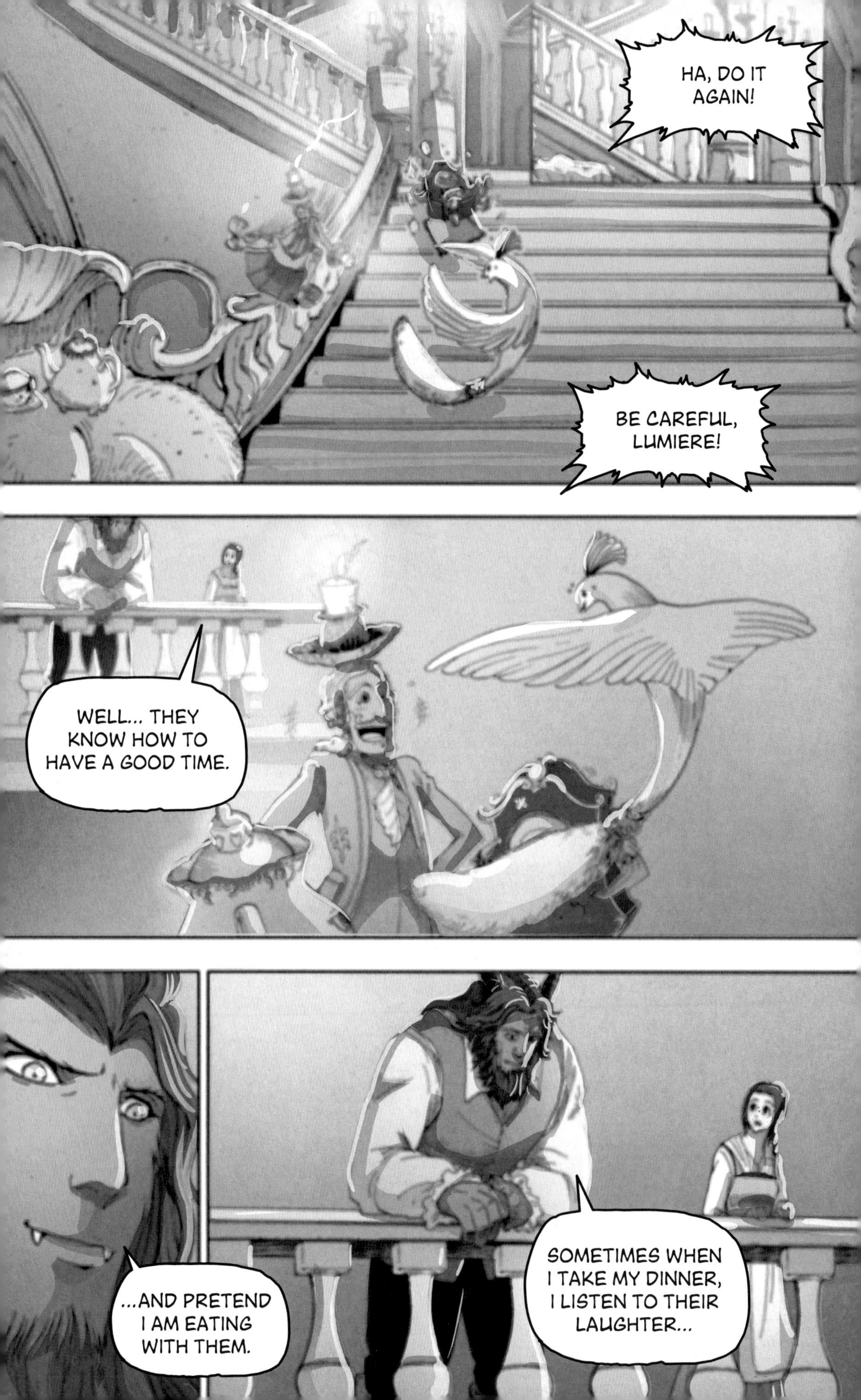
HA, DO IT AGAIN!
BE CAREFUL, LUMIERE!
WELL... THEY KNOW HOW TO HAVE A GOOD TIME.
SOMETIMES WHEN I TAKE MY DINNER, I LISTEN TO THEIR LAUGHTER...
...AND PRETEND I AM EATING WITH THEM.

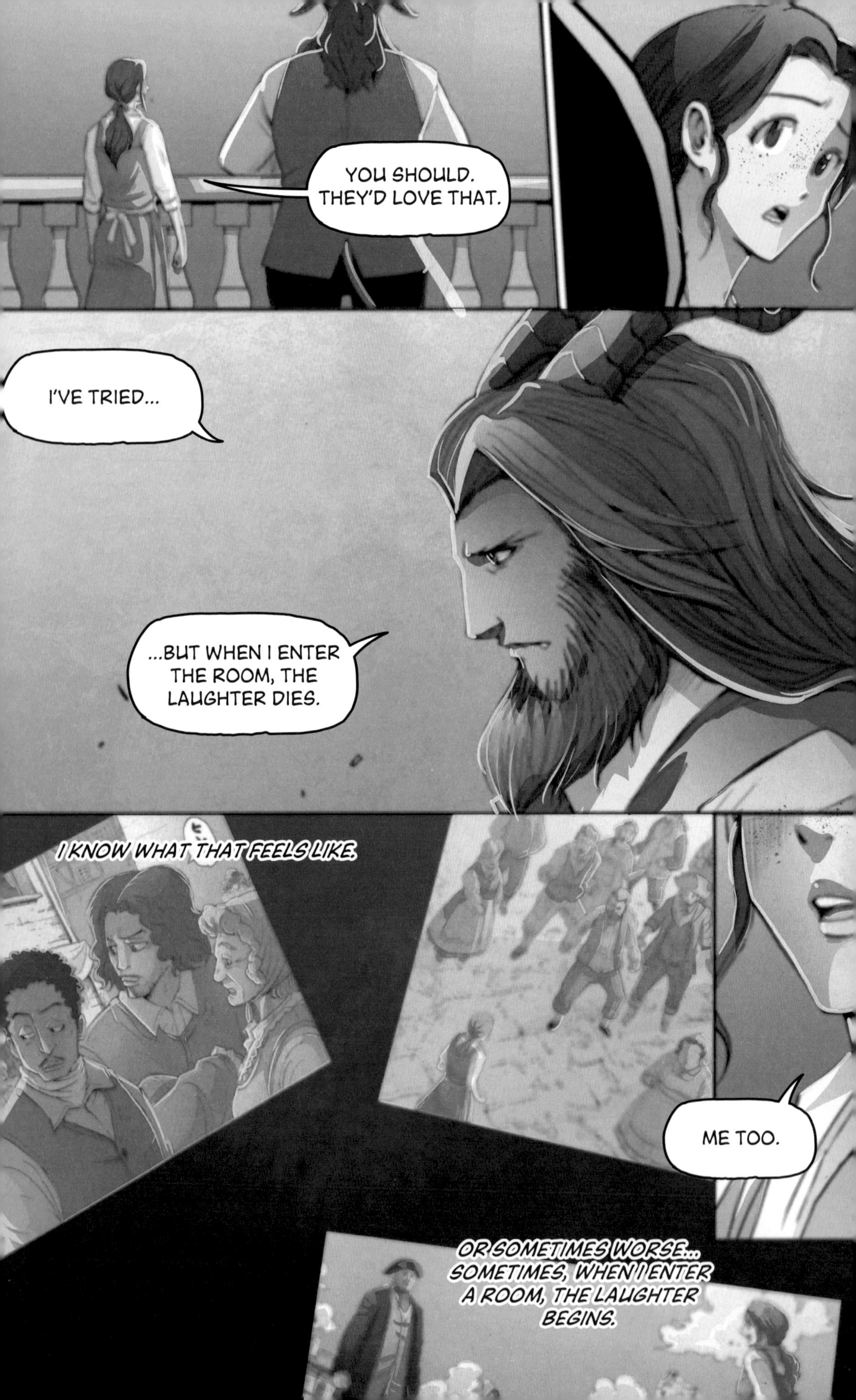
YOU SHOULD. THEY'D LOVE THAT.
I'VE TRIED...
...BUT WHEN I ENTER THE ROOM, THE LAUGHTER DIES.
ME TOO.
I KNOW WHAT THAT FEELS LIKE.
OR SOMETIMES WORSE... SOMETIMES, WHEN I ENTER A ROOM, THE LAUGHTER BEGINS.

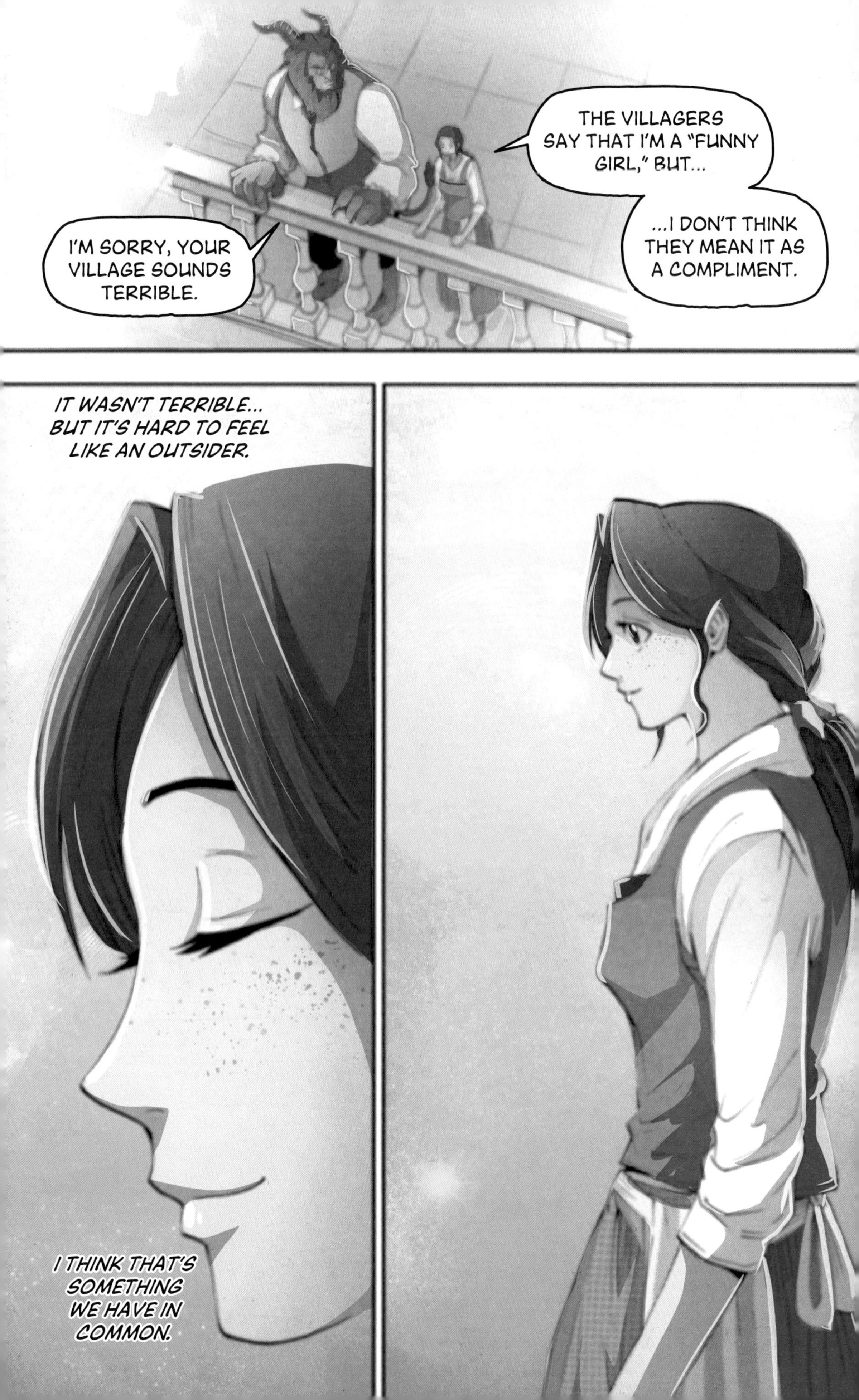
THE VILLAGERS SAY THAT I'M A "FUNNY GIRL," BUT...
...I DON'T THINK THEY MEAN IT AS A COMPLIMENT.
I'M SORRY, YOUR VILLAGE SOUNDS TERRIBLE.
IT WASN'T TERRIBLE... BUT IT'S HARD TO FEEL LIKE AN OUTSIDER.
I THINK THAT'S SOMETHING WE HAVE IN COMMON.

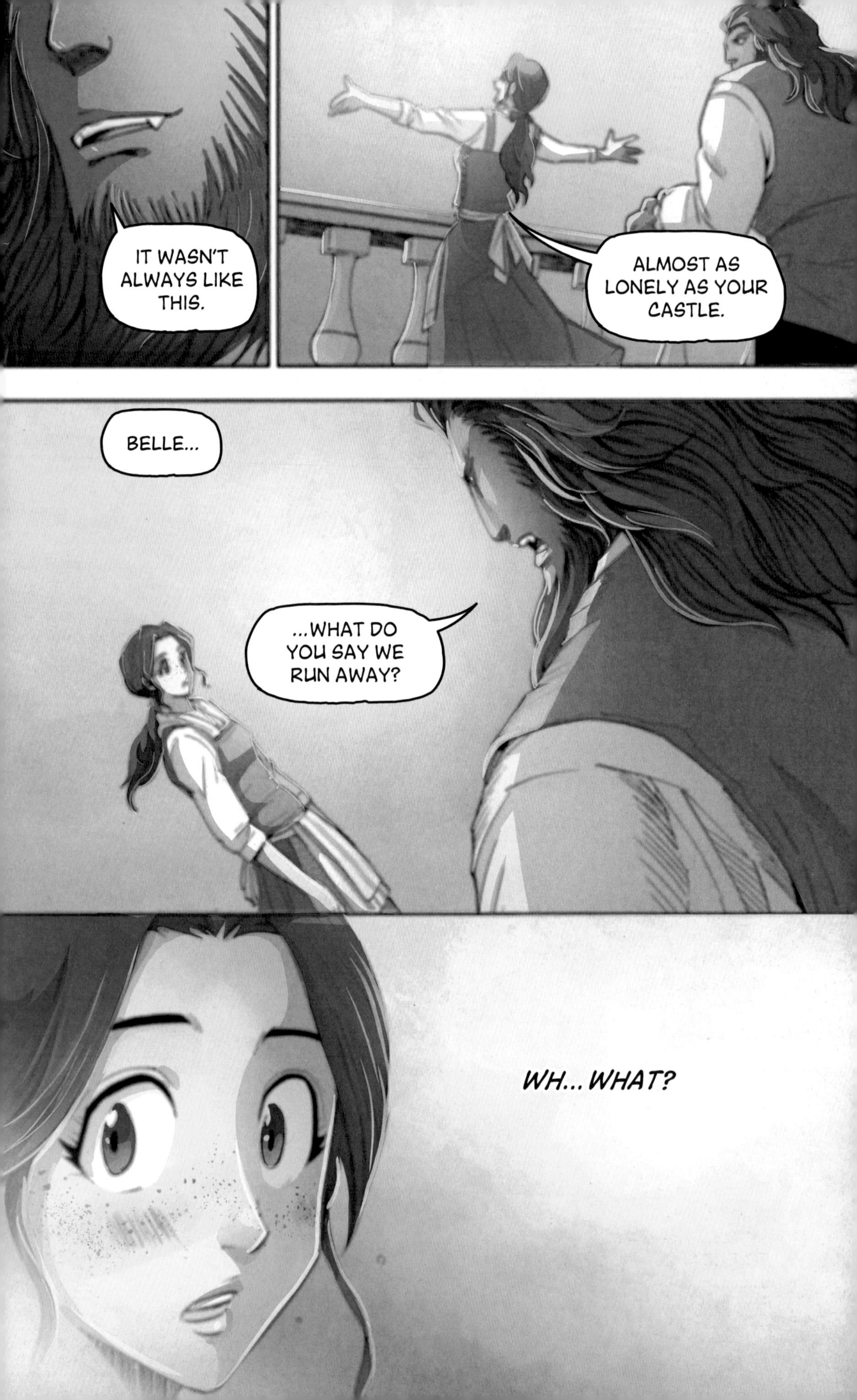
ALMOST AS LONELY AS YOUR CASTLE.
IT WASN'T ALWAYS LIKE THIS.
BELLE...
...WHAT DO YOU SAY WE RUN AWAY?
WH...WHAT?

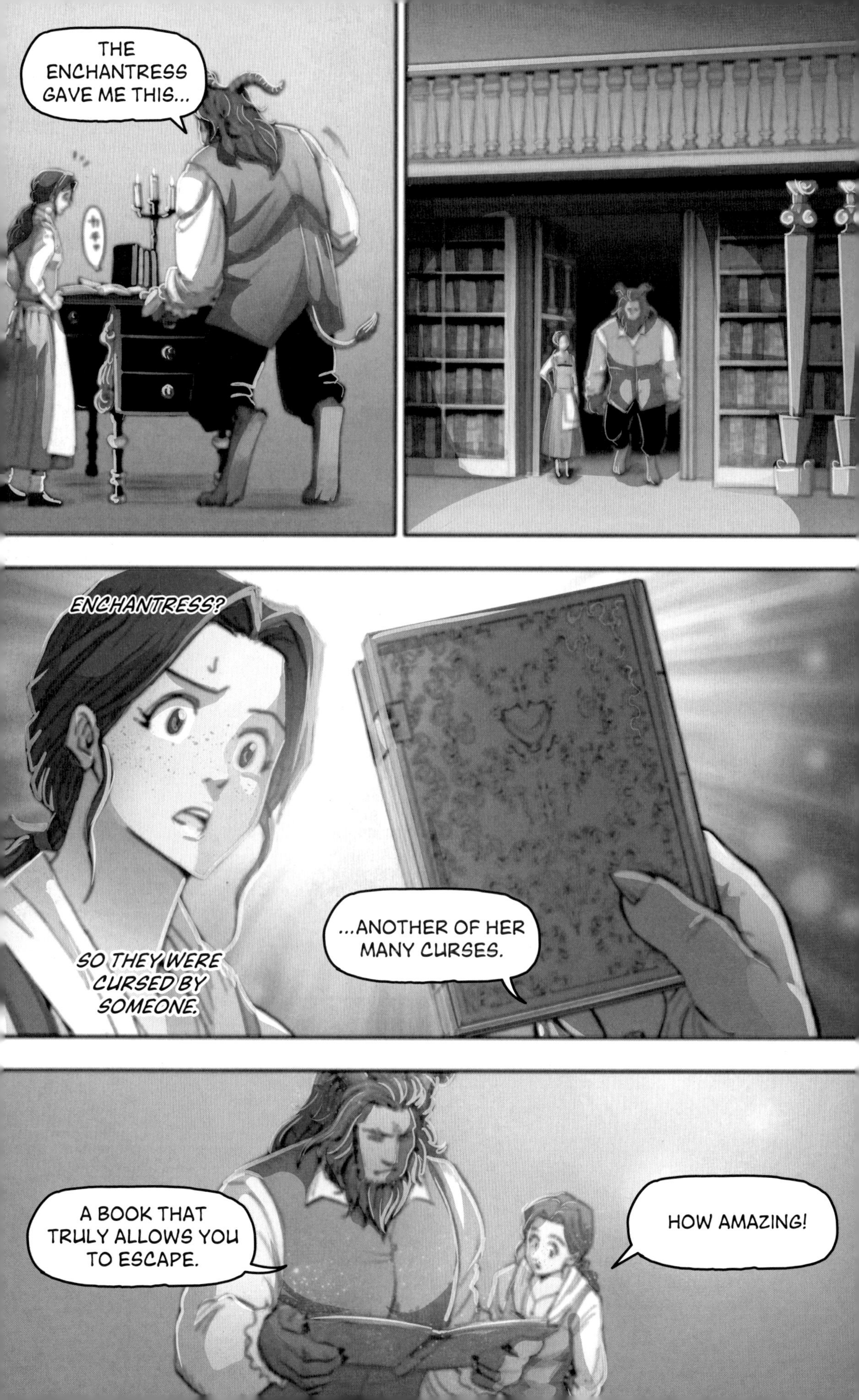
THE ENCHANTRESS GAVE ME THIS...
ENCHANTRESS?
...ANOTHER OF HER MANY CURSES.
SO THEY WERE CURSED BY SOMEONE.
HOW AMAZING!
A BOOK THAT TRULY ALLOWS YOU TO ESCAPE.

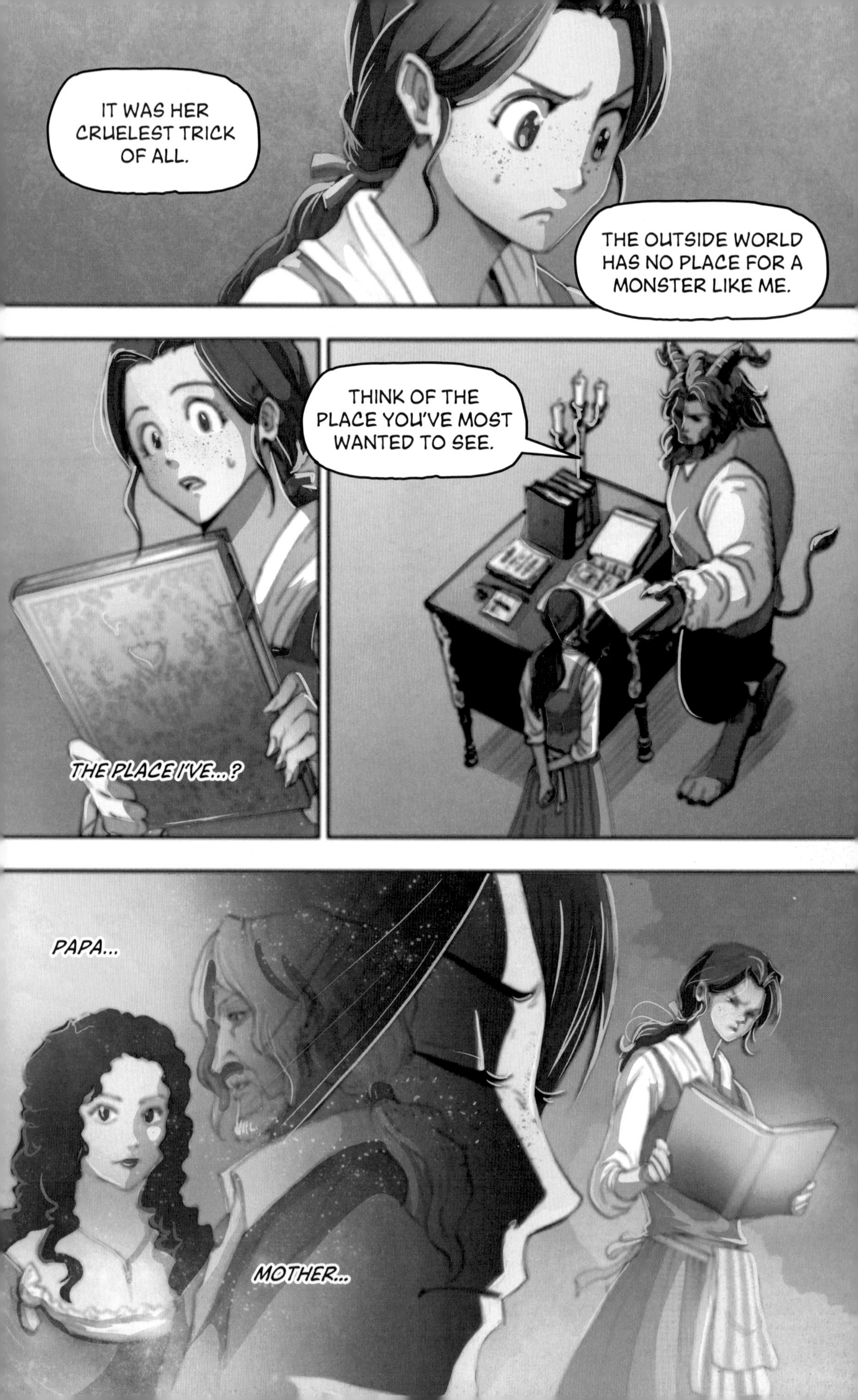
IT WAS HER CRUELEST TRICK OF ALL.
THE OUTSIDE WORLD HAS NO PLACE FOR A MONSTER LIKE ME.
THINK OF THE PLACE YOU'VE MOST WANTED TO SEE.
THE PLACE I'VE...?
PAPA...
MOTHER...

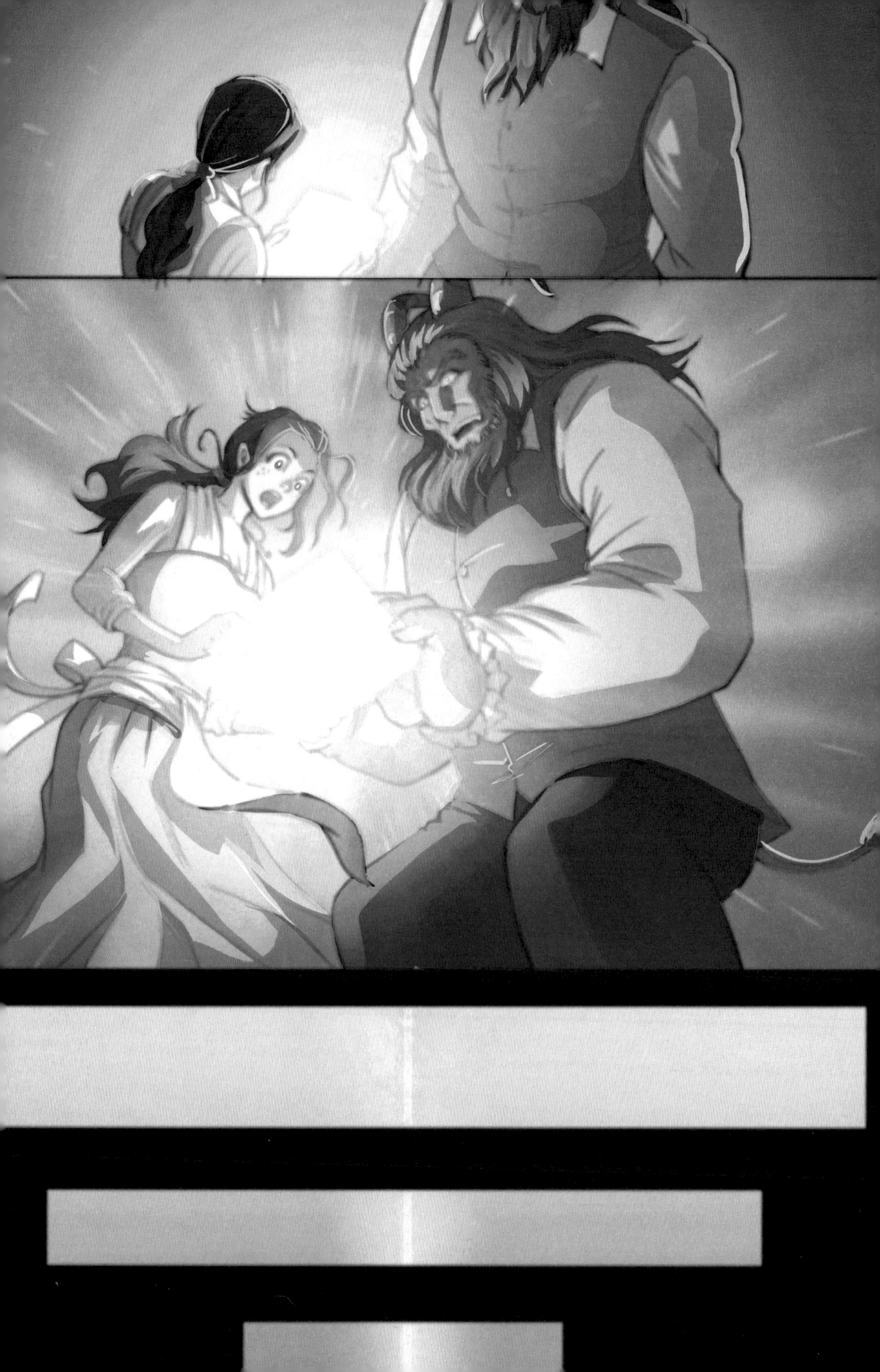

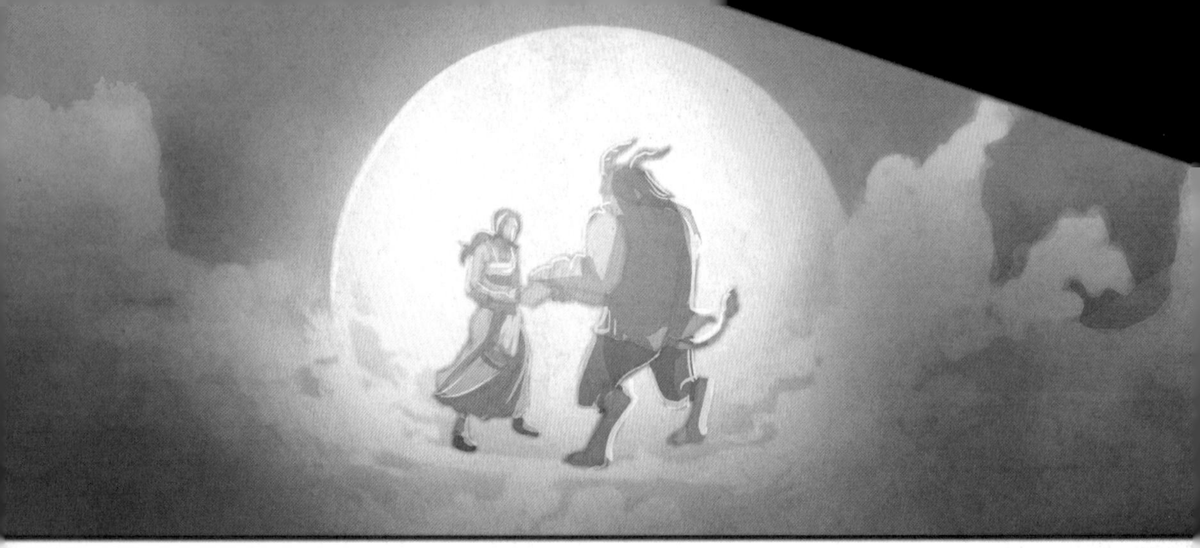

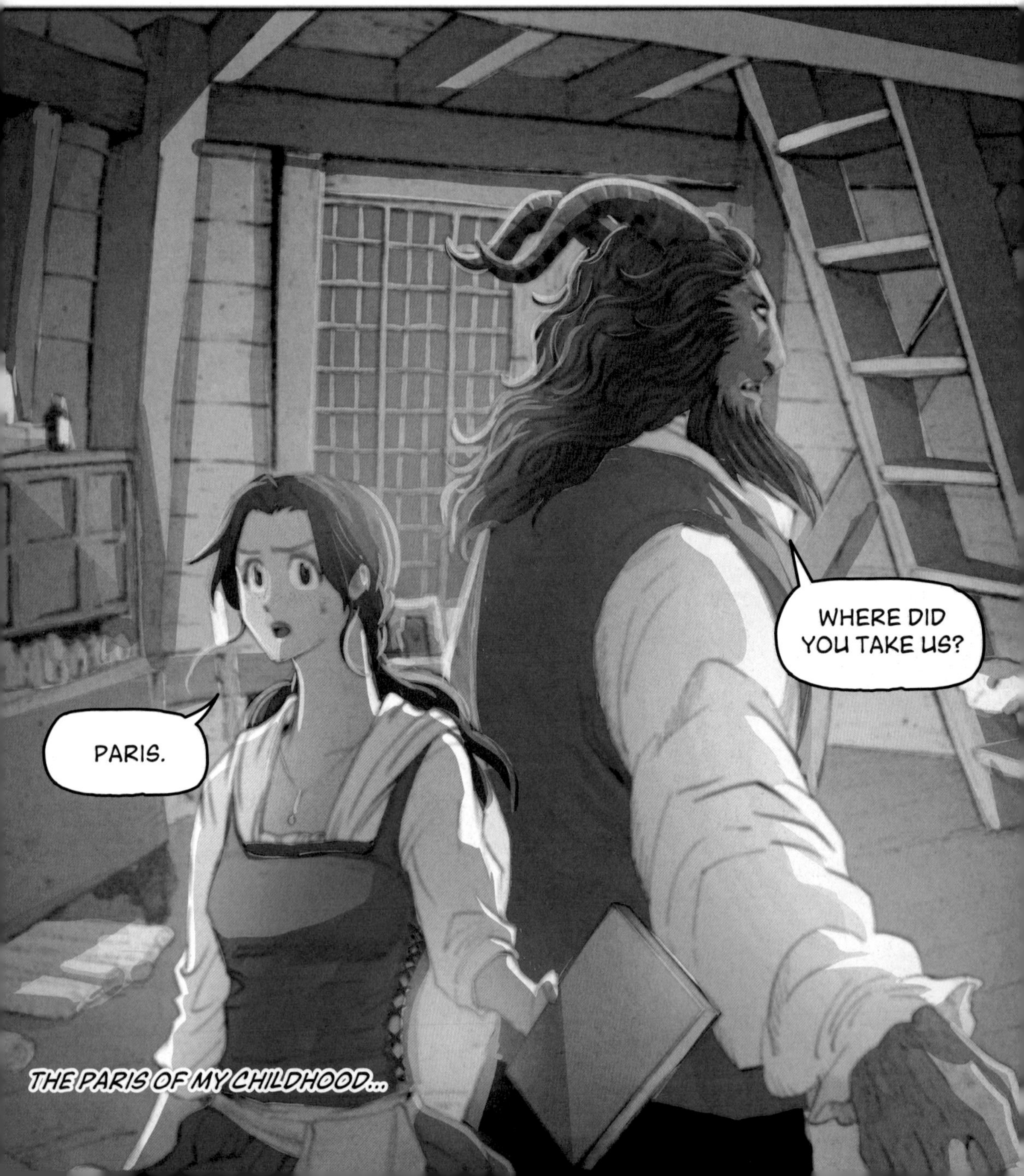
WHERE DID YOU TAKE US?
PARIS.
THE PARIS OF MY CHILDHOOD...

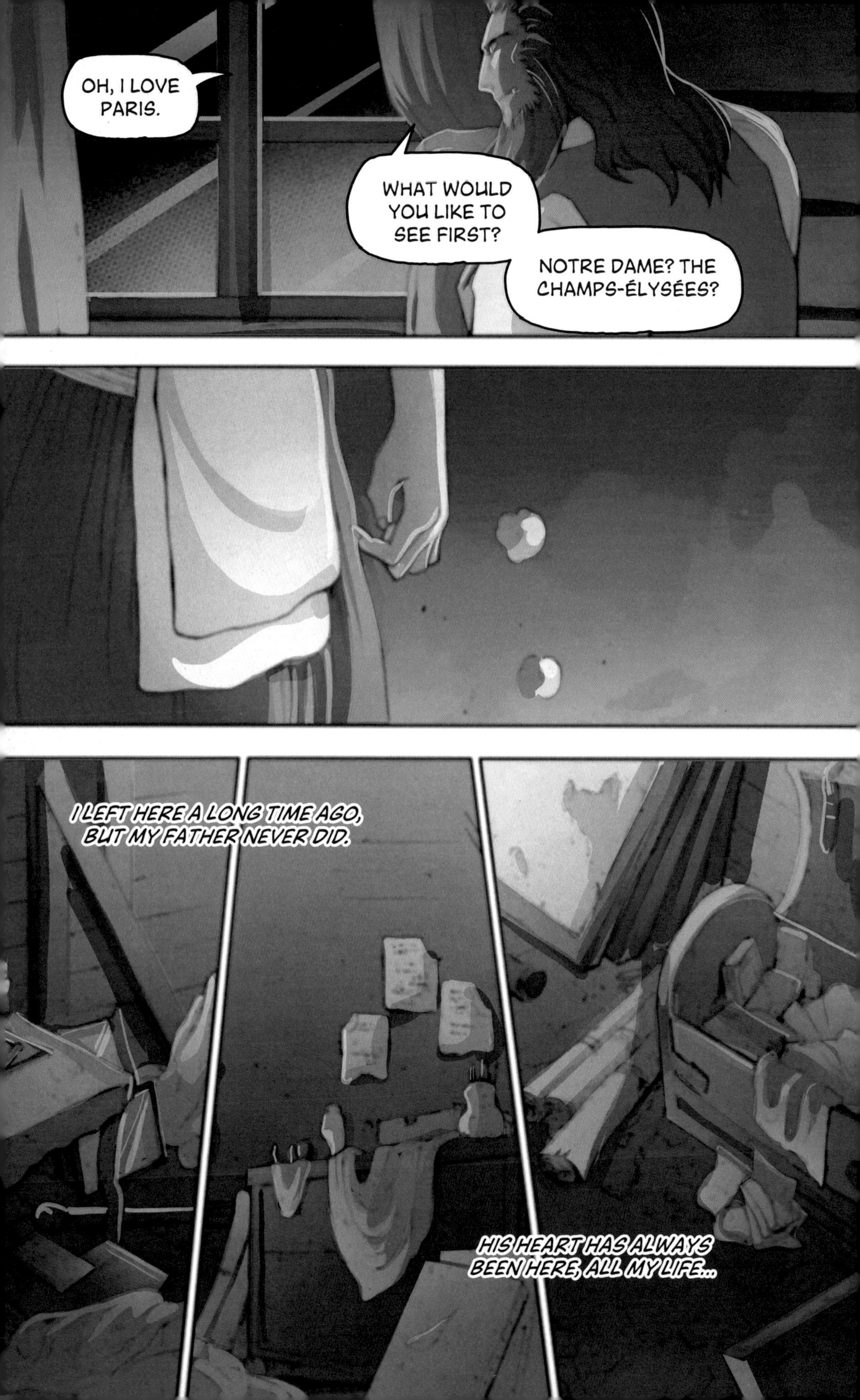
OH, I LOVE PARIS.
WHAT WOULD YOU LIKE TO SEE FIRST?
NOTRE DAME? THE CHAMPS-ÉLYSÉES?
I LEFT HERE A LONG TIME AGO, BUT MY FATHER NEVER DID.
HIS HEART HAS ALWAYS BEEN HERE, ALL MY LIFE...

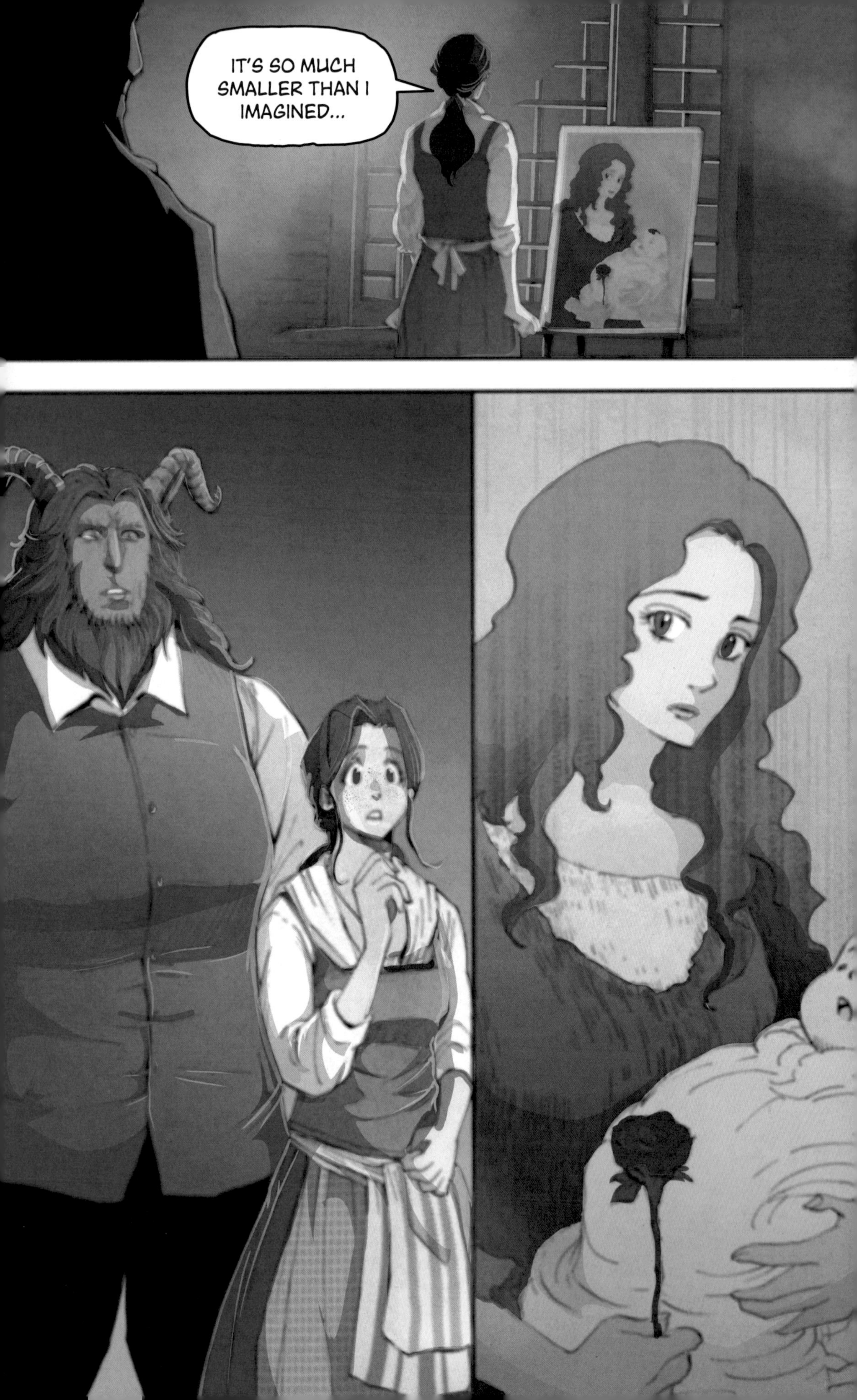
IT'S SO MUCH SMALLER THAN I IMAGINED...

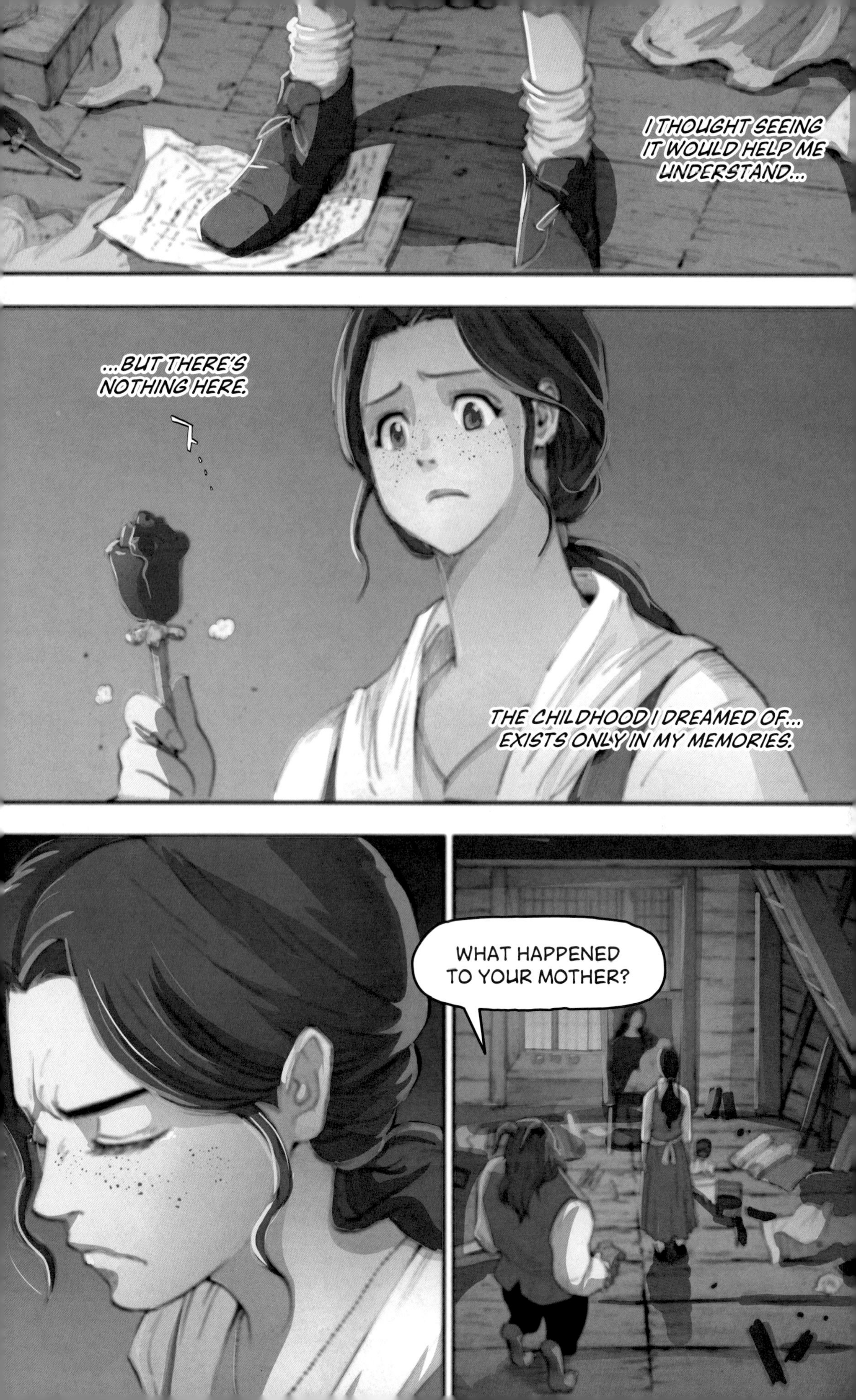
I THOUGHT SEEING IT WOULD HELP ME UNDERSTAND...
...BUT THERE'S NOTHING HERE.
THE CHILDHOOD I DREAMED OF... EXISTS ONLY IN MY MEMORIES.
WHAT HAPPENED TO YOUR MOTHER?

THAT'S THE ONLY STORY...

...PAPA COULD NEVER BRING HIMSELF TO TELL ME.

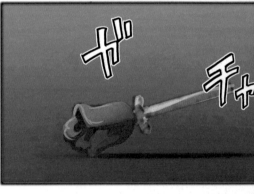

THAT'S...

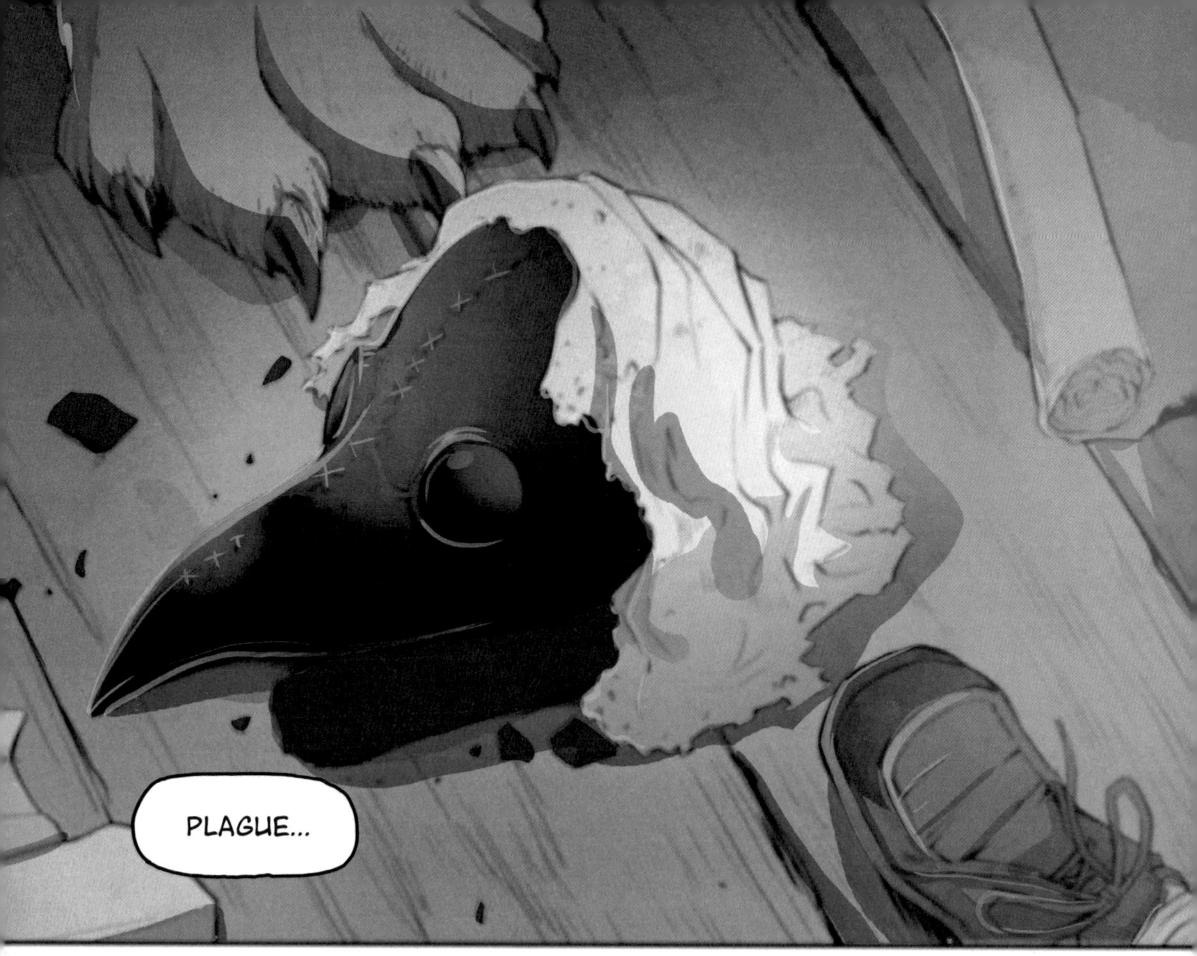
PLAGUE...
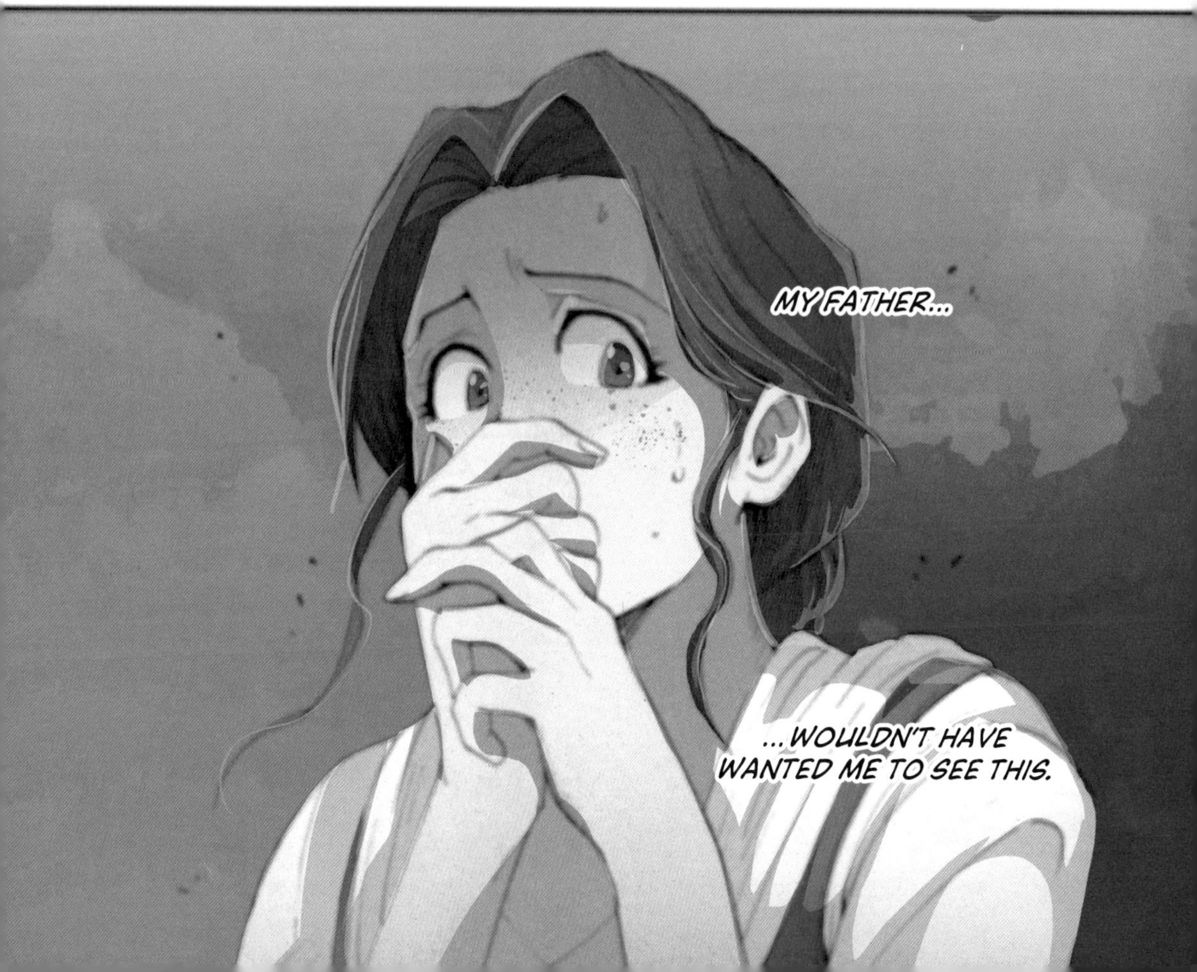
MY FATHER...
...WOULDN'T HAVE WANTED ME TO SEE THIS.

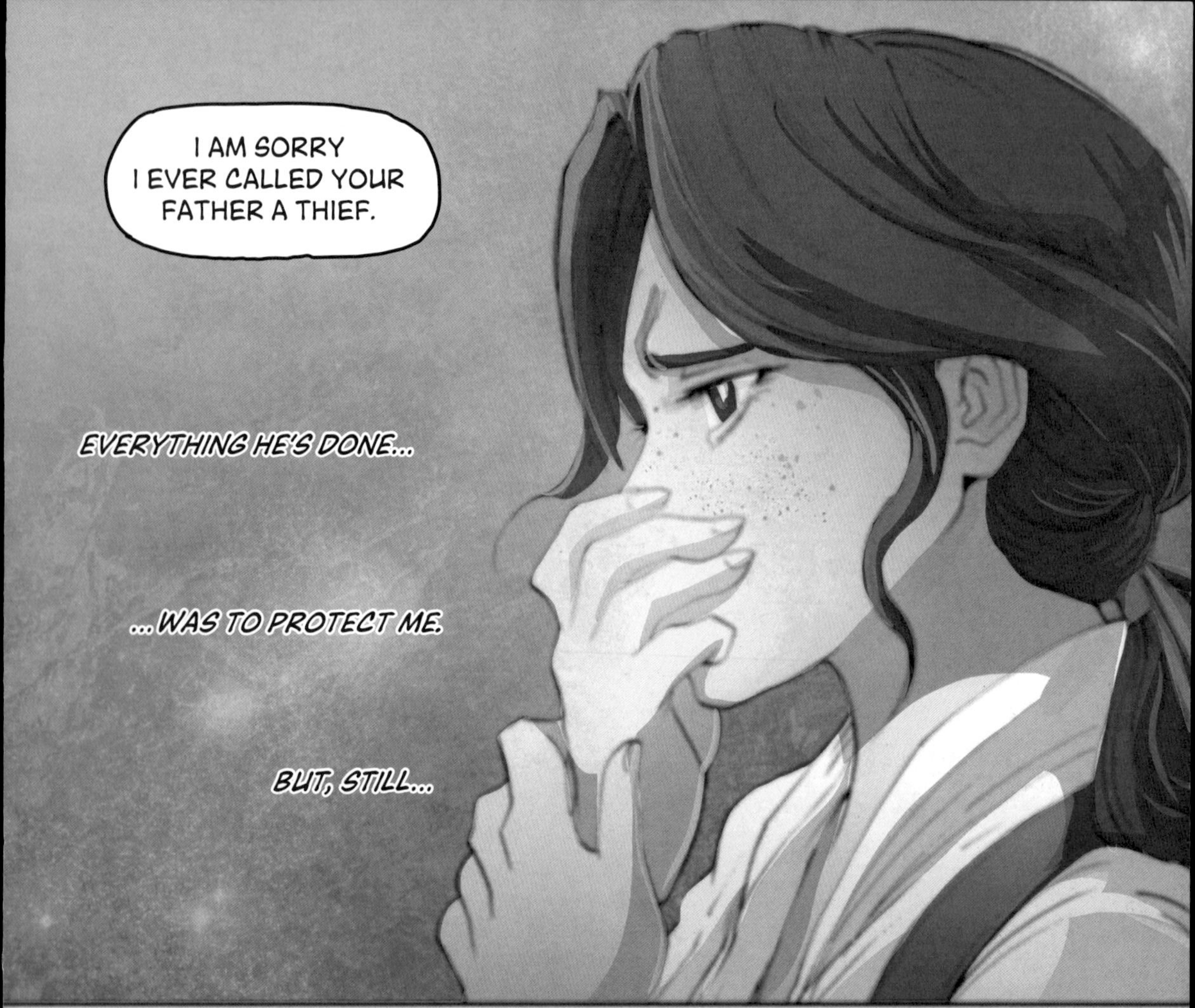
I AM SORRY I EVER CALLED YOUR FATHER A THIEF.
EVERYTHING HE'S DONE...
...WAS TO PROTECT ME.
BUT, STILL...

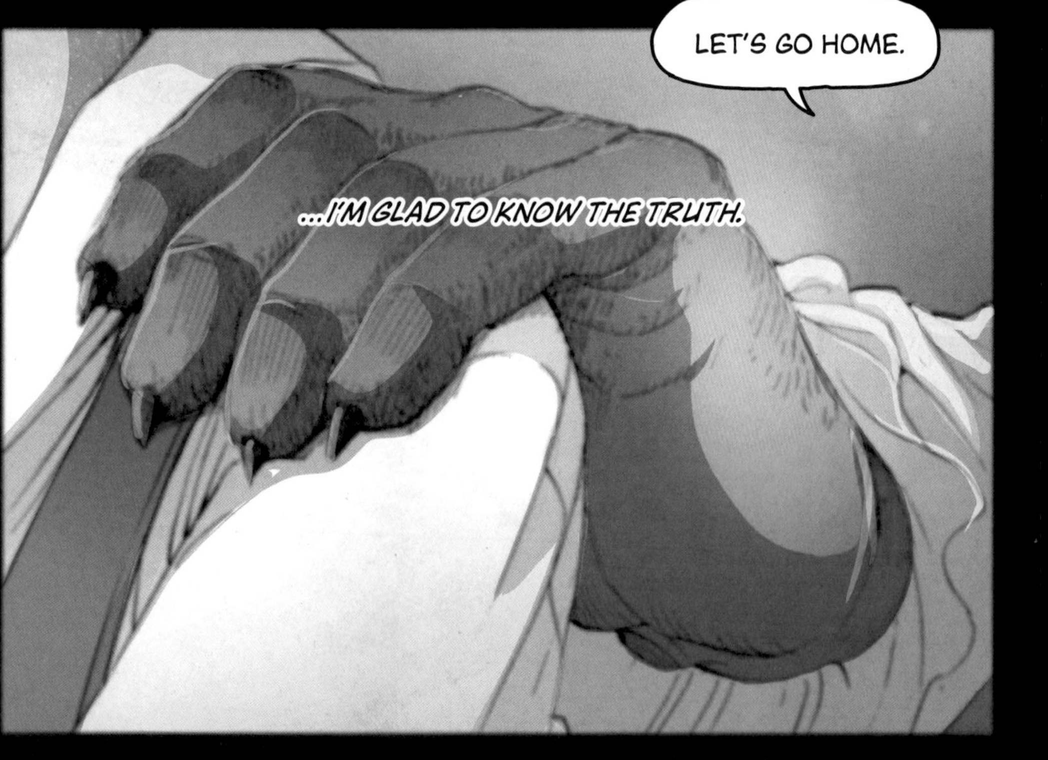
LET'S GO HOME.
...I'M GLAD TO KNOW THE TRUTH.

THANK YOU, CHIP!

WELCOME!

Chapter 6

HURRY UP NOW, DEAR.

MADAME ALMOST HAS YOUR DRESS READY!

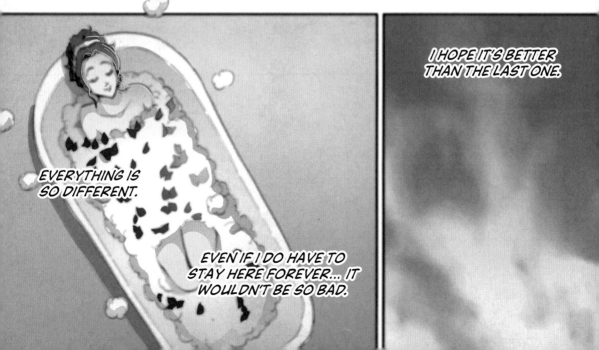

I HOPE IT'S BETTER THAN THE LAST ONE.

EVERYTHING IS SO DIFFERENT.

EVEN IF I DO HAVE TO STAY HERE FOREVER... IT WOULDN'T BE SO BAD.

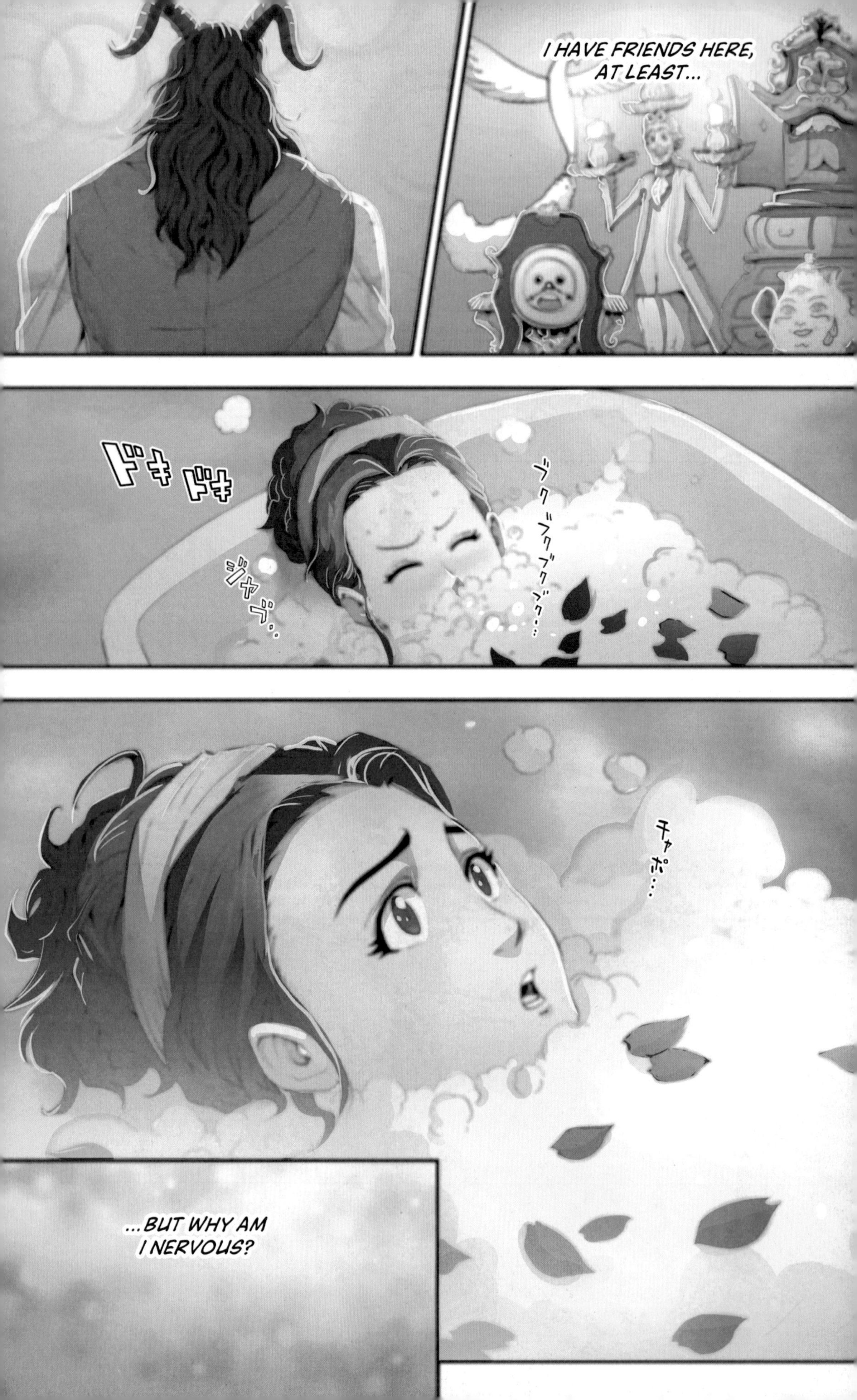
I HAVE FRIENDS HERE, AT LEAST...
ブクブクブクブク…
ドキドキ
ジャブ。
チャポ…
...BUT WHY AM I NERVOUS?

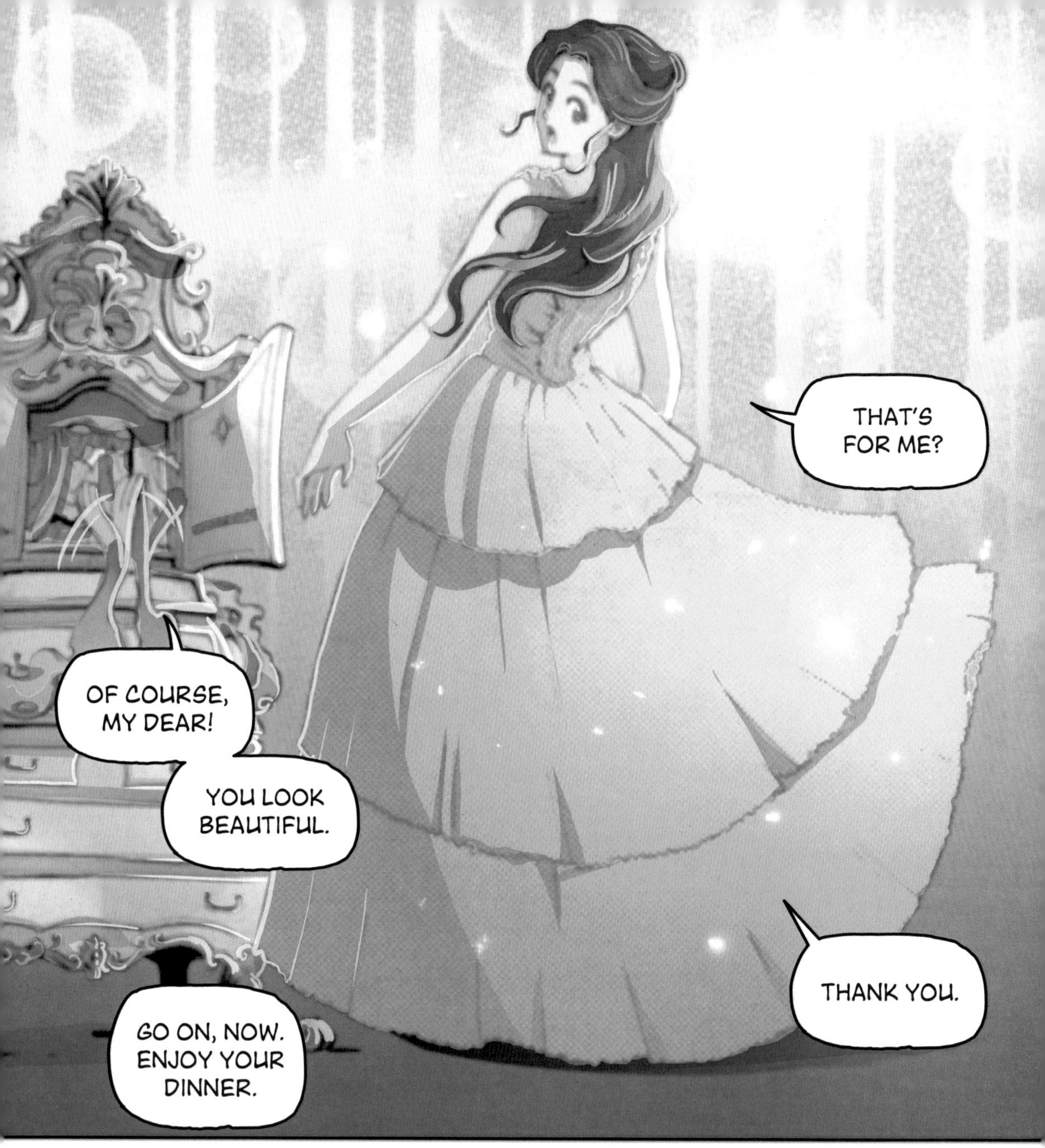
THAT'S FOR ME?
OF COURSE, MY DEAR!
YOU LOOK BEAUTIFUL.
THANK YOU.
GO ON, NOW. ENJOY YOUR DINNER.
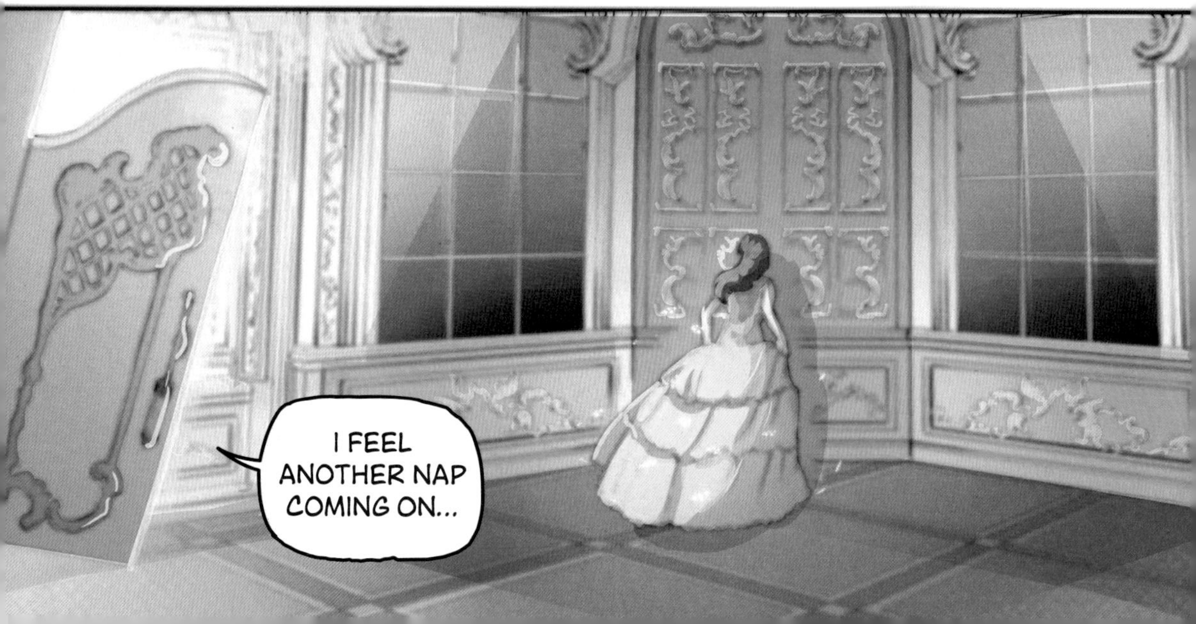
I FEEL ANOTHER NAP COMING ON...

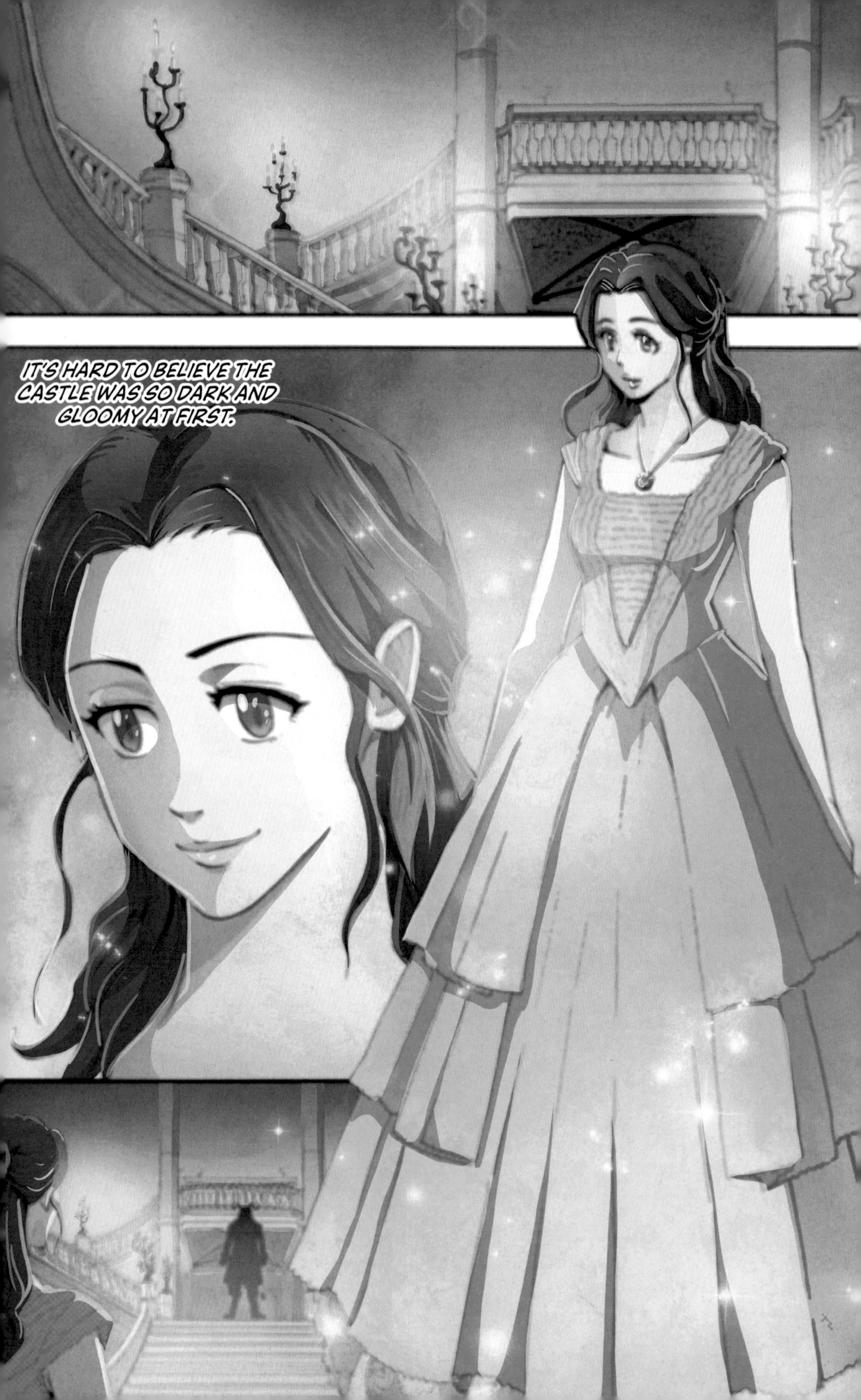
IT'S HARD TO BELIEVE THE CASTLE WAS SO DARK AND GLOOMY AT FIRST.

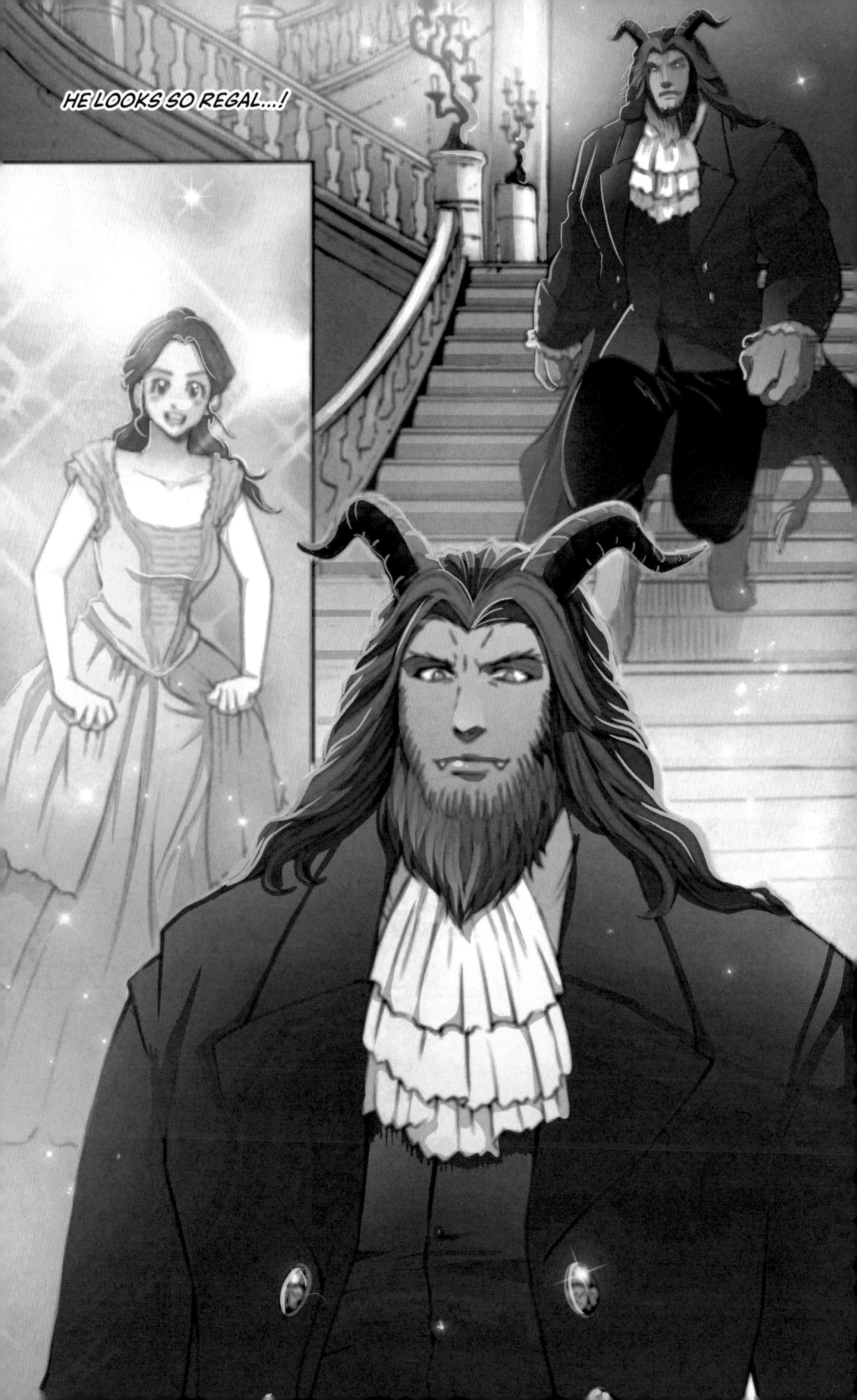
HE LOOKS SO REGAL...!

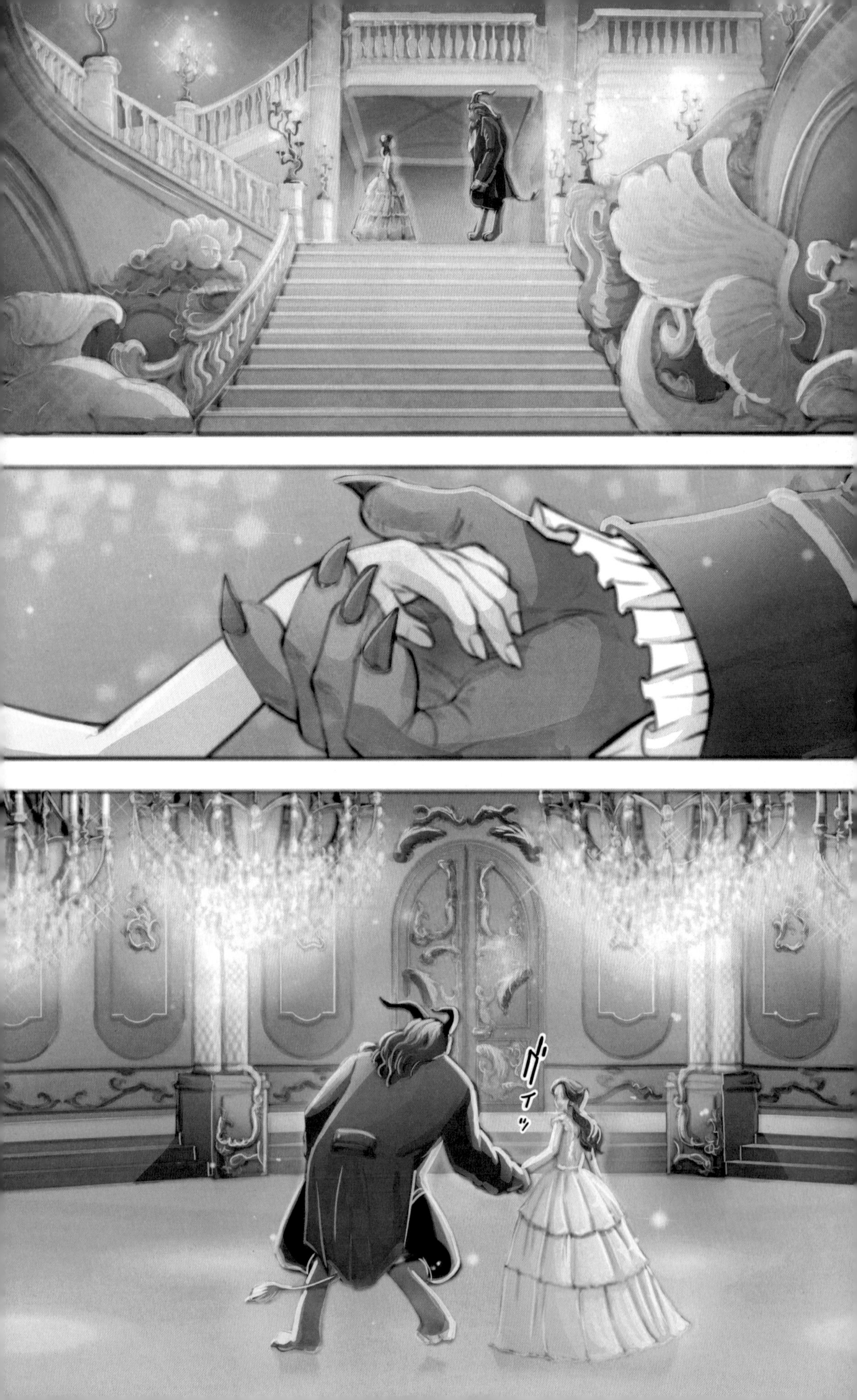
グイッ

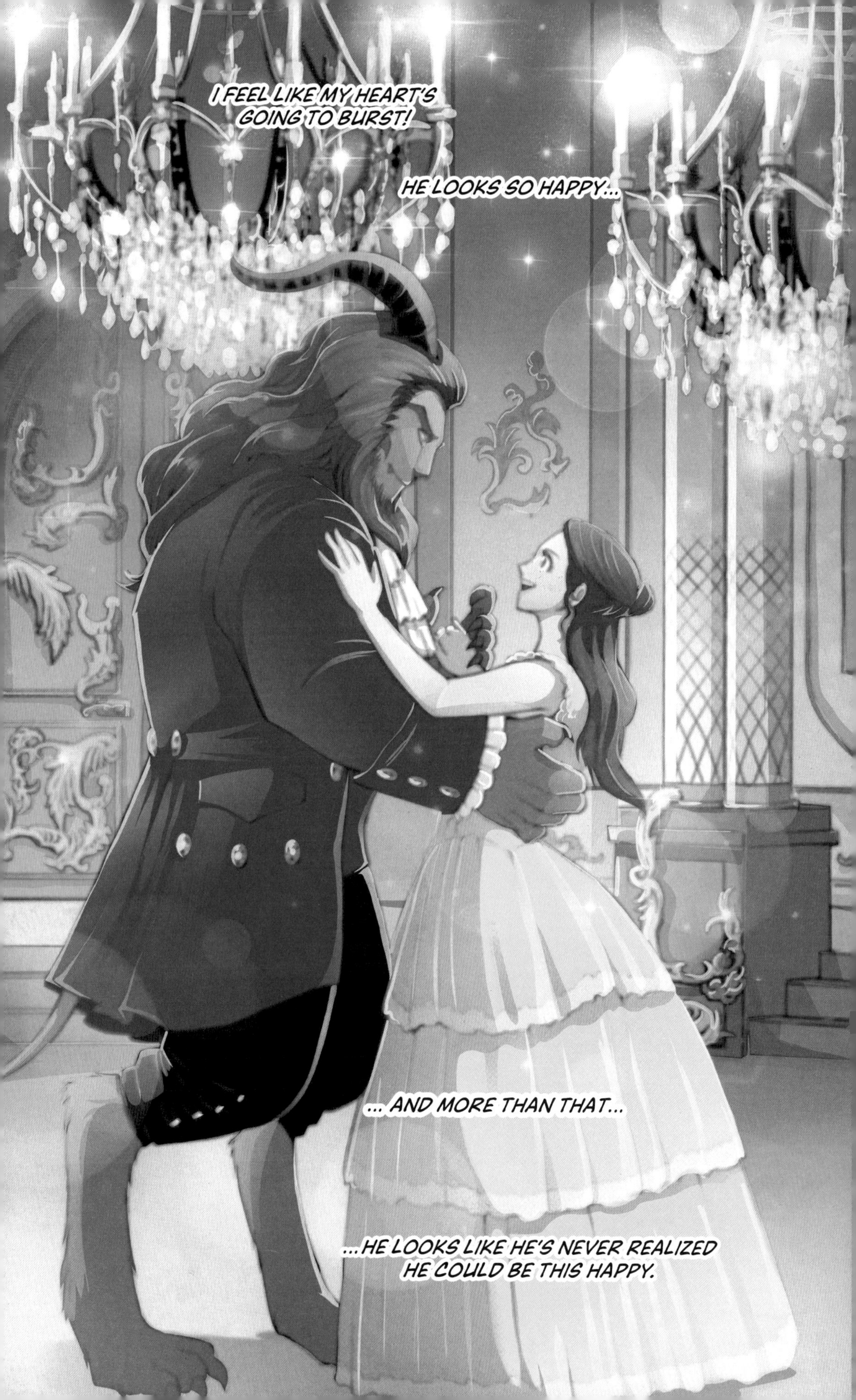
I FEEL LIKE MY HEART'S GOING TO BURST!
HE LOOKS SO HAPPY...
... AND MORE THAN THAT...
...HE LOOKS LIKE HE'S NEVER REALIZED HE COULD BE THIS HAPPY.

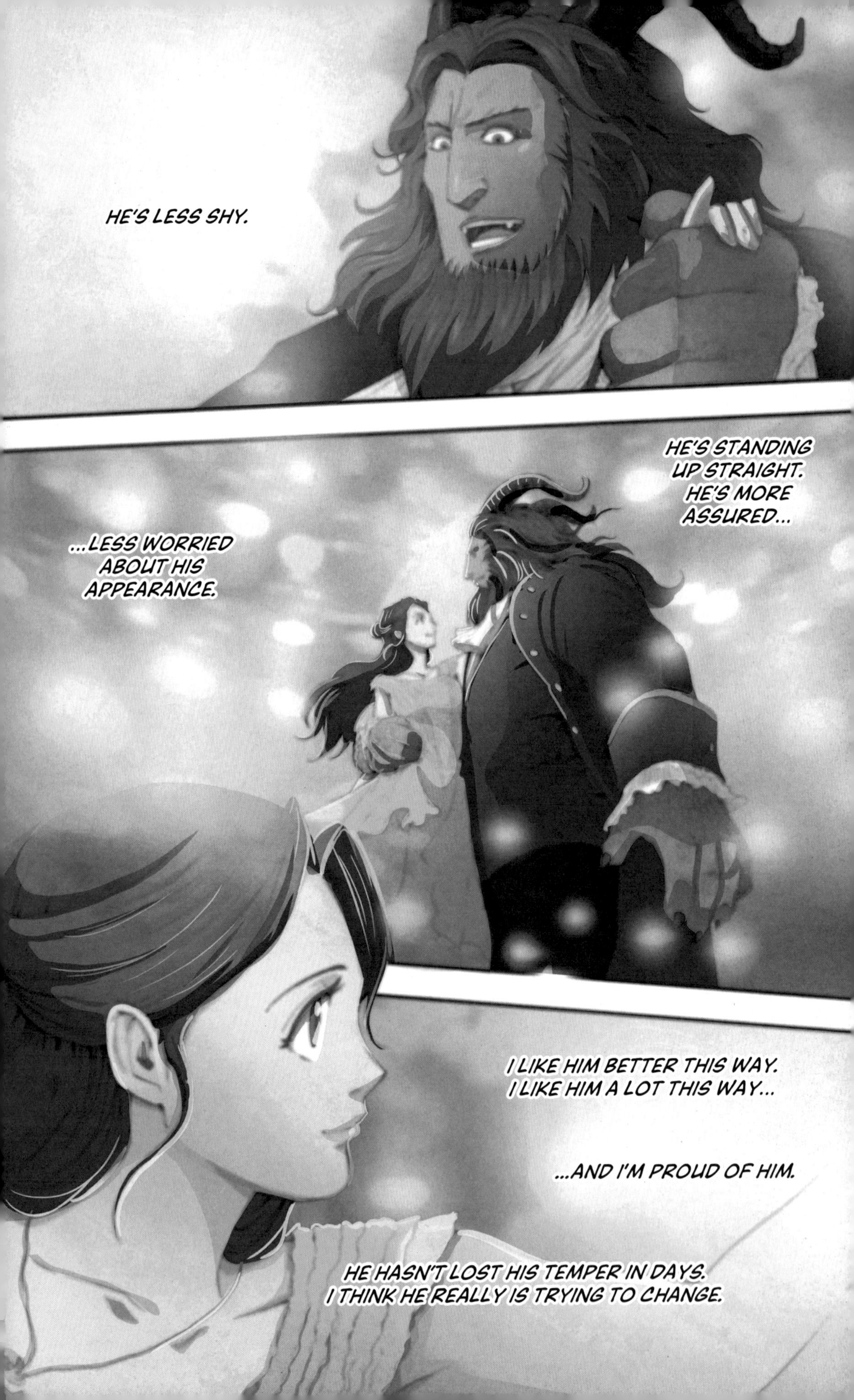
HE'S LESS SHY.
HE'S STANDING UP STRAIGHT. HE'S MORE ASSURED...
...LESS WORRIED ABOUT HIS APPEARANCE.
I LIKE HIM BETTER THIS WAY. I LIKE HIM A LOT THIS WAY...
...AND I'M PROUD OF HIM.
HE HASN'T LOST HIS TEMPER IN DAYS. I THINK HE REALLY IS TRYING TO CHANGE.

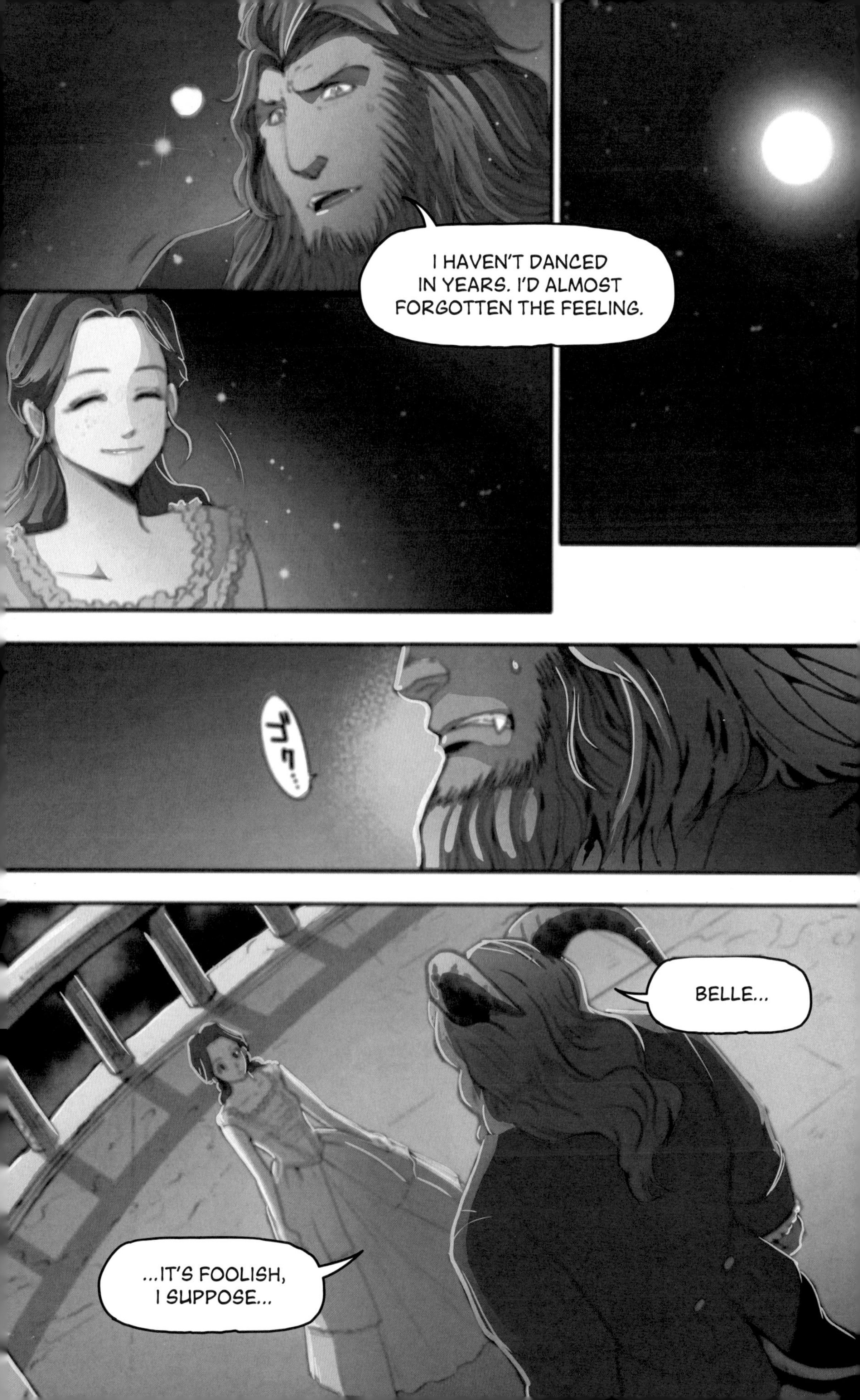
I HAVEN'T DANCED IN YEARS. I'D ALMOST FORGOTTEN THE FEELING.
BELLE...
...IT'S FOOLISH, I SUPPOSE...

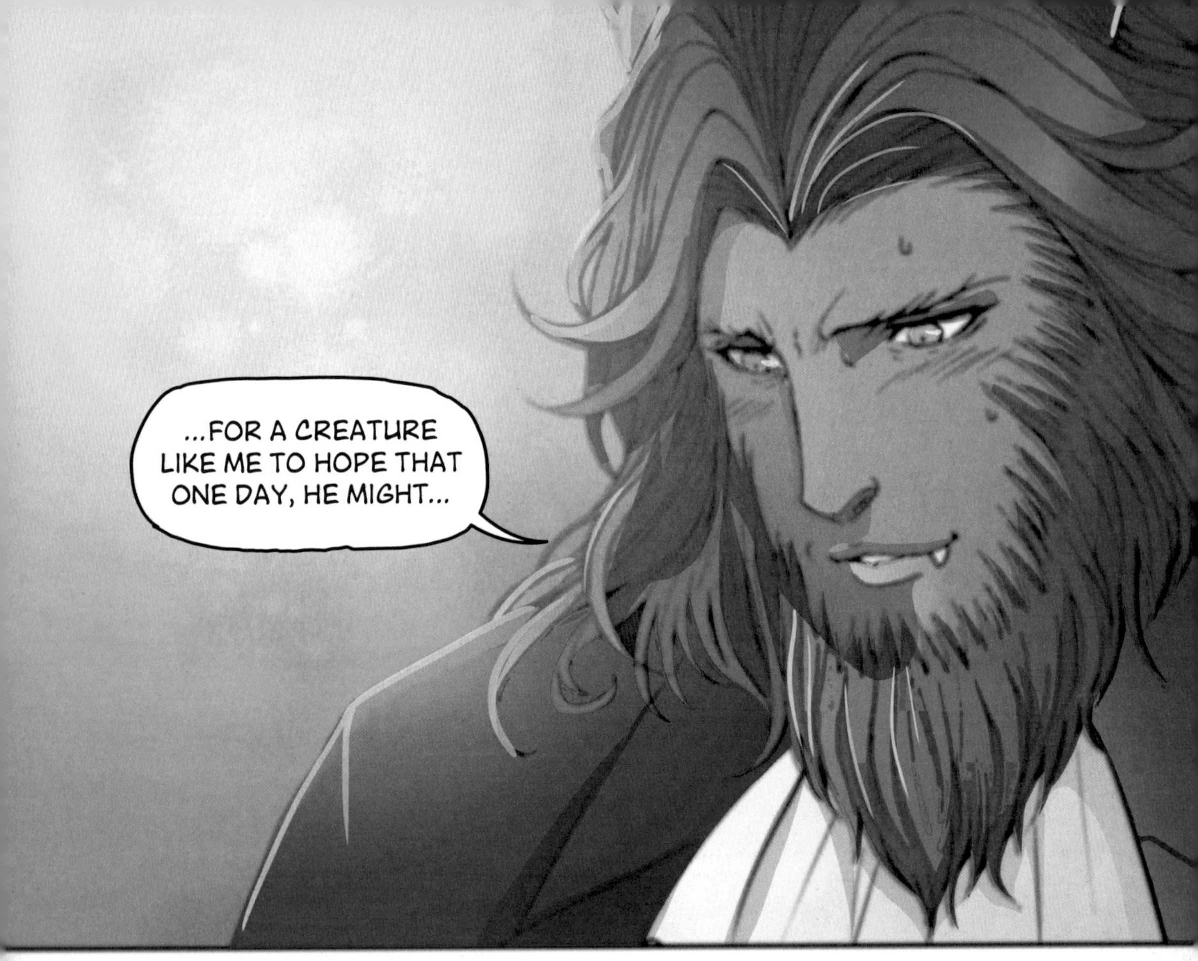
...FOR A CREATURE LIKE ME TO HOPE THAT ONE DAY, HE MIGHT...
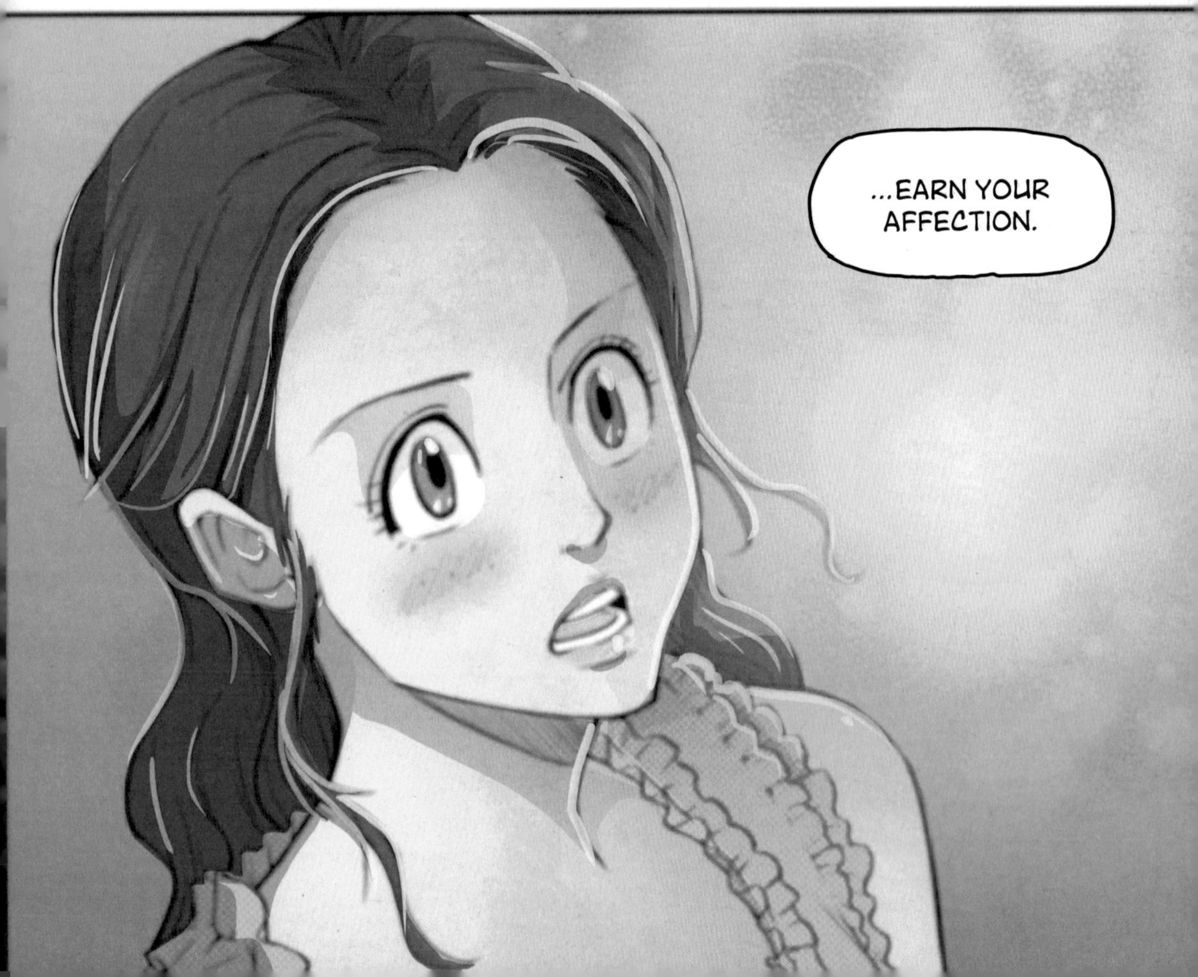
...EARN YOUR AFFECTION.

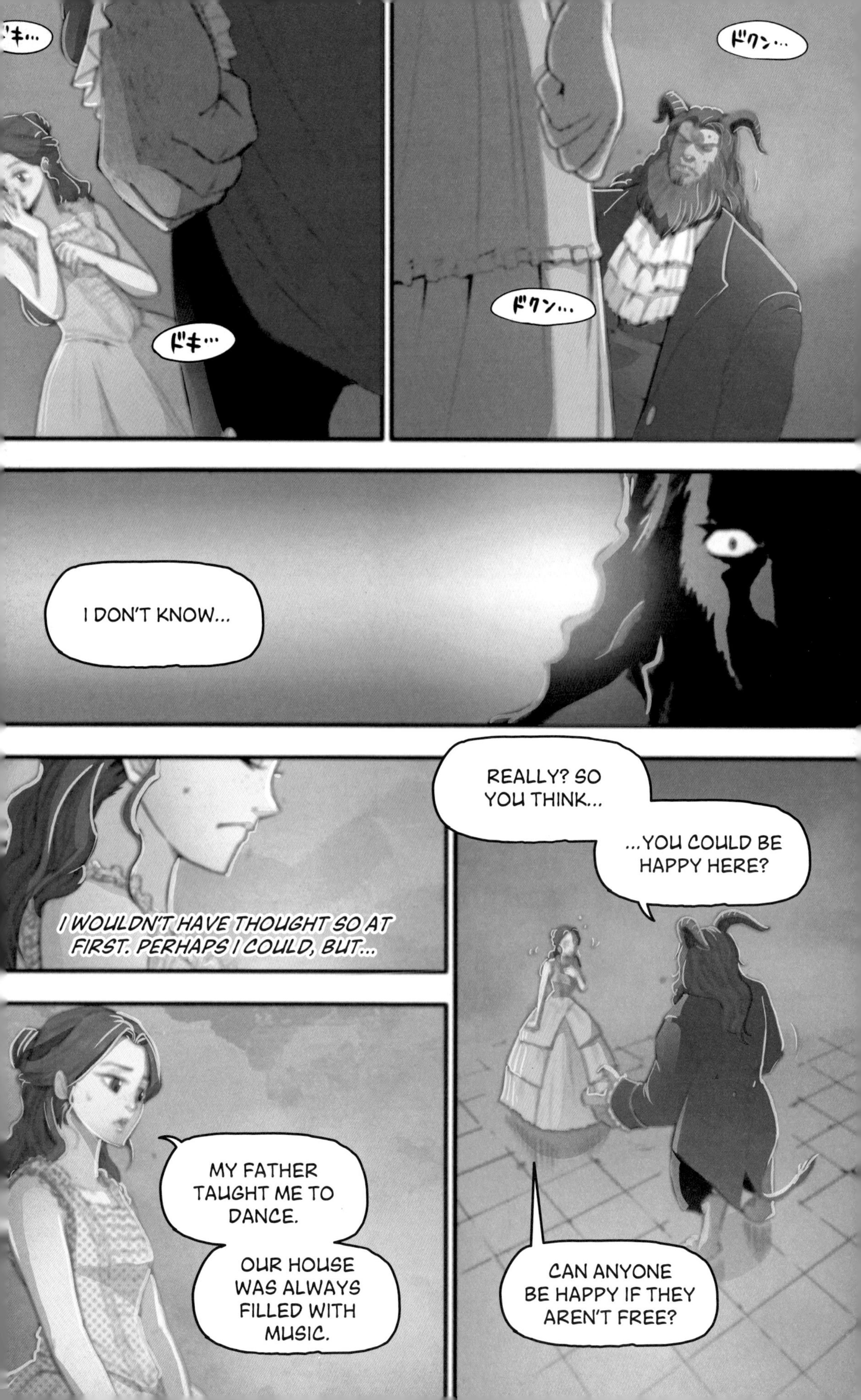
ドクン…
ドクン…
キ…
ドキ…
I DON'T KNOW...
REALLY? SO YOU THINK...
...YOU COULD BE HAPPY HERE?
CAN ANYONE BE HAPPY IF THEY AREN'T FREE?
I WOULDN'T HAVE THOUGHT SO AT FIRST. PERHAPS I COULD, BUT...
MY FATHER TAUGHT ME TO DANCE.
OUR HOUSE WAS ALWAYS FILLED WITH MUSIC.

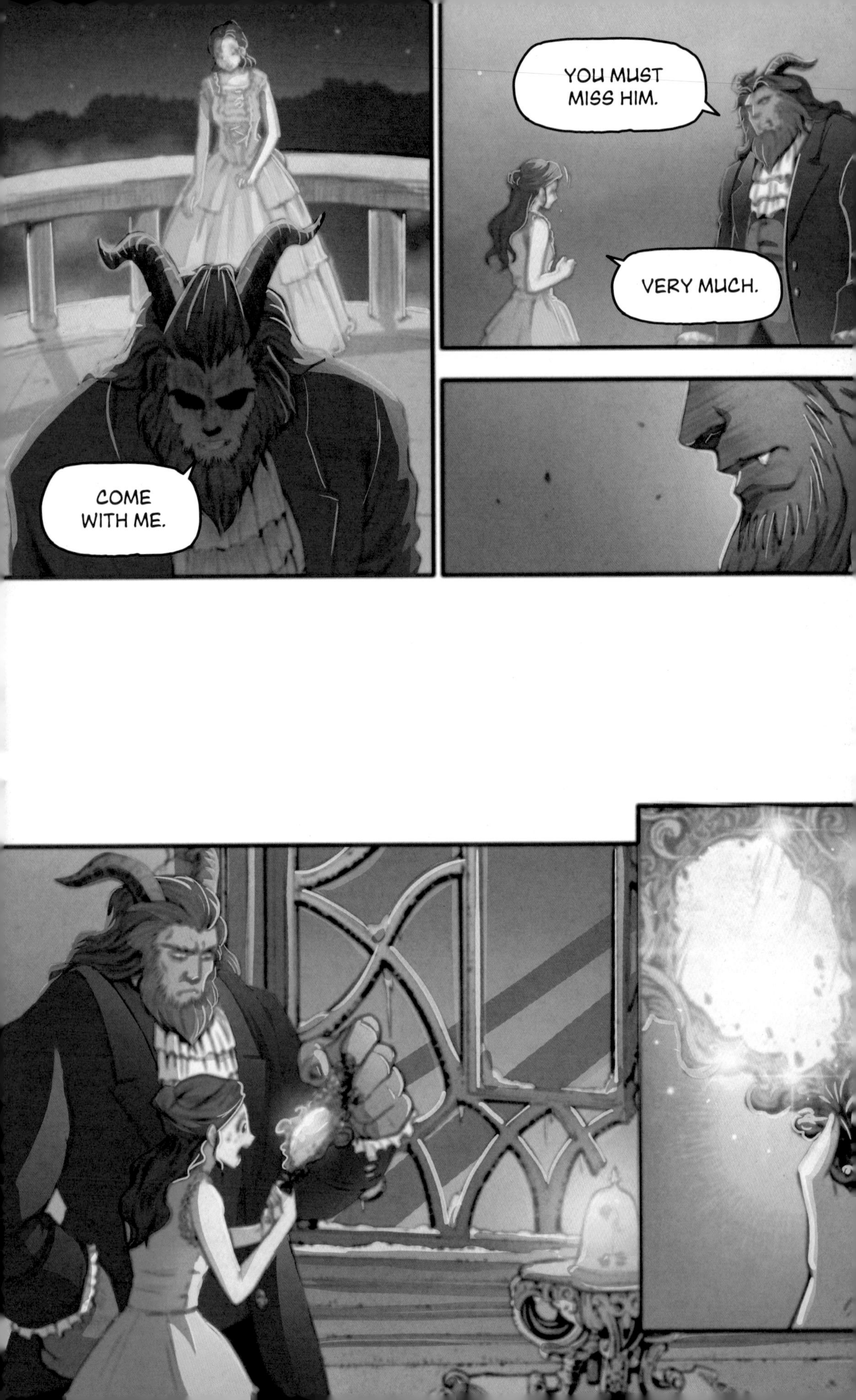
YOU MUST MISS HIM.
VERY MUCH.
COME WITH ME.

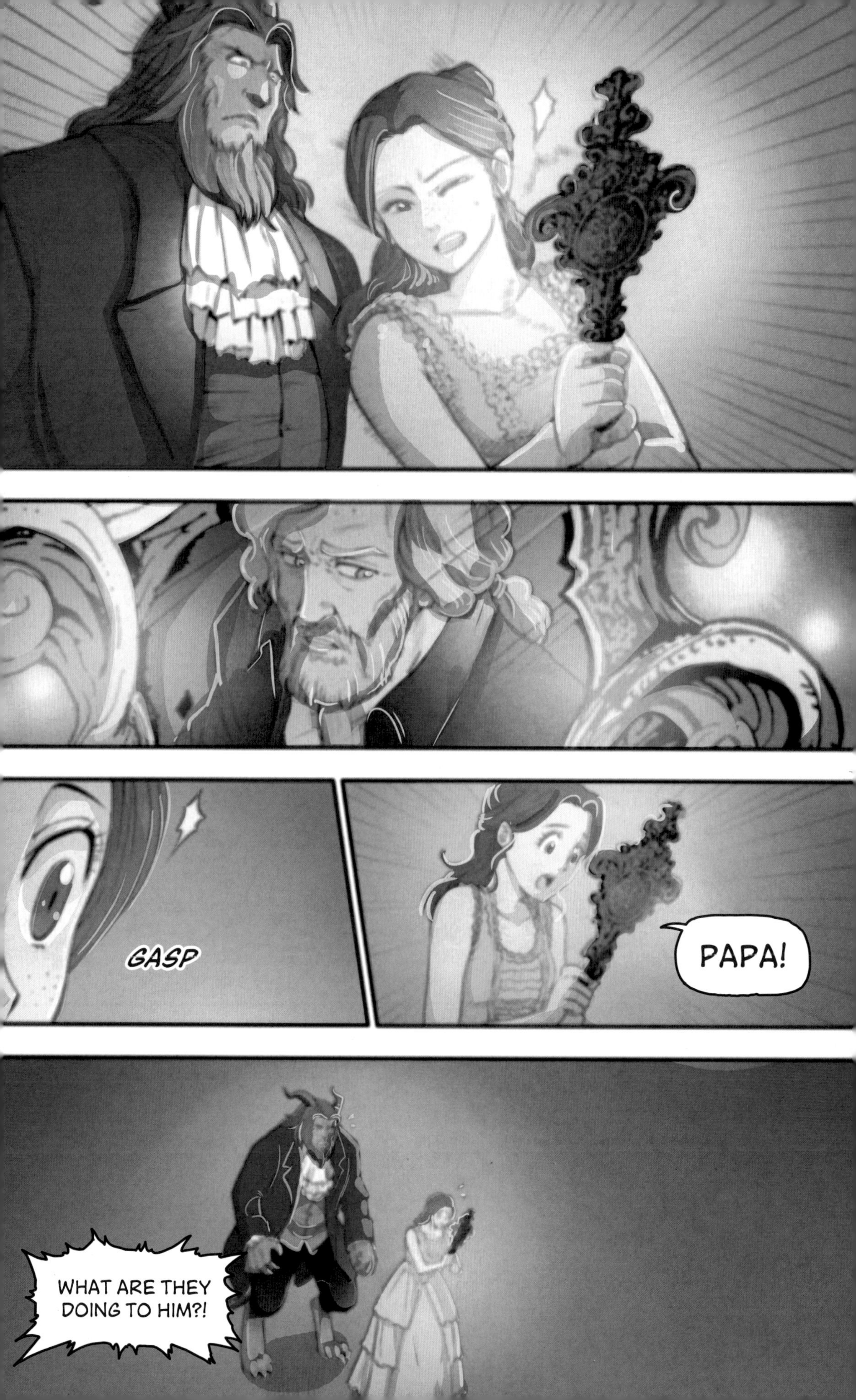
PAPA!
GASP
WHAT ARE THEY DOING TO HIM?!

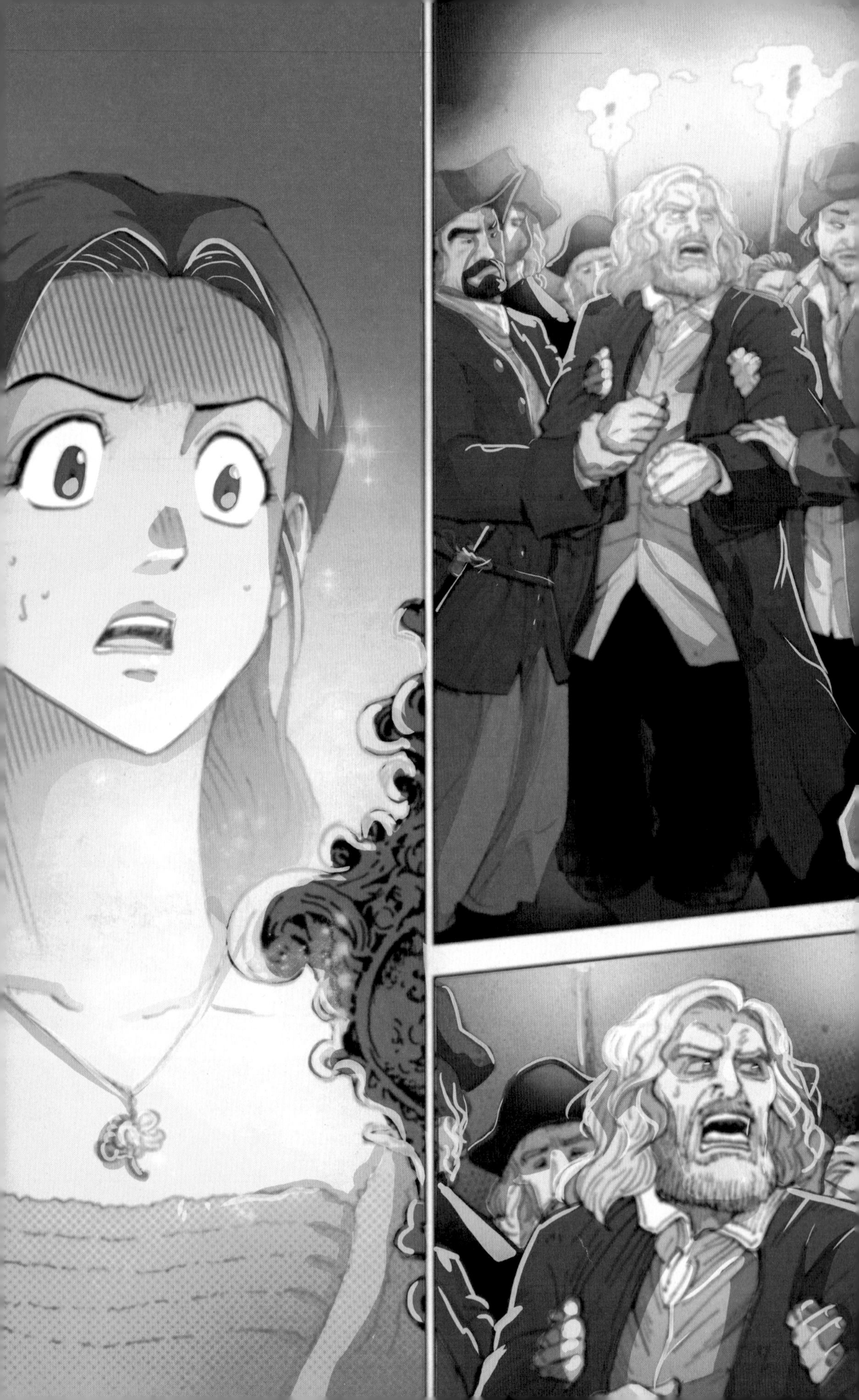

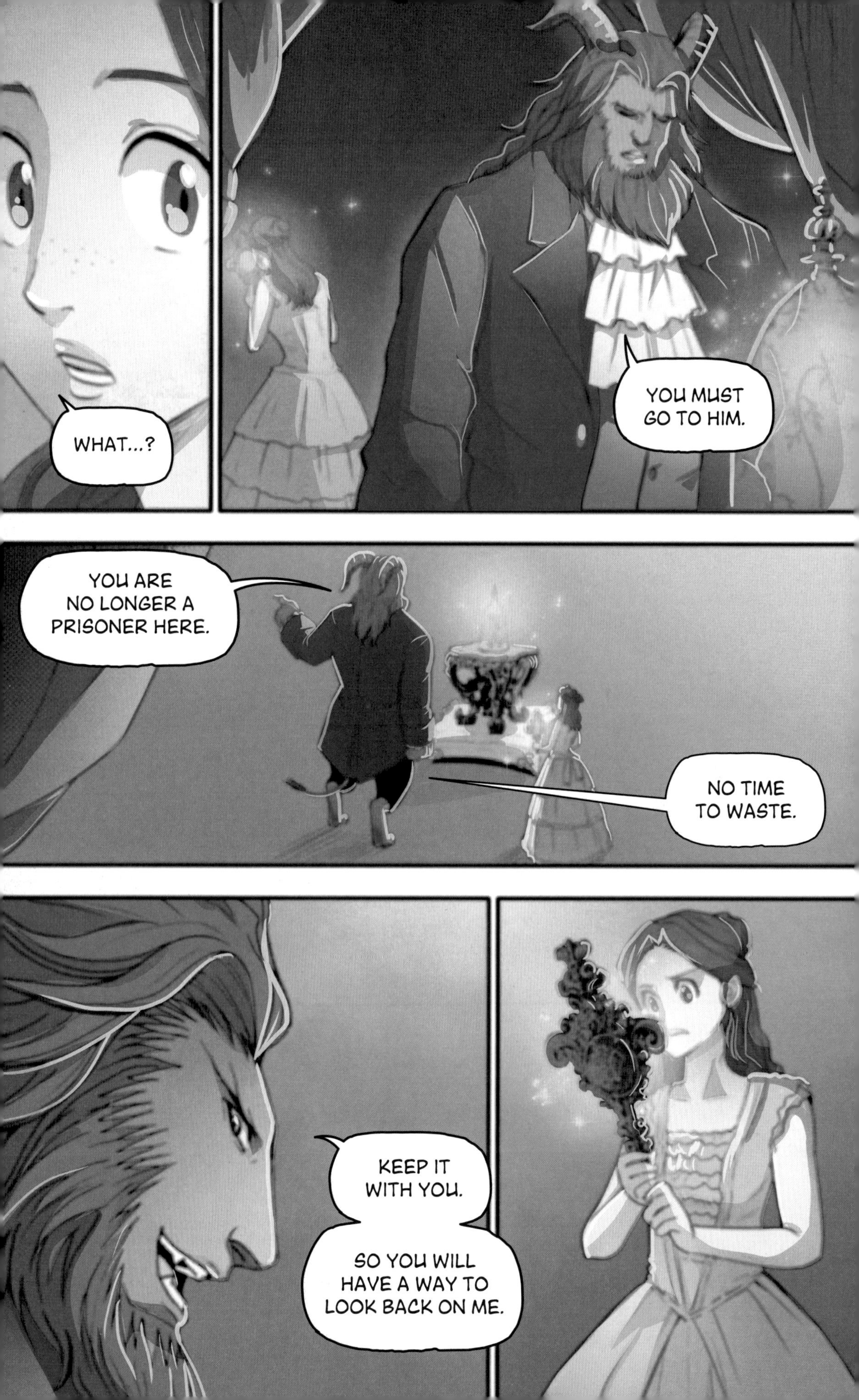
YOU MUST GO TO HIM.
WHAT...?
YOU ARE NO LONGER A PRISONER HERE.
NO TIME TO WASTE.
KEEP IT WITH YOU.
SO YOU WILL HAVE A WAY TO LOOK BACK ON ME.

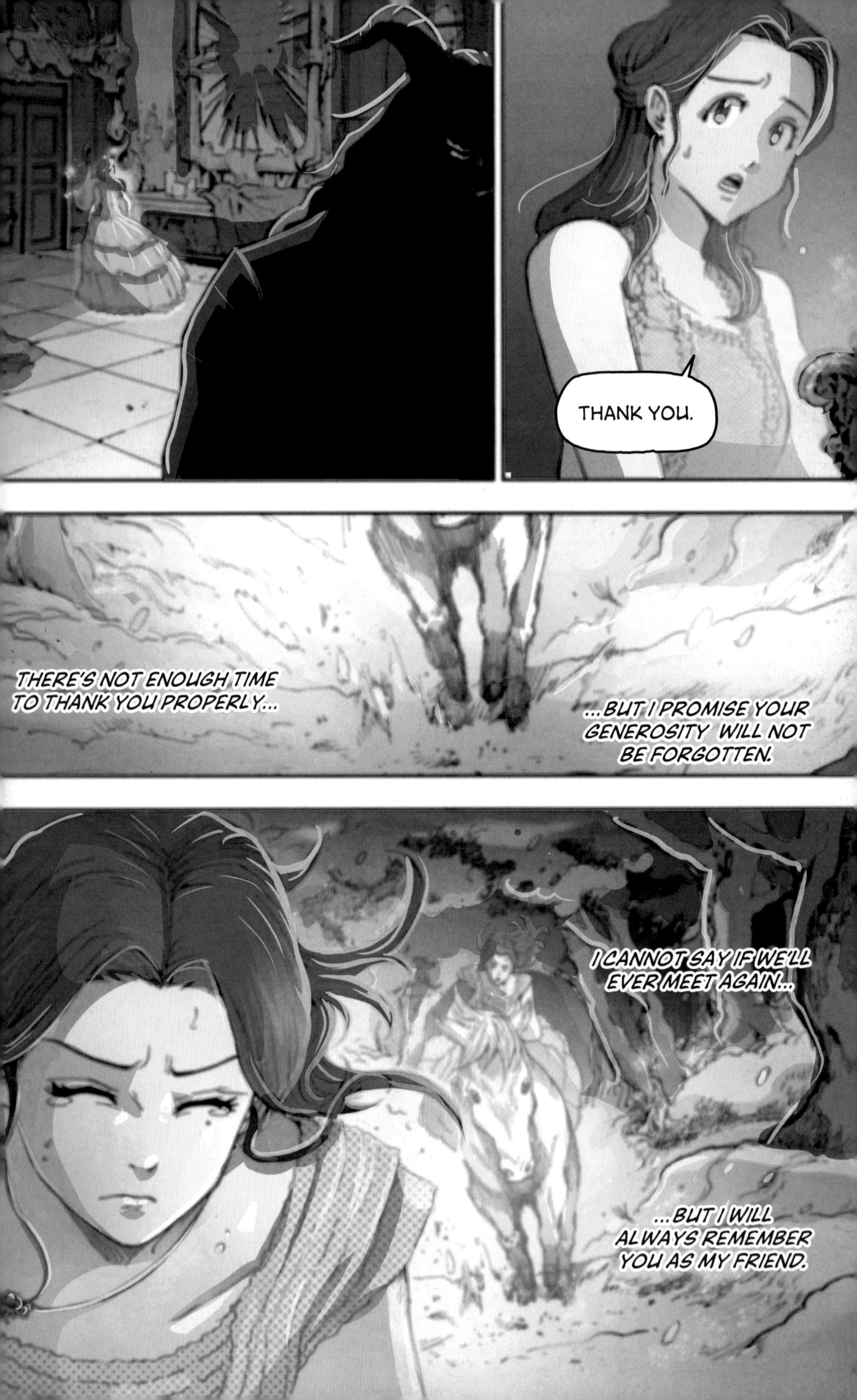
THANK YOU.
THERE'S NOT ENOUGH TIME TO THANK YOU PROPERLY...
...BUT I PROMISE YOUR GENEROSITY WILL NOT BE FORGOTTEN.
I CANNOT SAY IF WE'LL EVER MEET AGAIN...
...BUT I WILL ALWAYS REMEMBER YOU AS MY FRIEND.

Chapter 7

STOP THIS RIGHT NOW!

BELLE?

I'M AFRAID WE CAN'T DO THAT, MISS...

OPEN THIS DOOR! HE'S HURT.

...BUT WE'LL TAKE GOOD CARE OF HIM.

MY FATHER'S NOT CRAZY!

GASTON, TELL HIM!

BELLE, YOU KNOW HOW LOYAL I AM TO YOUR FAMILY...

...BUT YOUR FATHER HAS BEEN RAVING ABOUT A BEAST IN A CASTLE.

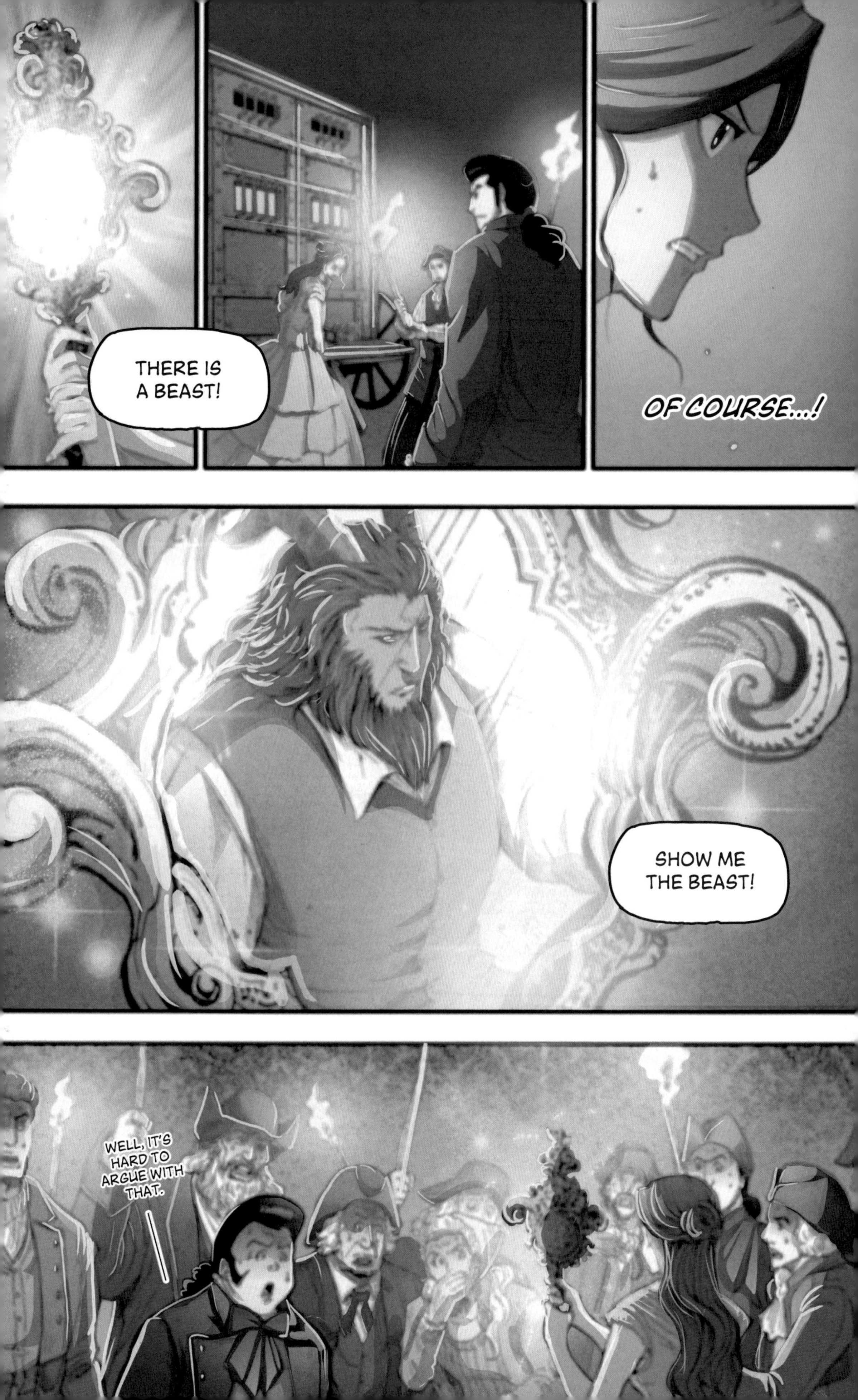
OF COURSE...!
THERE IS A BEAST!
SHOW ME THE BEAST!
WELL, IT'S HARD TO ARGUE WITH THAT.

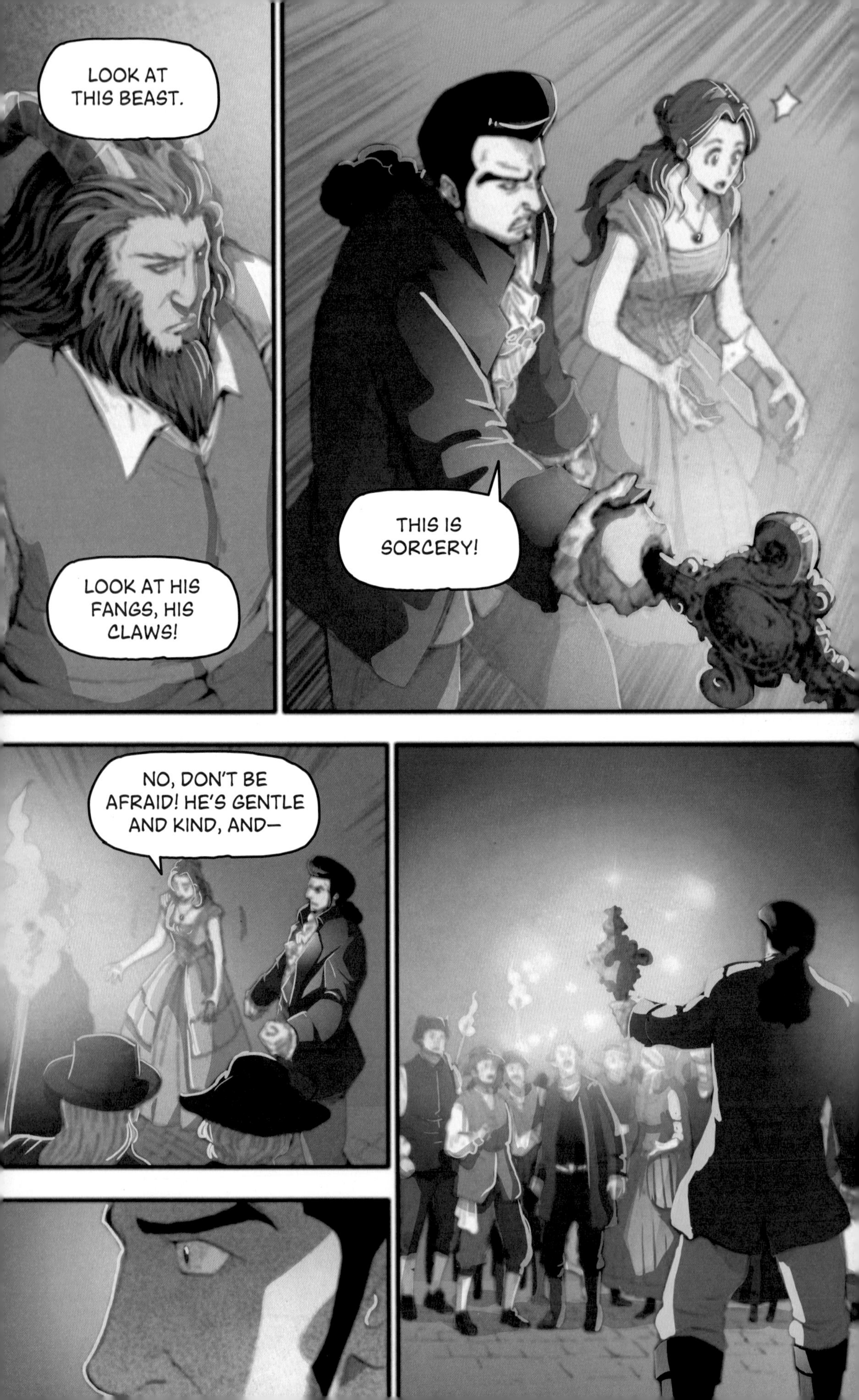
THIS IS SORCERY!
LOOK AT THIS BEAST.
LOOK AT HIS FANGS, HIS CLAWS!
NO, DON'T BE AFRAID! HE'S GENTLE AND KIND, AND—

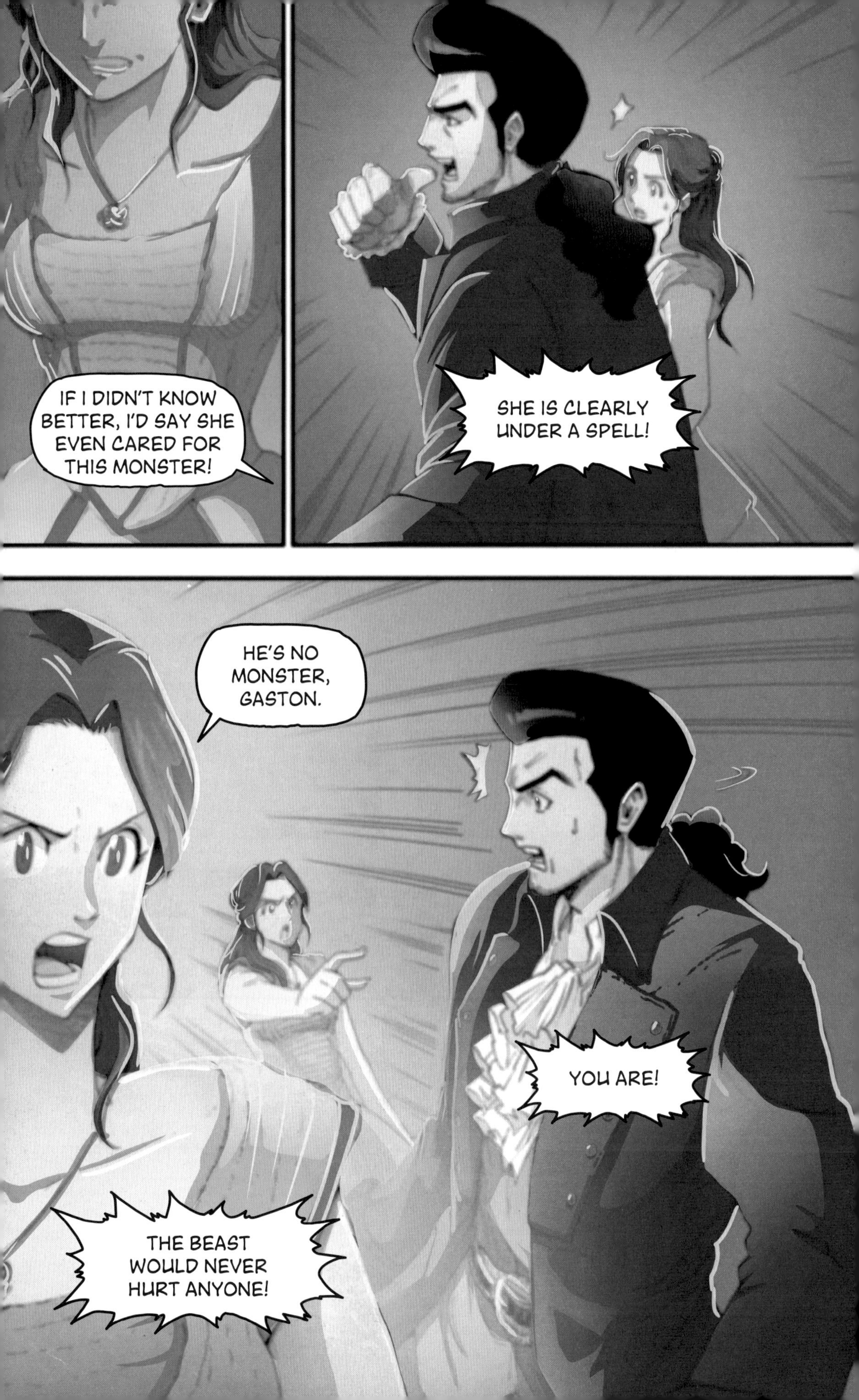
SHE IS CLEARLY UNDER A SPELL!
IF I DIDN'T KNOW BETTER, I'D SAY SHE EVEN CARED FOR THIS MONSTER!
HE'S NO MONSTER, GASTON.
YOU ARE!
THE BEAST WOULD NEVER HURT ANYONE!

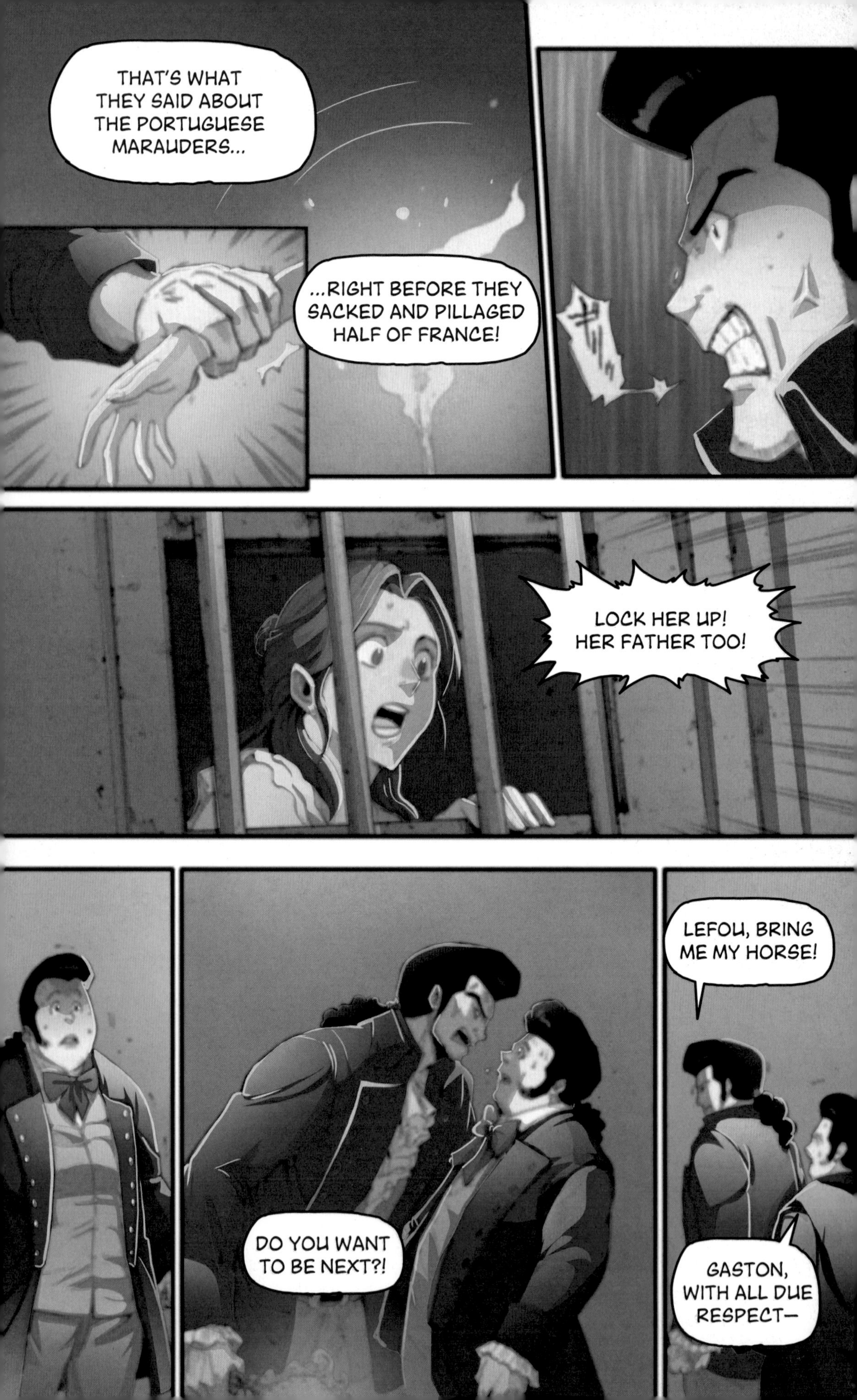
THAT'S WHAT THEY SAID ABOUT THE PORTUGUESE MARAUDERS...
...RIGHT BEFORE THEY SACKED AND PILLAGED HALF OF FRANCE!
LOCK HER UP! HER FATHER TOO!
LEFOU, BRING ME MY HORSE!
GASTON, WITH ALL DUE RESPECT—
DO YOU WANT TO BE NEXT?!

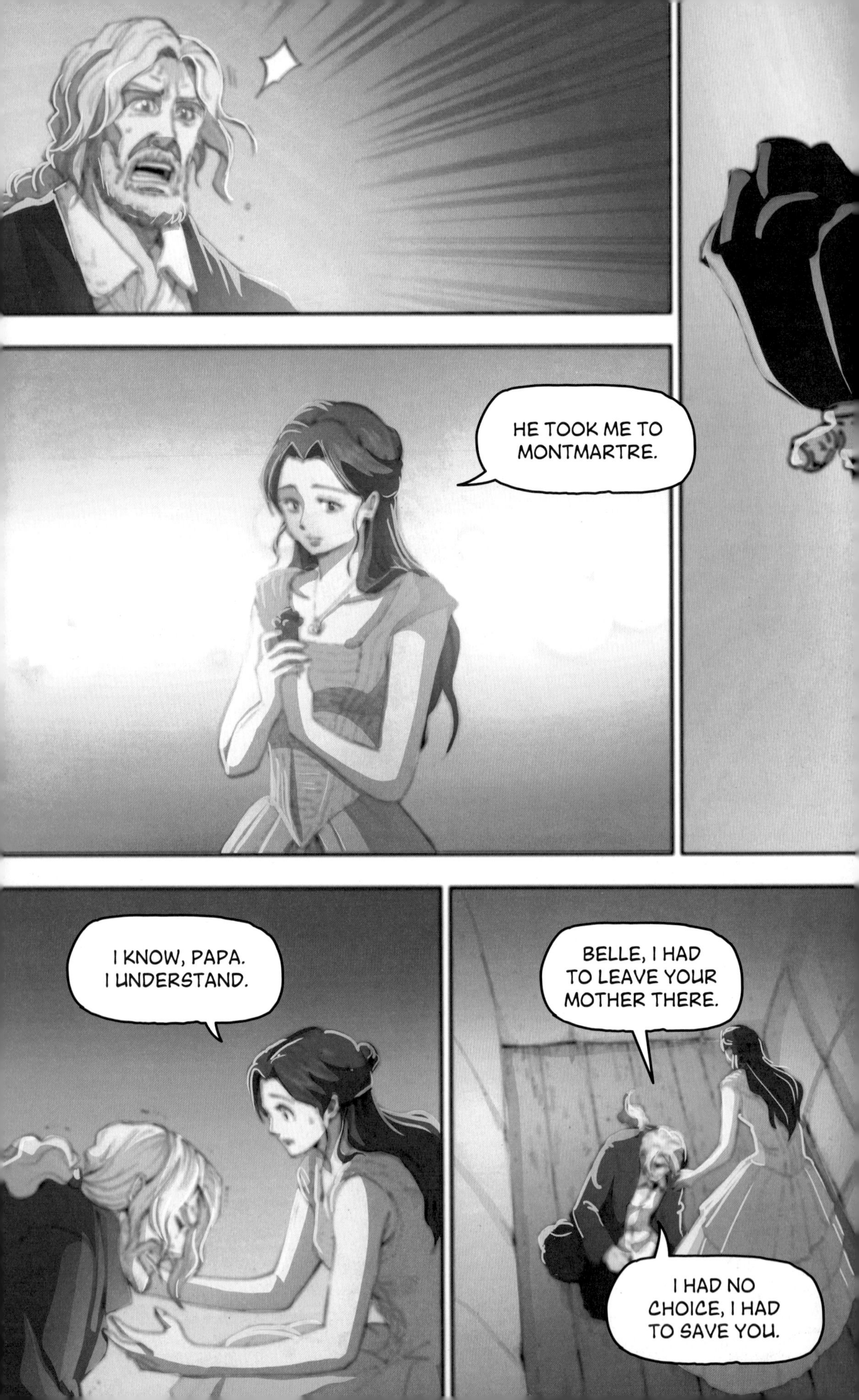
HE TOOK ME TO MONTMARTRE.
BELLE, I HAD TO LEAVE YOUR MOTHER THERE.
I HAD NO CHOICE, I HAD TO SAVE YOU.
I KNOW, PAPA. I UNDERSTAND.

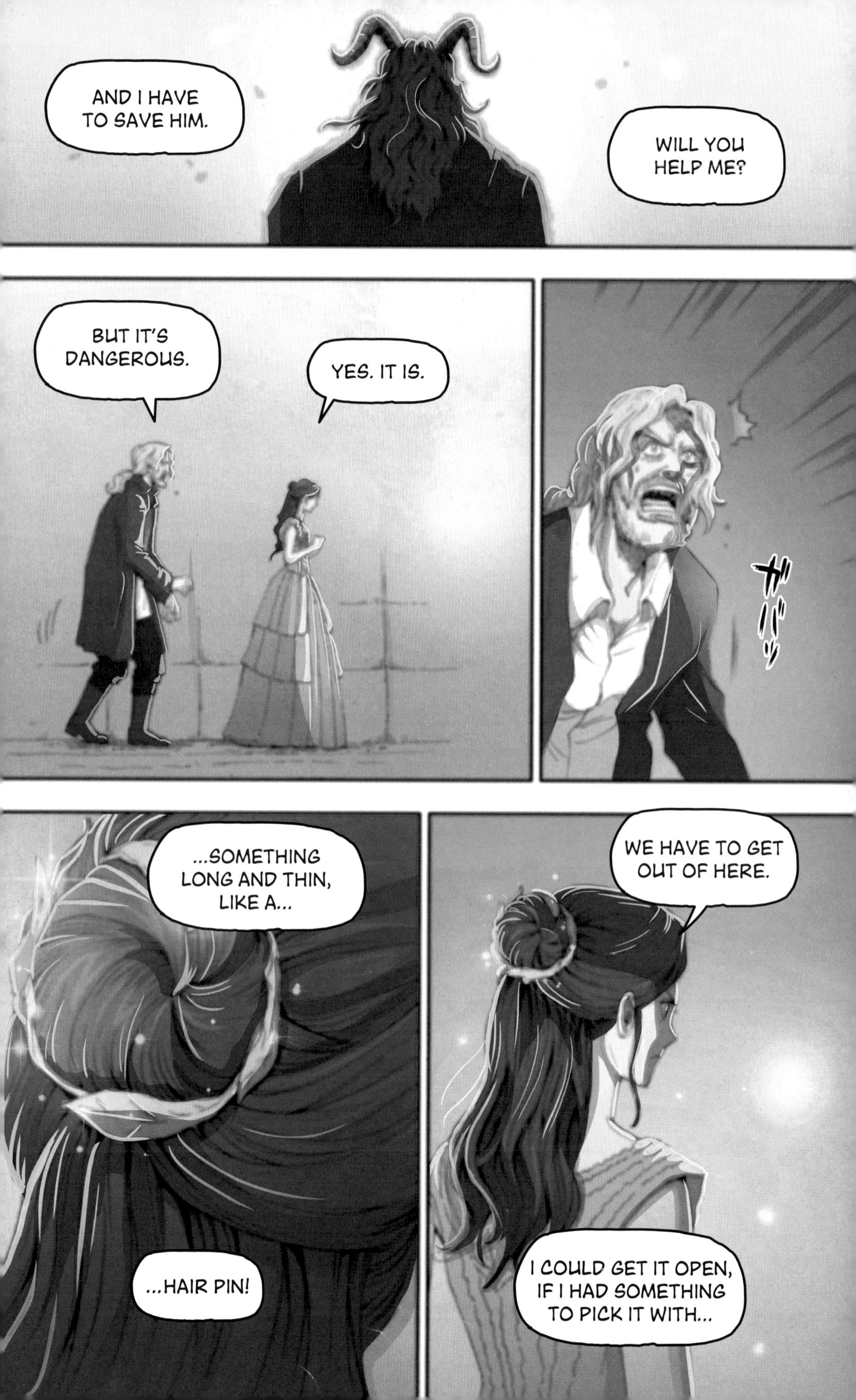
AND I HAVE TO SAVE HIM.
WILL YOU HELP ME?
ガバッ
BUT IT'S DANGEROUS.
YES. IT IS.
WE HAVE TO GET OUT OF HERE.
I COULD GET IT OPEN, IF I HAD SOMETHING TO PICK IT WITH...
...SOMETHING LONG AND THIN, LIKE A...
...HAIR PIN!

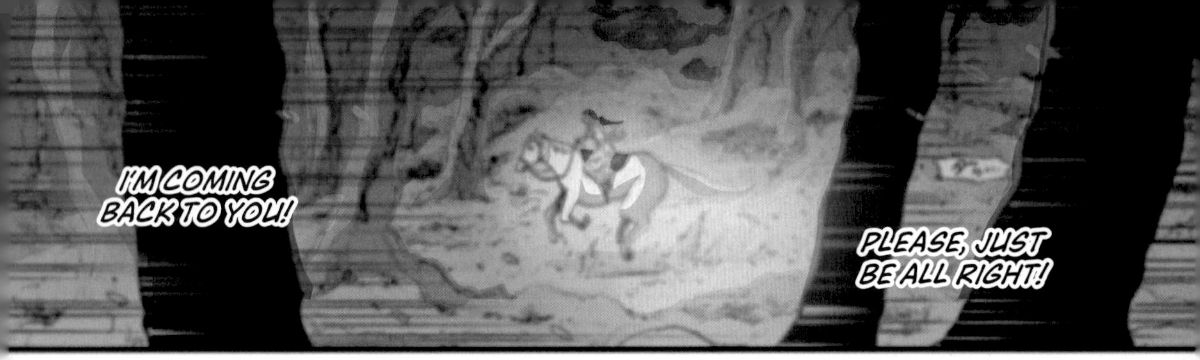
I'M COMING BACK TO YOU!
PLEASE, JUST BE ALL RIGHT!
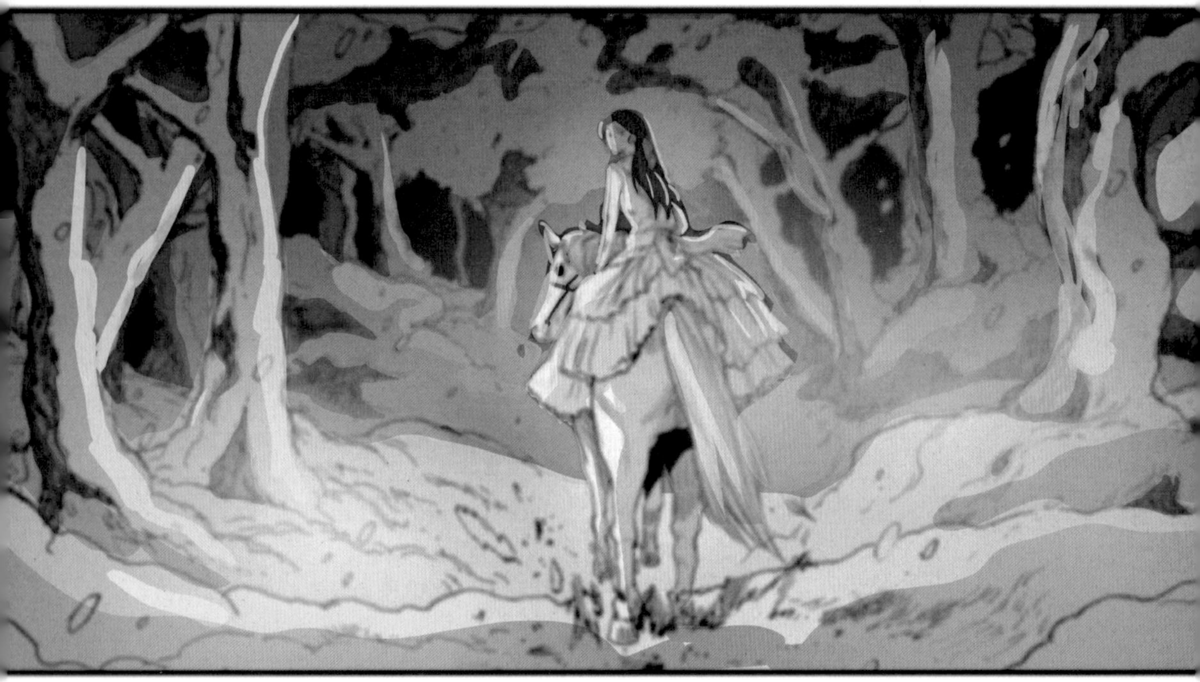
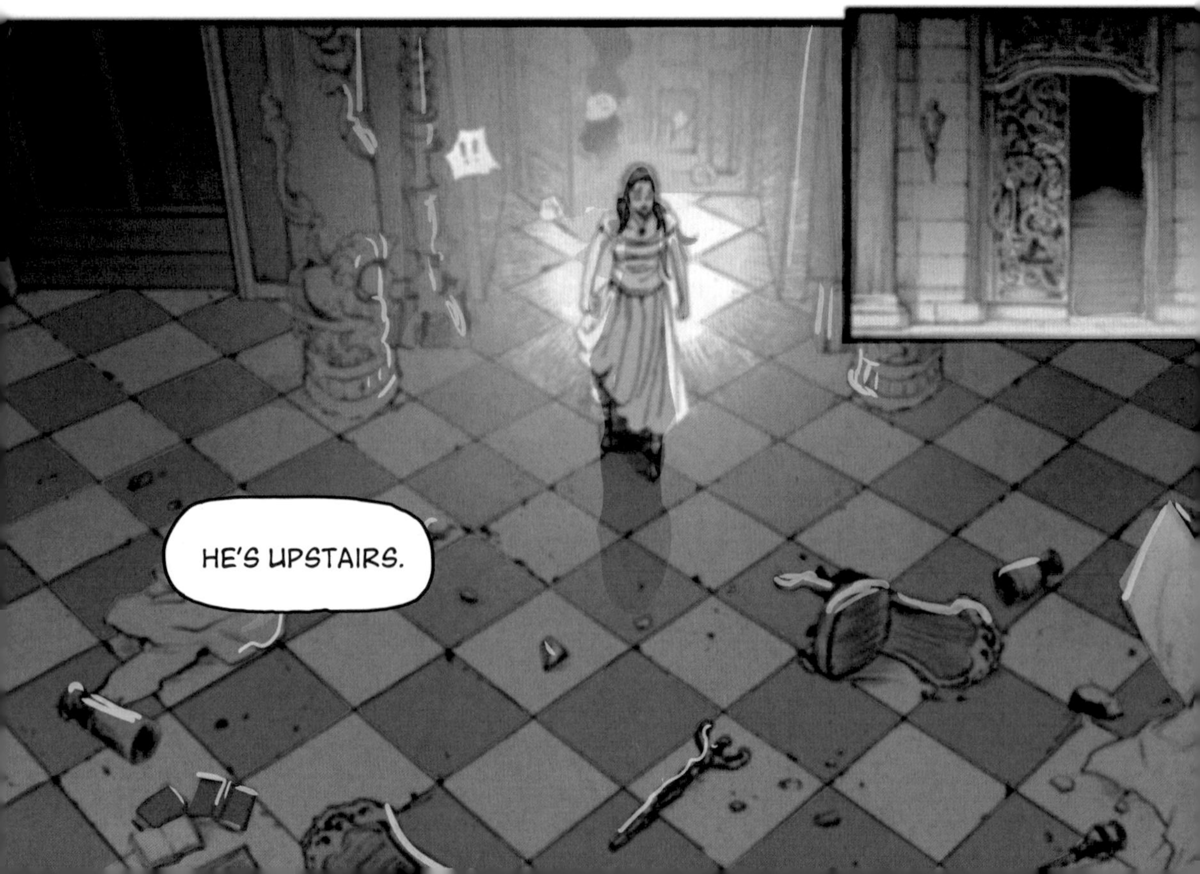
!!
HE'S UPSTAIRS.

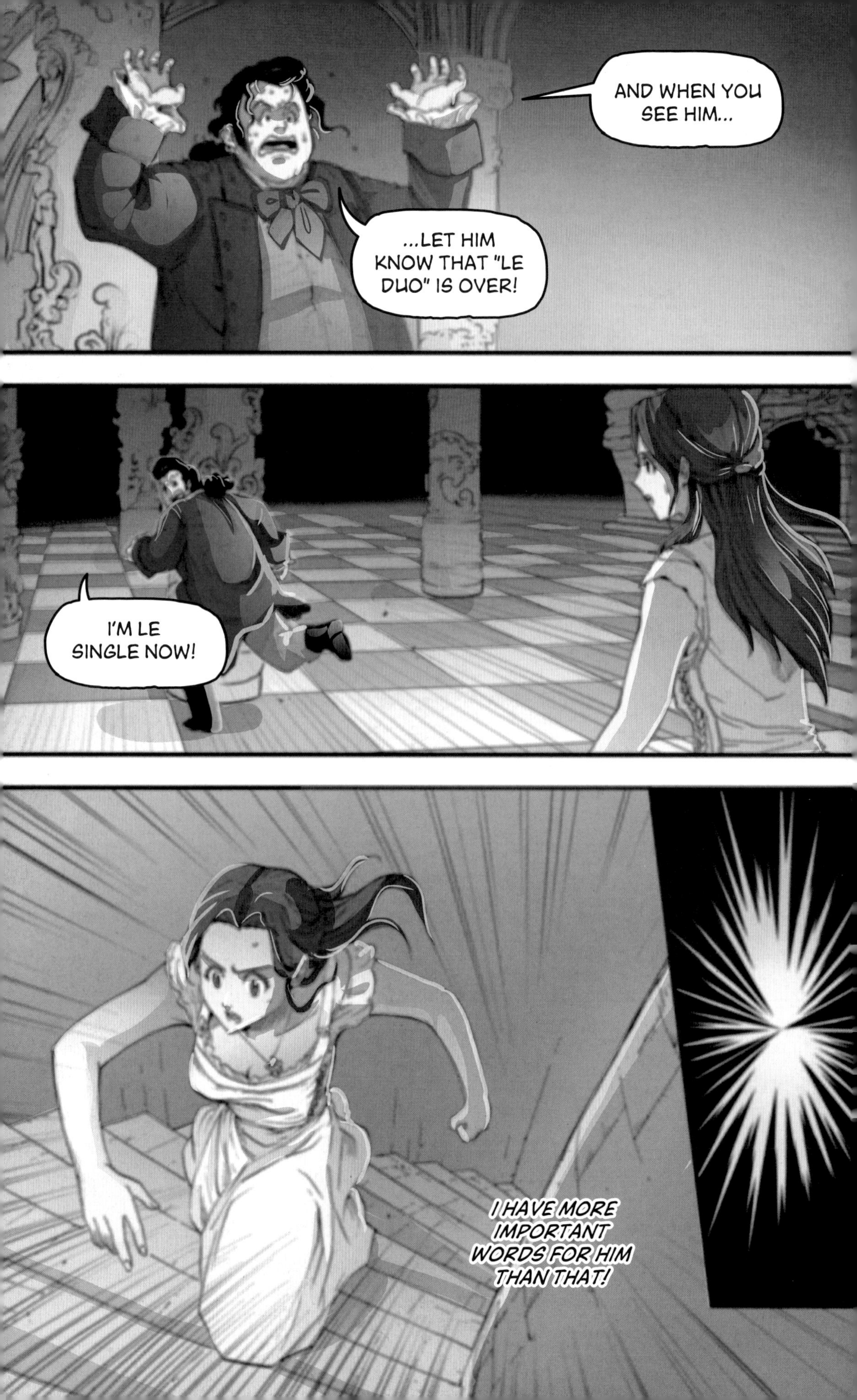
AND WHEN YOU SEE HIM...
...LET HIM KNOW THAT "LE DUO" IS OVER!
I'M LE SINGLE NOW!
I HAVE MORE IMPORTANT WORDS FOR HIM THAN THAT!

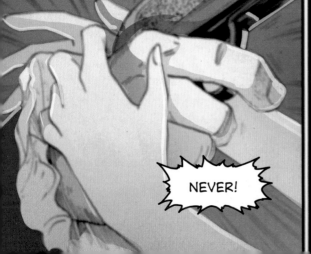

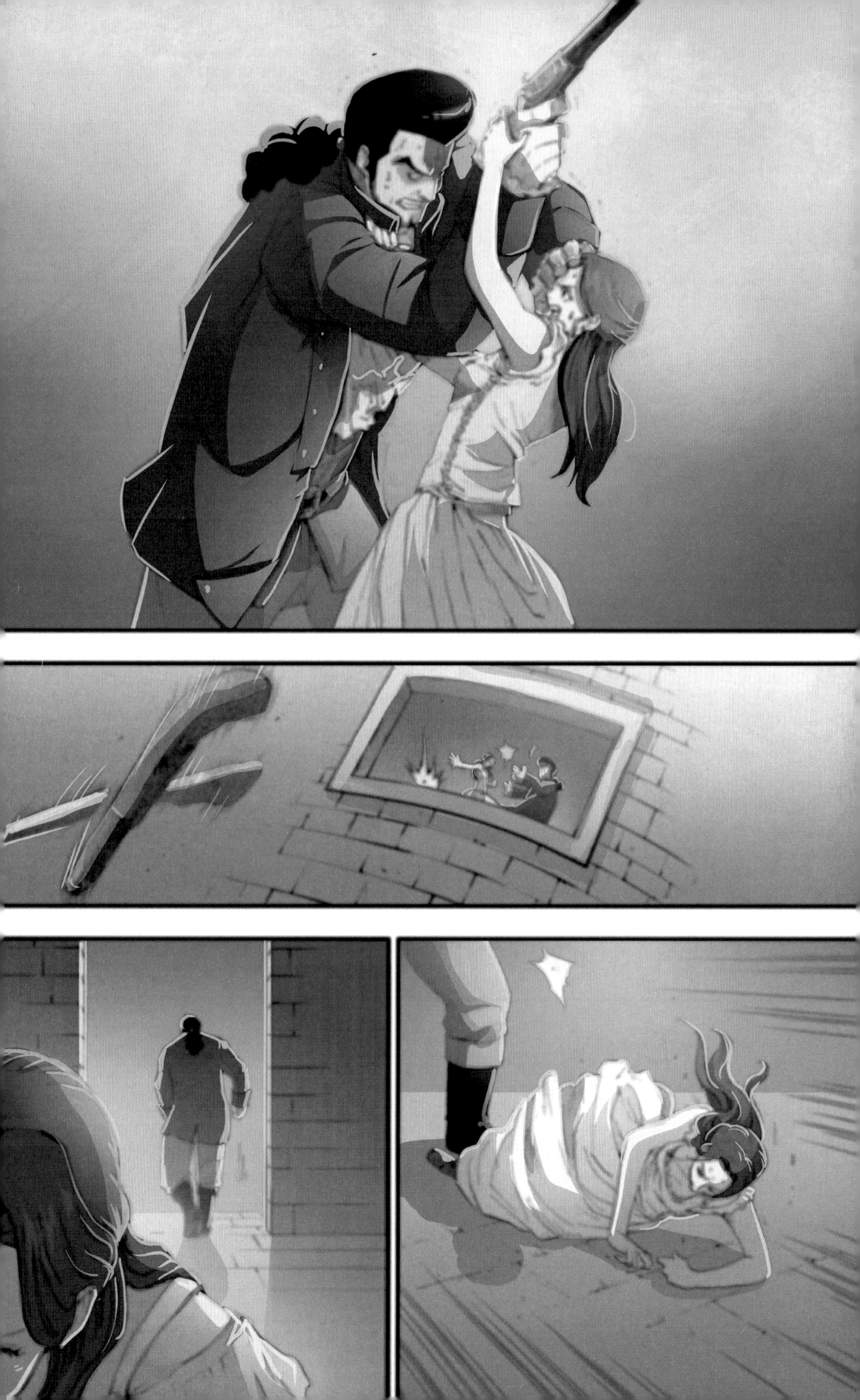

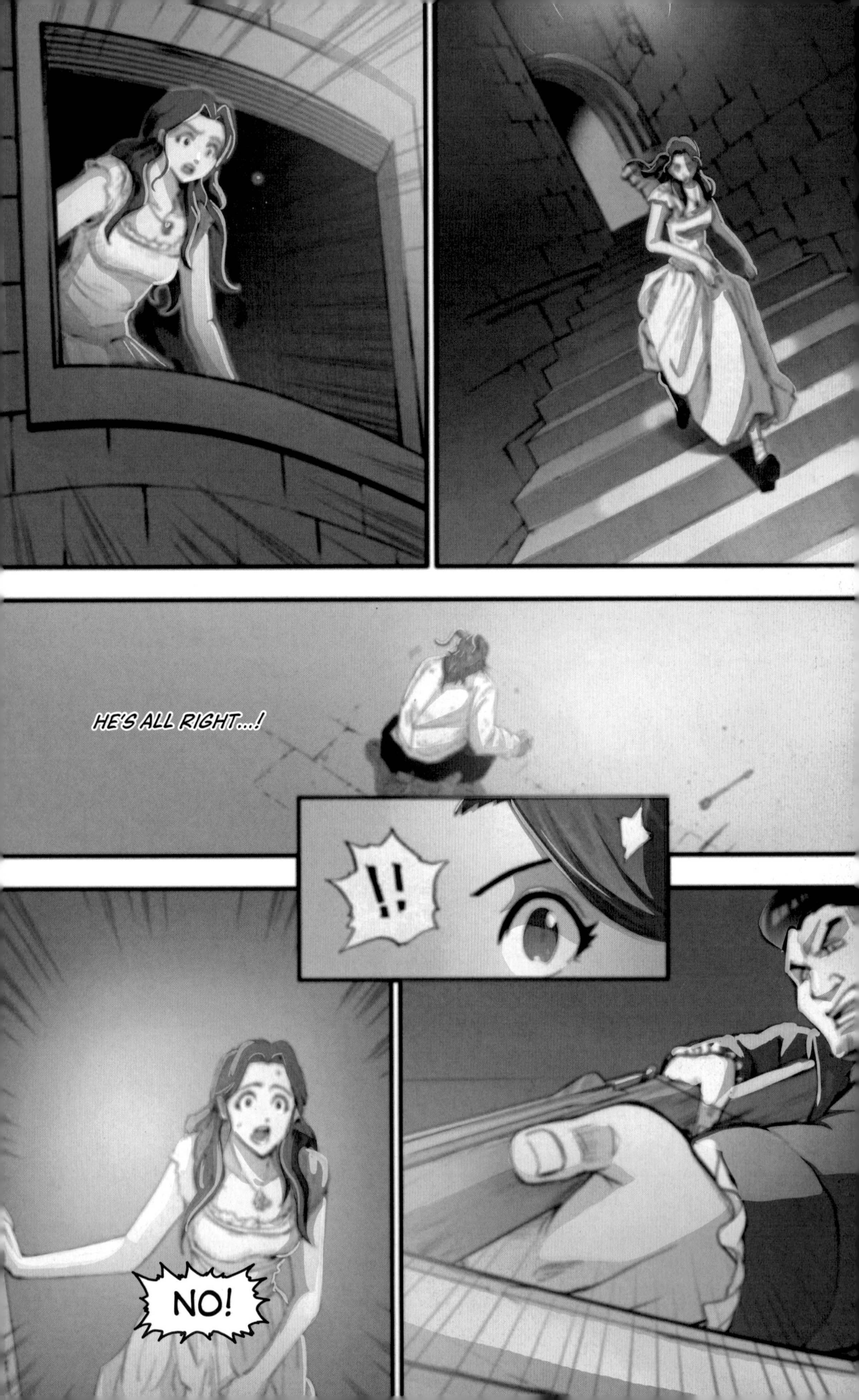
HE'S ALL RIGHT...!
!!
NO!

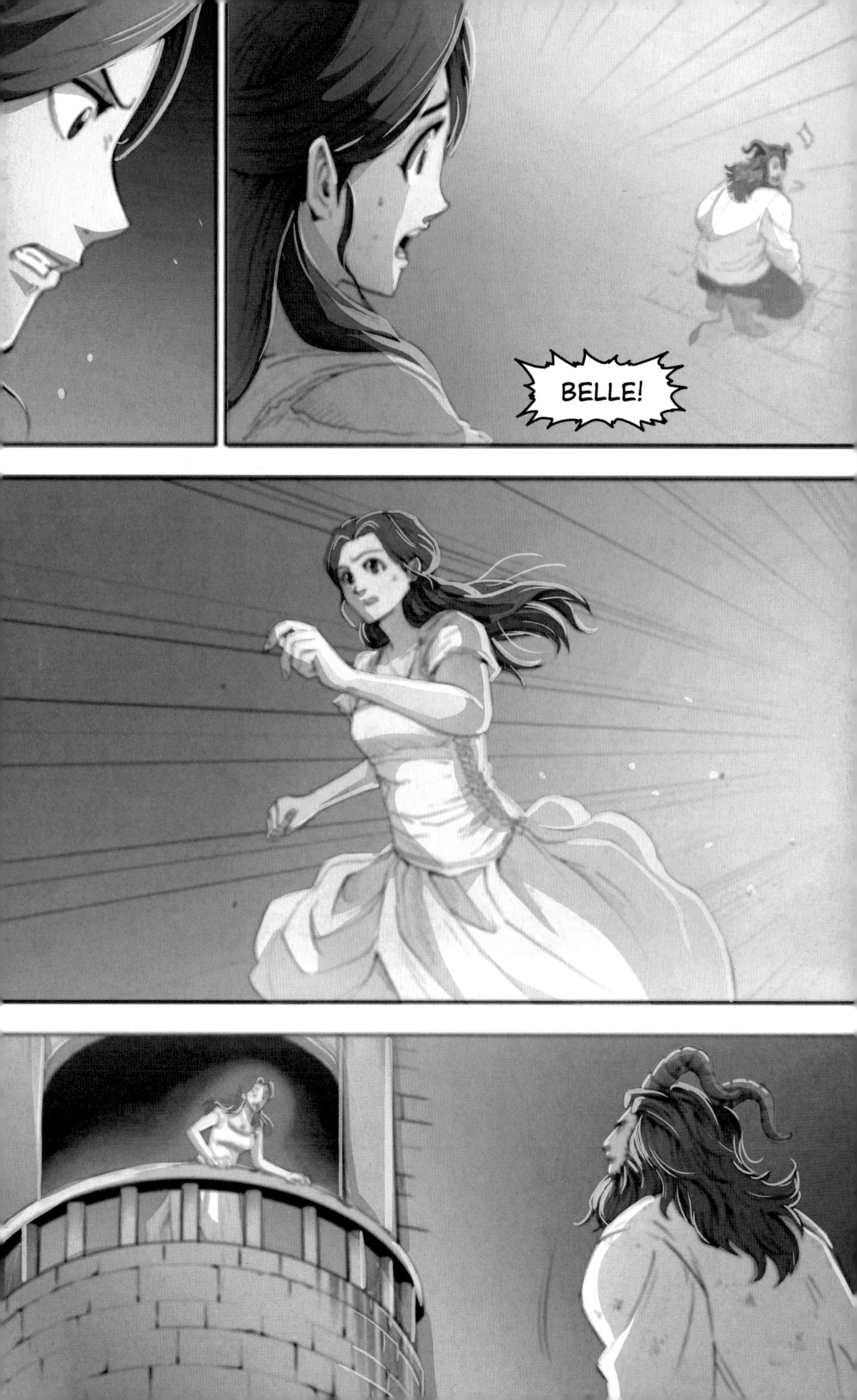
BELLE!

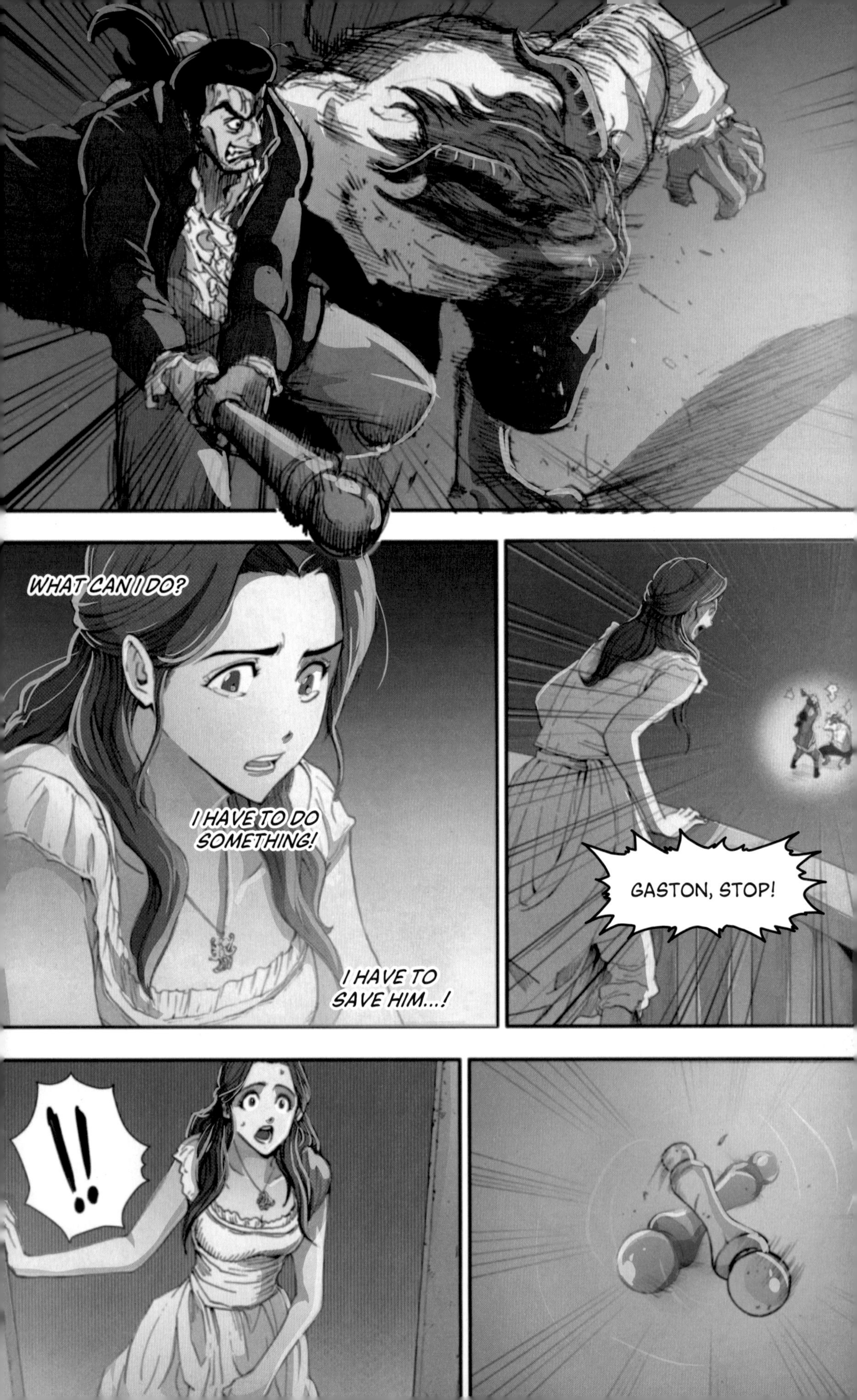
GASTON, STOP!
WHAT CAN I DO?
I HAVE TO DO SOMETHING!
I HAVE TO SAVE HIM...!
!!

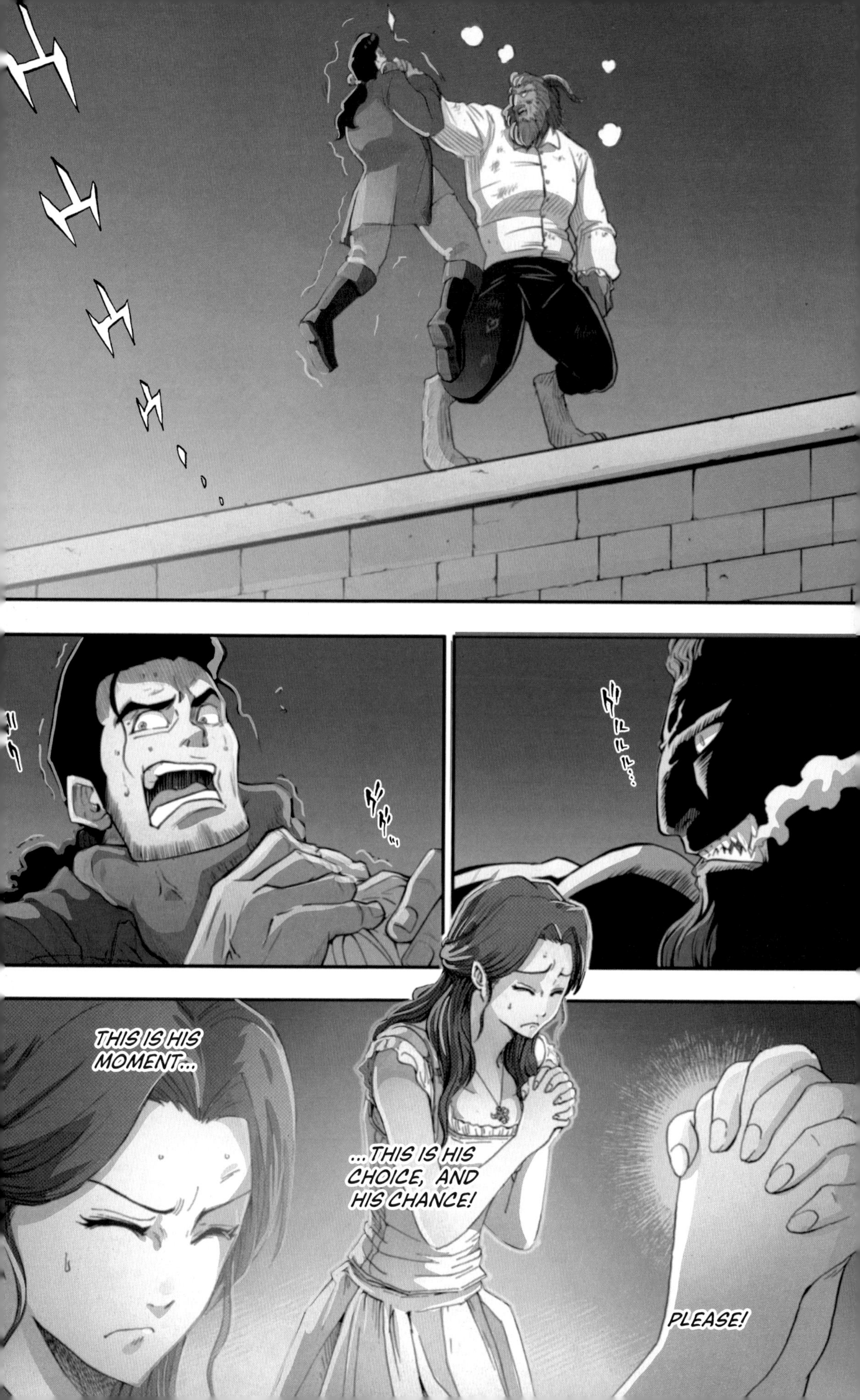
THIS IS HIS MOMENT...
...THIS IS HIS CHOICE, AND HIS CHANCE!
PLEASE!

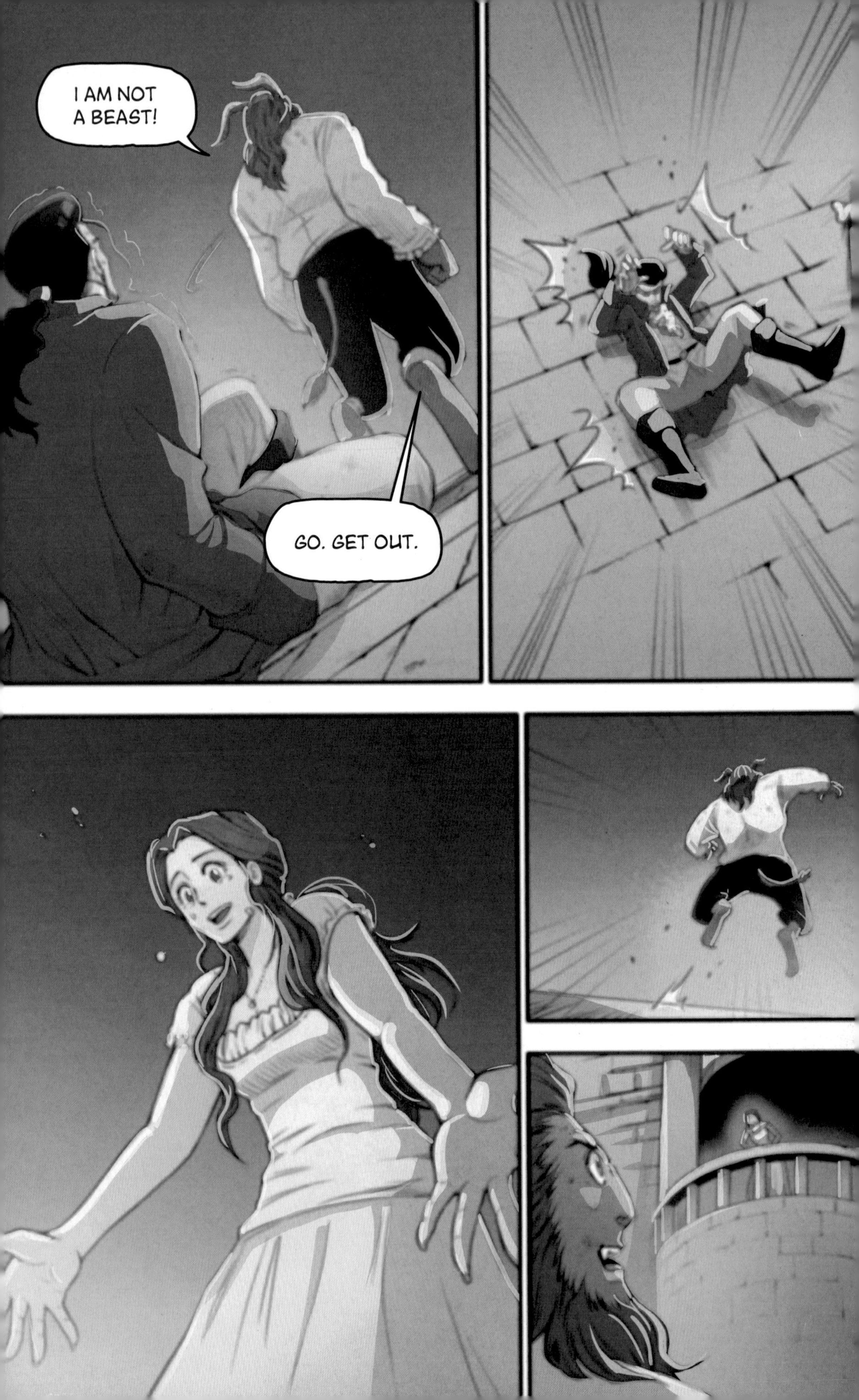
I AM NOT A BEAST!
GO. GET OUT.

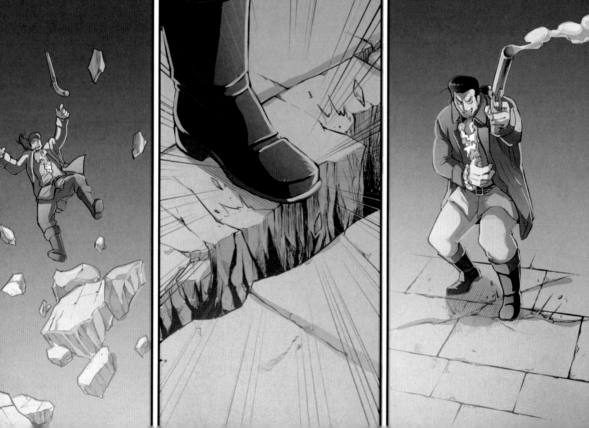

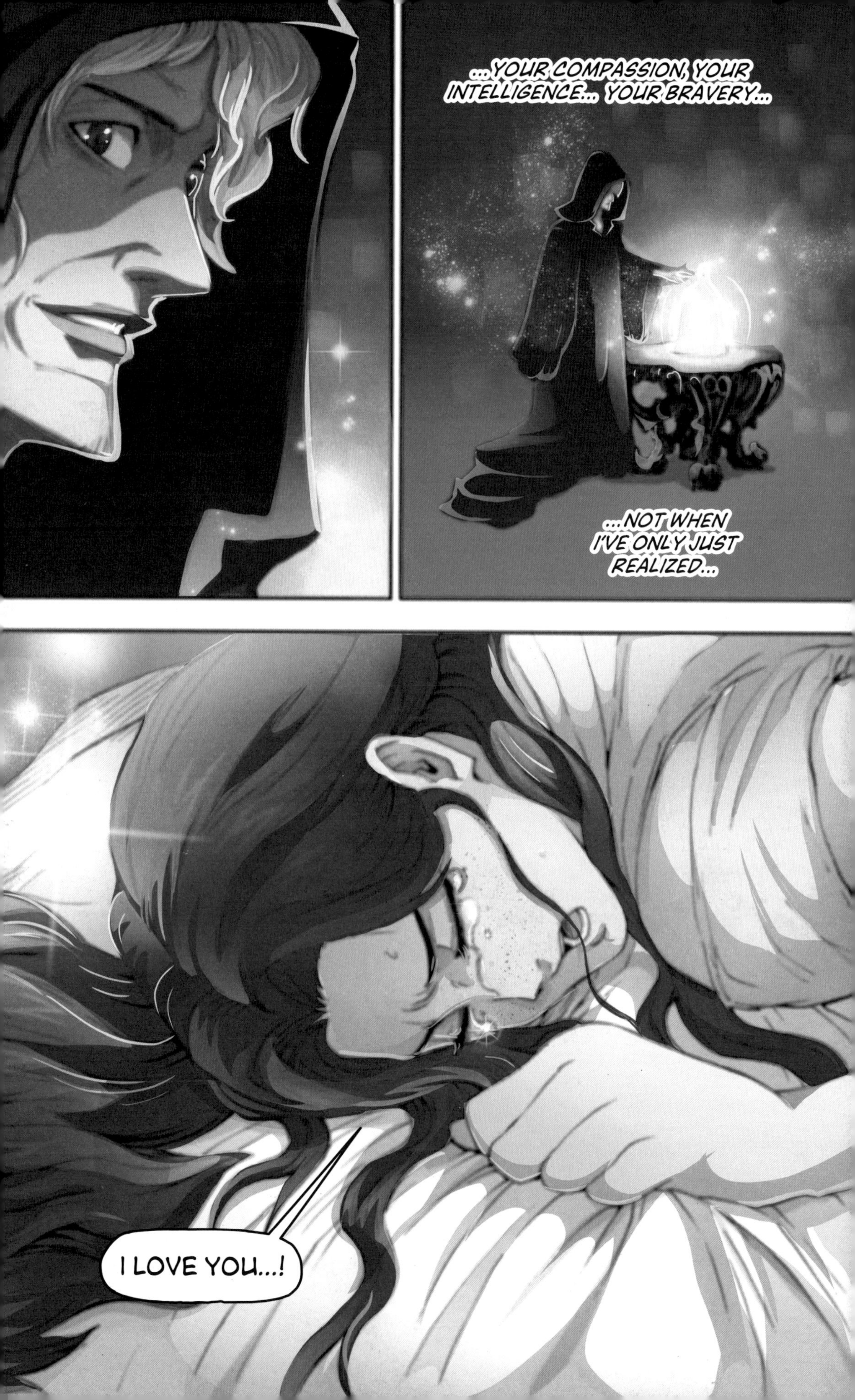
...YOUR COMPASSION, YOUR INTELLIGENCE... YOUR BRAVERY...
...NOT WHEN I'VE ONLY JUST REALIZED...
I LOVE YOU...!

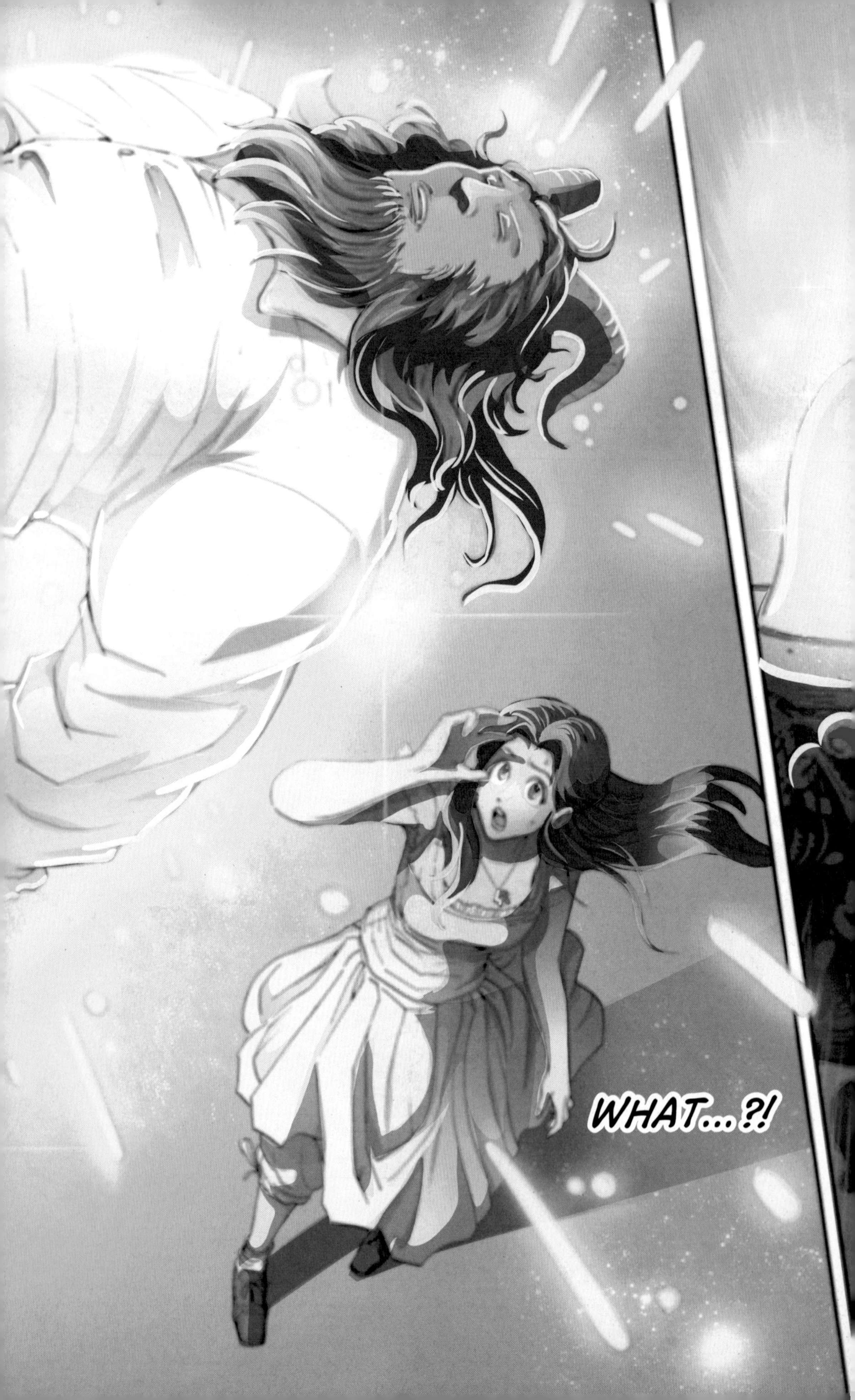
WHAT...?!

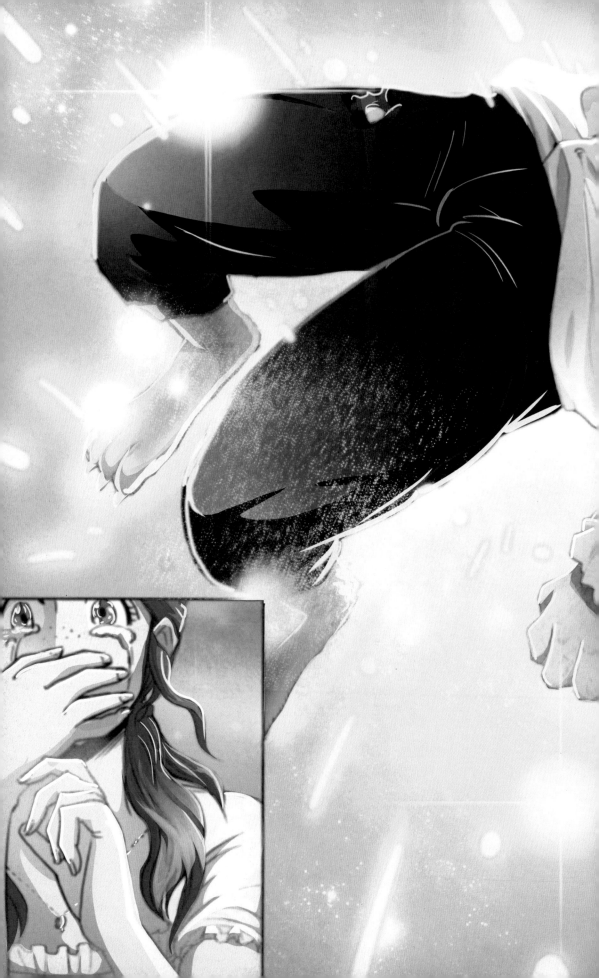

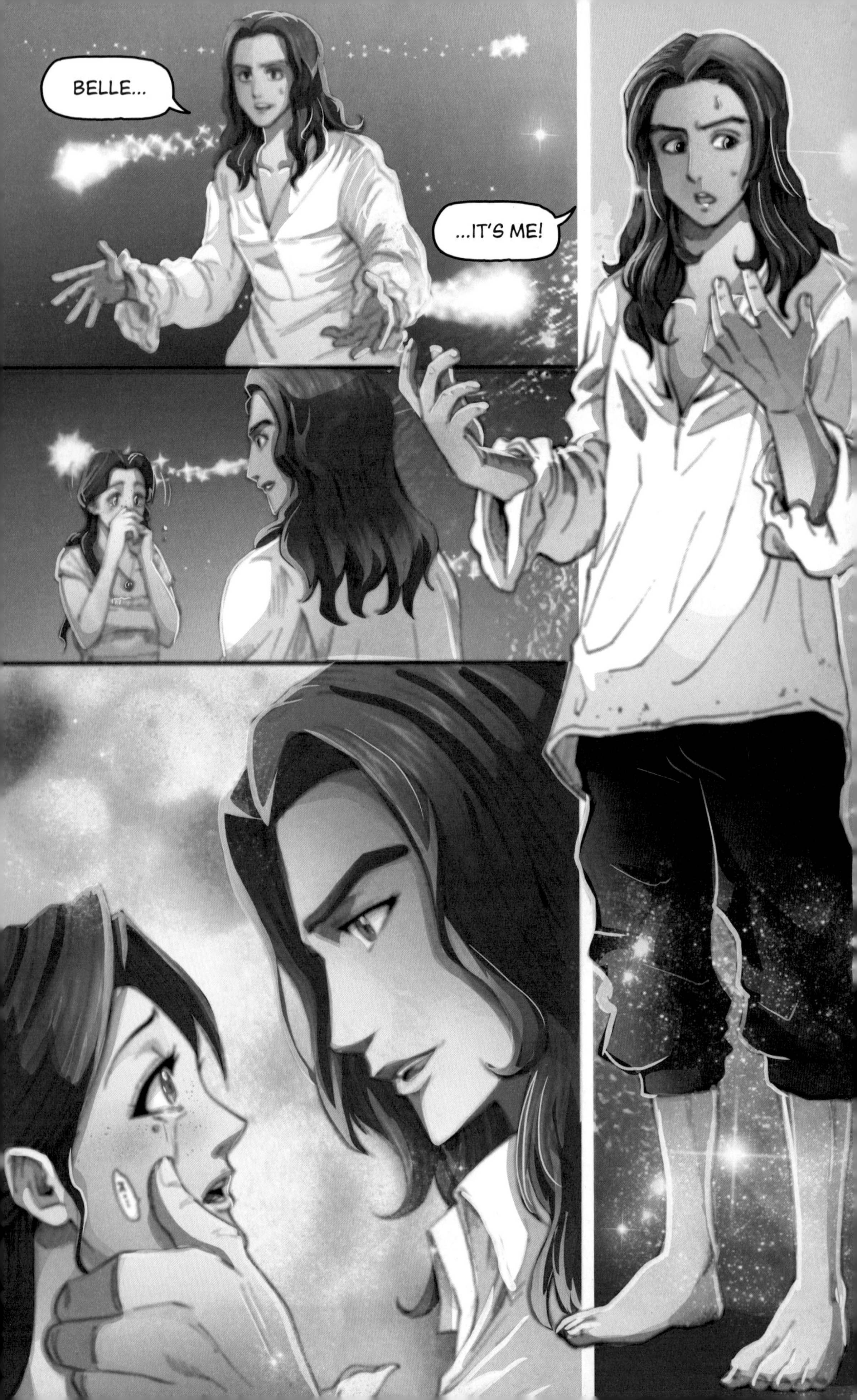
BELLE...
...IT'S ME!

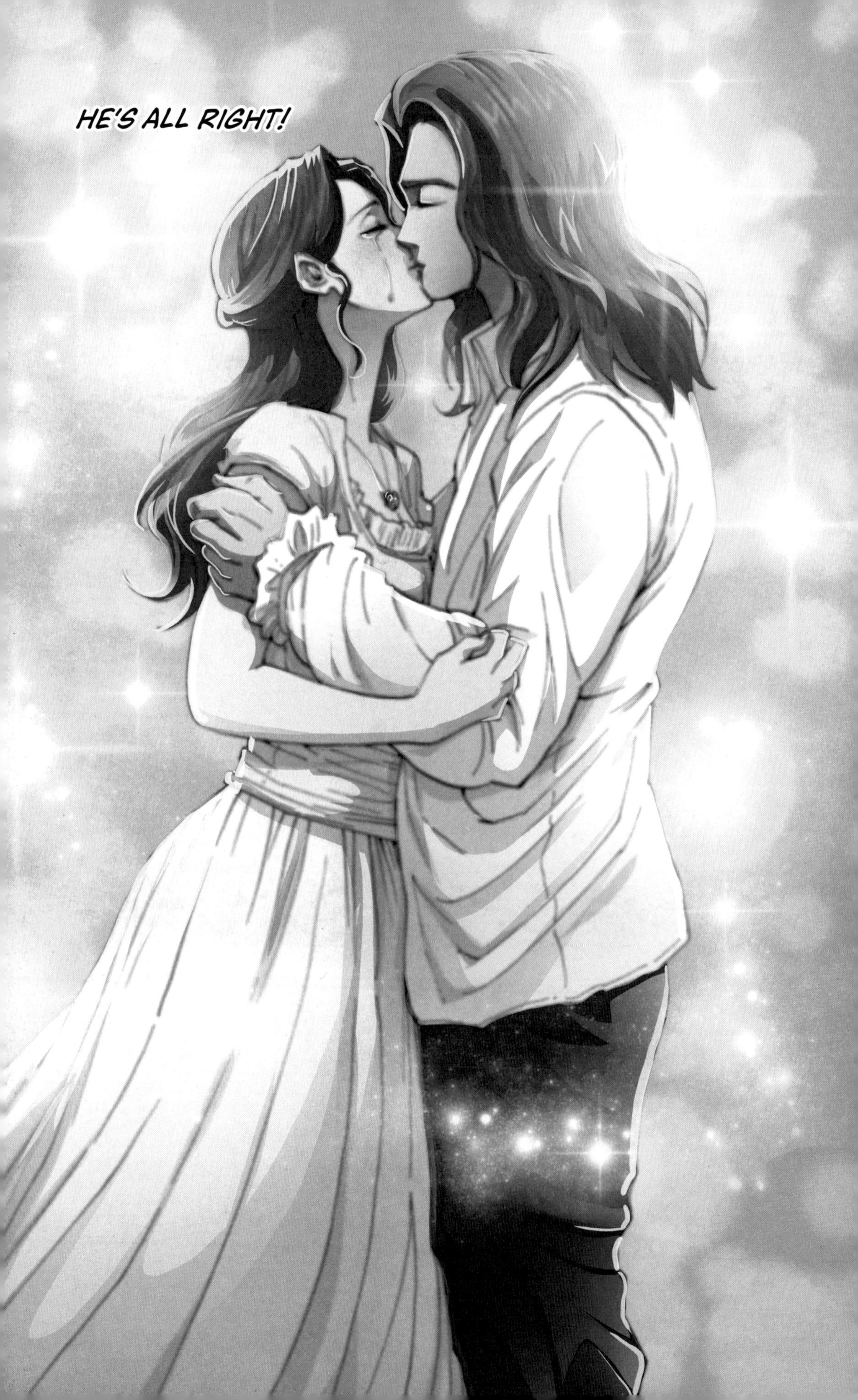
HE'S ALL RIGHT!

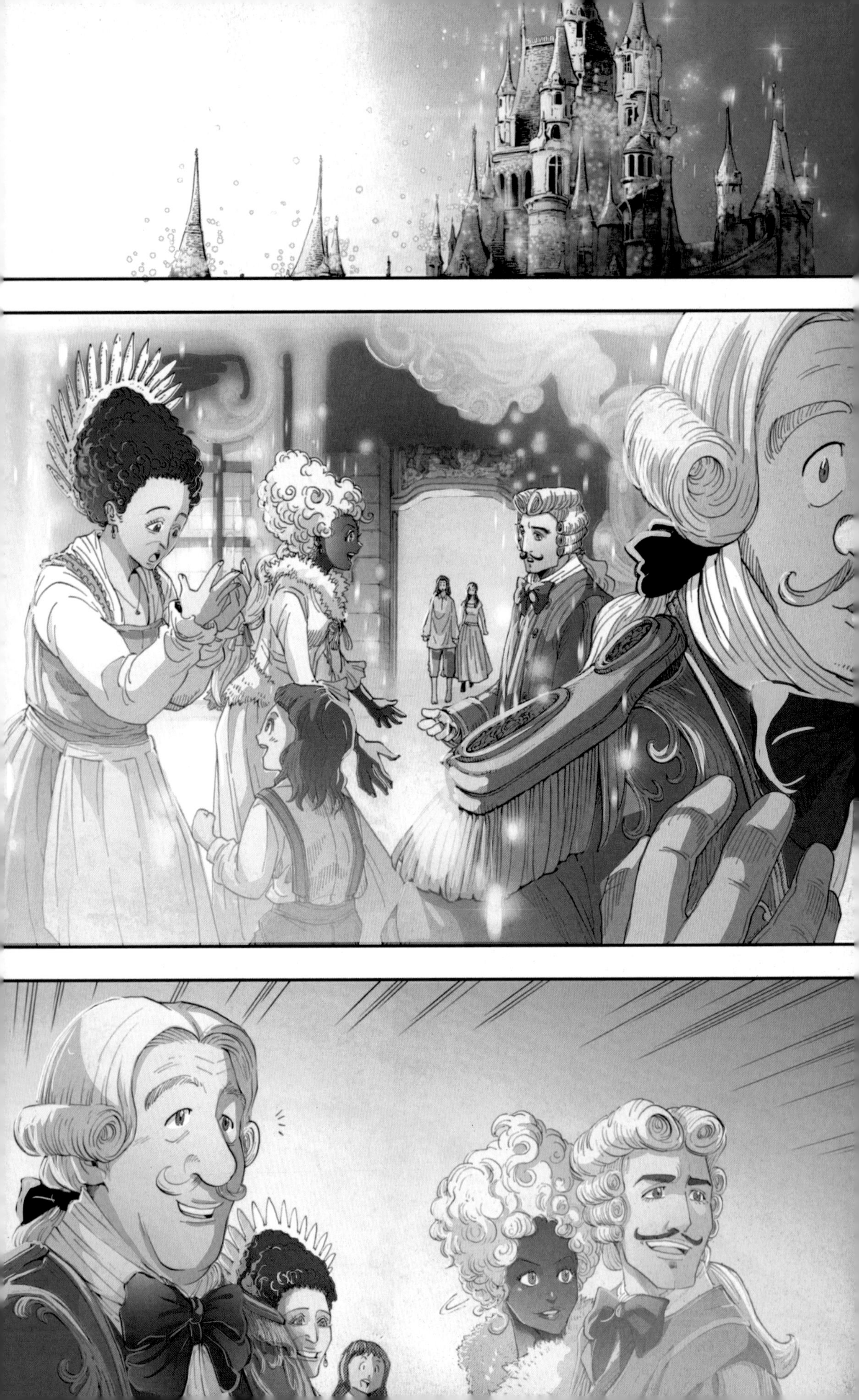

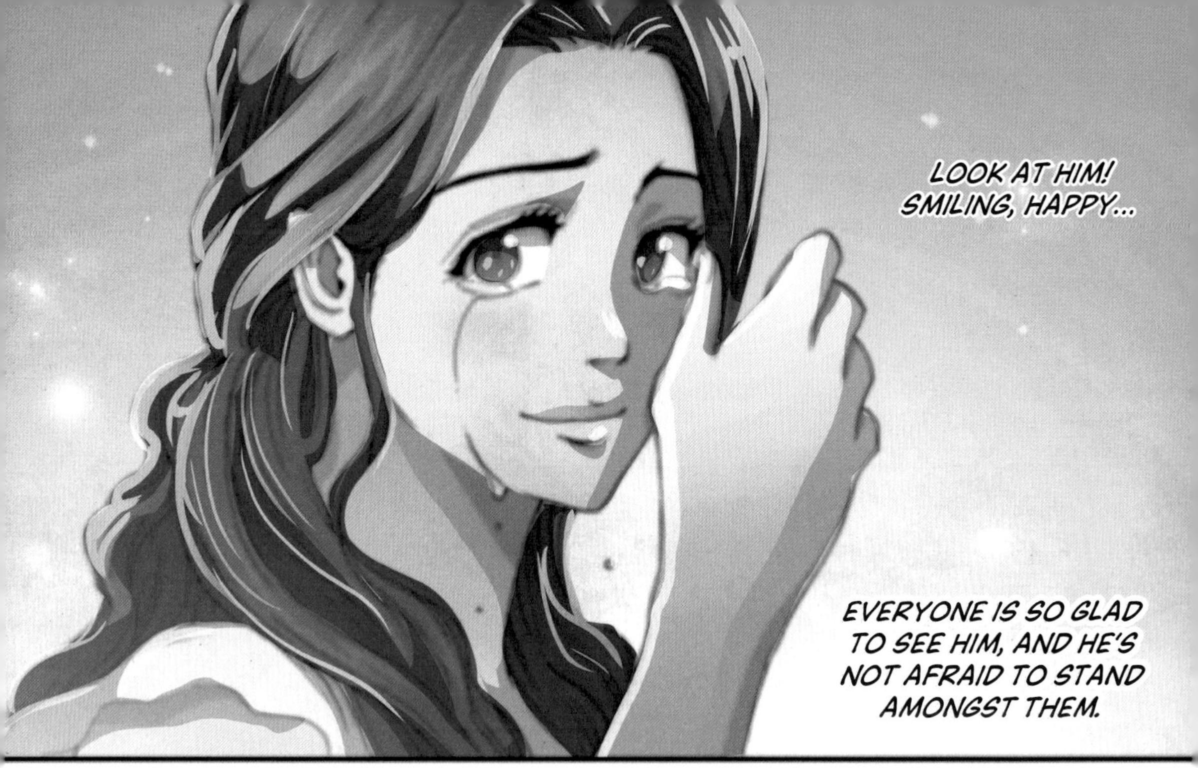
LOOK AT HIM!
SMILING, HAPPY...
EVERYONE IS SO GLAD TO SEE HIM, AND HE'S NOT AFRAID TO STAND AMONGST THEM.

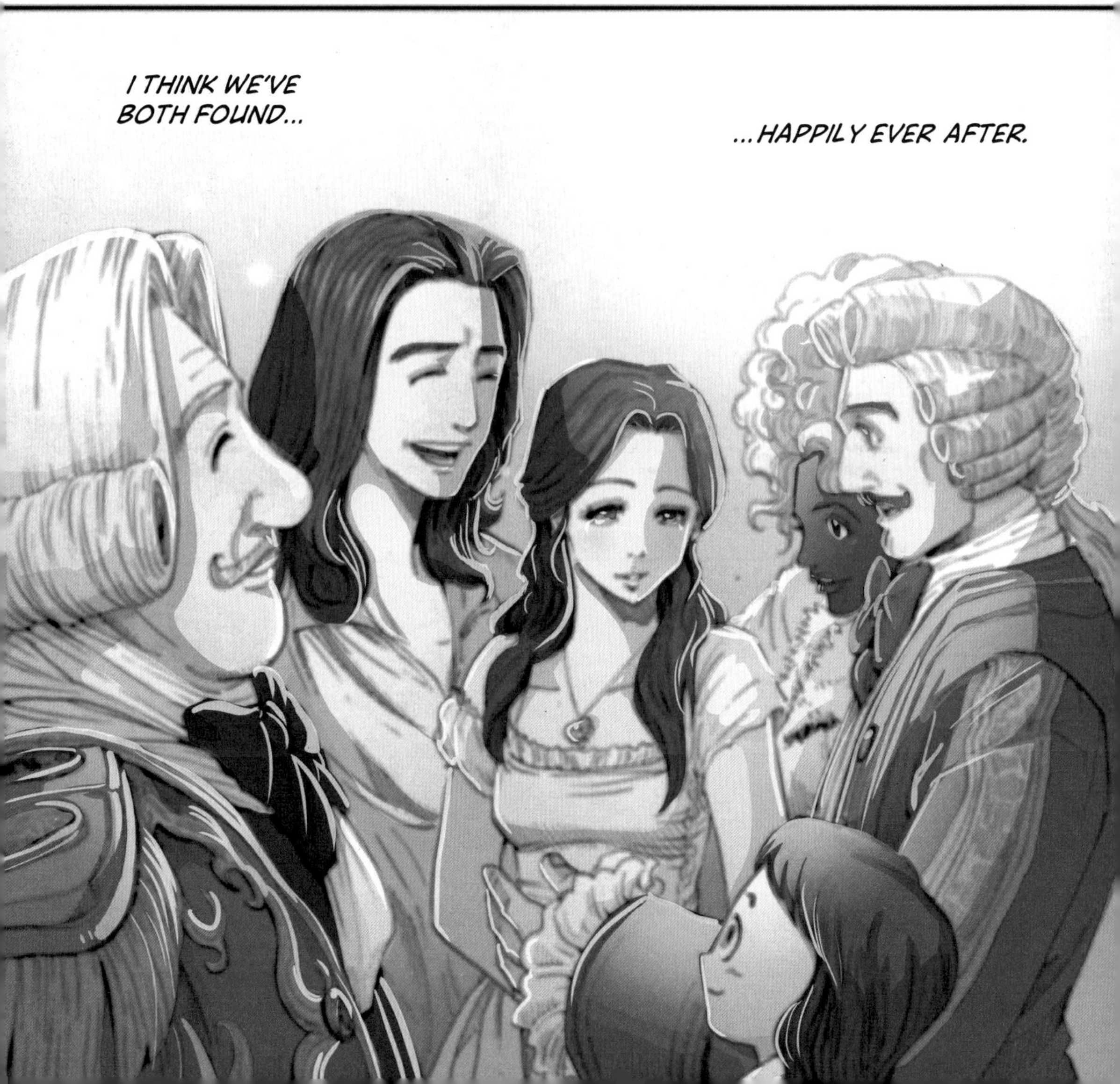
I THINK WE'VE BOTH FOUND...
...HAPPILY EVER AFTER.

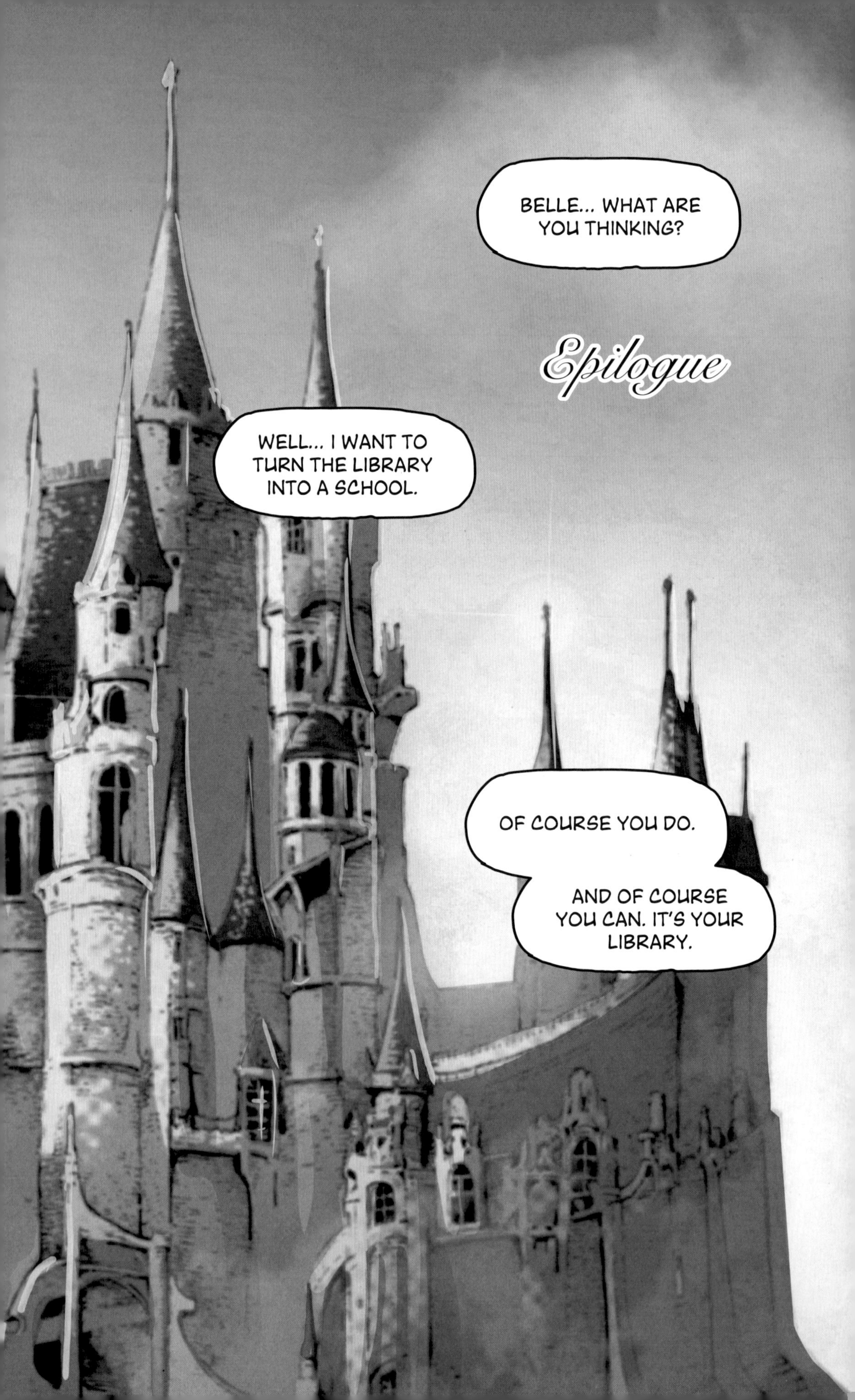
BELLE... WHAT ARE YOU THINKING?
Epilogue
WELL... I WANT TO TURN THE LIBRARY INTO A SCHOOL.
OF COURSE YOU DO.
AND OF COURSE YOU CAN. IT'S YOUR LIBRARY.

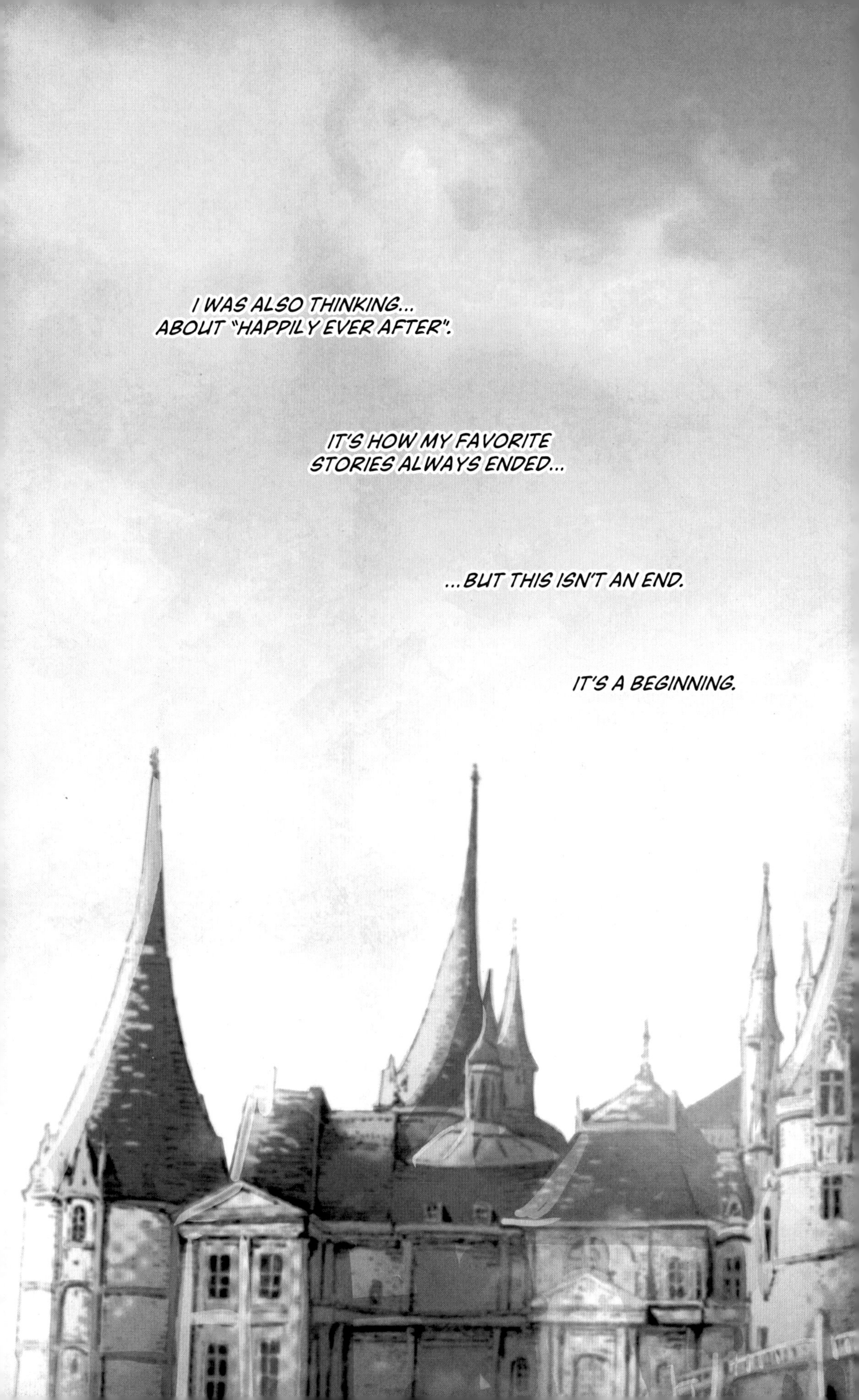
I WAS ALSO THINKING... ABOUT "HAPPILY EVER AFTER".
IT'S HOW MY FAVORITE STORIES ALWAYS ENDED...
...BUT THIS ISN'T AN END.
IT'S A BEGINNING.

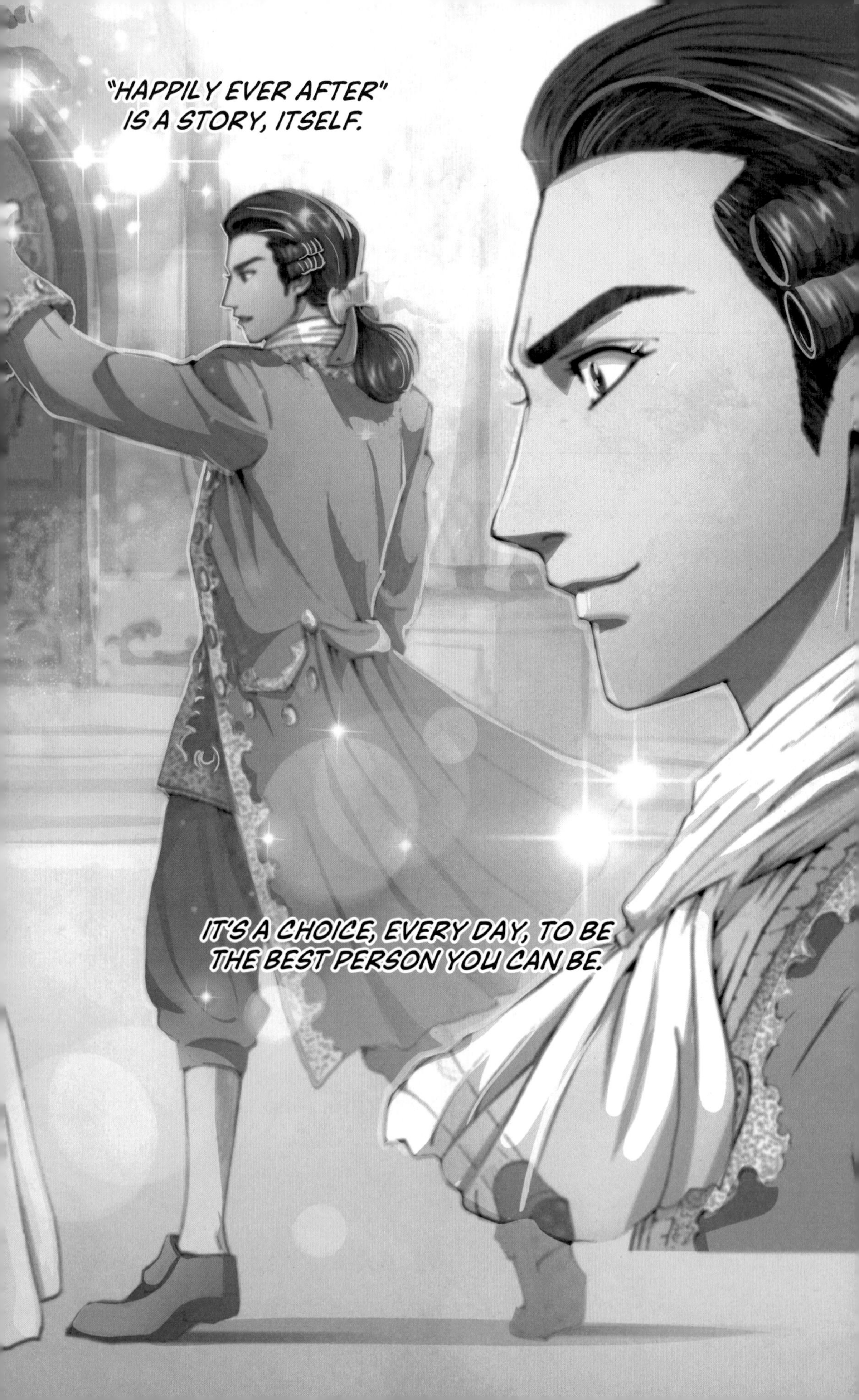
"HAPPILY EVER AFTER" IS A STORY, ITSELF.
IT'S A CHOICE, EVERY DAY, TO BE THE BEST PERSON YOU CAN BE.

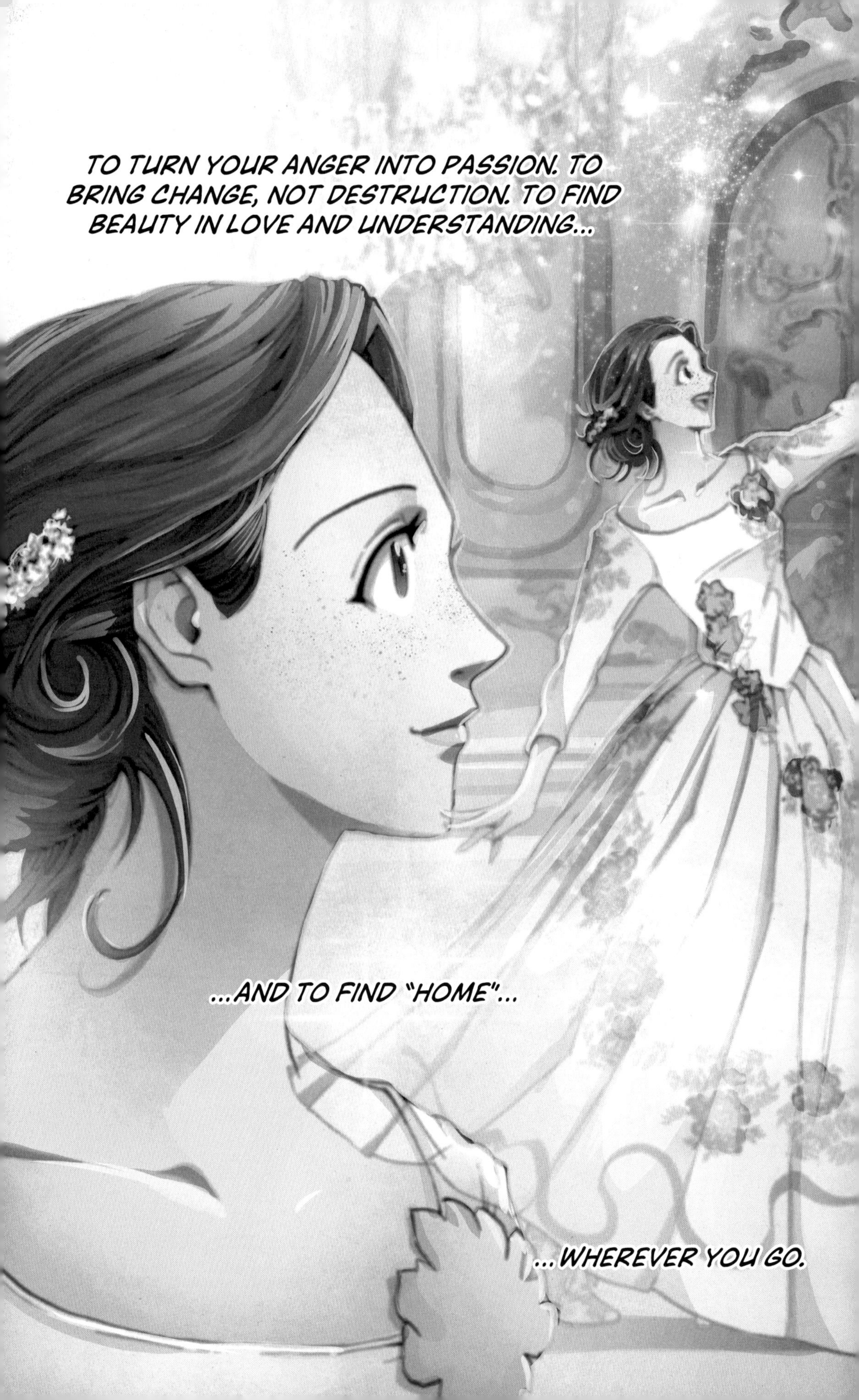
TO TURN YOUR ANGER INTO PASSION. TO BRING CHANGE, NOT DESTRUCTION. TO FIND BEAUTY IN LOVE AND UNDERSTANDING...
...AND TO FIND "HOME"...
...WHEREVER YOU GO.

Disney

Beauty and the Beast

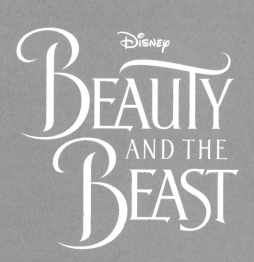

COVER COLOR CONCEPTS

When creating this manga, it was very important that the two covers come together like these two pieces of a puzzle. During the development process, we worked with artists to create a lot of different versions of this cover concept. Take a look at a few designs from the all-new full-color manga version!

Final Cover Inks

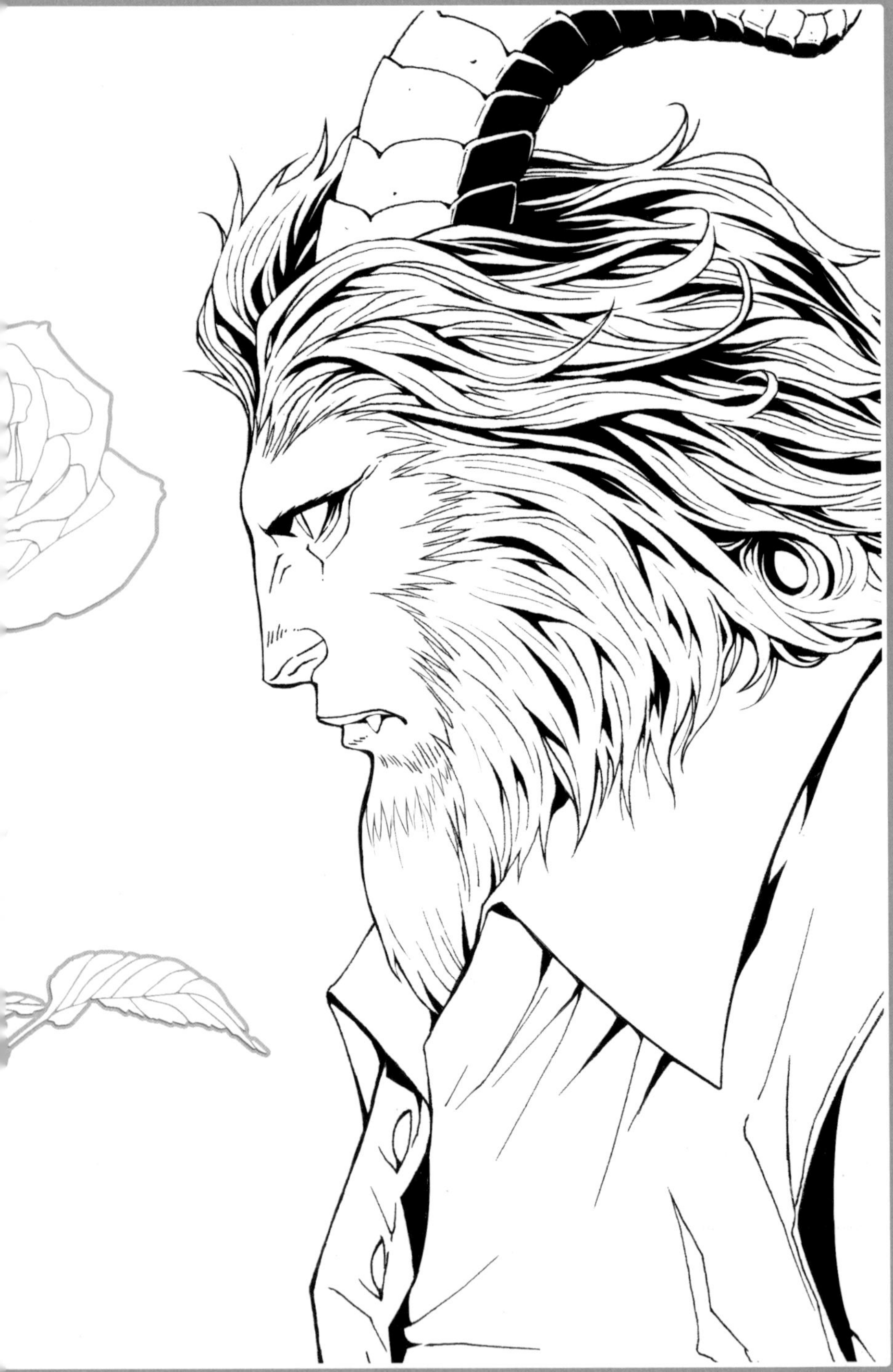

Cover Option #1

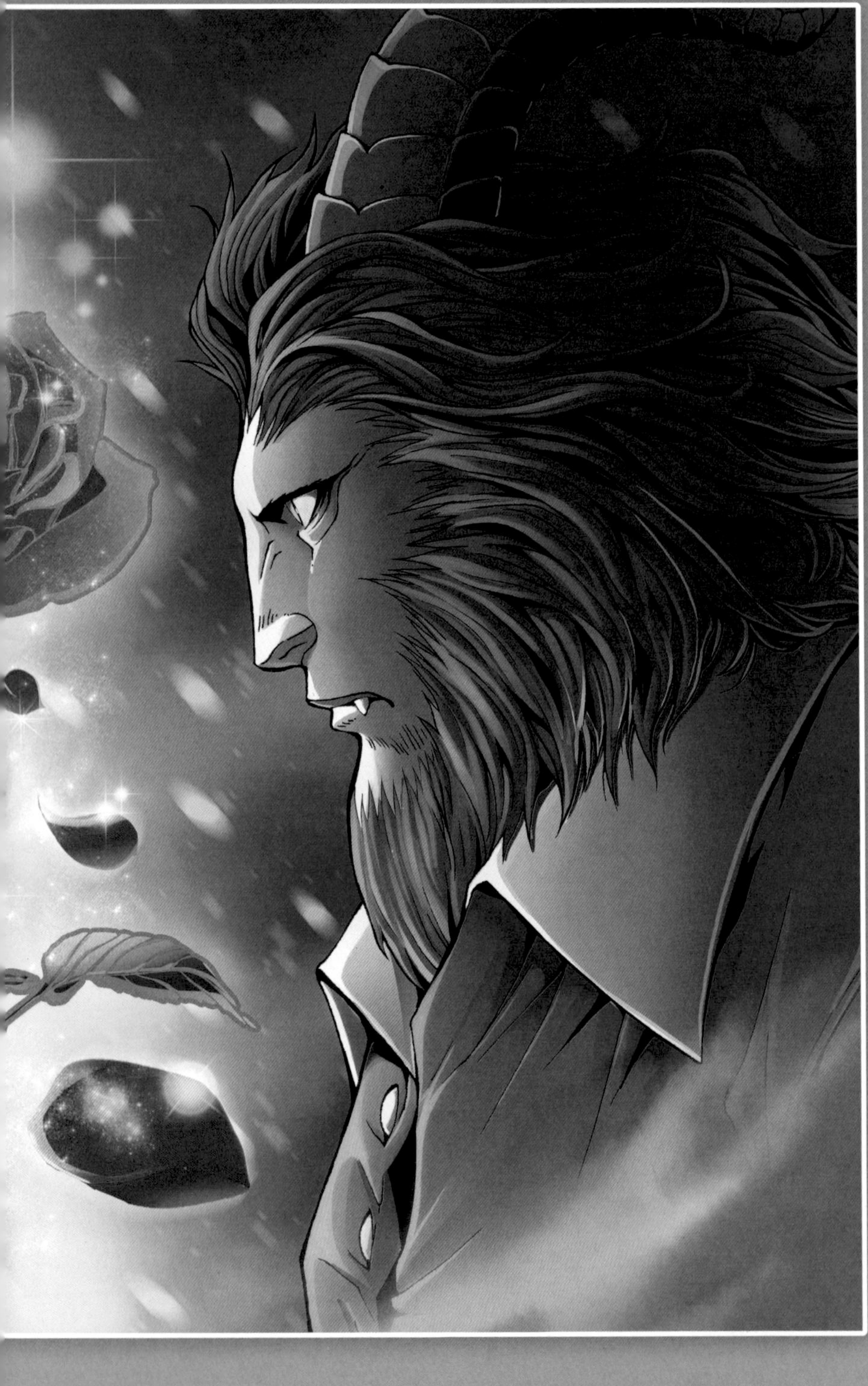

The artist made four versions of the cover in order to pick the best option!

Ultimately Option #1 went to print! So,
this is the final image on the covers.

Cover Option #2

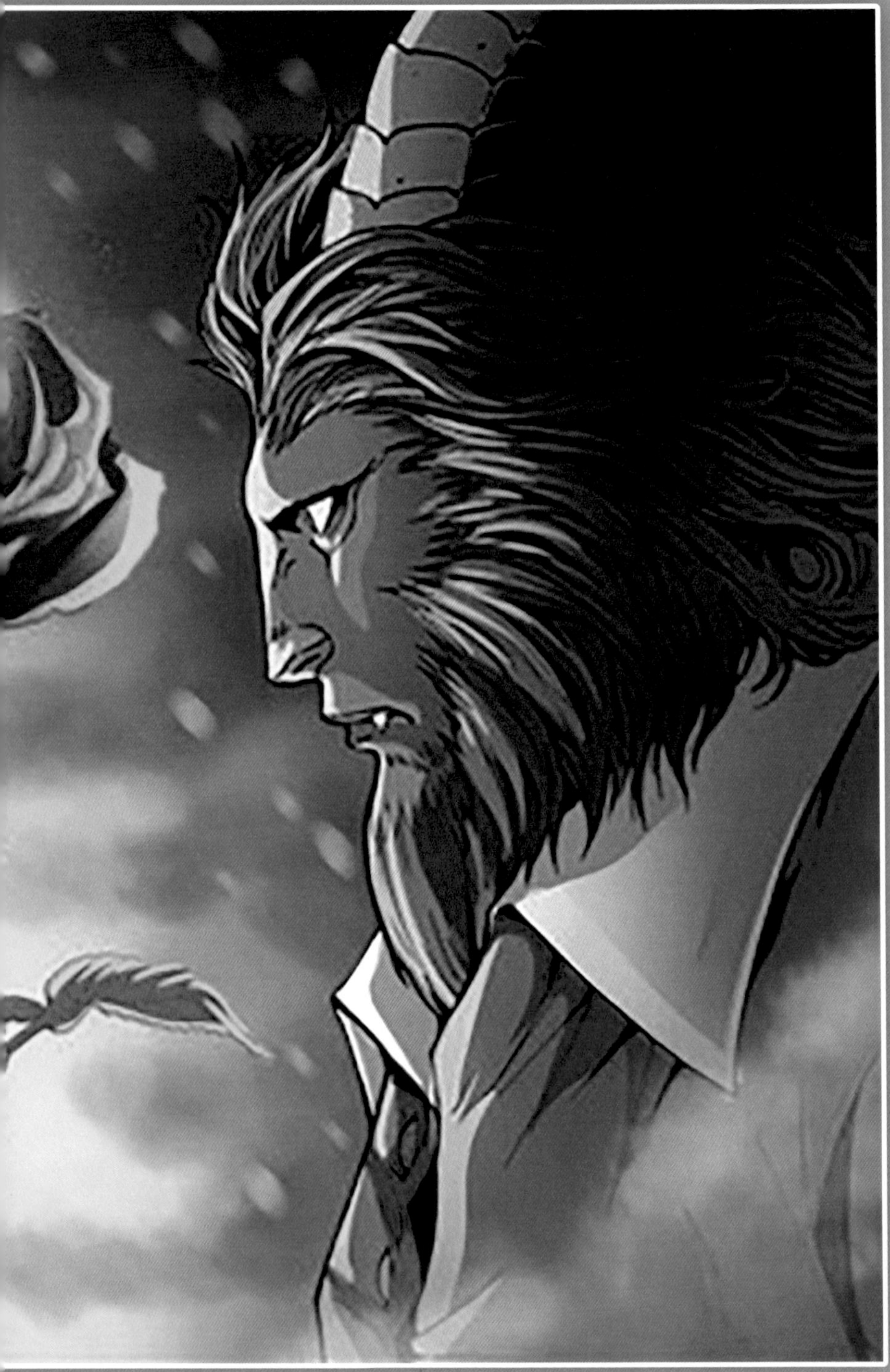

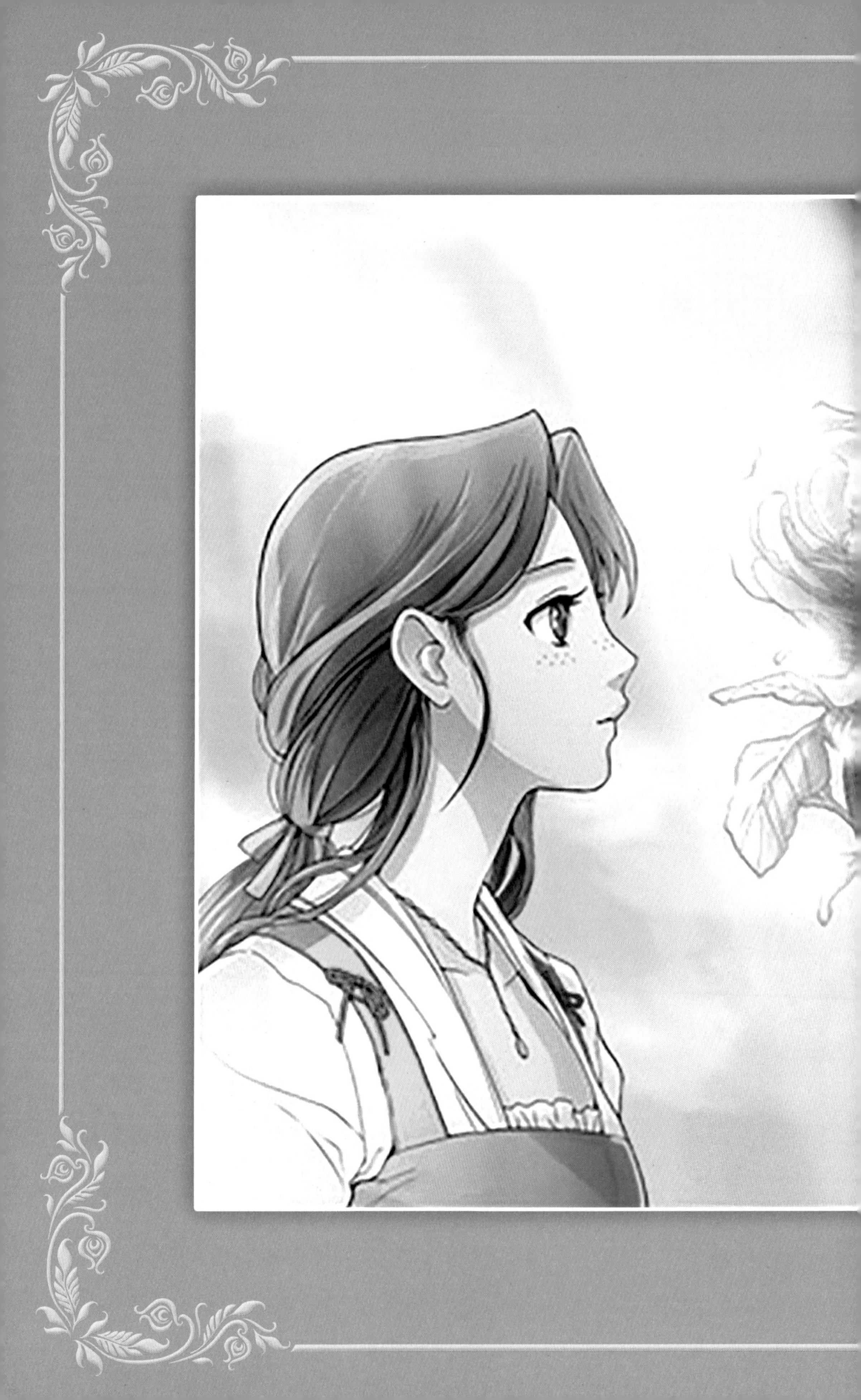

Cover Option #3

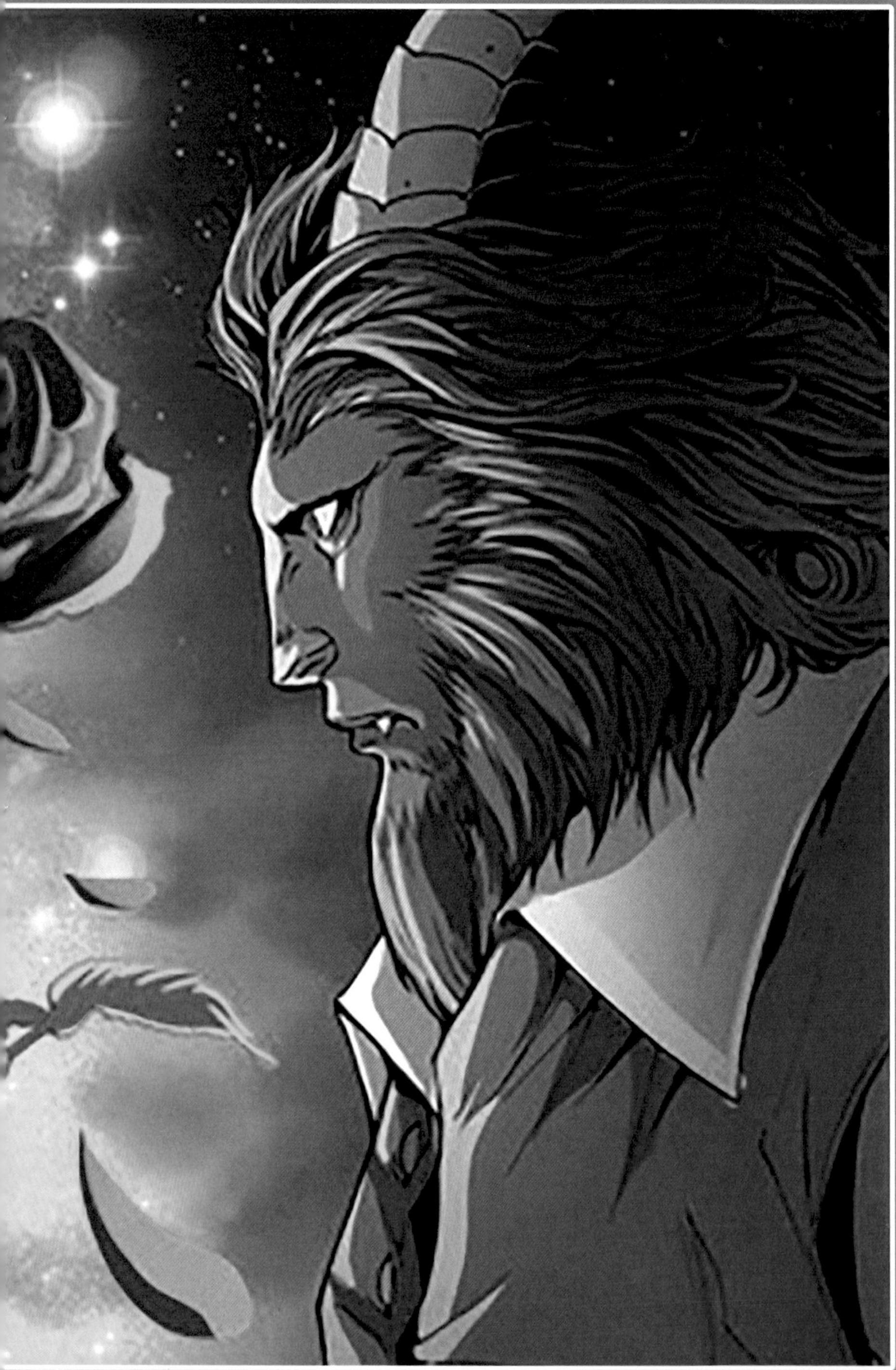

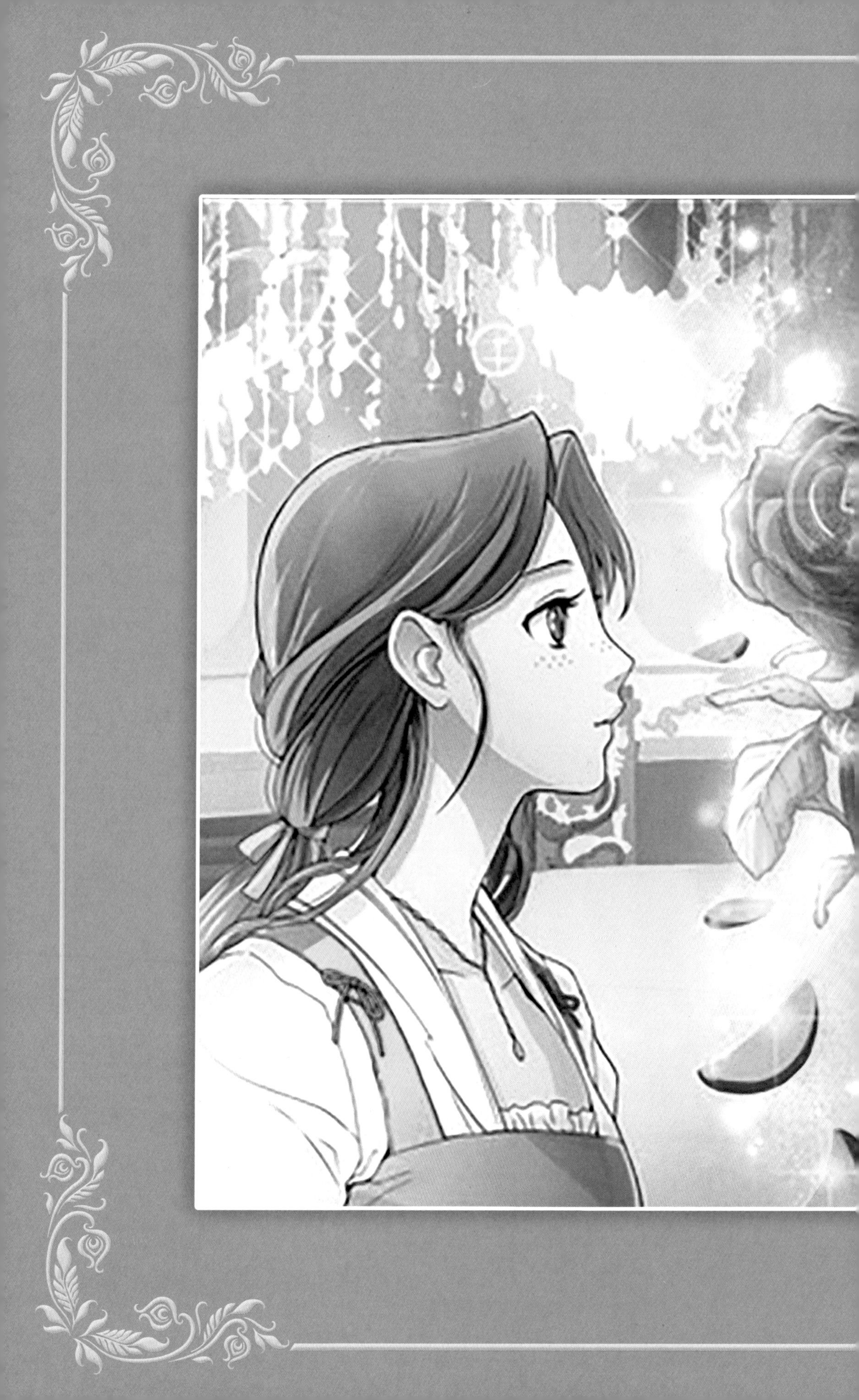

Cover Option #4

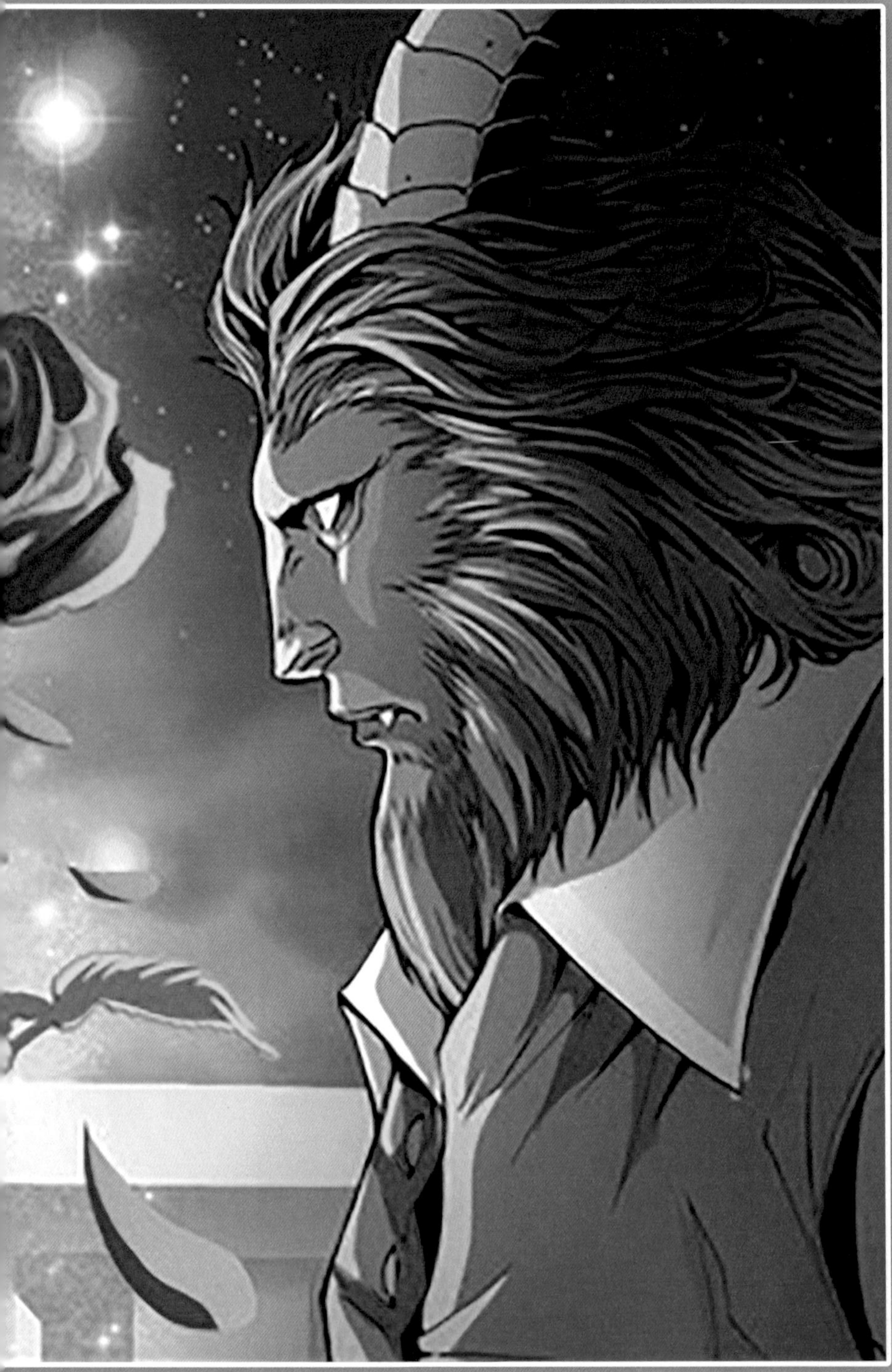

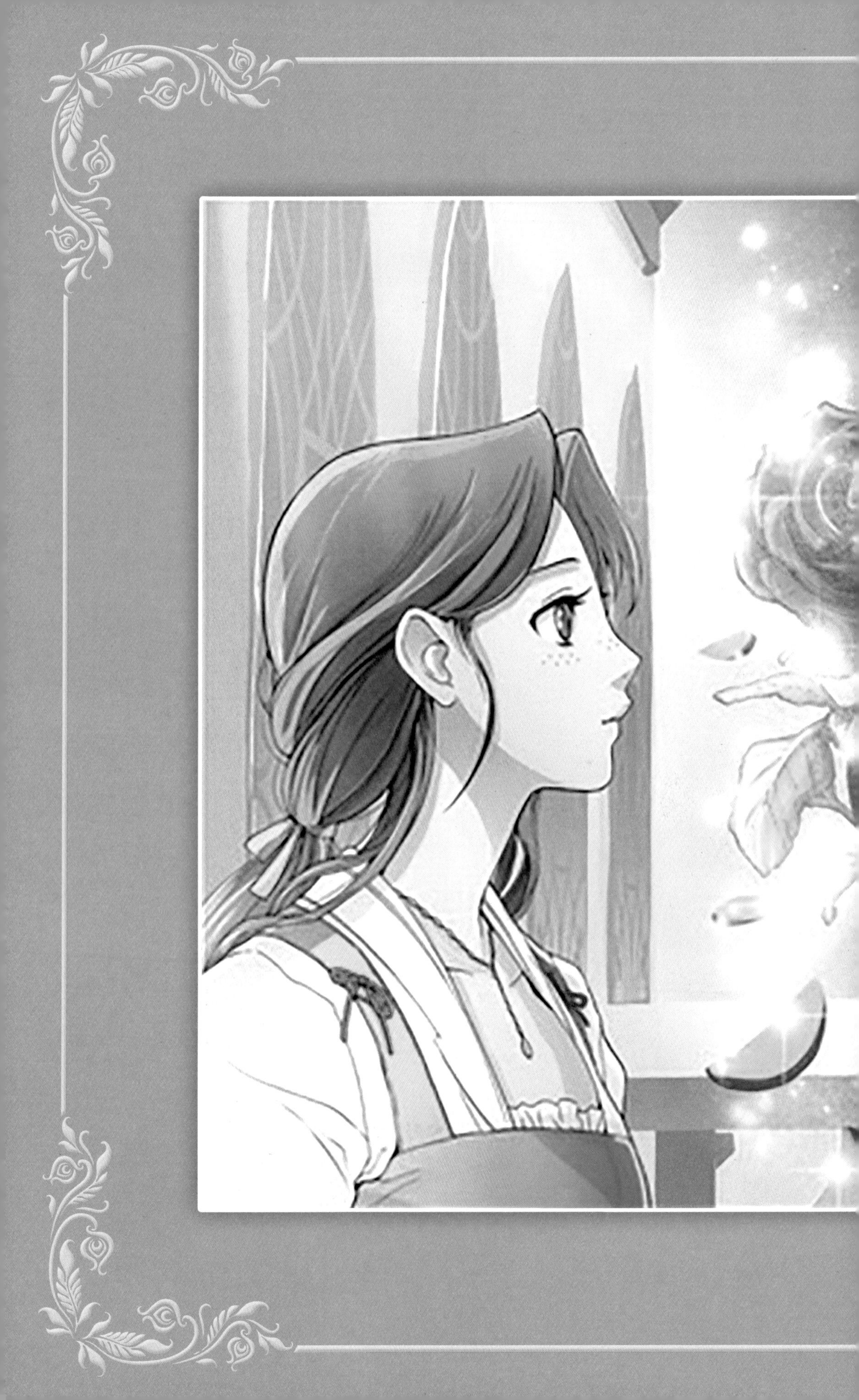

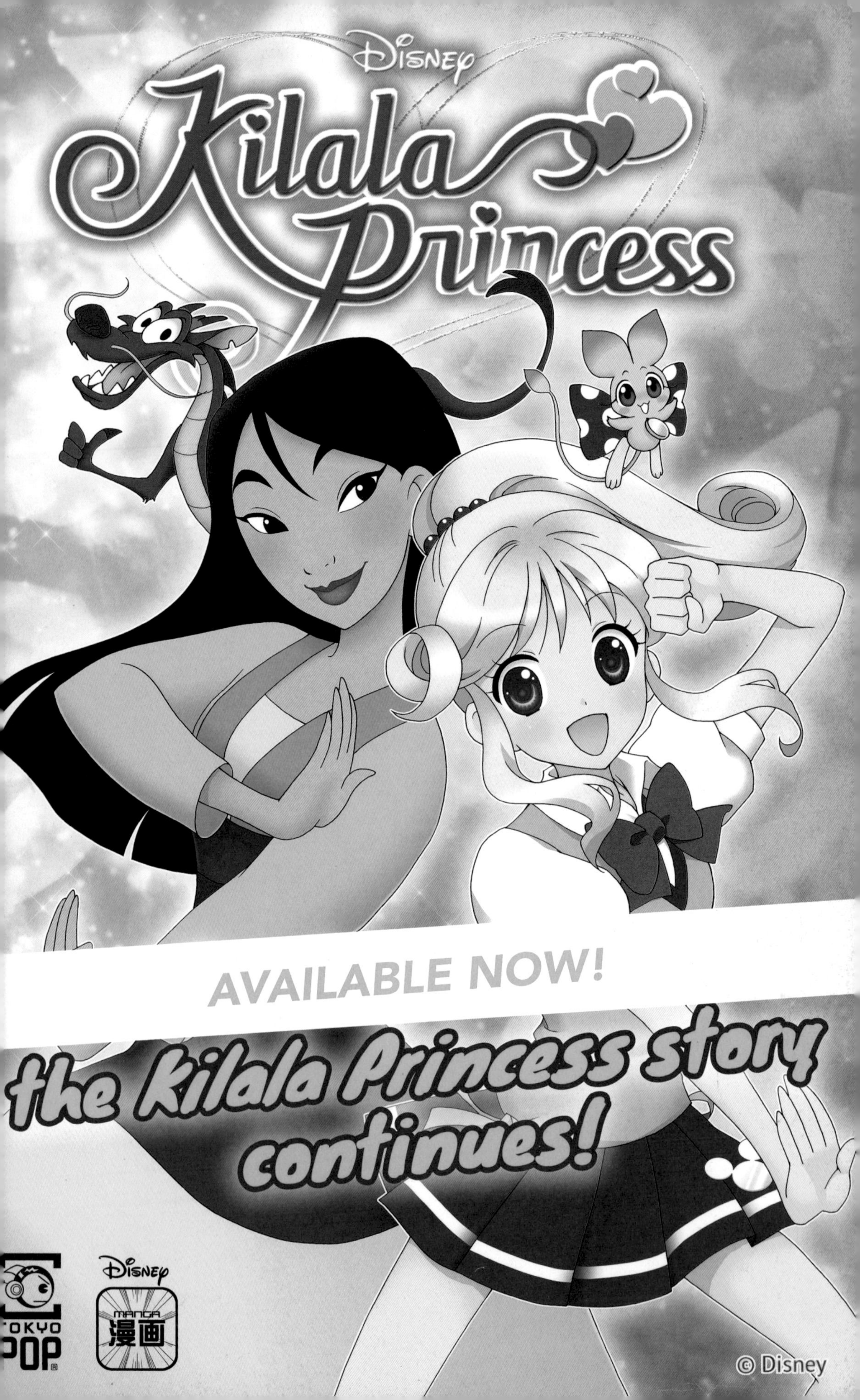
Disney
Kilala Princess
AVAILABLE NOW!
the Kilala Princess story continues!
TOKYOPOP
Disney
MANGA
漫画
© Disney

DISNEY DESCENDANTS

Full color manga trilogy based on the hit Disney Channel original movie

Experience this spectacular movie in manga form!

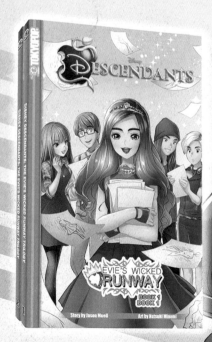

Disney Beauty and the Beast: Belle's Tale (Full-Color Edition)
Art by: Studio Dice
Story Adapted by: Mallory Reaves
Colors by: Gabriella Sinopoli

Editorial Associate - Janae Young
Marketing Associate - Kae Winters
Retouching and Lettering - Vibrraant Publishing Studio
Project Manager - Antonio Solinas
Editor - Janae Young
Graphic Designer - Sol DeLeo
Editor-in-Chief & Publisher - Stu Levy

Studio DICE

Hachi Mizuno

Pon Tachibana   Masashi Kuju   Rie Osanai
Kousuke Takezawa   Tatsuyuki Maeda   Sachika Aoyama
Eriko Terao   Shiori Soya   Takao Yabuno
Hisashi Nosaka

Concept Art by Hachi Mizuno
Cover Art by Hisashi Nosaka
Cover Art Colors by Gabriella Sinopoli

Coordination by MITCHELL PRODUCTION, LLC
http://mitchellprod.com/en

A  Manga

TOKYOPOP and 🔘 are trademarks or registered trademarks of TOKYOPOP Inc.

TOKYOPOP Inc.
5200 W. Century Blvd. Suite 705
Los Angeles, 90045

E-mail: info@TOKYOPOP.com
Come visit us online at www.TOKYOPOP.com

f www.facebook.com/TOKYOPOP
🐦 www.twitter.com/TOKYOPOP
📷 www.instagram.com/TOKYOPOP

ISBN: 978-1-4278-6808-4
First TOKYOPOP Printing: February 2022
Printed in Canada

STOP

THIS IS THE BACK OF THE BOOK!

How do you read manga-style? It's simple!
Let's practice -- just start in the top right
panel and follow the numbers below!

READ RIGHT -TO- LEFT